T3-BWP-132

Praise for No. 1 *New York Times*
bestselling author

"Her stories have fueled the dreams
of twenty-five million readers."
—*Entertainment Weekly*

"Roberts is indeed a word artist, painting her story
and her characters with vitality and verve."
—*Los Angeles Daily News*

"Roberts creates exceptional characters who...
live on in the reader's imagination and heart."
—*Publishers Weekly*

"Roberts...is at the top of her game."
—*People* magazine

"Roberts' bestselling novels are
some of the best in the romance genre."
—*USA TODAY*

"Everything Nora Roberts writes turns to gold."
—*Romantic Times*

NORA ROBERTS

From This Day

First Published 1983
Second Australian Paperback Edition 2004
ISBN 0 733 55160 2

Published by
Harlequin Mills & Boon
3 Gibbes Street
CHATSWOOD NSW 2067
AUSTRALIA

Printed and bound in Australia by
McPherson's Printing Group

NORA ROBERTS

No. 1 *New York Times* bestselling author Nora Roberts is "a word artist, painting her story and characters with vitality and verve," according to the *Los Angeles Daily News.* She has published over a hundred and forty novels, and her work has been optioned and made into films, excerpted in *Good Housekeeping* and has been translated into over twenty-five different languages and published all over the world.

In addition to her amazing success in mainstream, Nora has a large and loyal category-romance audience, which took her to their hearts in 1981 with her very first book.

With over 200 million copies of her books in print worldwide and a total of at least eighty-seven *New York Times* bestsellers, twenty-two of them reaching No. 1, she is truly a publishing phenomenon.

Chapter One

Spring comes late to New England. Snow lingers in isolated patches. Trees begin their greening hesitantly, tiny closed buds of leaves against naked branches. Early blooms of color burst from the earth's womb. The air is fresh with promise.

B.J. tossed open her window with a flourish and welcomed the early breeze into her room. *Saturday,* she thought with a grin, and began to braid her long, wheat-colored hair. The Lakeside Inn was half-full, the summer season three weeks away, and if all followed her well-ordered plans, her duties as manager would be light for the duration of the weekend.

Her staff was loyal, though somewhat temperamental. Like a large family, they squabbled, sulked, teased and stuck together like mortar and brick when the need arose. And I, she mused with a rueful grin, am head counselor.

Pulling on faded jeans, B.J. did not pause to consider the incongruity of the title. A small, childlike woman reflected in her glass, curves disguised by casual attire, braids hanging impishly astride a heart shaped, elfin face with huge smoky eyes dominant. Her only large feature, they swamped the tip-tilted nose and cupid's bow mouth and were prone to smolder or sparkle with the fluctuations of her mood. After lacing dilapidated sneakers, she jogged from the room, intending to check on breakfast preparations before stealing an hour for a solitary walk.

The main staircase of the inn was wide and uncarpeted, connecting its four sprawling stories without curve or angle, as straight and sturdy as the building itself. She saw with satisfaction the lobby was both tidy and deserted. The curtains were drawn to welcome the sun, needlepoint pillows plumped, and a vase of fresh wildflowers adorned the high, well-polished registration desk. The clatter of cutlery carried from the dining room as she passed through the downstairs hall, and she heard, with a long suffering sigh, the running argument between her two waitresses.

"If you really like a man with small, pig eyes, you should be very happy."

B.J. watched Dot shrug her thin shoulders with the words as she rolled a place setting in white linen.

‘‘Wally does not have pig eyes,’’ Maggie insisted. ‘‘They’re very intelligent. You’re just jealous,’’ she added with grim relish as she filled the sugar dispensers.

‘‘Jealous! Ha! The day I’m jealous of a squinty-eyed little runt…Oh, hello, B.J.’’

‘‘Good morning, Dot, Maggie. You rolled two spoons and a knife at that setting, Dot. I think a fork might be a nice touch.’’

Accompanied by her companion’s snickers, Dot unrolled the linen. ‘‘Wally’s taking me to a double feature at the drive-in tonight.’’ Maggie’s smug statement followed B.J. into the kitchen, and she allowed the door to swing shut on the ensuing retort.

Unlike the casual, old fashioned atmosphere of the remainder of the inn, the kitchen sparkled with twentieth century efficiency. Stainless steel glimmered everywhere in the oversized room, the huge stove attesting that the inn’s main attraction was its menu. Cupboards and cabinets stood like veteran soldiers, walls and linoleum gleaming with fresh cleaning. B.J. smiled, pleased with the room’s perfection and the drifting scent of coffee.

‘‘Morning, Elsie.’’ She received an absent mutter from the round woman working at a long, well-scrubbed counter. ''If everything's under control, I'm going out for a couple of hours.''

''Betty Jackson won't send any blackberry jelly.''

''What? Well, for goodness sake why not?'' Annoyed by the complication, B.J. plucked a fresh muffin from a basket and began to devour it. ''Mr. Conners always asks for her jelly, and we're down to the last jar.''

''She said if you couldn't be bothered to pay a lonely old woman a visit, she couldn't be bothered to part with any jelly.''

''Lonely old woman?'' B.J.'s exclamation was hampered by a mouthful of muffin. ''She runs more news items through that house of hers than the Associated Press. Blast it, Elsie, I really need that jelly. I was too busy last week to go listen to the latest special bulletins.''

''The new owner coming Monday got you worried?''

''Who's worried? I'm not worried.'' Scowling, she confiscated another muffin. ''It's simply that as manager of the inn, I want everything to be in order.''

''Eddie said you were muttering and slamming around your office after you got the letter saying he was coming.''

''I was not…muttering….'' Moving to the refrigerator, B.J. poured a glass of juice and spoke to Elsie's wide back. "Taylor Reynolds has a perfect right to inspect his property. It's just, blast it, Elsie, it was all those vague comments about modernizing. Mr. Taylor Reynolds better keep his hands off the Lakeside Inn and play with his other hotels. We don't need to be modernized," she continued, rapidly working herself up into a temper. "We're perfectly fine just the way we are. There's not a thing wrong with us, we don't need anything." She finished by folding her arms across her chest and glaring at the absent Taylor Reynolds.

"Except blackberry jelly," Elsie said mildly. B.J. blinked and brought herself back to the present.

"Oh, all right," she muttered and stalked toward the door. "I'll go get it. But if she tells me one more time that Howard Beall is a fine boy and good husband material, I'll scream. Right there in her living room with the doilies and chintz, I'll scream!"

Leaving this dire threat hanging in the air, B.J. stepped out into the soothing yellow sunlight.

"Blackberry jelly," she mumbled as she hopped on a battered red bike. "New owners with fancy notions...." Lifting her face to the sky, she tossed a pigtail behind her shoulder.

Pedaling down the maple lined drive, quicksilver temper ebbed, her resilient spirits were lifted with the beauty of the day. The valley was stirring with life. Small clusters of fragile violets and red clover dotted the rolling meadows. Lines of fresh laundry waved in the early breeze. The boundary of mountains was topped by a winter's coat, not yet the soft, lush green it would be in a month's time, but patched with stark black trees and the intermittent color of pines. Clouds scudded thin and white across the sky, chased by the teasing wind which whispered of spring and fresh blossoms.

Good humor restored, B.J. arrived in town with pink cheeks and a smile, waving to familiar faces along the route to Betty Jackson's jelly. It was a small town with tidy lawns, picket fences and old, well-kept homes. The dormers and gables were typical of New England. Nestled like a contented cat in the rolling valley, and the brilliant shimmer of Lake Champlain to the west, Lakeside remained serene and untouched by big city bustle. Having been raised on its outskirts had not dulled its magic for B.J.: she felt, as always when entering its limits, a gratitude that somewhere life remained simple.

Parking her bike in front of a small, green-shuttered house, B.J. swung through the gate and prepared to negotiate for her jelly supply.

"Well, B.J., what a surprise." Betty opened the door and patted her gray permanent. "I thought you'd gone back to New York."

"Things have been a bit hectic at the inn," she returned, striving for the proper humility.

"The new owner." Betty nodded with a fortune teller's wisdom and gestured B.J. inside. "I hear he wants to spruce things up."

Resigned that Betty Jackson's communications system was infallible, B.J. settled herself in the small living room.

"You know Tom Myers is adding another room to his house." Brushing off the seat of an overstuffed chair, Betty shifted her ample posterior and sat. "Seems Lois is in the family way again." She clucked her tongue over the Myers' profligacy. "Three babies in four years. But you like little ones, don't you, B.J.?"

"I've always been fond of children, Miss Jackson," B.J. acknowledged, wondering how to turn the conversation toward preserves.

"My nephew, Howard, just loves children."

B.J. braced herself not to scream and met the bland smile, calmly. "We've a couple at the inn now. Children do love to eat." Pleased with the maneuver, she pressed on. "They've simply devoured your jellies. I'm down to my last jar. Nobody has the touch you do with jellies, Miss Jackson; you'd put the big manufacturers out of business if you opened your own line."

"It's all in the timing," Betty preened under the praise, and B.J. tasted the hint of victory.

"I'd just have to close down if you didn't keep

me supplied.'' Gray eyes fluttered ingenuously. ''Mr. Conners would be crushed if I had to serve him store-bought goods. He simply raves about your blackberry jelly. *''Ambrosia,''* she added, relishing the word. ''He says it's *ambrosia.*''

''Ambrosia.'' Betty nodded in self-satisfied agreement.

Ten minutes later, B.J. placed a box of a dozen jars of jelly in the basket of her bike and waved a cheerful goodbye.

''I came, I saw, I conquered,'' she told the sky with audacious pride. ''And I did not scream.''

''Hey, B.J.!''

She twisted her head at the sound of her name, waving to the group playing sand lot ball as she pedaled to the edge of the field. ''What's the score?'' she asked the young boy who ran to her bike.

''Five to four. Junior's team's winning.''

She glanced over to where Junior stood, tall and gangly on the pitcher's mound, tossing a ball in his glove and grinning.

''Little squirt,'' she mumbled with reluctant affection. ''Let me pinch hit once.'' Confiscating the boy's battered cap, she secured it over her pigtails and walked onto the field.

''You gonna play, B.J.?'' Suddenly surrounded

by young bodies and adolescent faces, B.J. lifted a bat and tested it.

''For a minute. I have to get back.''

Junior approached, hands on hips, and grinned down from his advantage of three inches. ''Wanna bet I strike you out?''

She spared him a brief glance and swung the bat to her shoulder. ''I don't want to take your money.''

''If I strike you out,'' he yanked a pigtail with fifteen-year-old audacity, ''you gotta kiss me.''

''Get on the mound, you apprentice lecher, and come back in ten years.''

His grin remained unabashed, as B.J. watched, stifling a smile as he sauntered into position. He squinted, nodded, wound up and pitched. B.J. swung a full circle.

''Strike one!''

She turned and scowled at Wilbur Hayes who stood as umpire. Stepping up to the plate again, the cheers and taunts grew in volume. She stuck out her tongue at Junior's wink.

''Strike two!'' Wilbur announced as she watched the pitch sail by.

''Strike?'' Turning, she placed her hands on her hips. ''You're crazy, that was chin high. I'm going to tell your mother you need glasses.''

''Strike two,'' Wilbur repeated and frowned with adolescent ferocity.

Muttering, B.J. stepped again into the batter's box.

"You might as well put the bat down," Junior shouted, cradling the ball in the mitt. "You're not even coming close to this one."

"Take a good look at the ball, Junior, 'cause it's the last time you'll see it." Shifting the hat lower on her head, B.J. clutched the bat. "It's going clear to New York."

She connected with a solid crack of bat and watched the ball begin its sail before she darted around the bases. Running full steam, head down, she heard the shouts and cheers to slide as she rounded third. Scott Temple crouched at the plate, mitt opened for reception, as she threw herself down, sliding into home in a cloud of dust and frenzied shouts.

"You're out!"

"Out!" Scrambling to her feet, she met Wilbur's bland blue stare, eye to eye and nose to nose. "Out, you little squirt, I was safe by a mile. I'm going to buy you some binoculars."

"Out," he repeated with great dignity, and folded his arms.

"What we need here is an umpire with two working eyes." She turned to her crowd of supporters and threw out her hands. "I demand a second opinion."

"You were out."

Spinning at the unfamiliar voice, B.J. frowned up at the stranger. He stood leaning on the backstop, a small lift to his well-formed mouth and amusement shining from his dark brown eyes. He pushed a lock of curling black hair from his brow and straightened a long, lean frame.

"You should have been content with a triple."

"I was safe," she retorted, rubbing more dirt on her nose. "Absolutely safe."

"Out," Wilbur repeated.

B.J. sent him a withering glance before turning back to the man who approached the heated debate between teams. She studied him with a mixture of resentment and curiosity.

His features were well defined, sculptured with planes and angles, the skin bronzed and smooth, the faintest hint of red in his dark hair where the sun caught it. She saw that though his buff-colored suit was casual, it was obviously well tailored and expensive. His teasing smile widened at her critical survey, and her resentment deepened.

"I've got to get back," she announced, brushing at her jeans. "And don't think I'm not going to mention an eye exam to your mother," she added, giving Wilbur a final glare.

"Hey, kid." She straddled her bike and looked around idly, then smiled as she realized the man had grouped her with the teenagers. Restraining her smile, she looked up with what she hoped was the insolence of youth.

"Yeah?"

"How far is it to the Lakeside Inn?"

"Look, mister, my mother told me not to talk to strange men."

"Very commendable. I'm not offering you candy and a ride."

"Well." She frowned as if debating pros and cons. "O.K. It's about three miles up the road." Making her gesture vague, she finished with the obligatory codicil. "You can't miss it."

He gave a long stare into her wide gray eyes, then shook his head. "That's a big help. Thanks."

"Any time." She watched him wander toward a silver-blue Mercedes and, unable to prevent herself, called after him. "And I was safe. Absolutely safe." Tossing the borrowed hat back to its owner, B.J. cut across the meadow and headed toward the inn.

The four stories of red brick, with their gabled roof and neat shutters, loomed ahead of her. Pedaling up the wide, curving drive, she noted with satisfaction that the short cut had brought her ahead of the Mercedes.

I wonder if he's looking for a room, she thought. Parking her bike, she hauled out her treasure of jellies from the basket. Maybe he's a salesman. No, she contradicted her own thoughts, *that was no salesman.* Well, if he wants a room, we'll oblige him, even if he is an interfering busybody with bad eyes.

"Good morning." B.J. smiled at the newlyweds who strolled across the lawn.

"Oh, good morning, Miss Clark. We're going for a walk by the lake," the groom answered politely.

"It's a lovely day for it," B.J. acknowledged, parking her bike by the entrance. She entered the small lobby, and moving behind the front desk, set down the crate of jelly and reached for the morning mail. Seeing a personal letter from her grandmother, she opened it and began to read with pleasure.

"Get around, don't you?"

Her absorption was rudely broken. Dropping the letter, she lifted her elbows from the counter and stared into dark brown eyes. "I took a short cut." Unwilling to be outmatched by his height or faultless attire, she straightened and lifted her chin. "May I help you?"

"I doubt it, unless you can tell me where to find the manager."

His dismissive tone fueled her annoyance. She struggled to remember her job and remain pleasant. "Is there some problem? There's a room available if you require one."

"Be a good girl and run along." His tone was

patronizing. "And fetch the manager for me while you're about it. I'd like to see him."

Drawing herself to her full height she crossed her arms over her chest. "You're looking at her."

His dark brows rose in speculation as his eyes swept over her incredulously. "Do you manage the inn before school and on Saturdays?" he asked sarcastically.

B.J. flushed with anger. "I have been managing the Lakeside Inn for nearly four years. If there's a problem, I shall be delighted to take it up with you here, or in my office. If you require a room," she gestured toward the open register, "we'll be more than happy to oblige you."

"B.J. Clark?" he asked with a deepening frown.

"That's correct."

With a nod, he lifted a pen and signed the register. "I'm sure you'll understand," he began, raising his eyes again in fresh study. "Your morning activity on the baseball diamond and your rather juvenile appearance are deceptive."

"I had the morning free," she said crisply, "and my appearance in no way reflects on the inn's quality. I'm sure you'll see that for yourself during your stay, Mr...." Turning the register to face her, B.J.'s stomach lurched.

"Reynolds," he supplied, smiling at her astonished expression. "Taylor Reynolds."

Struggling for composure, B.J. lifted her face and assumed a businesslike veneer. ''I'm afraid we weren't expecting you until Monday, Mr. Reynolds.''

''I changed my plans,'' he countered, dropping the pen back in its holder.

''Yes, well...Welcome to Lakeside Inn,'' she said belatedly and flicked a pigtail behind her back.

''Thank you. I'll require an office during my stay. Can you arrange it?''

''Our office space is limited, Mr. Reynolds.'' Cursing Betty Jackson's blackberry jelly, she pulled down the key to the inn's best room and rounded the desk. ''However, if you don't mind sharing mine, I'm sure you'll find it adequate.''

''Let's take a look. I want to see the books and records anyway.''

''Of course,'' she agreed, gritting her teeth at the stranger's hold over her inn. ''If you'll just come with me.''

''B.J., B.J.'' She watched with an inward shudder as Eddie hurtled down the stairs and into the lobby. His glasses were slipping down his nose, his brown hair was flopping around his ears.

''B.J.,'' he said again, breathless, ''Mrs. Pierce-Lowell's T.V. went out right in the middle of her cartoons.''

''Oh, blast. Take mine in to her and call Max for the repair.''

''He's away for the weekend,'' Eddie reminded her.

''All right, I'll survive.'' Giving his shoulder an encouraging pat, she guided him to the door. ''Leave me a memo to call him Monday and get mine into her before she misses Bugs Bunny.'' Feeling the new owner's penetrating stare in the back of her head, B.J. explained apologetically. ''I'm sorry, Eddie has a tendency toward the dramatic, and Mrs. Pierce-Lowell is addicted to Saturday morning cartoons. She's one of our regulars, and we make it a policy to provide our guests with what pleases them.''

''I see,'' he replied, but she could find nothing in his expression to indicate that he did.

Moving quickly to the back of the first floor, B.J. opened the door to her office and gestured Taylor inside. ''It's not very big,'' she began as he surveyed the small room with desk and file cabinets and bulletin board, ''but I'm sure we can arrange it to suit your needs for the few days you will be here.''

''Two weeks,'' he stated firmly. He strolled across the room, picking up a bronzed paperweight of a grinning turtle.

"Two weeks?" she repeated, and the alarm in her voice caused him to turn toward her.

"That's right, Miss Clark. Is that a problem?"

"No, no, of course not." Finding his direct stare unnerving, she lowered her eyes to the clutter on her desk.

"Do you play ball every Saturday, Miss Clark?" He perched on the edge of the desk. Looking up, B.J. found her face only inches from his.

"No, certainly not," she answered with dignity. "I simply happened to be passing by, and—"

"A very courageous slide," he commented, shocking her by running a finger down her cheek. "And your face proves it."

Somewhat dazed, she glanced at the dust on his finger. "I was safe," she said in defense against a ridiculously speeding pulse. "Wilbur needs an optometrist."

"I wonder if you manage the inn with the same tenacity with which you play ball." He smiled, his eyes very intent on hers. "We'll have a look at the books this afternoon."

"I'm sure you'll find everything in order," she said stiffly. The effect was somewhat spoiled as she backed into the file cabinet. "The inn runs very smoothly, and as you know, makes a nice profit." She continued struggling to maintain her dignity.

"With a few changes, it should make a great deal more."

"Changes?" she echoed, apprehension in her voice. "What sort of changes?"

"I need to look over the place before I make any concrete decisions, but the location is perfect for a resort." Absently, he brushed the dust off his fingers on the windowsill and gazed out. "Pool, tennis courts, health club, a face lift for the building itself."

"There's nothing wrong with this building. We don't cater to the resort set, Mr. Reynolds." Furious, B.J. approached the desk again. "This is an inn, with all the connotations that includes. Family-style meals, comfortable lodgings and a quiet atmosphere. That's why our guests come back."

"The clientele would increase with a few modern attractions," he countered coolly. "Particularly with the proximity to Lake Champlain."

"Keep your hot tubs and disco lounges for your other acquisitions." B.J. bypassed simmer and went straight to boil. "This is Lakeside, Vermont, not L.A. I don't want any plastic surgery on my inn."

Brows rose, and his mouth curved in a grim smile. "Your inn, Miss Clark?"

"That's right," she retorted, "You may hold the purse strings, Mr. Reynolds, but I know this place, and our guests come back year after year because of what we represent. There's no way you're going to change one brick."

"Miss Clark." Taylor stood menacingly over her. "If I choose to tear down this inn brick by brick, that's precisely what I'll do. Whatever alterations I make or don't make, remain my decision, and my decision alone. Your position as manager does not entitle you to a vote."

"And your position as owner doesn't entitle you to brains!" she was unable to choke back as she stomped from the office in a flurry of flying braids.

Chapter Two

With relish, B.J. slammed the door to her room. Arrogant, interfering, insufferable man. Why doesn't he go play Monopoly somewhere else? Doesn't he already have enough hotels to tinker with? There must be a hundred in the Reynolds chain in the states alone, plus all those elegant foreign resorts. Why doesn't he open one in Antarctica?

Abruptly, she caught sight of her reflection in the mirror and stared in disbelief. Her face was smudged. Dust clung to her sweatshirt and jeans. Her braids hung to her shoulders. All in all, she thought grimly, I look like a rather dim-witted ten-year-old. She suddenly noticed a line down her cheek, and lifting her hand, recalled Taylor's finger resting there.

"Oh, blast." Shaking her head, she began to quickly unbind her hair. "I made a mess of it," she muttered and stripped off her morning uniform. "Looking like a grimy teenager and then losing my temper on top of it. Well, he's not going to fire me," she vowed fiercely and stalked to the shower. "I'll quit first! I'm not staying around and watching my inn mutilated."

Thirty minutes later, B.J. pulled a brush through her hair and studied the new reflection with satisfaction. Soft clouds of wheat floated on her shoulders. She wore an ivory dress, nipped at the waist, belted in scarlet to match tiny blazing rubies at her ears. Heels gave her height a slight advantage. She felt confident she could no longer be mistaken for sixteen. Lifting a neatly written page from her dresser, she moved purposefully from the room, prepared to confront the bear in his den.

After a brief excuse for a knock, B.J. pushed open the office door and slowly and purposefully advanced toward the man sitting behind the desk. Shoving the paper under his nose, she waited for his brown eyes to meet hers.

"Ah, B.J. Clark, I presume. This is quite a transfiguration." Leaning back in his chair, Taylor allowed his eyes to travel over the length of her. "Amazing," he smiled into her resentful gray eyes, "what can be concealed under a sweatshirt and baggy pants.... What's this?'' He waved the paper idly, his eyes still appraising her.

''My resignation.'' Placing her palms on the desk, she leaned forward and prepared to give vent to her emotions. ''And now that I am no longer in your employ, Mr. Reynolds, it'll give me a great deal of pleasure to tell you what I think. You are,'' she began as his brow rose at her tone, ''a dictatorial, capitalistic opportunist. You've bought an inn which has for generations maintained its reputation for quality and personal service, and in order to make a few more annual dollars, you plan to turn it into a live-in amusement park. In doing so, you will not only have to let the current staff go, some of whom have worked here for twenty years, but you'll succeed in destroying the integrity of the entire district. This is not your average tourist town, it's a quiet, settled community. People come here for fresh air and quiet, not for a brisk tennis match or to sweat in a sauna, and—''

''Are you finished, Miss Clark?'' Taylor questioned. Instinctively she recognized the danger in his lowered tones.

''No.'' Mustering her last resources of courage, she set her shoulders and sent him a lethal glare. ''Go soak in your Jacuzzi!''

On her heel, she spun around and made for the

door only to find her back pressed into it as she was whirled back into the room.

''Miss Clark,'' Taylor began, effectively holding her prisoner by leaning over her, arms at either side of her head. ''I permitted you to clear your system for two reasons. First, you're quite a fabulous sight when your temper's in full gear. I noticed that even when I took you for a rude teenager. A lot of it has to do with your eyes going from mist to smoke, it's very impressive. That, of course,'' he added as she stared up at him, unable to form a sound, ''is strictly on a personal level. Now on a professional plane, I am receptive to your opinions, if not to your delivery.''

Abruptly, the door swung open, dislodging B.J. and tumbling her into a hard chest. ''We found Julius's lunch,'' Eddie announced cheerfully and disappeared.

''You have a very enthusiastic staff,'' Taylor commented dryly as his arms propped her up against him. ''Who the devil is Julius?''

''He's Mrs. Frank's Great Dane. She doesn't… she won't go anywhere without him.''

''Does he have his own room?'' His tone was gently mocking.

''No, he has a small run in the back.''

Taylor smiled suddenly, his face close to hers. Power shot through her system like a bolt of electricity down a lightning rod. With a jerk, she pulled away and pushed at her tumbled hair.

"Mr. Reynolds," she began, attempting to retrieve her all too elusive dignity. He claimed her hand and pulled her back toward the desk, then pushed her firmly down on the chair.

"Do be quiet, Miss Clark," he told her in easy tones, settling behind the desk. "It's my turn now." She stared with a melding of astonishment and indignation.

"What I ultimately do with this inn is my decision. However, I will consider your opinion as you are intimate with this establishment and with the area and I, as yet, am not." Lifting B.J.'s resignation, Taylor tore it in half and dropped the pieces on the desk.

"You can't do that," she sputtered.

"I have just done it." The mild tone vibrated with authority.

B.J.'s eyes narrowed. "I can easily write another."

"Don't waste your paper," he advised, leaning back in his chair. "I have no intention of accepting your resignation at the moment. Later, I'll let you know. However," he added slowly, shrugging, "if you insist, I shall be forced to close down the inn for the next few months until I've found someone to replace you."

"It couldn't possibly take months to replace me," B.J. protested, but he was looking up at the ceiling as though lost in thought.

"Six months perhaps."

"Six months?" she frowned. "But you can't. We have reservations, it's nearly the summer season. All those people can't be disappointed. And the staff—the staff would be out of work."

"Yes." With an agreeable smile, he nodded and folded his hands on the desk.

Her eyes widened. "But—that's blackmail!"

"I think that term is quite correct." His amusement increased. "You catch on very quickly, Miss Clark."

"You can't be serious. You," she sputtered. "You wouldn't actually close the inn just because I quit."

"You don't know me well enough to be sure, do you?" His eyes were unfathomable and steady. "Do you want to chance it?"

Silence hung for a long moment, each measuring the other. "No," B.J. finally murmured, then repeated with more strength, "No, blast it, I can't! You know that already. But I certainly don't understand why."

"You don't have to know why," he interrupted with an imperious gesture of his hand.

Sighing, B.J. struggled not to permit temper to

rule her tongue again. "Mr. Reynolds," she began in what she hoped was a reasonable tone, "I don't know why you find it so important for me to remain as manager of the inn, but—"

"How old are you, Miss Clark?" He cut her off again. She stared in perplexed annoyance.

"I hardly see..."

"Twenty, twenty-one?"

"Twenty-four," B.J. corrected, inexplicably compelled to defend herself. "But I don't see what that has to do with anything."

"Twenty-four," he repeated, obviously concluding she had finished one sentence and that was sufficient. "Chronologically, I have eight years on you, and professionally quite a bit more. I opened my first hotel when you were still leading cheers at Lakeside High."

"I never led cheers at Lakeside High," she said coldly.

"Be that as it may—" he gently inclined his head "—the arithmetic remains the same. My reason for wanting you to remain in your current position at the inn is quite simple. You know the staff, the clientele, the suppliers and so forth...during this transition period I need your particular expertise."

"All right, Mr. Reynolds." B.J. relaxed slightly, feeling the conversation had leveled off to a more professional plane. "But you should be aware, I will give you absolutely no cooperation in changing any aspect which I feel affects the inn's personality. In point of fact, I will do my best to be uncooperative.''

''I'm sure you're quite skillful at that,'' Taylor said easily. B.J. was unsure whether the smile in his eyes was real or in her imagination. ''Now that we understand each other, Miss Clark, I'd like to see the place and get an idea of how you run things. I should be fairly well briefed in two weeks.''

''You can't possibly understand all I've been trying to tell you in that amount of time.''

''I make up my mind quickly,'' he told her. Smiling, he studied her face. ''When something's mine, I know what to do with it.'' His smile widened at her frown, and he rose. ''If you want the inn to remain as is, you'd best stick around and make your sales pitch.'' Taking her arm, he hauled her up from the chair. ''Let's take a look around.''

With all the warmth of a January sky, B.J. took Taylor on a tour of the first floor, describing storage closets in minute detail. Throughout, he kept a hand firmly on her arm as if to remind her of his authority. The continued contact made her vaguely uneasy. His scent was musky and essentially male and he moved with a casualness which she felt was deceptive. His voice rolled deep and smooth, and several times, she found herself listening more to its cadence than to his words. Annoyed, she added to the layers of frost coating her tone.

It would be easier, she decided, if he were short and balding with a generous middle, or, perhaps, if he had a sturdy mole on his left cheek and a pair of chins. It's absolutely unfair for a man to look the way he does and have to fight him, she thought resentfully.

"Have I lost you, Miss Clark?"

"What?" Looking up, she collected her wits, inwardly cursing him again for possessing such dark, magnetic eyes. "No, I was thinking perhaps you'd like lunch." A very good improvisation, she congratulated herself.

"Fine." Agreeably, he allowed her to lead the way to the dining room.

It was a basic, rustic room, large and rectangular with beamed ceilings and gently faded wallpaper. Its charm was old and lasting; amber globed lamps, graceful antiques and old silver. Local stone dominated one wall in which a fireplace was set. Brass andirons guarded the empty hearth. Tables had been set to encourage sociability, with a few more secluded for intimate interludes. The air was humming with easy conversation and clattering dishes. A smell of fresh baking drifted toward them. In silence, Taylor studied the room, his eyes roaming from corner to corner until B.J. was certain he had figured the precise square footage.

"Very nice," he said simply.

A large, round man approached, lifting his head with a subtle dramatic flourish.

"'If music be the food of love, play on.'"

"'Give me excess of it, that, surfeiting, the appetite may sicken, and so die.'"

Chuckling at B.J.'s response, he rolled with a regal, if oversized, grace into the dining room.

"Shakespeare at lunch?" Taylor inquired. B.J. laughed; against her will her antagonism dissolved. "That was Mr. Leander. He's been coming to the inn twice a year for the past ten years. He used to tour with a low budget Shakespearean troupe, and he likes to toss lines at me for me to cap."

"And do you always have the correct response?"

"Luckily, I've always been fond of Shakespeare, and as insurance, I cram a bit when he makes his reservation."

"Just part of the service?" Taylor inquired, tilting his head to study her from a new angle.

"You could say that."

Prudently, B.J. scanned the room to see where the young Dobson twins were seated, then steered Taylor to a table as far distant as possible.

"B.J." Dot sidled to her side, eyes lighting on Taylor in pure feminine avarice. "Wilbur brought the eggs, and they're small again. Elsie's threatening to do permanent damage.''

''All right, I'll take care of it.'' Ignoring Taylor's questioning stare, she turned to her waitress. ''Dot, see to Mr. Reynold's lunch. Please excuse me, Mr. Reynolds, I'll have to tend to this. Just send for me if you have any questions or if something is not to your satisfaction. Enjoy your meal.''

Seeing Wilbur's eggs as a lucky escape hatch, B.J. hurried to the kitchen.

''Wilbur,'' she said with wicked enjoyment as the door swung shut behind her. ''This time, I'm umpire.''

A myriad of small demands dominated B.J.'s afternoon. The art of diplomacy as well as the ability to delegate and make decisions was an intricate part of her job, and B.J. had honed her skills. She moved without breaking rhythm from a debate with the Dobson twins on the advisability of keeping a frog in their bathtub to a counseling service with one of the maids who was weeping into the fresh linen supply over the loss of a boyfriend. Through the hours of soothing and listening and laying down verdicts, she was still conscious of the presence of Taylor Reynolds. It was a simple matter to avoid him physically, but his presence seemed to follow her everywhere. He had made himself known, and she could not forget about him. Perversely, she found herself fretting to know where he was and what he was doing. Probably, she thought with a fresh flash of resentment, probably he's even now in my office poring over my books with a microscope, deciding where to put in his silly tennis courts or how to concrete the grove.

The dinner hour came and went. B.J. had decided to forego supervising the dining room to have a few hours of peace. When she came downstairs to the lounge the lighting was muted, the hour late. The three-piece band hired for the benefit of the Saturday crowd had already packed their equipment. The music had been replaced by the murmurs and clinking glasses of the handful of people who remained. It was the quiet time of the evening, just before silence. B.J. allowed her thoughts to drift back to Taylor.

I've got two weeks to make him see reason, she reminded herself, exchanging goodnights as stragglers began to wander from the lounge. That should be plenty of time to make even the most insensitive businessman understand. I simply went about things in the wrong way. Tomorrow, I'll start my campaign with a brand new strategy. I'll keep my temper under control and use a great many smiles. I'm good at smiling when I put my mind to it.

Practicing her talent on the middle-aged occupant in room 224, B.J.'s confidence grew at his rapidly blinking appreciation. Yes, she concluded, smiles are much better than claws at this stage. A few smiles, a more sophisticated appearance, and a brisk, businesslike approach, and I'll defeat the enemy before the war's declared. Rejuvenated, she turned to the bartender who was lackadaisically wiping the counter. "Go on home, Don, I'll clear up the rest."

"Thanks, B.J." Needing no second urging, he dropped his rag and disappeared through the door.

"It's no trouble at all," she told the empty space with a magnanimous gesture of one hand. "I really insist."

Crossing the room, she began to gather half filled baskets of peanuts and empty glasses, switching on the small eye-level television for company. Around her, the inn settled for sleep, the groans and creaks so familiar, they went unnoticed. Now that the day was over, B.J. found the solitude for which she yearned.

Low, eerie music poured out of the television, drifting and floating through the darkened room. Glancing up, B.J. was soon mesmerized by a horror film. Kicking off her shoes, she slid onto a stool. The story was old and well-worn, but she was caught by a shot of clouds drifting over a full moon. She reached one hand absently for a basket of peanuts, settling them into her lap as the fog began to clear on the set to reveal the unknown terror, preceded by the rustle of leaves, and heavy breathing. With a small moan at the stalking monster's distorted face, B.J. covered her eyes and waited for doom to claim the heroine.

"You'd see more without your hand in front of your eyes."

As the voice came, disembodied in the darkness, B.J. shrieked, dislodging a shower of peanuts from her lap. "Don't ever do that again!" she commanded, glaring up at Taylor's grinning face.

"Sorry." The apology lacked conviction. Leaning on the bar, he nodded toward the set. "Why do you have it on if you don't want to watch?"

"I can't help myself, it's an obsession. But I always watch with my eyes closed. Now look, watch this part, I've seen it before." She grabbed his sleeve with one hand and pointed with the other. "She's going to walk right outside like an idiot. I ask you, would anyone with a working brain cell walk out into the pitch darkness when they hear something scraping at the window? Of course not," she answered for him. "A smart person would be huddled under the bed waiting for it to go away. Oh." She pulled him closer, burying her face against his chest as the monster's face loomed in a close-up. "It's horrible, I can't watch. Tell me when it's over."

Slowly, it dawned on her that she was burrowing

into his chest, his heartbeat steady against her ear. His fingers tangled in her hair, smoothing and soothing her as though comforting a child. She stiffened and started to pull back, but the hand in her hair kept her still.

"No, wait a minute, he's still stalking about and leering. There." He patted her shoulder and loosened his grip. "Saved by commercial television."

Set free, B.J. fumbled off the stool and began gathering scattered peanuts and composure. "I'm afraid things got rather out of hand this afternoon, Mr. Reynolds." Her voice was not quite steady, but she hoped he would attribute the waver to cowardice. "I must apologize for not completing your tour of the inn."

He watched as she scrambled over the floor on her hands and knees, a curtain of pale hair concealing her face. "That's all right. I wandered a bit on my own. I finally met Eddie when not in motion. He's a very intense young man."

She shifted away from him to search for more far reaching nuts. "He'll be good at hotel management in a couple years. He just needs a little more experience." Keeping her face averted, B.J. waited for the heat to cool from her cheeks.

"I met quite a few of the inn's guests today. Everyone seems very fond of B.J." He closed the distance between them and pushed back the hair which lay across her cheek. "Tell me, what does it stand for?"

"What?" Diverted by the fingers on her skin, she found it hard to concentrate on the conversation.

"B.J." He smiled into bemused eyes. "What does it stand for?"

"Oh." She returned the smile, stepping strategically out of reach. "I'm afraid that's a closely guarded secret. I've never even told my mother."

Behind her, the heroine gave a high-pitched, lilting scream. Scattering nuts again, B.J. threw herself into Taylor's arms.

"Oh, I'm sorry, that caught me off guard." Mortified, she lifted her face and attempted to pull away.

"No, this is the third time in one day you've been in this position." One hand lifted, and traveled down the length of her hair as he held her still. "This time, I'm going to see what you taste like."

Before she could protest, his mouth lowered to hers, at once firm and possessing. His arm around her waist brought her close to mold against him. His tongue found hers, and she was unaware whether he had parted her lips or if they had done so of their own volition. He lingered over her mouth, savoring its softness, deepening the kiss until she clung to him for balance. She told herself the sudden spiraling of her heartbeat was a reaction to the horror movie, the quick dizziness, the result of a missed dinner. Then she told herself nothing and only experienced.

''Very nice.'' Taylor's murmured approval trailed along her cheekbone, moving back to tease the corner of her mouth. ''Why don't we try it again?''

In instinctive defense, she pressed her hand into his chest to ward him off. *Lightly* she told herself, praying for the earth to stop trembling, *treat it lightly.* ''I'm afraid I don't come in thirty-two flavors, Mr. Reynolds, and...''

''Taylor,'' he interrupted, smiling down at the hand which represented no more of an obstacle than a blade of grass. ''I decided this morning, when you stalked me in the office, that we're going to know each other very well.''

''Mr. Reynolds...''

''Taylor,'' he repeated, his eyes close and compelling. ''And my decisions are always final.''

''Taylor,'' she agreed, not wanting to debate a minor point when the distance between them was lessening despite the pressure against his chest. ''Do you engage in this sort of activity with all the managers of your hotels?'' Hoping to wound him with a scathing remark, B.J. was immediately disappointed when he tossed back his head and laughed.

''B.J., this current activity has nothing whatever to do with your position at the inn. I am merely indulging my weakness for women who look good in pigtails.''

''Don't you kiss me again!'' she ordered, struggling with a sudden desperation which surprised him into loosening his hold.

''You'll have to choose between being demure or being provocative, B.J.'' His tone was mild, but she saw as she backed away, his eyes had darkened with temper. ''Either way we play, I'm going to win, but it would make the game easier to follow.''

''I don't play this sort of game,'' she retorted, ''and I am neither demure nor provocative.''

''You're a bit of both.'' His hands slipped into his pockets, and he rocked gently on his heels as he studied her furious face. ''It's an intriguing combination.'' His brow lifted in speculation. An expression of amusement flitted over his features. ''But I suppose you already know that or you wouldn't be so good at it.''

Forgetting her fears, B.J. took a step toward him. ''The only thing I know is that I have absolutely no desire to intrigue you in any way. All that I want you to do is to keep your resort builder's hands off this inn.'' Her hands balled into tight fists. ''I wish you'd go back to New York and sit in your penthouse.''

Before he could answer, B.J. turned and darted from the room. She hurried through the darkened lobby without even a backward glance.

Chapter Three

B.J. decided that making a fool of herself the previous evening had been entirely Taylor Reynolds' responsibility. Today, she resolved, slipping a gray blazer over a white silk shirt, I will be astringently businesslike. Nonetheless, she winced at the memory of her naive plea that he not kiss her again, the absurd way her voice had shaken with the words. *Why didn't I come up with some cool, sophisticated retort?* she asked herself. *Because I was too busy throwing peanuts around the room and making a fool of myself,* she answered the question to her frowning mirror image. *Why did a simple kiss cloak my brain with layers of cheesecloth?* The woman in the mirror stared back without answering.

He had caught her off guard, B.J. decided as she arranged her hair in a neat, businesslike roll at her neck's nape. It was so unexpected, she had overreacted. Despite herself, she relived the sensation of his mouth claiming hers, his breath warm on her cheek. The knee trembling, brain spinning feeling never before experienced, washed over her again, and briskly, she shook her head to dispel it. It was simply a matter of the unexpected creating a false intenseness, like pricking your thumb with a needle while sewing.

It was important, she knew, to refrain from thinking of Taylor Reynolds on a personal level, and to remember he held the fate of the Lakeside Inn in his hands.

Dirty pool, her mind muttered, recalling his easy threat to close the inn if she pressed her resignation. Emotional blackmail. He knew he held all the aces, and waited, with that damnably appealing smile, for her to fold or call. *Well*, she decided, and smoothed the charcoal material of her skirt, *I play a pretty mean game of poker myself, Taylor Reynolds.* After trying out several types of smiles in the mirror, polite, condescending, dispassionate, she left the room with brisk steps.

Sunday mornings were usually quiet. Most of the guests slept late, rising in dribbles to wander downstairs for breakfast. Traditionally, B.J. spent these quiet hours closeted in her office with whatever paperwork she felt merited attention. From experience, she had found this particular system worked well, being the least likely time for calamities, minor or major, to befall guests or staff.

She grabbed a quick coffee in the kitchen before plunging into the sea of invoices and account books.

''How providential.'' She jerked slightly as a hand captured her arm, and she found herself being led to the dining room. ''Now, I won't have to have breakfast alone.''

The dozens of flaming retorts which sprang to mind at Taylor's presumptuousness were dutifully banked down. B.J. answered with her seasoned polite smile. ''How kind of you to ask. I hope you spent a pleasant night.''

''As stated in your public relations campaign, the inn is conducive to restful nights.''

Waving aside her hostess, B.J. moved through the empty tables to a corner booth. ''I think you'll find all my publicity is based on fact, Mr. Reynolds.'' Sliding in, B.J. struggled to keep her voice light and marginally friendly. Remnants of their argument in her office and their more personal encounter in the lounge clung to her, and she attempted to erase both from her mind.

''So far I find no discrepancies.''

Maggie hovered by the table, her smile dreamily

absent. No doubt she was thinking of her date last night with Wally, B.J. thought. ''Toast and coffee, Maggie,'' she said kindly, breaking the trance. The waitress scribbled on her pad, her cheeks flushed.

''You know,'' Taylor observed after giving his order, ''you're very good at your job.''

B.J. chided herself for her pleasure at the unexpected praise. ''Why do you say that?''

''Not only are your books in perfect order, but you know your staff and handle them with unobtrusive deftness. You just managed to convey a five-minute lecture with one brief look.''

''It makes it easier when you understand your staff and their habits.'' Her brows lifted in easy humor. ''You see, I happen to know Maggie's mind is still focused on the double feature she and Wally didn't watch last night.''

His grin flashed, boyish and quick.

''The staff is very much like a family.'' B.J. was careful to keep her tone casual, her hands busy pouring coffee. ''The guests feel that. They enjoy the informality which is always accompanied by quality service. Our rules are flexible, and the staff is trained to adjust to the individual needs of the guests. The inn is a basic place, not for those who require formal entertainment or unlimited luxury. Fresh air, good food and a pleasant atmosphere are our enticements, and we deliver.''

She paused as Maggie placed their breakfast order on the table.

"Do you have a moral objection to resorts, B.J.?"

The unexpectedness of Taylor's question put her off. Blinking in confusion at the long, lean fingers as they held a knife, spreading Betty Jackson jelly on toast, she stammered, "No...why of course not." Those fingers, she recalled irrelevantly, had tangled in her hair. "No," she repeated more firmly, meeting his eyes. "Resorts are fine if they are run correctly, as yours are. But their function is entirely different from ours. In a proper resort there's an activity for every minute of the day. Here, the atmosphere is more relaxed, a little fishing or boating, skiing, and above all the menu. The Lakeside Inn is perfect exactly as it is," she concluded more fiercely than she had intended and watched one brow rise, nearly meeting the curling thickness of his hair.

"That's yet to be determined." He lifted his cup to his lips.

His tone was mild, but B.J. recognized traces of anger in the disconcertingly direct eyes. She dropped her eyes to her own cup as if enticed by the rich, black liquid.

"'The gray-eyed morn smiles on the frowning night.'"

The quote brought her head up sharply, and looking into Mr. Leander's smiling, expectant face, B.J.

searched her brain. "'Chequering the eastern clouds with streaks of light.'"

Thank goodness I've read *Romeo and Juliet* a dozen times, she thought, watching his pleased saunter as he moved to his table.

"One day, he's going to catch you, and you're going to draw a blank."

"Life's a series of risks," she returned flippantly. "Better to accept its challenges."

Reaching over, he tucked a stray lock behind her ear, and she jerked away from his touch, unexpectedly shy.

"For the most part," he drew the words out with infuriating emphasis, "I believe you do. It should make things very interesting. More coffee?" His question was pleasant and easy as if they had shared the morning meal on a regular basis. B.J. shook her head in refusal.... She felt uneasily inept at parrying words with this domineering, sophisticated man....

Sunlight poured through the many-paned windows, spilling in patchwork patterns on the floor, a lawn mower hummed along the outer edges of lawn, and somewhere close, a bird sang his enjoyment of a golden day. Closeted in the office with Taylor, B.J. tuned even these small pleasures out, keeping her mind firmly on the business at hand. Here, with the impersonal wedges of invoices and account books between them, she felt confident and assured. In discussing the inn's procedure, her feet were on solid ground. Honesty forced her to admit that Taylor Reynolds knew his profession down to the finest detail. He skimmed through her books with the sharp eye of an accountant, shifted and sorted invoices with the ease of a business manager.

At least, B.J. told herself, he doesn't treat me like an empty-headed imbecile who can't tally monthly accounts. Rather, she found him listening to her explanations with attentive respect. Soothed by his obvious appreciation of her intelligence B.J. decided if he did not yet look on the Lakeside Inn as she did, perhaps that too would come.

"I see you deal with a great many small businesses and local farms."

"That's right." She searched the bottom drawer of her desk for an ashtray as he lit a cigarette. "It's advantageous on all sides. We get more personal service and fresher produce, and it boosts local economy." Finding a small ceramic ashtray under a pile of personal correspondence, B.J. placed it on the desk. "The Lakeside Inn is essential to this district. We provide employment and a market for local products and services."

"Umm."

Finding his response less than illuminating, B.J.

opened her mouth to continue when the door burst open.

"B.J." Eddie stood, bottom lip trembling. "It's the Bodwins."

"I'll be right there." Suppressing a sigh, she made a mental note to tell Eddie to knock during Taylor's stay.

"Is that a natural disaster or a plague?" Taylor asked, watching Eddie's speedy exit.

"It's nothing, really." She edged toward the door. "Excuse me, I'll just be a minute."

Shutting the door behind her, B.J. hurried to the lobby.

"Hello, Miss Patience, Miss Hope." She greeted the elderly Bodwin sisters with a wary smile.

Tall and lean as two aged willows, the Bodwins were long-standing guests.

"It's so nice to see you both again."

"It's always a pleasure to come back, Miss Clark," Miss Patience announced, and Miss Hope murmured in agreement. Habitually Miss Patience announced, and Miss Hope murmured. It was one of the few things which separated them. Over the years they had melded into mirror images from their identical wire rimmed spectacles to their identical orthopedic shoes.

"Eddie, see that the luggage is taken up, please." Miss Patience flashed a knowing smile which B.J.

tried not to notice. B.J. saw her sharp-eyed glance drift over her head. Turning, she spotted Taylor.

"Miss Patience, Miss Hope, this is Taylor Reynolds, the owner of the inn." Miss Patience shot her a meaningful look.

"A pleasure, ladies." Gallantly, he took each thin-boned hand in his. A blush, dormant for twenty-five years, rose to Miss Hope's wrinkled cheek.

"You're a very fortunate young man." Miss Patience gave Taylor a thorough survey, then nodded as if satisfied. "I'm sure you know what a treasure you have in Miss Clark. I hope you appreciate her."

B.J. resisted grinding her teeth for fear the sound would be audible. With a smile, Taylor laid a hand on her shoulder.

"I'm quite convinced Miss Clark is indispensable and my appreciation inadequate."

Satisfied, Miss Patience nodded.

B.J. shook the offending hand from her shoulder and assumed a coolly professional manner. "You have your regular table, number 2."

"Of course." Miss Patience moved her lips into a smile and patted B.J.'s cheek. "You're a good girl, Miss Clark." Smiling vaguely, the two ladies drifted away.

"Surely, B.J." Taylor turned to B.J. with an infuriating smile, "you're not going to give those two dotty old girls the second table?"

"The Lakeside Inn," she said coldly, turning to precede him to the office, "makes it a habit to please its guests. I see no reason why the Bodwins shouldn't sit wherever they want. Mr. Campbell always seated them at number 2."

"Mr. Campbell," Taylor countered with infuriating calm, "no longer owns the inn. I do."

"I'm well aware of that." Her chin tilted higher in defiance. "Do you want me to turn out the Bodwin sisters and place them at the table near the kitchen? Don't they look fancy enough for you? Why don't you think of them as people rather than little black numbers in the bloody account book?"

Her tirade was sharply cut off as he gripped her shoulders. She found she had swallowed the remaining words before she could prevent herself.

"You have," he began in an ominously low voice, "a very unfortunate temper and some very odd ideas. No one tells me how to run my business. Absolutely no one. Advice is accepted upon request, but I only make the decisions, and I alone give the orders."

He moved toward her. She could only stare, fascinated and faintly terrified.

"Do we understand each other?"

B.J. nodded, wide-eyed, then gathered courage to answer audibly. "Yes, perfectly. What would you like me to do about the Bodwins?"

"You've already done it. When you do something which displeases me, B.J., I'll let you know." The underlying threat brought storm warnings to her eyes. "Of course you know," Taylor continued, his tone softening, "you're a very ingenious lady. You've managed to share my breakfast table and work with me throughout the morning without once using my name. You've skirted around it, jumped over it and crawled under it, fascinating me with the acrobatics."

"That's ridiculous." She attempted to shrug, but his hands were firm on her shoulders. "Your imagination needs re-oiling."

"Then perhaps..." His arms moved to capture her waist. She arched away only to be brought steadily closer. "You'd say it now." His mouth hovered above hers. She felt the unfamiliar sweet flow of weakness, the trembling warmth just under her skin.

"Taylor." She failed to bring her voice above a whisper.

"Very good, you'll use it more often." His mouth curved, but she saw the smile only in his eyes. "Do I frighten you, B.J.?"

"No." Her denial was faint. "No," she repeated with more firmness.

"Liar." His laugh was both amused and pleased as his mouth teased hers. It rubbed lightly, holding back the promise until with a moan she drew him closer and took it.

Her breasts crushed against his chest, her lips instinctively found his. She felt herself tumbling in helpless cartwheels down an endless shaft where lights whirled in speeding colors. His hands moved from her waist to her hips, his strong fingers discovering the secrets of subtle curves as his mouth took everything she offered. Craving more, she strained against him until her sharpened senses began to dim, and the world spun hazily around her and vanished.

Fear rose like a phoenix from the flames of passion, and she struggled away, stunned and confused. ''I...I need to check how lunch is going.'' She fumbled behind for the doorknob.

His hands in his pockets, Taylor rocked back on his heels and held her gaze with steady assurance. ''Of course.... Now run away to your duties. But you understand, B.J., that I intend to have you sooner or later. I can be patient up to a point.''

Her hand connected with the knob. She found her voice. ''Of all the appalling nerve! I'm not a piece of property you can have your agent pick up for you.''

''No, I'm handling this strictly on my own.'' He smiled at her. ''I know when something's going to be mine. Acquiring it is simply a matter of timing.''

“I’m not an it.” More outraged than she had thought possible, she took a step toward him. “I have no intention of being acquired and added to your trophies! And timing will get you nowhere!”

His smile was maddeningly confident. B.J. slammed the door full force behind her.

Chapter Four

Mondays always kept B.J. busy. She was convinced that if a major calamity were to fall, it would fall on a Monday simply because that would be the time she would be least able to cope with it. Taylor Reynolds' presence in her office was an additional Monday morning burden. His calm statement of the previous day was still fresh in her mind, and she was still seething with resentment. In an icy voice, she explained to him each phone call she made, each letter she wrote, each invoice she filed. He would not, she decided, accuse her of being uncooperative. Frigid perhaps, she thought with wicked pleasure, but not uncooperative.

Taylor's impeccable, businesslike attitude did

nothing to endear him to her. She was well aware that her cold politeness bordered on the insulting.

Never had she met a man more in control or more annoying. Briefly, she considered pouring her coffee into his lap just to get a reaction. The thought was satisfying.

"Did I miss a joke?" Taylor asked as an involuntary smile flitted over B.J.'s face.

"What?" Realizing her lapse, B.J. struggled to compose her features. "No, I'm afraid my mind was wandering. You'll have to excuse me," she went on, "I have to make sure that all the rooms are made up by this time of day. Will you be wanting lunch in here or in the dining room?"

"I'll come to the dining room." Leaning back, Taylor studied her as he tapped his pencil against the corner of the desk. "Are you joining me?"

"Oh, I'm terribly sorry." B.J.'s tone was falsely saccharine. "I'm swamped today. I recommend the roast beef, though. I'm sure you'll find it satisfactory." Satisfied with her delivery, she closed the door quietly behind her.

With ingenuity and luck, B.J. managed to avoid Taylor throughout the afternoon. The inn was nearly empty as most of the guests were outdoors enjoying the mild spring weather. B.J. was able to slip down the quiet corridors without running into Taylor. She kept her antenna tuned for his presence, however.

Though she knew it was childish, she found herself enjoying the one-way game of hide and seek. It became a self-imposed challenge that she keep out of his sight until nightfall.

In the pre-dinner lull, the inn was drowsy and silent. Humming to herself, B.J. carefully checked off linens in the third floor supply room. She was confident Taylor would not venture into that area of the inn, and relaxed her guard. Her mind traveled from her task, touching on pictures of boating on the lake, walks in the woods, and long summer evenings. Though her daydreams were pleasant, they were underlined by a nagging dissatisfaction. She tried to shrug it off but found it stubborn. There was something missing from the images, or rather someone. Whom would she be boating with on the lake? Whom would she be walking with in the woods? Who would be there to make the long summer evenings special? A distressing image began to form in B.J.'s brain, and she squeezed her eyes tight until it faded.

"I don't need him," she muttered, giving a pile of freshly laundered sheets a pat. "Absolutely not." B.J. backed from the tiny room and quietly pulled the door shut. When she backed into a solid object, she shrieked and fell forward against the closed door.

''Jumpy, aren't you?'' Taylor took her shoulders and turned her to face him. His expression was amused. ''Muttering to yourself, too. Maybe you need a vacation.''

''I...I...''

''A long vacation,'' he concluded, giving her cheek a fatherly pat.

Finding her tongue, B.J. responded with reasonable calm. ''You startled me, sneaking around that way.''

''I thought it was a rule of the house,'' he countered as his grin broke out. ''You've been doing it all afternoon.''

Furious that her cunning had fallen short of the mark, she spoke with frosty dignity. ''I have no idea what you're talking about. Now, if you'll excuse me...''

''Did you know you get a half-inch vertical line between your eyebrows when you're annoyed?''

''I'm very busy.'' She kept her voice cool as she did her best to keep the space between her brows smooth. *Blast the man!* she thought as his engaging smile began to have its effect on her. ''Taylor, if there is something specific you want...'' She stopped as she saw his grin widen until it nearly split his face. ''If there's some business you want to discuss—'' she amended.

''I took a message for you,'' he informed her,

then lifted a finger to smooth away the crease between her brows. ''A very intriguing message.''

''Oh?'' she said casually, wishing he would back up so that she did not feel so imprisoned between his body and the closed store-room door.

''Yes, I wrote it down so there'd be no mistake.'' He took a slip of paper from his pocket and read. ''It's from a Miss Peabody. She wanted you to know that Cassandra had her babies. Four girls and two boys. Sextuplets.'' Taylor lowered the paper and shook his head. ''Quite an amazing feat.''

''Not if you're a cat.'' B.J. felt the color lacing her cheeks. *Why would he have to be the one to take the message? Why couldn't Cassandra have waited?* ''Miss Peabody is one of our oldest guests. She stays here twice a year.''

''I see,'' said Taylor, his mouth twitching. ''Well, now that I've done my duty, it's your turn to do yours.'' Taking her hand, Taylor began to lead her down the corridor. ''This country air gives me quite an appetite. You know the menu, what do you recommend we have?''

''I can't possibly,'' she began.

''Of course you can,'' he interrupted mildly. ''Just think of me as a guest. Inn policy is to give the guests what pleases them. It pleases me to have dinner with you.''

Cornered by her own words, B.J. offered no argument. Within minutes, she found herself seated across from the man she had so successfully avoided during the afternoon.

B.J. thought dinner a relatively painless affair. She felt too, as it neared an end, that she had done her duty and done it superbly. It was, however, difficult to resist the pull of Taylor's charm when he chose to put it into use. The charm itself was so natural and understated that she often found herself captivated before she realized what was happening. Whenever she felt her walls of indifference crumbling, she retreated a step and shored up the holes. *What a shame he isn't someone else,* she mused as he recounted an anecdote. *It would be so nice to enjoy a quiet dinner with him if there weren't any boundaries. But there are,* she reminded herself, quickly pulling out of the range of his charm. *Very definite, very important boundaries. This is war,* she reflected, thinking of their conversation of the previous day. *I can't afford to get caught behind enemy lines.* As Taylor raised his glass and smiled at her, B.J. wondered if Mata Hari had ever been faced with a tougher assignment.

They had reached the coffee stage when Eddie approached their table. "Mr. Reynolds?" B.J. looked on with approval as Eddie neither fidgeted nor seemed ready to burst with the tidings he bore. "There's a phone call for you from New York."

"Thank you, Eddie. I'll take it in the office. I shouldn't be long," Taylor told her as he rose.

"Please, don't rush on my account." B.J. gave him a careful smile, resigning herself to the fact she was a coward. "I still have several things to see to this evening."

"I'll see you later," Taylor returned in a tone that brooked no argument. Their eyes met in a quick clash of wills. In a swift change of mood, Taylor laughed and bent down to kiss B.J. on the forehead before he strolled away.

Mouth agape, B.J. rubbed the spot with her fingertips, wondering why she suddenly felt lightheaded. Forcing herself back to earth, she drank her coffee and hurried off to the lounge.

Monday nights at the inn were an old tradition. The lounge was the center of activity for the weekly event. As B.J. paused in the doorway, she ran a critical eye over the room. The candles had been lit inside each of the coach lanterns which sat on the huddled tables. The lights flickered against the wood. Scents of polish, old wood and smoke melded. The dance floor was gently lit with amber spotlights. Satisfied that the mood was set, B.J. crossed the room and halted next to an ancient Victrola. The faithful mechanism was housed in a rich mahogany cabinet. With affection, B.J. trailed a finger over the smooth lid before opening it.

People began to wander in as she sorted through the collection of old 78s. The hum of conversation behind her was so familiar, it barely tickled her consciousness. Glasses chinked, ice rattled, and an occasional laugh echoed along the walls. With the absentminded skill of an expert, B.J. wound the Victrola into life and set a thick, black record on the turntable. The music which drifted out was scratchy, tinny and charming. Before the record was half over, three couples were on the dance floor. Another Monday night was launched.

During the next half hour, B.J. played an unbroken stream of nineteen-thirty tunes. Over the years, she had noted that no matter what the mean age of the audience, the response to a trip through the past was positive. *Perhaps,* she mused, *it's because the simplicity of the music suits the simplicity of the inn.* With a shrug, she abandoned her analysis and grinned at a couple fox-trotting over the dance floor to the strains of "Tea For Two."

"What the devil is going on in here?"

B.J. heard the demanding question close to her ear and whirled to find herself face to face with Taylor. "Oh, I see you're finished with your call. I hope there isn't any trouble?"

"Nothing important." He waited until she had switched records before he asked again, "B.J., I asked you what's going on in here?"

''Why, just what it looks like,'' she answered vaguely, hearing from the tone of the record that it was time to replace the needle. ''Sit down, Taylor, I'll have Don mix you a drink. You know I'd swear there hasn't been time for this needle to wear out.'' Delving into her spares, B.J. began the task of changing needles.

''When you're finished, perhaps you'd take a look at my carburetor.''

Engrossed in the intricacies of her job, B.J. remained untouched by Taylor's mockery. ''We'll see,'' she murmured, then carefully placed the new needle on the record. ''What would you like, Taylor?'' As she straightened, she glanced toward the bar.

''Initially, an explanation.''

''An explanation?'' she repeated, finally giving him her full attention. ''An explanation about what?''

''B.J.'' Impatience was beginning to thread through his tone. ''Are you being deliberately dense?''

Liking neither his tone nor his question, B.J. stiffened. ''Perhaps if you would be a bit more specific, I would be a bit less dense.''

''I was under the impression that this lounge possessed a functional P.A. system.''

''Well, of course it does.'' As she became more

confused, B.J. pushed away the thought that perhaps she actually was dense. ''What does that have to do with anything?''

''Why isn't it being used?'' He glanced down at the Victrola. ''And why are you using this archaic piece of equipment?''

''The P.A. system isn't being used,'' she explained in calm, reasonable tones, ''because it's Monday.''

''I see.'' Taylor glanced toward the dance floor where one couple was instructing another on the proper moves of a two step. ''That, of course, explains everything.''

His sarcasm caused indignation to flood through her. Clamping her teeth on a stream of unwise remarks, B.J. began to sift rapidly through records. ''On Monday nights, we use the Victrola and play old records. And it is not an archaic piece of equipment,'' she added, unable to prevent herself. ''It's an antique, a museum quality antique.''

''B.J.'' Taylor spoke to the top of her head as she bent to change records. ''Why?''

''Why what?'' she snapped, furious with his ambiguity.

''Why do you use the Victrola and play old records on Monday nights?'' He spoke very clearly, spacing his words as if speaking to someone whose brain was not fully operative.

''Because,'' B.J. began, her eyes flowing, her fists clenching.

Taylor held up a hand to halt the ensuing explanation. ''Wait.'' After the one word command, he crossed the room and spoke to one of the guests. Seething, B.J. watched him use his most charming smile. It faded as he moved back to join her. ''You're being relieved of Victrola duty for a bit. Outside.'' With this, he took her arm and pulled her to the side door. The cool night air did nothing to lower B.J.'s temperature. ''Now.'' Taylor closed the door behind him and leaned back against the side of the building. He made a small gesture with his hand. ''Go right ahead.''

''Oh, you make me so mad I could scream!'' With this dire threat, B.J. began pacing up and down the porch. ''Why do you have to be so…so…''

''Officious?'' Taylor offered.

''Yes!'' B.J. agreed, wishing passionately that she had thought of the word herself. ''Everything's moving along just fine, and then you have to come in and look down your superior nose.'' For some moments, she paced in silence. The romance of the moonlight filtering through the trees seemed sadly out of place. ''People are enjoying themselves in there.'' She swung her hand toward the open window. A Cole Porter number drifted back to her. ''You don't have any right to criticize it. Just because we're not using a live band, or playing top forty numbers, doesn't mean we're not entertaining the guests. I really don't see why you have to..." She broke off abruptly as he grabbed her arm.

"O.K., time's up." As he spun her around, the hair fell over B.J.'s face, and she brushed it back impatiently. "Now, suppose we start this from the beginning."

"You know," she said between her teeth, "I really hate it when you're calm and patient."

"Stick around," he invited. It began to sink into her brain that his voice was dangerously low. "You might see the other end of the scale." Glaring at him did not seem to improve her situation, but B.J. continued to do so. "If you'll think back to the beginning of this remarkable conversation, you'll recall that I asked you a very simple question. And, I believe, a very reasonable one."

"And I told you," she tossed out, then faltered. "At least, I think I did." Frustrated, she threw both hands up in the air. "How am I supposed to remember what you said and what I said? It took you ten minutes to come to the point in the first place." She let out a deep breath as she realized she did not yet have control of her temper. "All right, what was your very simple, very reasonable question?"

"B.J., you would try the patience of a saint." She heard the amused exasperation in his voice and tried not to be charmed. ''I would like to know why I stepped into nineteen-thirty-five when I came into the lounge.''

''Every Monday night,'' she began in crisp, practical tones, ''the inn offers this sort of entertainment. The Victrola was brought here more than fifty years ago, and it's been used every Monday night since. Guests who've been here before expect it. Of course,'' she went on, too involved in her story to realize she was being drawn closer into Taylor's arms, ''the P.A. system was installed years ago. The other six nights of the week, we switch off between it and a live band, depending on the season. The Monday night gathering is almost as old as the inn itself and an important part of our tradition.''

The low, bluesy tones of ''Embraceable You'' were floating through the open window. B.J. was swaying to its rhythm, as yet unaware that Taylor was leading her in a slow dance. ''The guests look forward to it. I've found since I've worked here, that's true no matter how old or how young the clientele is.'' Her voice had lost its crispness. She found her trend of thought slipping away from her as their bodies swayed to the soft music.

''That was a very reasonable answer.'' Taylor drew her closer, and she tilted back her head, unwilling to break eye contact. ''I'm beginning to see the advantages of the idea myself.'' Their faces were close, so close she could feel the touch of his breath on her lips. ‘‘Cold?’’ he asked, feeling her tremble. Though she shook her head, he gathered her closer until the warmth of his body crept into hers. Their cheeks brushed as they merged into one gently swaying form.

‘‘I should go back in,’’ she murmured, making no effort to move away. She closed her eyes and let his arms and the music guide her.

‘‘Um-hum.’’ His mouth was against her ear.

Small night sounds added to the lull of the music from the lounge; a whisper of leaves, the quiet call of a bird, the flutter of moth wings against window glass. The air was soft and cool on B.J.’s shoulders. It was touched with the light scent of hyacinth. Moonlight sprinkled through the maples, causing the shadows to tremble. She could feel Taylor’s heartbeat, a sure, steady rhythm against her own breast. He trailed his mouth along her temple, brushing it through her hair as his hands roamed along her back.

B.J. felt her will dissolving as her senses grew more and more acute. She could hear the sound of his breathing over the music, feel the texture of his skin beneath his shirt, taste the male essence of him on her tongue. Her surroundings were fading like an old photograph with only Taylor remaining sharp and clear. Untapped desire swelled inside her. Suddenly, she felt herself being swallowed by emotions she was not prepared for, by needs she could not understand.

"No, please." Her bid for freedom was so swift and unexpected that she broke from Taylor's arms without a struggle. "I don't want this." She clung to the porch rail and faced him.

Closing the distance between them in one easy motion, Taylor circled the back of her neck with his hand. "Yes, you do." His mouth lowered, claiming hers. B.J. felt the porch tilt under her feet.

Longing, painfully sweet, spread through her until she felt she would suffocate. His hands were bringing her closer and closer. With some unexplained instinct, she knew if she were wrapped in his arms again, she would never find the strength to resist him.

"No!" Lifting both hands, she pushed against his chest and freed herself. "I don't!" she cried in passionate denial. Turning, she streaked down the porch steps. "Don't tell me what I want," she flung back at him before she raced around the side of the building.

She paused before she entered the inn to catch her breath and to allow her pounding heart to slow down. Certainly not the usual Monday evening at Lakeside Inn, she thought, smiling wryly to herself. Unconsciously, she hummed a few bars of "Embraceable You,'' but caught herself with a self-reprimanding frown before she entered the kitchen to remind Dot about the bud vases on the breakfast tables.

Chapter Five

There are days when nothing goes right. The morning, blue and clear and breezy, looked deceptively promising. Clad in a simple green shirtdress and low heels, B.J. marched down the stairs running the word *businesslike* over and over in her mind. Today, she determined, she would be the manager of the inn conducting business with the owner of the inn. There was no moonlight, no music, and she would not forget her responsibilities again. She strolled into the dining room, prepared to greet Taylor casually, then use the need to oversee breakfast preparations as an excuse not to share the morning meal with him. Taylor, however, was already well into a fluffy mound of scrambled eggs and deep into a conversation with Mr. Leander. Taylor gave B.J. an absent wave as she entered, then returned his full attention to his breakfast companion.

Perversely, B.J. was annoyed that her well-planned excuse was unnecessary. She scowled at the back of Taylor's head before she flounced into the kitchen. Ten minutes later, she was told in no uncertain terms that she was in the way. Banished to her office, she sulked in private.

For the next thirty minutes, B.J. occupied herself with busy work, all the while keeping her ears pricked for Taylor's approach. As the minutes passed, she felt a throbbing tension build at the base of her neck. The stronger the ache became, the deeper became her resentment toward Taylor. She set the reason for her headache and her glum mood at his doorstep, though she could not have answered what he had done to cause either. *He was here,* she decided, then broke the point of her pencil. *That was enough.*

"B.J.!" Eddie swirled into the office as she stood grinding her teeth and sharpening her pencil. "There's trouble."

"You bet there is," she muttered.

"It's the dishwasher." Eddie lowered his eyes as if announcing a death in the family. "It broke down in the middle of breakfast."

B.J. let out her breath in a quick sound of annoyance. ‘‘All right, I’ll call Max. With any luck it’ll be going full swing before lunch.’’

Luck, B.J. was to find, was a mirage.

An hour later, she stood by as Max the repairman did an exploratory on the dishwasher. She found his continual mutters, tongue cluckings and sighs wearing on her nerves. Time was fleeting, and it seemed to her that Max was working at an impossibly slow pace. Impatient, she leaned over his shoulder and stared at tubes and wires. Bracing one hand on Max’s back, she leaned in further and pointed.

‘‘Couldn’t you just…’’

‘‘B.J.’’ Max sighed and removed another screw. ‘‘Go play with the inn and let me do my job.’’

Straightening, B.J. stuck out her tongue at the back of his head, then flushed scarlet as she spotted Taylor standing inside the doorway.

‘‘Have a problem?’’ he asked. Though his voice and mouth were sober, his eyes laughed at her. She found his silent mockery infuriating.

‘‘I can handle it,’’ she snapped, wishing her cheeks were cool and her position dignified. ‘‘I’m sure you must be very busy.’’ She cursed herself for hinting at his morning involvement. This time he did smile, and she cursed him as well.

‘‘I’m never too busy for you, B.J.’’ Taylor crossed the room, then took her hand and raised it to his lips before she realized his intent. Max cleared his throat.

''Cut that out.'' She tore her hand away and whipped it behind her back. ''There's no need to concern yourself with this,'' she continued, struggling to assume the businesslike attitude she had vowed to take. ''Max is fixing the dishwasher before the lunch rush.''

''No, I'm not.'' Max sat back on his heels and shook his head. In his hand was a small-toothed wheel.

''What do you mean, no you're not?'' B.J. demanded, forgetting Taylor in her amazement. ''You've got to. I need…''

''What you need is one of these,'' Max interrupted, holding up the wheel.

''Well, all right.'' B.J. plucked the part from his hand and scowled at it. ''Put one in. I don't see how a silly little thing like this could cause all this trouble.''

''When the silly little thing has a broken tooth, it can cause a lot of trouble,'' Max explained patiently, and glanced at Taylor for masculine understanding. ''B.J., I don't carry things like this in stock. You'll have to get it from Burlington.''

''Burlington?'' Realizing the situation was desperate B.J. used her most pleading look. ''Oh, but, Max.''

Though well past his fiftieth birthday, Max was not immune to huge gray eyes. He shifted from one foot to the other, sighed and took the part from B.J.'s palm. "All right, all right, I'll drive into Burlington myself. I'll have the machine fixed before dinner, but lunch is out. I'm not a magician."

"Thank you, Max." Rising on her toes, B.J. pecked his cheek. "What would I do without you?" Mumbling, he packed up his tools and started out of the room. "Bring your wife in for dinner tonight, on the house." Pleased with her success, B.J. smiled as the door swung shut. When she remembered Taylor, she cleared her throat and turned to him.

"You should have those eyes registered with the police department," he advised, tilting his head and studying her. "They're a lethal weapon."

"I don't know what you're talking about." She sniffed with pretended indifference while she wished she could have negotiated with Max in private.

"Of course you do." With a laugh, Taylor cupped her chin in his hand. "That look you aimed at him was beautifully timed."

"I'm sure you're mistaken," she replied, wishing his mere touch would not start her heart pounding. "I simply arranged things in the best interest of the inn. That's my job."

"So it is," he agreed, and leaned on the injured

dishwasher. ‘‘Do you have any suggestions as to what’s to be done until this is fixed?’’

‘‘Yes.’’ She glanced at the double stainless steel sink. ‘‘Roll up your sleeves.’’

It did not occur to B.J. to be surprised that she and Taylor washed the dozens of breakfast dishes side by side until it was *fait accompli.* The interlude had been odd, B.J. felt, because of the unusual harmony which existed between them. They had enjoyed a companionable banter, an easy partnership without the tension which habitually entered their encounters. When Elsie returned to begin lunch preparations, they scarcely noticed her.

‘‘Not one casualty,’’ Taylor proclaimed as B.J. set the last plate on its shelf.

‘‘That’s only because I saved two of yours from crashing on the floor.’’

‘‘Slander,’’ Taylor stated and swung an arm over her shoulder as he led her from the room. ‘‘You’d better be nice to me. What’ll you do if Max doesn’t fix the dishwasher before dinner? Think of all those lunch dishes.’’

‘‘I’d rather not. However, I’ve already given that possibility some consideration.’’ B.J. found the handiest chair in her office and dropped into it. ‘‘I know a couple of kids in town that we could recruit in a pinch. But Max won’t let me down.’’

''You have a lot of faith.'' Taylor sat behind the desk, then lifted his feet to rest on top of it.

''You don't know Max,'' B.J. countered. ''If he said he'd have it fixed before dinner, he will. Otherwise, he'd have said I'll try, or maybe I can, or something of that sort. When Max says I will, he does. That,'' she added, seeing the opportunity to score a point, ''is an advantage of knowing everyone you deal with personally.''

Taylor inclined his head in acknowledgement as the phone rang on the desk. Signaling for Taylor not to bother, B.J. rose and answered it.

''Lakeside Inn. Oh, hello, Marilyn. No, I've been tied up this morning.'' She eased a hip down on the edge of the desk and shuffled through her papers. ''Yes, I have your message here. I'm sorry, I just got back into the office. No, you let me know when you have all your acceptances back, then we'll have a better idea of how to plan the food and so on. There's plenty of time. You've got well over a month before the wedding. Trust me; I've handled receptions before. Yes, I know you're nervous. It's all right, prospective brides are meant to be nervous. Call me when you have a definite number. You're welcome, Marilyn. Yes, yes, you're welcome. 'Bye.''

B.J. hung up the phone and stretched her back before she realized Taylor was waiting for an explanation. "That was Marilyn," B.J. informed him. "She was grateful."

"Yes, I rather got that impression."

"She's getting married next month." B.J. lifted a hand to rub at the stiffness in the back of her neck. "If she makes it without a nervous breakdown, it'll be a minor miracle. People should elope and not put themselves through all this."

"I'm sure there are countless fathers-of-the-bride who would agree with you after paying the expenses of the wedding." He rose, moving around the desk until he stood in front of her. "Here, let me." Lifting his hands, he massaged her neck and shoulders. B.J.'s protest became a sigh of pleasure. The word *businesslike* floated quietly out of her mind. "Better?" Taylor asked, smiling at her closed eyes.

"Mmm. It might be in an hour or two." She stretched under his hands like a contented kitten. "Ever since Marilyn set the date, she's been on the phone three times a week to check on the reception. It's hard to believe someone could get that excited about getting married."

"Well, not everyone is as cool and collected as you," Taylor remarked as he ran his thumbs along her jawline, stroking his other fingers along the base of her neck. "And, by the way, I wouldn't spread that eloping idea of yours around if I were you. I imagine the inn makes a good profit doing wedding receptions.''

''Profit?'' B.J. opened her eyes and tried to concentrate on what they had been saying. It was difficult to think with his hands so warm and strong on her skin. ''Profit?'' she said again and swallowed as her brain cleared. ''Oh well…yes.'' She scooted off the desk and out of his reach. ''Yes, usually…that is…sometimes.'' She wandered the room wishing the interlude in the kitchen had not made her forget who he was. ''It depends, you see, on… Oh boy.'' She ended on a note of disgust and blew out a long breath.

''Perhaps you'd translate all that into English?'' Taylor suggested. With a twinge of uneasiness, B.J. watched him seat himself once more behind the desk. *Owner to manager* again, she thought bitterly.

''Well, you see,'' she began, striving for nonchalance. ''There are occasions when we do wedding receptions or certain parties without charge. That is,'' she rushed on as his face remained inscrutable, ''we charge for the food and supplies, but not for the use of the lounge…''

''Why?'' The one word interruption was followed by several seconds of complete silence.

''Why?'' B.J. repeated and glanced briefly at the ceiling for assistance. ''It depends, of course, and it is the exception rather than the rule.'' *Why?* she demanded of herself. *Why don't I learn to keep my mouth shut?* "In this case, Marilyn is Dot's cousin. You met Dot, she's one of our waitresses," she continued as Taylor remained unhelpfully silent. "She also works here during the summer season. We decided, as we do on certain occasions, to give Marilyn the reception as a wedding present."

"We?"

"The staff," B.J. explained. "Marilyn is responsible for the food, entertainment, flowers, but we contribute the lounge and our time, and," she added, dropping her voice to a mumble, "the wedding cake."

"I see." Taylor leaned back in the chair and laced his fingers together. "So, the staff donates their time and talent and the inn."

"Just the lounge." B.J. met his accusatory glance with a glare. "It's something we do only a couple of times a year. And if I must justify it from a business standpoint, it's good public relations. Maybe it's even tax deductible. Ask your C.P.A." She began to storm around the office as her temper rose, but Taylor sat calmly. "I don't see why you have to be so picky. The staff works on their own time. We've been doing it for years. It's…"

"Inn policy," Taylor finished for her. "Perhaps I should have you list all the eccentricities of inn policy for me. But I should remind you, B.J., that the inn's policy is not carved in stone."

"You're not going to drop the axe on Marilyn's reception," B.J. stated, prepared for a fight to the finish.

"I've misplaced my black hood, B.J., so I can't play executioner. However," he continued before the look of satisfaction could be fully formed on her face, "you and I will have to have a more detailed discussion on the inn's public relations."

"Yes, sir," she replied in her most wintry voice, and was saved from further argument by the ringing of the phone.

Taylor motioned for her to answer it. "I'll get us some coffee."

B.J. watched him stroll from the room as she lifted the phone to her ear.

When Taylor returned a few moments later, she was seated behind the desk just replacing the receiver. With a sound of annoyance, she supported her chin on her elbows.

"The florist doesn't have my six dozen daffodils."

"I'm sorry to hear that." Taylor placed her coffee on the desk.

"Well, you should be. It's your inn, and they are actually your daffodils."

"It's kind of you to think of me, B.J.," Taylor

said amiably. ''But don't you think six dozen is a bit extreme?''

''Very funny,'' she muttered and picked up her coffee cup. ''You won't think it's such a joke when there aren't any flowers on the tables.''

''So, order something besides daffodils.''

''Do I look like a simpleton?'' B.J. demanded. ''He won't have anything in that quantity until next week. Some trouble at the greenhouse or something. Blast it!'' She swallowed her coffee and scowled at the far wall.

''For heaven's sake, B.J., there must be a dozen florists in Burlington. Have them delivered.'' Taylor dismissed the matter of daffodils with an airy wave.

B.J. gave him an opened mouth look of astonishment. ''Delivered from Burlington? Do you have any idea how much those daffodils would cost?'' Rising, she paced the room while she considered her options. ''I simply can't tolerate artificial flowers,'' she muttered while Taylor sipped his coffee and watched her. ''They're worse than no flowers at all. I hate to do it,'' she said with a sigh. ''It's bad enough having to beg for her jelly, now I'm going to have to beg for her flowers. There's absolutely nothing else I can do. She's got the only garden in town that can handle it.'' Making a complete circle of the room, B.J. plopped down behind the desk again.

''Are you finished?''

''No,'' B.J. answered, picking up the phone. ''I still have to talk her out of them.'' Grimly, she set her teeth. ''Wish me luck.''

Deciding all would be explained in due time, Taylor sat back to watch. ''Luck,'' he said agreeably and finished off his coffee.

When B.J. had completed her conversation, he shook his head in frank admiration. ''That,'' he said as he toasted her with his empty cup, ''was the most blatant con job I've ever witnessed.''

''Subtlety doesn't work with Betty Jackson.'' Smug, B.J. answered his toast, then rose. ''I'm going to go pick up those flowers before she changes her mind.''

''I'll drive you,'' Taylor offered, taking her arm before she reached the door.

''Oh, you needn't bother.'' The contact reminded her how slight was her will when he touched her.

''It's no bother,'' he countered, leading her through the inn's front door. ''I feel I must see the woman who, how did you put it? 'Raises flowers with an angel's touch.'''

''Did I say that?'' B.J. struggled to prevent a smile.

''That was one of your milder compliments.''

''Desperate circumstances call for desperate measures,'' B.J. claimed and slid into Taylor's Mercedes. ''Besides, Miss Jackson does have an extraordinary garden. Her rosebush won a prize last year. Turn left here,'' she instructed as he came to a fork in the road. ''You know, you should be grateful to me instead of making fun. If you'd had your way, we'd be eating up a healthy percentage of the inn's profits in delivery fees.''

''My dear Miss Clark,'' Taylor drawled, ''if there's one thing I can't deny, it's that you are a top flight manager. Of course, I'm also aware that a raise is in order.''

''When I want a raise, I'll ask for one,'' B.J. snapped. As she gave her attention to the view out the side window, she missed Taylor's glance of speculation. She had not liked his use of her surname, nor had she liked being reminded again so soon of the status of their positions. He was her employer, and there was no escaping it. Closing her eyes, she chewed on her lower lip. The day had not run smoothly, perhaps that was why she had been so acutely annoyed over such a small thing. *And so rude,* she added to herself. Decidedly, it was her responsibility to offer the olive branch. Turning, she gave Taylor a radiant smile.

''What sort of raise?''

He laughed, and reached over to ruffle her hair. ''What an odd one you are, B.J.''

''Oh, I know,'' she agreed, wishing she could understand her own feelings. ''I know. There's the house.'' She gestured as they approached. ''Third from the corner.''

They alighted from opposite sides of the car, but Taylor took her arm as they swung through Betty Jackson's gate. This visit, B.J. decided, thinking of the silver blue Mercedes and Taylor's elegantly simple silk shirt, should keep Miss Jackson in news for six months. The doorbell was answered before it had stopped ringing.

''Hello, Miss Jackson,'' B.J. began and prepared to launch into her first thank you speech. She closed her mouth as she noticed Betty's attention was focused well over her head. ''Oh, Miss Jackson, this is Taylor Reynolds, the owner of the inn. Taylor, Betty Jackson.'' B.J. made introductions as Betty simultaneously pulled her apron from her waist and metal clips from her hair.

''Miss Jackson.'' Taylor took her free hand as Betty held the apron and clips behind her back. ''I've heard so much about your talents, I feel we're old friends.'' Blushing like a teenager, Betty was, for the first time in her sixty odd years, at a loss for words.

''We came by for the flowers,'' B.J. reminded her, fascinated by Betty's reaction.

''Flowers? Oh, yes, of course. Do come in.'' She ushered them into the house and into her living room, all the while keeping her hand behind her back.

''Charming,'' Taylor stated, gazing around at chintz and doilies. Turning, he gave Betty his easy smile. ''I must tell you, Miss Jackson, we're very grateful to you for helping us out this way.''

''It's nothing, nothing at all,'' Betty said, fluttering her hand with the words. ''Please sit down. I'll fix us a nice pot of tea. Come along, B.J.'' She scurried from the room, leaving B.J. no choice but to follow. Safely enclosed in the kitchen, Betty began to move at lightning speed. ''Why didn't you tell me you were bringing *him?*'' she demanded, flourishing a teapot.

''Well, I didn't know until…''

''Goodness, you could have given a person a chance to comb her hair and put her face on.'' Betty dug out her best china cups and inspected them for chips.

B.J. bit the inside of her lip to keep a grin from forming. ''I'm sorry, Betty. I had no idea Mr. Reynolds was coming until I was leaving.''

''Never mind, never mind.'' Betty brushed aside the apology with the back of her hand. ''You did bring him after all. I'm positively dying to talk to him. Why don't you run out and get your flowers now before tea?'' She produced a pair of scissors.

''Just pick whatever you need.'' She dismissed B.J. with a hasty wave. ''Take your time.''

After the back door had closed firmly in her face, B.J. stood for a moment, torn between amusement and exasperation before heading towards Betty's early spring blooms.

When she re-entered the kitchen about twenty minutes later, armed with a selection of daffodils and early tulips, she could hear Betty laughing. Carefully placing her bouquet on the kitchen table, she walked into the living room.

Like old friends, Taylor and Betty sat on the sofa, a rose patterned teapot nestled cozily on the low table. ''Oh, Taylor,'' Betty said, still laughing, ''you tell such stories! What's a poor woman to believe?''

B.J. looked on in stunned silence. She was certain Betty Jackson had not flirted this outrageously in thirty years. And, she noted with a shake of her head, Taylor was flirting with equal aplomb. As Betty leaned forward to pour more tea, Taylor glanced over her head and shot B.J. a grin so endearingly boyish it took all her willpower not to cross the room and throw herself into his arms. He was, she thought with a curious catch in her heart, impossible. No female under a hundred and two was safe around him. Unable to do otherwise, B.J. answered his grin.

''Miss Jackson,'' B.J. said, carefully readjusting her features. ''Your garden is lovely as always.''

''Thanks, B.J. I really do work hard on it. Did you get all that you wanted?''

''Yes, thank you. I don't know how I would have managed without you.''

''Well.'' Betty sighed as she rose. ''I'll just get a box for them.''

Some fifteen minutes later, after Betty had exacted a promise from Taylor that he drop by again, B.J. was in the Mercedes beside him. In the back seat were the assortment of flowers and a half a dozen jars of jelly as a gift to Taylor.

''You,'' B.J. began in the sternest voice she could manage, ''should be ashamed.''

''I?'' Taylor countered, giving her an innocent look. ''Whatever for?''

''You know very well what for,'' B.J. said severely. ''You very near had Betty swooning.''

''I can't help it if I'm charming and irresistible.''

''Oh, yes, you can,'' she disagreed. ''You were deliberately charming and irresistible. If you'd said the word, she'd have ripped up her prize rosebush and planted it at the inn's front door.''

''Nonsense,'' Taylor claimed. ''We were simply having an enjoyable conversation.''

''Did you enjoy the camomile tea?'' B.J. asked sweetly.

''Very refreshing. You didn't get a cup, did you?''

''No.'' B.J. sniffed and folded her arms across her chest. ''I wasn't invited.''

''Ah, now I see.'' Taylor sighed as he pulled in front of the inn. ''You're jealous.''

''Jealous?'' B.J. gave a quick laugh and brushed the dust from her skirt. ''Ridiculous.''

''Yes, I see it now,'' he said smugly, repressing a grin. ''Silly girl!'' With this, he stopped the car, and turning to B.J. lowered his smiling mouth to hers. Imperceptibly, his lips lost their teasing quality, becoming warm and soft on her skin. B.J.'s playful struggles ceased, and she stiffened in his arms.

''Taylor, let me go.'' She found it was more difficult now to catch her breath than it had been when she had been laughing. A small moan escaped her as his lips trailed to her jawline. ''No,'' she managed, and putting her fingers to his lips, pushed him away. He studied her, his eyes dark and full of knowledge as she fought to control her breathing. ''Taylor, I think it's time we established some rules.''

''I don't believe in rules between men and women, and I don't follow any.'' He said this with such blatant arrogance, B.J. was shocked into silence. ''I'll let you go now, because I don't think it's wise to make love with you in broad daylight in the front seat of my car. However, the time will come when the circumstances will be more agreeable."

B.J. narrowed her eyes and found her voice. "You seriously don't think I'll agree to that, do you?"

"When the time comes, B.J.," he said with maddening confidence, "you'll be happy to agree."

"Fat chance," she said as she struggled out of the car. "We're never going to agree about anything." Slamming the door gave her some satisfaction.

As she ran up the front steps and into the inn, B.J. decided she never wanted to hear the word *businesslike* again.

Chapter Six

B.J. was standing on the wide lawn enjoying the warmth of the spring sun. She had decided to avoid Taylor Reynolds as much as possible and concentrate on her own myriad responsibilities. Unfortunately, that had not been as easy as she had hoped: she had been forced to deal with him on a daily business basis.

Though the inn was relatively quiet, B.J. knew that in a month's time, when the summer season began, the pace would pick up. Her gaze traveled the length and height of the inn, admiring the mellowed bricks serene against the dark pines, the windows blinking in the bright spring sun. On the back porch, two guests were engaged in an undemanding game of checkers. From where she was standing, B.J. could barely hear the murmur of their conversation without hearing the words.

All too soon, this peace would be shattered by children shouting to each other as they raced across the lawn, by the purr of motorboats as they sped past the inn. Yet, somehow, the inn never lost its informal air of tranquility. Here, she mused, the shade was for relaxing, the grass invited bare feet, the drifting snow for sleigh rides and snow men. Elegance had its place, B.J. acknowledged, but the Lakeside Inn had a charm of its own. *And Taylor Reynolds was not going to destroy it.*

You've only got ten days left. He leaves in ten days, she reminded herself. She sighed.

The sigh was as much for herself as for the inn's fate. *I wish he'd never come. I wish I'd never laid eyes on him.* Scowling, she headed back towards the inn.

"That face is liable to turn guests away." Startled, B.J. stared at Taylor as he blocked the doorway. "I think it's best for business if I get you away from here for a while." Stepping forward, he took her hand and pulled her across the lawn.

"I have to go in," she protested. "I…I have to phone the linen supplier."

"It'll keep. Your duties as guide come first."

‘‘Guide? Would you please let me go? Where are we going?’’

‘‘Yes. No. And we’re going to enjoy one of Elsie’s famous picnics.’’ Taylor held up the hamper he held in his free hand. ‘‘I want to see the lake.’’

‘‘You don’t need me for that. You can’t miss it. It’s the huge body of water you come to at the end of the path.’’

‘‘B.J.’’ He stopped, turning directly to face her. ‘‘For two days you’ve avoided me. Now, I’m well aware we have differences in our outlook on the inn.’’

‘‘I hardly see…’’

‘‘Be quiet,’’ he said pleasantly. ‘‘I am willing to give you my word that no major alterations will be started without your being notified. Whatever changes I decide upon will be brought to your attention before any formal plans are drawn up.’’ His tone was brisk and businesslike even while he ignored her attempts to free her hand. ‘‘I respect your dedication and loyalty to the inn.’’ His tone was coolly professional.

‘‘But…’’

‘‘However,’’ he cut her off easily, ‘‘I do own the inn, and you are in my employ. As of now you have a couple hours off. How do you feel about picnics?’’

‘‘Well, I…’’

‘‘Good. I’m fond of them myself.’’ Smiling easily, he began to move down the well worn path through the woods.

The undergrowth was still soft from winter. Beneath the filtered sunlight wild flowers were a multicolored carpet, bright against their brown background of decaying leaves. Squirrels darted up the trunks of trees where birds had already begun to nest.

"Do you always shanghai your companions?" B.J. demanded, angry and breathless at keeping pace with Taylor's long strides.

"Only when necessary," he replied curtly.

The path widened, then spread into the grassy banks of the lake. Taylor stopped, surveying the wide expanse of lake with the same absorption that B.J. had observed in him earlier.

The lake was unruffled, reflecting a few clouds above it. The mountains on its opposite edge were gently formed. They were not like the awesome, demanding peaks of the West, but sedate and well behaved. The silence was broken once by the quick call of a chickadee, then lay again like a calming hand on the air.

"Very nice," Taylor said at length, and B.J. listened for but heard no condescension in his tone. "A very lovely view. Do you ever swim here?"

"Only since I was two," B.J. answered, groping for a friendly lightness. She wished he would not continue to hold her hand as if he had done so a thousand times before, wished hers did not fit into his as if molded for the purpose.

"Of course." He turned his head, switching his study from the lake to her face. "I'd forgotten, you were born here, weren't you?"

"I've always lived in Lakeside." Deciding that setting up the picnic things was the most expedient way to break the hand contact, B.J. took the hamper and began spreading Elsie's neatly folded cloth. "My parents moved to New York when I was nineteen, and I lived there for almost a year. I transferred colleges at mid-term and enrolled back here."

"How did you find New York?" Taylor dropped down beside her, and B.J. glimpsed at the bronzed forearms which his casually rolled up sleeves revealed.

"Noisy and confusing," she replied, frowning at a platter of crisp golden chicken. "I don't like to be confused."

"Don't you?" His swift grin appeared at her frown. With one deft motion, he pulled out the ribbon which held her hair neatly behind her back. "It makes you look like my adolescent niece." He tossed it carelessly out of reach as B.J. grabbed for it.

"You are an abominably rude man." Pushing

back her newly liberated hair, she glared into his smiling face.

"Often," he agreed and lifted a bottle of wine from the hamper. He drew the cork with the ease of experience while B.J. fumed in silence. "How did you happen to become manager of the Lakeside Inn?"

The question took her off guard. For a moment she watched him pour the inn's best Chablis into Dixie cups. "I sort of gravitated to it." Accepting the offered cup, she met the directness of his gaze and realized he would not be content with the vagueness of her answer. "I worked summers at the inn when I was in high school, sort of filling in here and there at first. By the time I graduated, I was assistant manager. Anyway," she continued, "when I moved back from New York, I just slid back in. Mr. Blakely, the old manager, recommended me when he retired, and I took over." She shrugged and bit into a drumstick.

"Between your education and your dedication to your career, where did you find the time to learn how to swing a bat like Reggie Jackson?"

"I managed to find a few moments to spare. When I was fourteen," she explained, grinning at the memory, "I was madly in love with this older man. He was seventeen." She gave Taylor a sober nod. "Baseball oozed from his pores, so I enthusiastically took up the game. He'd call me shortstop, and my toes would tingle.''

Taylor's burst of laughter startled a slumbering blue jay who streaked across the sky with an indignant chatter. ''B.J., I don't know anyone like you. What happened to the toe tingler?''

Overcome by the pleasure his laughter had brought her, she fumbled for the thread of the conversation. ''Oh...he...uh...he's got two kids and sells used cars.''

''His loss,'' Taylor commented, cutting a thin wedge of cheese.

B.J. broke a fragrant hunk of Elsie's fresh bread and held it out to Taylor for a slice of cheese. ''Do you spend much time at your other hotels?'' she asked, uncomfortable at the personal tone the conversation seemed to be taking.

''Depends.'' His eyes roamed over her as she sat cross legged on the grass, her soft hair tumbling over her shoulders, her lips slightly parted.

''Depends?'' she inquired. He stared a moment at her and she fought not to fidget under his encompassing gaze.

''I make certain my managers are competent.'' He broke the silence with a smile. ''If there's a specific problem, I'll deal with it. First, I like to get the feel of a new acquisition, determine if a policy change is warranted.''

"But you work out of New York?" The trend of the conversation was much more to her liking. The tension eased from her shoulders.

"Primarily. I've seen fields in Kansas that looked less like wheat than your hair." He captured a generous handful. B.J. swallowed in surprise. "The fog in London isn't nearly as gray or mysterious as your eyes."

B.J. swallowed and moistened her lips. "Your chicken's getting cold."

His grin flashed at her feeble defense but his hand relinquished its possession of her hair. "It's supposed to be cold." Lifting the wine bottle, Taylor refilled his cup. "Oh, by the way, there was a call for you."

B.J. took a sip of Chablis with apparent calm. "Oh, was it important?"

"Mmm." Taylor moved his shoulders under his cream colored tailored shirt. "A Howard Beall. He said you had his number."

"Oh." B.J. frowned, recalling it was about time for her duty date with Betty Jackson's nephew. Her sigh was automatic.

"My, you simply reek of enthusiasm."

Taylor's dry comment brought on a smile and a shrug. "He's just a man I know."

Taylor contented himself with a slight raising of his brow.

The sky was now an azure arch, without even a puff of cloud to spoil its perfection. Replete and relaxed, B.J. rolled over on her back to enjoy it. The grass was soft and smelled fresh. Overhead, the maple offered a half-shade. Its black branches were touched with young, tender leaves. Through the spreading cluster of trees, dogwoods bloomed white.

"In the winter," she murmured, half to herself, "it's absolutely still here after a snowfall. Everything's white. Snow hangs and drips from the trees and carpets the earth. The lake's like a mirror. The ice is as clear as rain water. You almost forget there's any place else in the world, or that spring will come. Do you ski, Taylor?" She rolled over on her stomach, her elbows supporting her head to smile at him, all animosity forgotten.

"I've been known to." He returned her smile, studying the soft drowsy face, rosy from the sun and the unaccustomed wine.

"The skiing's marvelous here." She tossed back her hair with a quick movement of her shoulders. "Snow skiing's so much more exciting than water skiing, I think. The food at the inn brings the skiing crowd. There's nothing like Elsie's stew after a day on the slopes." Plucking a blade of grass, she twirled it idly.

Taylor moved to lie down beside her. She was too content to be alarmed at his proximity.

"Dumplings?" he inquired, and she grinned down into his face.

"Of course. Hot buttered rum or steaming chocolate."

"I'm beginning to regret I missed the season."

"Well, you're in time for strawberry shortcake," she offered in consolation. "And the fishing's good year round."

"I've always favored more active sports." His finger ran absently up her arm, and B.J. tried hard to ignore the pleasure it gave her.

"Well." Her brow creased as she considered. "There's a good stable about fifteen miles from here, or boats for rent at the marina, or…"

"Those aren't the sports I had in mind." With a swift movement, he dislodged her elbows and brought her toppling onto his chest. "Are they the best you can do?" His arms held her firmly against him, but she was already captured by the fascination of his eyes.

"There's hiking," she murmured, unaware of the strange husky texture of her own voice.

"Hiking," Taylor murmured, before altering their positions in one fluid motion.

"Yes, hiking's very popular." She felt her consciousness drifting as she gazed up at him and struggled to retain some hold on lucidity. "And…and swimming."

“Mmm.” Absently, his fingers traced the delicate line of her cheek.

“And there’s…uh…there’s camping. A lot of people like camping. We have a lot of parks.” Her voice faltered as his thumb ran over her lips.

“Parks?” he repeated, prompting her.

“Yes, a number of parks, quite a number. The facilities are excellent for camping.” She gave a small moan as his mouth lowered to tease the curve of her neck.

“Hunting?” Taylor asked conversationally as his lips traveled over her jawline to brush the corner of her mouth.

“I, yes. I think…what did you say?” B.J. closed her eyes on a sigh.

“I wondered about hunting,” he murmured, kissing closed lids as his fingers slid under her sweater to trace her waist.

“There’s bobcat in the mountains to the north.”

“Fascinating.” He rubbed his mouth gently over hers as his fingers trailed lightly up her flesh to the curve of her breast. “The chamber of commerce would be proud of you.” Lazily, his thumb ran over the satin swell. Pleasure became a need as warmth spread from her stomach to tremble in her veins and cloud her brain.

“Taylor.” Unable to bring her voice above a

whisper, her hand sought the thick mass of his hair. ‘‘Kiss me.’’

‘‘In a minute,’’ he murmured, obviously enjoying the taste of her neck, until with devastating leisure, he moved his mouth to hers.

Trembling with a new, unfamiliar hunger, B.J. pulled him closer until his mouth was no longer teasing but avid on hers. Warmth exploded into fire. His tongue was searching, demanding all of her sweetness, his body as taut as hers was fluid. He took possession of her curves with authority, molding them with firm, strong hands. His mouth no longer roamed from hers but remained to devour what she offered. The heat grew to an almost unbearable intensity, her soul melting in it to flow into his. For a moment, she was lost in the discovery of merging, feeling it with as much clarity as she felt his hands and mouth. Soaring freedom and the chains of need were interchangeable. As time ceased to flow, she plunged deeper and deeper into the all-enveloping present.

His hands took more, all gentleness abandoned. It flashed across the mists in her brain that beneath the control lay a primitive, volatile force from which she had no defense. She struggled weakly. Her protests were feeble murmurs against the demands of his mouth. Feeling her tense, Taylor lifted his head, and she felt the unsteady rhythm of his breathing on her face.

''Please, let me go.'' Hating the weak timbre of her own voice, she sank her teeth into the lip still tender from his.

''Why should I do that?'' Temper and passion threatened his control. She knew she had neither the strength nor the will to resist him if he chose to take.

''Please.''

It seemed an eternity that he studied her, searching the smoky depths of her eyes. She watched the anger fade from his eyes as he took in the fair hair spread across the grass, the vulnerable, soft mouth. Finally, he released her with a brief, muttered oath.

''It appears,'' he began as she scrambled to sit up, ''that pigtails suit you more than I realized.'' He took out a cigarette and lit it deliberately. ''Virginity is a rare commodity in a woman your age.''

Color flooded her cheeks as B.J. began to pack up the remains of the picnic. ''I hardly see what business that is of yours.''

''It doesn't matter,'' he countered easily and she cursed him for his ability to retain his composure so effortlessly while her entire body still throbbed with need. ''It will simply take a bit more time.'' At her uncomprehending stare, he smiled and folded the cloth. ''I told you I always win, B.J. You'd best get used to it.''

"You listen to me." Storming, she sprang to her feet. "I am not about to be added to your list. This was…this was…" Her hands spread out to sweep away the incident while her brain searched for the proper words.

"Just the beginning," he supplied. Rising with the hamper, he captured her arm in a firm grip. "We haven't nearly finished yet. I wouldn't argue at the moment, B.J.," he warned as she began to sputter. "I might decide to take what you so recently offered here and now, rather than giving you some time."

"You are the most arrogant—" she began. Her voice sounded hopelessly childish even to her own ears.

"That's enough for now, B.J." Taylor interrupted pleasantly. "There's no point saying anything you might regret." He leaned down and kissed her firmly before helping her to her feet. With an easy swing, he reached for the hamper. B.J. was too dazed to do anything but meekly follow him as he led the way toward the homeward wooded path.

Chapter Seven

Once back at the inn, B.J. wanted nothing more than to disengage her arm from Taylor's grasp and find a dark, quiet hole in which to hide. She knew all too well that she had responded completely to Taylor's demands. Moreover, she knew she had made demands of her own. She was confused by her own reactions. Never before had she had difficulty in avoiding or controlling a romantic interlude, but she was forced to admit that from the moment Taylor had touched her, her mind had ceased to function.

Biology, she concluded, darting Taylor a sidelong glance as they approached the skirting porch. It was simply a matter of basic biology. Any woman would naturally be attracted to a man like Taylor Reynolds. He has a way of looking at you, B.J. mused, that makes your mind go fuzzy, then blank. He has a way of touching you that makes you feel as though you never had been touched before. He's nothing like any other man I've ever known. And *I asked him to kiss me.* Color rose to her cheeks. *I actually asked him to kiss me.* It must have been the wine.

Soothed by this excuse, B.J. turned to Taylor as they entered the side door. "I'll take the basket back to the kitchen. Do you need me for anything else?"

"That's an intriguing question," he drawled.

B.J. shot him a quelling glance. "I have to get back to work now," she said briskly. "Now, if you'll excuse me?"

B.J.'s dignified exit was aborted by a flurry of activity in the lobby. Curiosity outweighing pride, she allowed Taylor to lead her toward the source.

A tall, svelte brunette stood by the desk, surrounded by a clutter of shocking pink luggage. Her pencil-slim form was draped in a teal blue suit of raw silk. The scent of gardenias floated toward B.J.

"If you'll see to my luggage, darling, and tell Mr. Reynolds I'm here, I'd be very grateful." She addressed these requests in a low, husky voice to Eddie who stood gaping beside her.

"Hello, Darla. What are you doing here?"

At Taylor's voice, the dark head turned. B.J.

noted the eyes were nearly the same shade as the exquisite suit.

"Taylor." Impossibly graceful on four-inch heels, Darla glided across the lobby to embrace Taylor warmly. "I'm just back from checking on the job in Chicago. I knew you'd want me to look this little place over and give you my ideas."

Disengaging himself, Taylor met Darla's glowing smile with an ironic smile. "How considerate of you. B.J. Clark, Darla Trainor. Darla does the majority of my decorating, B.J. manages the inn."

"How interesting." Darla gave B.J.'s sweater and jeans a brief, despairing glance and patted her own perfectly styled hair. "From what I've seen so far, my work is certainly cut out for me." With a barely perceptible shudder, Darla surveyed the lobby's hand hooked rugs and Tiffany lamps.

"We've had no complaints on our decor." B.J. leaped to the inn's defense.

"Well." She was given a small, pitying smile from deeply colored lips. "It's certainly quaint, isn't it? Rather sweet for Ma and Pa Kettle. You'll have to let me know, Taylor, if you plan to enlarge this room." Transferring her attention, Darla's expression softened and warmed. "But, of course, red's always an eye-catcher. Perhaps red velvet drapes and carpeting."

B.J.'s eyes darkened to flint. "Why don't you take your red velvet drapes and..."

"I believe we'll discuss this later," Taylor said diplomatically, tightening his hold on B.J.'s arm. Struggling to prevent herself from crying with the pain, B.J. found argument impossible.

"I'm sure you'd like to get settled in," she forced out between clenched lips.

"Of course." Darla viewed B.J.'s brief outburst with a fluttering of heavy lashes. "Come up for a drink, Taylor. I assume this place has room service."

"Of course. Have a couple of martinis sent up to Miss Trainor's room," Taylor said to Eddie. "What's your room number, Darla?"

"I don't believe I have one yet." Again using her extensive lashes to advantage, Darla turned to a still dazed Eddie. "There seems to be a small communication problem."

"Give Miss Trainor 314, Eddie, and see to her bags." The sharp command in B.J.'s voice snapped Eddie's daydream, and he scurried to comply. "I hope you find it suitable." B.J. turned her best managerial smile on her new and unwelcome guest. "Please let me know if there's anything you need. I'll see to your drinks."

Taylor's hand held her still another moment. "I'll speak with you later."

"Delighted," B.J. returned, feeling the circulation slowly returning to her arm as he released it. "I'll wait to be summoned at your convenience, Mr. Reynolds. Welcome to the Lakeside Inn, Miss Trainor. Have a nice stay."

It was a simple matter to avoid a private meeting with Taylor as he spent the remainder of the day in Darla Trainor's company. They were closeted in 314 for what seemed to B.J. a lifetime. To boost her ego B.J. decided to phone Howard. They arranged a date for the following evening. *Well, at least Howard doesn't closet himself downing martinis with Miss Glamorpuss,* she thought. Somehow this knowledge was not as comforting as it should have been.

The dress B.J. had chosen for dinner was black and sleek. It molded her subtle curves with a lover's intimacy, falling in a midnight pool around her ankles, with a gentle caress for thighs and calves. Small pearl buttons ran from her throat to her waist. The high, puritanical neckline accentuated her firm, small breasts and emphasized her slender neck. She left her hair loose to float in a pale cloud around her shoulders. She touched her scent behind her ears before leaving her room to descend to the dining room.

The candle-lit, corner table where Taylor sat with Darla was intimate and secluded. Glancing in their direction, B.J. could not suppress a scowl. There was no denying that they were a handsome couple. *Made for each other,* she thought bitterly. Darla's vermilion sheath plunged to reveal the creamy swell of her breasts. Taylor's dark suit was impeccably cut. In spite of herself, B.J.'s eyes were drawn to the breadth of his shoulders. She drew in her breath sharply, recalling the feel of his corded muscles now expertly concealed by the fine tailoring, and shivered involuntarily.

Taylor glanced over, his expression indefinable as he made a slow, exacting survey, his eyes lingering on the gentle curves draped in the simplicity of unrelieved black. Though her skin grew warm, B.J. met his eyes levelly. Examination complete, Taylor lifted one brow, whether in approval or disapproval, she could not determine. With a brief gesture of his hand, he ordered B.J. to his table.

Fuming at the casual insolence of the command, she schooled her features into tranquility. She wove her way through the room, deliberately stopping to speak with diners along the route.

"Good evening." B.J. greeted Taylor and his companion with a professional smile. "I hope you're enjoying your meal."

"As always, the food is excellent." Taylor rose and pulled up a chair expectantly. His eyes narrowed in challenge. It was not the moment to cross him, B.J. decided.

"I trust your room pleases you, Miss Trainor," she said pleasantly, as she sat down.

"It's adequate, Miss Clark. Though I must say, I was rather taken aback by the decorating scheme."

"You'll join us for a drink," Taylor stated, motioning a waitress over without waiting for B.J.'s consent. She glared at him for a moment before she glanced up at Dot.

"My usual," she said, not feeling obliged to explain this was a straight ginger ale. She turned back to Darla, coating her voice with polite interest. "And what is it about the decorating which took you aback, Miss Trainor?"

"Really, Miss Clark," Darla began as though the matter was obvious. "The entire room is *provincial,* don't you agree? There are some rather nice pieces, I admit, if one admires American antiques, but Taylor and I have always preferred a modern approach."

Fighting her annoyance and an all too unwanted spasm of jealousy, B.J. said sarcastically, "I see. Perhaps you'd care to elaborate on the modern approach for this country bumpkin. I so seldom get beyond the local five and dime."

Dot set B.J.'s drink in front of her and scurried away, recognizing storm warnings.

"In the first place," Darla began, immune to her frosty gray eyes, "the lighting is all wrong. Those glass domed lamps with pull chains are archaic. You need wall to wall carpeting. The hand hooked rugs and faded Persians will have to go. And the bathroom…Well, needless to say, the bathroom is hopeless." With a sigh, Darla lifted her champagne cocktail and sipped. "Footed tubs belong in period comedies, not in hotels."

B.J. chewed on a piece of ice to keep her temper from boiling over. "Our guests have always found a certain charm in the baths."

"Perhaps," Darla acknowledged with a depreciating shrug. "But with the proper changes and improvements, you'll be catering to a different type of clientele." She drew out a slim cigarette, giving Taylor a brief flutter of lashes as he lit it.

"Do you have any objections to footed tubs and pull chains?" B.J. asked him, voice precise, eyes stormy.

"They suit the present atmosphere of the inn." His voice was equally precise, his eyes cool.

"Maybe I've got a few fresh ideas for you, Miss Trainor, if and when you pull out your little book of samples." Setting down her glass, B.J. watched from the corner of her eye as Taylor flicked his lighter at the end of his cigarette. "Mirrors should be good on the ceiling in particular. Just a light touch of decadence. Lots of chrome and glass to give the rooms that spacious, symmetrical look. And white, plenty of white as well, perhaps with fuchsia accents. The bed, of course,'' she continued with fresh inspiration. ''A large circular bed with fuchsia coverings. Do you like fuchsia, Taylor?''

''I don't believe I asked for your advice on decorating tonight, B.J.'' Taylor drew casually on his cigarette. The smoke traveled in a thin column toward the exposed beam ceiling.

''I'm afraid, Miss Clark,'' Darla commented, spurred on by Taylor's mild reproof, ''that your taste runs to the vulgar.''

''Oh really?'' B.J. blinked as if surprised. ''I suppose that's what comes from being a country bumpkin.''

''I'm sure whatever I ultimately decide will suit you, Taylor.'' Darla placed a hand with easy familiarity on his as B.J.'s temper rose. ''But it will take a bit longer than usual as the alterations will be so drastic.''

''Take all the time you need.'' B.J. gestured with magnanimity as she rose. ''In the meantime, keep your hands off my footed tubs.''

The dignity of her exit was spoiled by a near collision with Dot who had been discreetly eavesdropping.

''An order of arsenic for table three…on the

house,'' B.J. muttered, skirting around the wide eyed waitress and sweeping from the room.

B.J.'s intention to stalk straight to her room and cool off was undone by a series of small, irritating jobs. It was after ten when the last had been dealt with and she was able to shut the door to her room and give vent to suppressed temper.

''Country bumpkin,'' she hissed through clenched teeth. Her eyes rested on a William and Mary table. *She'd* probably prefer plastic cubes in black and white checks. Her eyes moved from the dower chest to the schoolmaster's desk and on to the Bostonian rocker and wing chair in softly faded green. Each room of the inn was distinctive, with its own personality, its own treasures. Closing her eyes, B.J. could clearly see the room which Darla now occupied, the delicate pastel of the flowered wallpaper, the fresh gleam of the oak floor, the charm of the narrow, cushioned window seat. The pride of that particular room was an antique highboy in walnut with exquisite teardrop pulls. B.J. could not recall an occasion when a guest who had stayed in that room had done other than praise its comforts, its quiet charm, its timeless grace.

Darla Trainor, B.J. vowed, *is not getting her hands on my inn.* Walking to the mirrored bureau, she stared at her reflection, then let out a long disgusted breath. She's got a face that belongs on a cameo, and mine belongs on a milk commercial, she thought. Picking up her brush, she told herself that these reflections had nothing to do with the problem at hand.

How am I going to convince Taylor that the inn should stay as it is when she's already rattling off changes and giving him intimate smiles? I suppose, B.J. continued, giving her reflection a fierce scowl, *she's not just his decorator.* The kiss she gave him when she arrived wasn't very businesslike. I don't believe for a moment they spent all that time in her room discussing fabrics.

That's no concern of mine, she decided with a strong tug of the brush. But if they think they're going to start steaming off wallpaper without a fight, they're in for a surprise. She put down her brush and turned just as the door swung open to admit Taylor.

Before her astonished eyes, he closed and locked her door before placing the key in his pocket. As he advanced toward her, she could see that he was obviously angry.

''Being the owner doesn't give you the right to use the master key without cause,'' she snapped, as she backed against the bureau.

''It appears I haven't made myself clear.'' Taylor's voice was deceptively gentle. ''You have, for the time being, a free hand in the day to day managing of this inn. I have not, nor do I desire to infringe upon your routine. However—'' He took a step closer. B.J. discovered her hands were clutching the edge of the bureau in a desperate grip. ''All orders, all decisions, all changes in policy come from me, and only me.''

''Of all the dictatorial…''

''This isn't a debate,'' he cut her off sharply. ''I won't have you issuing orders over my head. Darla is employed by me. I tell her what to do, and when to do it.''

''But surely you don't want her to toss out all these lovely old pieces for gooseneck floor lamps and modular shelving. The server in the dining room is Hepplewhite. There're two Chippendale pieces in your room alone, and…''

The hand which moved from the back of her neck to circle her throat halted B.J.'s furious rush of words. She became uncomfortably aware of the strength of his fingers. No pressure was applied, but the meaning was all too evident.

''Whatever I want Darla to do is my concern, and my concern only.'' He tightened his grip, bringing her closer. Now B.J. read the extent of his anger in his eyes. Like two dark suns, they burned into hers. ''Keep your opinions to yourself until I ask for them. Don't interfere or you'll pay for it. Is that understood?''

"I understand perfectly. Your relationship with Miss Trainor has overruled any opinion of mine."

"That—" his brow lifted "—is none of your business."

"Whatever concerns the inn is my business," B.J. countered. "I offered you my resignation once, and you refused it. If you want to get rid of me now, you'll have to fire me."

"Don't tempt me." He lowered his hand and rested his fingers on the top button of her bodice. "I have my reasons for wanting you around, but don't push it. I agreed to keep you abreast of any alterations I decide on, but if you persist in being rude to others in my employ, you'll be out on your ear."

"I can't see that Darla Trainor needs protection from me," B.J. remarked resentfully.

"Don't you?" His temper appeared to drift toward amusement as he scanned her face. "A couple of centuries ago, you'd have been burned at the stake for looking as you do at this moment. Hell smoke in your eyes, your mouth soft and defiant, all that pale hair tumbling over a black dress." Deftly, his fingers undid the top button and moved down to the next as his eyes kept hers a prisoner. "That dress is just puritanical enough to be seductive. Was it accident or design that you wore it tonight?"

With casual ease, he unloosed half the range of

buttons, continuing his progress as his gaze remained fixed on hers.

"I don't know what you mean." Yet her traitorous feet refused to walk away. B.J. found herself powerless to move. "I want…I want you to go."

"Liar," he accused quietly, his hands slipping inside the opened front of her dress. His fingers traced lightly over her skin. "Tell me again you want me to go." His hands rose, his thumbs moving gently under the curve of her breasts. The room began to sway like the deck of a ship.

"I want you to go." Her voice was husky, her lids felt heavy with a tantalizing languor.

"Your body contradicts you, B.J." His hands claimed her breasts briefly before sliding to the smooth skin of her back. He brought her hard against him. "You want me just as much as I want you." His mouth lowered to prove his point.

Surrendering to a force beyond her understanding, B.J. rested in his arms. His demands increased with her submission, his mouth drawing the response she had no strength to withhold. While her mind screamed no, her arms drew him closer. The warnings to run were lost as his lips moved to the vulnerable skin of her throat, teasing the softness with tongue and teeth. She could only cling and fret for more. Mouth returned to mouth. While his hands roamed, arousing fresh pleasure, hers slipped under his jacket.

With a suddenness that gave her no time for defense, no thought of resistance, he fell deep into her heart. He claimed its untouched regions with the deftness of a seasoned explorer. The emotion brought B.J. to a spinning ecstasy which vied with a crushing, hopeless despair. To love him was certain disaster, to need him, undeniable misery, to be in his arms, both the darkness and the light. Trapped in the cage of her own desire, she would never find escape.

Helpless to do other than answer the hunger of his mouth, submit to the caressing journey of his hands, she felt the sting of emptiness behind her closed lids. Her arms pulled him closer to avert the insidious chill of reason.

"Admit it," he demanded, his lips moving again to savage her throat. "Admit you want me. Tell me you want me to stay."

"Yes, I want you." The words trembled on a sob as she buried her face in his shoulder. "Yes, I want you to stay."

She felt him stiffen and burrowed deeper until his hand forced her face to his. Her eyes were luminous, conquering the darkness with the glimmer of unshed tears. Her mouth was soft and tremulous as she fought the need to throw herself into his arms and weep out her newly discovered love. For eternity, he stared, and she watched without comprehension as his features hardened with fresh temper. When he spoke, however, his voice was calm and composed and struck like a fist on the jaw.

"It appears we've gotten away from the purpose of this meeting." Stepping away, his hands retreated to his pockets. "I believe I've made my wishes clear."

She shook her head in confusion. As her hand lifted to her tousled hair, the opening of her dress shifted in innocent suggestion over creamy skin. "Taylor, I…"

"Tomorrow—" she shivered as the coolness of his voice sapped the warmth from her skin "—I expect you to give Miss Trainor your complete co-operation, and your courtesy. Regardless of your disagreement, she is a guest of the inn and shall be treated as such."

"Of course." The hated tears began to flow as pain and rejection washed over her. "Miss Trainor shall be given every consideration." She sniffed, brushed at tears and continued with dignity. "You have my word."

"Your word!" Taylor muttered, taking a step toward her. B.J. streaked to the bath and locked the door.

"Go away!" No longer able to control the sobs,

one small fist pounded impotently against the panel. "Go away and leave me alone. I gave you my promise, now I'm off duty."

"B.J., open this door."

She recognized both anger and exasperation in his tone and wept more desperately. "No, go away! Go keep Miss Perfect company and let me alone. Your orders will be carried out to the letter. Just go. I don't have to answer to you until morning."

Taylor's swearing and storming around the room were quite audible, though to B.J. his muttered oaths and comments made little sense. Finally, the bedroom door slammed with dangerous force. In an undignified huddle on the tiled floor, B.J. wept until she thought her heart would break.

Chapter Eight

"Well, you did it again, didn't you?" B.J. stared at her reflection as the morning sun shone in without mercy. You made a total fool of yourself. With a weary sigh, she ran a hand through her hair before turning her back on the accusing face in the mirror. How could I have known I'd fall in love with him? she argued as she buttoned a pale green cap-sleeved blouse. I didn't plan it. I didn't want it.

"Blast," she muttered and pulled on a matching skirt. How can I control the way he makes me feel? The minute he puts his hands on me, my brain dissolves. To think that I would have let him stay last night knowing all he wanted from me was a quick affair! How could I be so stupid? And then, she added, shame warring with injured pride, *he didn't want me after all.* I suppose he remembered Darla. Why should he waste his time with me when she's available?

The next ten minutes were spent in fierce self-flagellation as B.J. secured her hair in a roll at the base of her neck. These tasks completed, she squared her shoulders and went out to meet whatever task the day brought.

A casual question to Eddie informed her Taylor was already closeted in the office, and Darla Trainor had not yet risen. B.J. was determined to avoid them both and succeeded throughout the morning.

The lunch hour found her in the lounge, conducting an inventory on the bar stock. The room was quiet, removed from the luncheon clatter. She found the monotony soothing on her nerves.

''So, this is the lounge.''

The intrusion of the silky voice jolted B.J.'s calm absorption. She whirled around, knocking bottles of liquor together.

Darla glided into the room looking elegantly businesslike in an oatmeal colored three piece suit, a pad and pencil in perfectly manicured hands. She surveyed the cluster of white clothed tables, the postage stamp dance floor, the vintage upright Steinway. Flicking a finger down the muted glow of knotty pine paneling, she advanced to the ancient oak bar.

''How incredibly drab.''

''Thank you,'' B.J. returned in her most courteous voice before she turned to replace a bottle on the mirrored shelves.

''Fix me a sweet vermouth,'' Darla ordered, sliding gracefully onto a stool and dropping her pad on the bar's surface.

B.J.'s mouth opened, furious retorts trembling on her tongue. Recalling her promise to Taylor, she clamped it shut and turned to comply.

''You must remember, Miss Clark,'' Darla's triumphant smile made B.J.'s hand itch to connect with ivory skin, ''I'm merely doing my job. There's nothing personal in my observations.''

Attempting to overcome her instinctive dislike, B.J. conceded. ''Perhaps that's true. But, I have a very personal feeling about the Lakeside Inn. It's more home than a place of business to me.'' She set the glass of vermouth at Darla's fingertips before turning back to count bottles.

''Yes, Taylor told me you're quite attached to this little place. He found it amusing.''

''Did he?'' Feeling her hand tremble, B.J. gripped the shelves until her knuckles whitened. ''What a strange sense of humor Taylor must have.''

''Well, when one knows Taylor as I do, one knows what to expect.'' Their eyes met in the mirror. Darla smiled and lifted her glass. ''He seems to think you're a valuable employee. What did he say…rather adept at making people comfortable.'' She smiled again and sipped. ''Taylor demands value from his employees as well as obedience. At times, he uses unorthodox methods to keep them satisfied.''

''I'm sure you'd know all about that.'' B.J. turned slowly, deciding wars should be fought face to face.

''Darling, Taylor and I are much more than business associates. And I, of course, understand his… ah…distractions with business.''

''How magnanimous of you.''

''It would never do to allow emotion to rule a relationship with Taylor Reynolds.'' Drawing a long, enameled nail over the rim of her glass, Darla gave B.J. a knowledgeable look. ''He has no patience with emotional scenes or complications.''

The memory of her weeping spell and Taylor's angry swearing played back in B.J.'s mind. ''Perhaps we've at last reached a point of agreement.''

''The first warning is always friendly, Miss Clark.'' Abruptly, Darla's voice hardened, throwing B.J. momentarily off balance. ''Don't get too close. I don't allow anyone to infringe on my territory for long.''

''Are we still talking about Taylor?'' B.J. inquired. ''Or did I lose part of this conversation?''

''Just take my advice.'' Leaning over the bar,

Darla took B.J.'s arm in a surprisingly strong grip. "If you don't, the next place you manage will be a dog kennel."

"Take your hand off me." B.J.'s tone was soft and ominous, as the well-shaped nails dug into her flesh.

"As long as we understand each other." With a pleasant smile, Darla released B.J.'s arm and finished her drink.

"We understand each other very well." Taking the empty glass, B.J. placed it under the bar. "Bar's closed, Miss Trainor." She turned her back to recount already counted bottles.

"Ladies." B.J. stiffened and watched Taylor's reflection enter the room. "I hadn't expected to find you at the bar at this time of day." His voice was light, but the eyes which met B.J.'s in the glass did not smile.

"I've been wandering around making notes," Darla told him. B.J. watched her hand rub lightly over the back of his. "I'm afraid the only thing this lounge has going for it is its size. It's quite roomy, and you could easily fit in double the tables. But then, you'll have to let me know if you want to go moody, or modern. Actually, it might be an idea to add another lounge and do both, along the lines of your place in San Francisco."

His murmur was absent as he watched B.J. move to the next shelf.

"I thought I'd get a good look at the dining room if the luncheon crowd is gone." Darla's smile was coaxing. "Why don't you come with me, Taylor, and you can give me a clearer picture of what you have in mind?"

"Hmm?" His attention shifted, but the imperceptible frown remained. "No, I haven't decided on anything yet. Go ahead and take a look, I'll get back to you."

Well arched brows rose at the dismissive tone, but Darla remained cool and composed. "Of course. I'll bring my notes to your office later and we can discuss it."

Her heels echoed faintly on the wooden floor. Her heavy perfume scent lingered in the air after she faded from view.

"Do you want a drink?" B.J. questioned, keeping her back to him and her voice remote.

"No, I want to talk to you."

With great care, B.J. avoided meeting his eyes in the mirror. She lifted a bottle, carefully examining the extent of its contents. "Haven't we covered everything?"

"No, we haven't covered everything. Turn around B.J., I'm not going to talk to your back."

"Very well, you're the boss." As she faced him, she caught a flash of anger in his eyes.

"Do you provoke me purposely, B.J., or is it just an accidental talent?"

"I have no idea. Take your choice." Suddenly, she was struck by inspiration. "Taylor," she said urgently. "I *would* like to talk to you. I'd like to talk to you about buying the inn. It can't be as important to you as it is to me. You could build a resort farther south that would suit you better. I could raise the money if you gave me some time."

"Don't be ridiculous." His abrupt words cooled her enthusiasm. "Where would you come up with the kind of money required to buy a property like this?"

"I don't know." She paced back and forth behind the bar. "Somewhere. I could get a loan for part of it, and you could hold a note for the rest. I've some money saved..."

"No." Standing, he skirted the bar and closed the distance between them. "I have no intention of selling."

"But, Taylor..."

"I said no. Drop it."

"Why are you being so stubborn? You won't even consider changing your mind? I might even be able to come up with a good offer if you gave me time—" Her voice trailed off uncertainly.

"I said I wanted to *talk* to you. At the moment I don't care to discuss the inn or any part of it."

He gripped her arm to spin her around, connecting with the flesh tender from Darla's nails. B.J. gave a cry of pain and jerked away. Taylor loosened his hold immediately, and she fell into the shelves, knocking glasses in a crashing heap on the floor.

"What the devil's got into you?" he demanded as her hand went automatically to nurse her bruised arm. "I barely touched you. Listen, B.J., I'm not tolerating you jumping like a scared rabbit every time I get close. I haven't hurt you. Stop that!" He pulled her hand away, then stared in confusion at the marks on her arm. "Good Lord. I didn't…I'd swear I barely touched you." Astonished, his eyes lifted to hers, darkened with emotions she could not understand. For a moment, she merely stared back, fascinated by seeing his habitual assurance rattled.

"No, I did it before." Dropping her eyes, B.J. busied herself by resecuring the pins in her hair. "It's just a bit sore. You startled me when you grabbed it."

"How did you do that?" He moved to take her arm for a closer examination, but B.J. stepped away quickly.

"I bumped into something. I've got to start looking where I'm going." She began to gather shards of broken glass, fresh resentment causing her head to ache.

"Don't do that," Taylor commanded. "You'll cut yourself."

Like an echo to his words, B.J. jerked as a piece of glass sliced her thumb. Moaning in pain and disgust, she dropped the offending glass back into the heap.

"Let me see." Taylor pulled her to her feet, ignoring her struggles for release. "Ah, B.J." With a sigh of exasperation, he drew a spotless white handkerchief from his pocket, dabbing at the cut. "I'm beginning to think I have to keep you on a very short leash."

"It's nothing," she mumbled, fighting the warmth of his fingers on her wrist. "Let me go, you'll have blood all over you."

"Scourges of war." He brought the wounded thumb briefly to his lips, then wrapped the cloth around it. "You will continue to bind up your hair, won't you?" With his free hand, he dislodged pins, clattering them among broken glass. Studying the flushed face and tumbled hair, his mouth lifted in a smile which brought B.J. new pain. "What is it about you that constantly pulls at my temper? At the moment, you look as harmless as a frazzled kitten."

His fingers combed lightly through her hair, then rested on her shoulders. She felt the sweet, drawing weakness seeping through her limbs. ''Do you know how close I came to kicking in that foolish bathroom door last night? You should be careful with tears, B.J., they affect men in strange ways.''

''I hate to cry.'' She lifted her chin, terrified she would do so again. ''It was your fault.''

''Yes, I suppose it was. I'm sorry.''

She stared, stunned by the unexpected apology. In a featherlight caress, he lowered his mouth to brush hers. ''It's all right...It doesn't matter.'' She backed away, frightened by her own need to respond, but found herself trapped against the bar. Taylor made no move toward her, but merely said, ''Have dinner with me tonight. Up in my room where we can talk privately.''

Her head shook before her lips could form a refusal. He closed the space between them before she could calculate an escape.

''B.J., I'm not going to let you run away. We need to talk somewhere where we won't be interrupted. You know that I want you, and...''

''You should be satisfied with your other acquisitions,'' she retorted, battling the creeping warmth.

''I beg your pardon?'' At her tone, his face hardened. The hand which had lifted to brush through her hair dropped back to his side.

''I'm sure you'll understand if you give it a bit of thought.'' She lifted her own hand to the sore flesh of her arm as if to keep the memory fresh. His eyes followed her gesture in puzzlement.

"It would be simpler if you elaborated."

"No, I don't think so. Just don't let your ego get out of hand, Taylor. I'm not running from you, I simply have a date tonight."

"A date?" He slipped his hands into his pockets as he rocked back on his heels. His voice was hard.

"That's right. I'm entitled to a personal life. I don't think it's included in my job contract that I have to spend twenty-four hours at your beck and call." Adding salt to her own wound, she continued, "I'm sure Miss Trainor will fill your requirements for the evening very well."

"Undoubtedly," he agreed with a slow nod. Stung by the ease of his answer, B.J.'s ice became fire.

"Well then, that's all decided, isn't it? Have a delightful evening, Taylor. I assure you, I intend to. If you'll excuse me, I've work to do." She brushed by him, only to be brought up short by a hand on her hair.

"Since we're both going to be otherwise engaged this evening, perhaps we can get this out of the way now."

His mouth took hers swiftly, and she could taste his smoldering fury. She made a futile attempt to clamp her lips tightly against his. Ruthlessly, his hand jerked her hair. As she gasped in pained surprise he invaded her mouth, conquering her senses one by one. Just as she had abandoned all semblance of resistance, he drew back, his hands moving with slow insistence from her waist to her shoulders.

''Are you through?'' Her voice was husky. Despising the longing to feel his mouth again, she forced herself rigid, keeping her eyes level.

''Oh no, B.J.'' The tone was confident. ''I'm a long way from through. But for now,'' he continued as she braced herself for another assault, ''you'd best tend to that cut.''

Too unnerved to answer, B.J. rushed from the lounge. She had left dignity to lay with the scattered pieces of glass.

She felt the kitchen would be the quietest sanctuary at that time of day and entered on the pretext of wanting a cup of coffee.

''What did you do to your hand?'' Elsie's question was off-handed as she completed the assembly line production of apple cobblers.

''Just a scratch.'' Frowning down at Taylor's handkerchief, B.J. shrugged and advanced on the coffee pot.

''Better put some iodine on it.''

''Iodine stings.''

Tongue clucking, Elsie wiped her hands on her

full apron before foraging in a small cabinet for medical supplies. ''Sit down and don't be a baby.''

''It's just a scratch. It's not even bleeding now.'' Helplessly, B.J. dropped into a chair as Elsie flourished a small bottle and a bandage. ''It's nothing at all. Ouch! Blast it, Elsie! I told you that wretched stuff stings.''

''There.'' Elsie secured the bandage with a satisfied smile. ''Out of sight, out of mind.''

''So you say.'' B.J. rested her chin on her hand and stared into the depth of her coffee cup.

''Miss Snooty tried to get into my kitchen,'' Elsie announced with an indignant sniff.

''Who? Oh, Miss Trainor.'' Throbbing thumb momentarily forgotten, B.J. gave her cook her full attention. ''What happened?''

''I tossed her out, of course.'' Elsie flicked flour from her abundant bosom and looked pleased.

''Oh.'' Leaning back in her chair, B.J. laughed at the picture of Elsie ordering sophisticated Darla out of her kitchen. ''Was she furious?''

''Fit to be tied,'' Elsie returned pleasantly. B.J.'s grin widened before she could prevent it. ''Going out with Howard tonight?''

''Yes.'' Her answer was automatic, not even vaguely surprised that communications had delivered this information to Elsie's ears. ''To the movies, I think.''

"Don't know why you're wasting your time going off with him when Mr. Reynolds is around."

"Well, it keeps Betty Jackson happy, and..." B.J. stopped and frowned as the complete sentence seeped through. "What does Taylor...Mr. Reynolds have to do with it?"

"I don't see why you're going out with Howard Beall when you're in love with Taylor Reynolds." Elsie's statement was matter-of-factly delivered as she poured herself a cup of coffee.

"I am not in love with Taylor Reynolds," B.J. declared, gulping down coffee and scalding both tongue and throat.

"Yes, you are," Elsie corrected, adding cooling cream to her own cup.

"I am not."

"Are too."

"I am not. I am absolutely not! Just what makes you so smart?" she added nastily.

"Fifty years of living, and twenty-four of knowing you." The reply was smug.

"La de da." B.J. attempted to appear sublimely unconcerned.

"Be real nice if you got married and settled down right here." Ignoring B.J.'s fit of choking, Elsie calmly sipped her coffee. "You could keep right on managing the inn."

"Stick to chicken and dumplings, Elsie," B.J. advised when she had recovered. "As a fortune teller, you're a complete failure. Taylor Reynolds would no more marry me and settle here than he would marry a porcupine and live on the moon. I'm a bit too countrified and inexperienced for his taste."

"Hmph." Elsie sniffed again and shook her head. "Sure does a lot of looking in your direction."

"I'm sure in the vast wisdom you've amassed in your famous fifty years, you know the difference between a physical attraction and the urge to marry and settle down. Even in our sheltered little town, we learn the difference between love and lust."

"My, my, aren't we all grown up and sassy," Elsie observed with the mild tolerance of an adult watching a child's tantrum. "Finish your coffee and scoot, I've got a prime rib that needs tending. And don't worry that bandage off your thumb," she ordered as B.J. swung through the door.

Obviously, B.J. decided as she prepared for her date that evening, I don't project an imposing enough authority figure. She frowned again as she recalled Elsie dismissing her like a bad tempered child. A breeze wafted through her opened window, billowing the curtains and wafting in the smell of freshly mowed grass. B.J. shrugged off her black mood. I'll simply change my image a bit.

She rooted through her closet and pulled out her

birthday present from her grandmother. The blouse was pure white silk and plunged deep to cling provocatively to every curve and plane before it tapered to the narrow waist of sleek black pants. The slacks continued a loving embrace over hips and down the length of shapely legs, molding her shape with the accuracy of a second skin.

"I'm not sure I'm ready for a new image," she muttered, turning sideways in front of her mirror. "I'm not sure Howard's ready either." The thought brought an irrepressible giggle as Howard's pleasantly homely face loomed in her mind.

He had the eyes of a faithful puppy, made all the more soulful by the attempt of a moustache which hung apologetically over his top lip. The main problem, B.J. decided, concentrating on his image, is that he lacks a chin. His face seemed to melt into his neck.

But he's a nice man, B.J. reminded herself. A nice, uncomplicated, predictable, undemanding man. Easing her feet into leather slides, she grabbed her bag and scurried from the room.

Her hopes to slip unseen outside to await Howard's arrival were shattered by a panic-stricken Eddie.

"B.J. Hey, B.J.!" He loped across the lobby and cornered her before she could reach the door.

''Eddie, if the place isn't burning down, hold it until tomorrow. I'm just leaving.''

''But, B.J.,'' he continued, grabbing her hand and ignoring her unconscious search of the room for a tall, dark man. ''Dot told Maggie that Miss Trainor is going to redecorate the inn, and that Mr. Reynolds plans to make it into a resort with saunas in every room and an illegal casino in the back.'' Horrified, his hand clung to hers for reassurance, his eyes pleading behind the thickness of his glasses.

''In the first place,'' B.J. began patiently, ''Mr. Reynolds has no intention of running an illegal casino.''

''He has one in Las Vegas,'' Eddie whispered in confidence.

''Gambling is a prerequisite in Las Vegas, it's not illegal.''

''But, B.J., Maggie said the lounge is going to be done in red and gold plush with nude paintings on the walls.''

''Nonsense.'' She patted his hand in amusement as color rose to his cheeks. ''Mr. Reynolds hasn't decided anything yet. When he does, I'm sure it won't run to red and gold plush, and nudes!''

''Thank you,'' Taylor said at her back. B.J. jumped. ''Eddie, I believe the Bodwin sisters are looking for you,'' he added.

"Oh, yes, sir." Face flaming, Eddie shot off, leaving B.J. in the very position she had sought to avoid.

"Well, well." Taylor surveyed her, an encompassing, thoroughly male examination, lingering on the point where her blouse joined above her breasts. "I trust your date has a high boiling point."

She started to snap that Howard had no boiling point at all, but changed her mind. "Do you really like it?" Tossing clouds of hair over her shoulder, B.J. gave Taylor the benefit of a melting, sultry smile.

"Let's say I might find it appealing under different circumstances," he said dryly.

Pleased to observe he was annoyed, B.J. recklessly gave his cheek a brief pat and glided to the door. "Good night, Taylor. Don't wait up now." Triumphant, she stepped out into the pink-clouded evening.

Howard's reaction to her appearance caused her ego to soar yet higher. He swallowed, eyes blinking rapidly, and stammered in small, incoherent sentences the entire distance to town. Finding this a pleasant change from self-assured amusement, B.J. basked in his admiration as she watched the hazy sun sink beyond the hills through the car window.

In town, the streets were already quiet with the mid-week, mid-evening hush which isolates small towns from the outside world. A few windows glowed like cats' eyes in the dark, but most of the houses had bedded down for the night like so many contented domestic pets.

At the far end of town where the theater was, there were more signs of activity. Howard pulled into the parking lot with his usual, plodding precision. The neon sign glowed somewhat ludicrously against the quiet sky. The *L* in PLAZA had been retired for the past six months.

"I wonder," B.J. mused as she alighted from Howard's sensible Buick, "if Mr. Jarvis will ever get that sign fixed or if each of the letters will die a quiet death." Howard's answer was muffled by the car door slam. She was faintly surprised as he took her arm with a possessive air and led her into the theater.

An hour through the feature, B.J decided Howard was not at all himself. He did not consume his popcorn with his usual voracity, nor did he shift throughout the film on the undeniably uncomfortable seats the Plaza offered. Rather, he sat in a glazed-eyed state that seemed almost catatonic.

"Howard." Keeping her voice low, B.J. placed her hand on his. To her surprise he jumped as though she had pinched him. "Howard, are you all right?"

Her astonishment changed to stunned disbelief when he grabbed her, scattering popcorn, and pressed a passionate if fumbling kiss to her mouth. At first, B.J. sat stunned. All other advances by Howard had consisted of a brotherly embrace at the door of the inn. Then, hearing a few snickers from the back of the theater, she wiggled from his arms and pushed against his stocky chest.

"Howard, behave yourself!" She gave an exasperated sigh and straightened in her seat.

Abruptly, Howard gripped her arm and pulled her to her feet, dragging her up the aisle and out of the theater.

"Howard, have you lost your mind?"

"I couldn't sit in there any more," he muttered, bundling her into his car. "It's too crowded."

"Crowded?" She blew an errant curl from her eyes. "Howard, there couldn't have been more than twenty people in there. I think you should see a doctor." She patted his shoulder then tested his brow for signs of fever. "You're a bit warm and not at all yourself. I can get a ride back, you'd better just go home."

"No!" There was no mistaking the vehemence of his tone.

B.J. gave Howard a long, searching stare before settling back uneasily into her seat. Though it was too dark to tell much, he appeared to be concentrating on his driving. He drove rapidly over the winding country road. Soon B.J. was able to distinguish the blinking lights of the hotel.

Suddenly, Howard pulled off the road and seized her. In the beginning, B.J. was more surprised than angry. "Stop it! Stop this, Howard! What in the world has gotten into you?"

"B.J." His mouth searched for hers, and this time his kiss was neither fumbling nor brotherly. "You're so beautiful." His groping hand reached for her blouse.

"Howard Beall, I'm ashamed of you!" B.J. remonstrated, pushing Howard firmly away and sliding toward the car door. "You get home right now and take a cold shower and go to bed!"

"But, B.J.—"

"I mean it." She wrenched open the car door and jumped out. Standing by the road, she tossed back her hair and adjusted her clothes. "I'm walking right back to the inn before you grow fangs again. Consider yourself lucky if I don't say something to your aunt about your temporary bout of insanity." Turning, she began the half-mile hike to the hotel.

Ten minutes later, shoes in hand and muttering disjointed imprecations toward the entire male sex, B.J. panted up the steep hill. The shadowy trees sighed softly in the moonlight. A lone owl hooted above her. But B.J. was in no mood for the beauties of the evening. "You be quiet," she commanded, glaring up at the bundle of feathers.

"I haven't said anything yet," a deep voice answered.

On the verge of screaming, B.J. found a hand over her mouth. Struggling to escape, she found a hard arm gripping her around the waist. "What the—?"

"Out for a stroll?" Taylor inquired mildly, releasing her. "It does seem an odd place to take a walk," he commented.

"Very funny." She managed two outraged steps before he caught her wrist.

"What's the matter? Your friend run out of gas?"

"Listen, I don't need this right now." Realizing she had dropped her shoes in her fright, B.J. searched the ground. "I've just walked a hundred miles after wrestling with a crazy man."

"Did he hurt you?" The grip on her wrist increased, as Taylor examined her more closely.

"Of course not." Tossing back her hair, B.J. let out a sigh of exasperation. "Howard wouldn't hurt a fly. I don't know what came over him. He's never acted like that before."

"Are you really that artless, or am I watching the second feature?" At her baffled expression, Taylor took her shoulders and administered a brief shake. "Grow up, B.J.! Look at yourself, the poor guy didn't have a chance."

"Don't be ridiculous." She shrugged out of his hold. "Howard's known me forever. He's never behaved like this before. He's just been reading too many romances or something. Good grief, I used to go skinny dipping with him when I was ten years old."

"Has anyone bothered to point out that you're no longer ten years old?"

Something in his voice made her raise her eyes to his.

"Stand still, B.J." He spoke in quiet command, and she felt her knees tremble. "I feel like a mountain lion stalking a house kitten."

For a moment, they stood apart, the stars glimmering above their heads, the moon a pale white guardian. Somewhere, a nightbird called to its mate, a plaintive sound. It echoed into silence as she melted in his arms.

She rose on her toes to offer him the gift of her mouth, her sigh of surrender merging with the wind's murmur. Her breasts crushed against his chest as his hands molded her hips closer. For this moment, she was his. Her heart sought no past or future but only the warmth and knowledge of now—the eternity of the present. She moaned with pleasure as his mouth sought the curve of her neck. Her fingers tangled with his dark hair as his mouth met hers again and she opened her lips to his kiss.

Locked together, they were oblivious to the sounds of night; the sigh of wind, the mellow call of an owl and the chirp of crickets. With a harsh suddenness, the inn door opened, pooling them in artificial light.

"Oh, Taylor, I've been waiting for you."

B.J. pulled away in humiliation as Darla leaned against the doorway, draped in a flowing black negligee. Her ivory skin gleamed against the lace. Her smooth, raven hair fell loose and full down her back.

"What for?" Taylor's question was abrupt.

Darla pouted and moved lace clad shoulders. "Taylor, darling, don't be a bear."

Devastated that he should have used her so blatantly while he had another woman waiting, B.J. stooped to retrieve her shoes.

"Where do you think you're going?" Taylor captured her wrist and aborted her quick escape.

"To my room," B.J. informed him with her last vestige of calm. "It appears you have a previous engagement."

"Just a minute."

"Please, let me go. I've done my quota of wrestling for one evening."

His fingers tightened on her flesh. "I'm tempted to wring your neck." Taylor tossed her wrist away as though the small contact was abhorrent.

Turning on bare heels, B.J. rushed up the steps and past a sweetly smiling Darla.

Chapter Nine

B.J. moved her files to her room. There, she determined, she could work in peace without Taylor's disturbing presence. She immersed herself in paperwork and tried to block all else from her mind. The gray, drizzling rain which hissed at her windows set the stage for her mood. Thick, low hanging clouds allowed no breath of sun. Still, her eyes were drawn to the misty curtain, her mind floating with the clear rivulets which ran down the glass. Shaking her head to bring herself to order, B.J. concentrated on her linen supply.

Her door swung open, and she turned from the slant top desk. With sinking heart, she watched Taylor enter.

"Hiding out?"

It was apparent from the set of his mouth that his mood had not mellowed since her departure the previous evening.

"No." The lifting of her chin was instinctive. "It's simply more convenient for me to work out of my room while you need the office."

"I see." He towered menacingly over her desk, making her feel small and insignificant. "Darla tells me you two had quite a session yesterday in the lounge."

B.J.'s mouth opened in surprise. She could not believe Darla would have disclosed her own behavior so readily.

"I warned you, B.J., that as long as Darla is a guest at the inn, you're to treat her with the same courtesy you show all other guests."

B.J. was astonished. "I'm sorry, Taylor, perhaps I'm dim. Would you mind explaining that?"

"She told me you were inexcusably rude, that you made some comments on her relationship with me, refused to serve her a drink, made yourself generally unpleasant, and told the staff not to cooperate with her."

"She said that, did she?" B.J.'s eyes darkened with rage. She set her pen down carefully and rose despite Taylor's proximity. "Isn't it odd how two people can view the same scene from entirely different perspectives! Well.'' She stuck her hand in her pockets and planted her feet firmly. "I have news for you—''

''If you've another version,'' Taylor returned evenly, ''I'd like to hear it.''

''Oh!'' Unable to prevent herself, she lifted her fist to give his chest a small, inadequate punch. His eyes dropped to it in amused indulgence. ''How generous of you. The condemned man is given a fair trial.'' Whirling, she paced the room in a swirl of agitation, debating whether to give him a verbatim account of her meeting with Darla. Finally, her pride won over her desire to clear herself in Taylor's eyes. ''No thanks, your honor. I'll just take the fifth.''

''B.J.'' Taylor took her shoulders and spun her to face him. ''Must you constantly provoke me?''

''Must you constantly pick on me?'' she countered.

''I wouldn't have said I was doing that.'' His tone had changed from anger to consideration.

''That's your opinion. I'm the one who's constantly in the position of justifying myself. I'm tired of having to explain my every move, of trying to cope with your moods. I never know from one minute to the next if you're going to kiss me or sit me in the corner with a dunce hat. I'm tired of feeling inadequate, naive and stupid. I never felt like any of those things before, and I don't like it.''

Her words tumbled out in a furious rush while Taylor merely looked on, politely attentive.

"And I'm sick of your precious Darla altogether. Sick of her criticizing every aspect of the inn, sick of her looking at me as though I were some straw-chewing hick from Dogpatch. And, I resent her running to you with fabricated stories, and, I detest your using me to boost your over-inflated ego while she's floating around half naked waiting to warm your bed. And…Oh, blast!"

Her torrent of complaints was interrupted by the shrill ringing of the phone. Ripping the receiver from its cradle, B.J. snapped into it.

"What is it? No, nothing's wrong. What is it, Eddie?" Pausing, she listened, her hand lifting to soothe the back of her neck where tension lodged. "Yes, he's here." She turned back to Taylor and held out the phone. "It's for you, a Mr. Paul Bailey."

He took the receiver in silence, his eyes still on her face. As she turned to leave the room, his hand caught her wrist. "Stay here." Waiting for her nod of agreement, he released her. B.J. moved to the far side of the room and stared out at the insistent rain.

Taylor's conversation consisted of monosyllabic replies which B.J. blocked from her mind. Frustrated by the inability to complete her outburst, she now felt the impetus fading. Just as well, she admitted with a sigh of weary resignation. I've already said enough to insure the job at that dog kennel Darla mentioned. Blast! She rested her forehead on the cool glass. Why did I have to fall in love with an impossible man?

"B.J." She started at the sound of her name, then twisted her head to watch Taylor cradle the phone. "Pack," he said simply and moved to the door.

Closing her eyes, she tried to tell herself it was better that she leave, better not to be connected with him even as an employee. Nodding mutely, she turned back to the window.

"Enough for three days," he added in after-thought as his hand closed over the knob.

"What?" Thrown into confusion, she turned, staring with a mixture of grief and bewilderment.

"We'll be gone for three days. Be ready in fifteen minutes." Halting, Taylor's features softened suddenly at her clouded expression. "B.J., I'm not firing you. Give me credit for a bit more class than that."

She shook her head, washed with relief and the knowledge of the inevitable. He started to cross the room, then paused and merely leaned against the closed door.

"That was a call from the manager of one of my resorts. There's a bit of a problem, and I've got to see to it. You're coming with me."

"Coming with you?" Her fingers lifted to her temple as if she could smooth in understanding. "What on earth for?"

"In the first place, because I say so." He folded his arms across his chest and became the complete employer. "And secondly, because I like my managers well rounded. No pun intended," he added, smiling as her color rose. "This is a good opportunity for you to see how my other hotels are run."

"But I can't just leave at a moment's notice," she objected, as her mind struggled to cope with the new development. "Who'll take care of things here?"

"Eddie will. It's about time he had a bit more responsibility. You let him lean on you too much. You let all of them lean on you too much."

"But we have five new reservations over the weekend, and..."

"You're down to ten minutes, B.J.," he informed her with a glance at his watch. "If you don't stop arguing, you'll only have the clothes on your back to take with you."

Seeing all of her objections would be overruled, she tried not to think of what going away with Taylor would do to her nervous system. *Business,* she reminded herself. *Just business.*

Somewhat annoyed that he was already walking through the door, having taken it for granted that she was going with him, she called after him, ''I can't simply pack because you say to.''

He turned back, his temper fraying. ''B.J.''

''You never said where,'' she reminded him. ''I don't know if I need mukluks or bikinis.''

A ghost of a smile played on his lips before he answered. ''Bikinis. We're going to Palm Beach.''

B.J. was to find her surprises were not yet over for the morning. First, her last minute flurry of instructions was cut off by Taylor's order as she was bundled out of the dripping rain and into his car. On the drive to the airport, she mentally reviewed every possible disaster which could occur during her absence. She opened her mouth to enlighten Taylor only to be given a quelling look which had her suffering in silence.

At the airport, she found herself confronted not with a commercial jet, but with Taylor's private one, already primed for take-off. B.J. stood motionless staring at the small trim plane as he retrieved their luggage.

''B.J., don't stand in the rain. Go on up.''

''Taylor.'' Unmindful of the rain which pelted her, B.J. turned to him. ''I think there's something you should know. I'm not very good at flying.''

''That's all right.'' He secured cases under his

arm and grabbed her hand. ''The plane does most of the work.''

''Taylor, I'm serious,'' she objected, as he dragged her inside the plane.

''Do you get air sick? You can take a pill.''

''No.'' She swallowed and lifted her shoulders. ''I get paralyzed. Stewardesses have been known to stow me in the baggage compartment so I don't panic the other passengers.''

He rubbed his hands briskly through her hair, scattering rain drops. ''So, I've found your weakness. What are you afraid of?''

''Mostly of crashing.''

''It's all in your head,'' he said easily as he helped her off with her jacket. ''There's a term for it.''

''Dying,'' she supplied, causing him to laugh again. Miffed by his amusement, she turned away to examine the plush luxury of the cabin. ''This looks more like an apartment than a plane.'' She ran a hand over the soft maroon of a chair. ''Everyone's entitled to a phobia,'' she muttered.

''You're absolutely right.'' His voice trembled on the edge of laughter. B.J. turned to snap at him but found his smile too appealing.

''You won't think it's so funny when I'm lying in a moaning heap on your shag carpet.''

''Possibly not.'' He moved toward her and she

stiffened in defense. Brooding down at her a moment, he searched her wary gray eyes. "B.J.," he began, "shall we call a moratorium on our disagreements? At least for the duration of the trip?"

"Well, I..." His voice was soft and persuasive, and she lowered her eyes to study the buttons of his shirt.

"An armed truce?" he suggested, capturing her chin between his thumb and forefinger and lifting her face. "With negotiations to follow?" He was smiling, his charming, utterly disarming smile. She knew resistance was hopeless.

"All right, Taylor." Unable to prevent her own smile from blossoming, she remained still as his finger lifted to trace it.

"Sit down and fasten your seat belt." He kissed her brow with an easy friendliness which left her weak.

B.J. found that the easy flow of his conversation from the moment of take off eased her tension. Incredibly, she felt no fear as the plane soared into the air.

"It's so flat and so warm!" B.J. exclaimed as she stepped off the plane steps and looked around her.

Taylor chuckled as he led the way to a sleek black Porsche. He exchanged a few words with a waiting attendant, accepted the keys, unlocked the door, and motioned B.J. inside.

"Where is your hotel?" she asked.

"In Palm Beach. This is West Palm Beach. We have to cross Lake Worth to get to the island."

"Oh!" Enchanted by roadside palms, she lapsed into silence.

The white, sandy soil and splashes of brilliant blossoms were so far removed from the scenery of her native New England, she felt as though she had entered another world. The waters of Lake Worth, separating Palm Beach from the mainland, sparkled blue and white under the afternoon sun. The ocean-side was lined with resort hotels. B.J. recognized the elaborate initials *T.R.* atop a sleek white building which rose twelve stories over the Atlantic. Hundreds of windows winked back at her. Taylor pulled into the semi-circular macadam drive and stopped the car. B.J. narrowed her eyes against the streaming rays of the sun. The archway which formed the entrance was guarded by palms and semi-tropical plants, their tangle of color obviously well planned and scrupulously tended. The lawn spread, perfectly level and unbelievably green.

"Come," said Taylor, coming around to open the door for her. He helped her out of the car and led her inside.

To B.J. the lobby was a tropical paradise. The

floor was flagstoned, the walls a half-circle of windows at the front. A center fountain played over a rocky garden, dotted with lush plants and ferns. B.J. saw that the interior was round, an open circle spiraling to the ceiling where a mural emulating the sky had been painted. The effect was one of limitless space. *How different from the cozy familiarity of the Lakeside Inn!* she thought.

''Ah, Mr. Reynolds.'' Her meditation was interrupted by the appearance of a slender, well dressed man with a shock of steel gray hair and a lean, bronzed face. ''So good to see you.''

''Paul.'' Taylor accepted the proffered hand and returned the smile of greeting. ''B.J., this is Paul Bailey, the manager. Paul, B.J. Clark.''

''A pleasure, Miss Clark.'' B.J.'s hand was engulfed by a smooth, warm grasp. His eyes surveyed her fresh, slender beauty with approval. She found herself smiling back.

''See to our bags and I'll take Miss Clark up. After we've settled in a bit, I'll get back to you.''

''Of course. Everything's quite ready.'' With another flash of teeth, he led the way to the registration desk and secured a key. ''Your bags will be right up, Mr. Reynolds. Is there anything else you'd like?''

''Not at the moment. B.J.?''

"What?" B.J. was still admiring the luxurious lobby.

"Would you like anything?" Taylor smiled at her and brushed a curl from her cheek.

"Oh…no, nothing. Thank you."

With a final nod for Bailey, Taylor secured her hand in his and led her to one of the three elevators. They glided up in a cage of octagon glass high above the cluster of greenery.

When they reached the top floor, Taylor moved along the thick carpeting to unlock the door. B.J. entered and crossing the silent plush of ivory carpet, stared down from the dizzying height at the white beach which jutted out into an azure span of sea. In the distance, she could see the churning whitecaps and the flowing grace of gulls as they circled and dove.

"What an incredible view. I'm tempted to dive straight off the balcony." Turning, she caught Taylor watching her from the center of the room. She could not decipher the expression in his eyes. "This is lovely," she said to break the long silence.

She ran a finger over the smooth surface of an ebony bar and wondered if Darla had decorated the room. Grudgingly, she admitted to herself if this were the case, Darla had done a good job.

"Would you like a drink?" Taylor pushed a button cunningly concealed in the mirror tiles on the wall behind the bar. A panel slid open to reveal a fully stocked bar.

"Very clever," B.J. smiled. "Some club soda would be nice," she said, leaning elbows on the bar.

"Nothing stronger?" he asked as he poured the soda over crackling ice. "Come in," he responded to the quiet knock on the door.

"Your luggage, Mr. Reynolds." A red-and-black-uniformed bellboy carried in the cases. B.J. was conscious of his curious gaze and blushed self-consciously.

"Fine, just leave them there." He accepted the tip from Taylor and vanished, closing the door with quiet respect.

B.J. eyed the cases. Taylor's elegant gray sat neatly beside her practical brown. "Why did he bring it all in here?" Setting down her glass, she lifted her eyes. "Shouldn't he have just taken mine to my room?"

"He did." Taylor secured another bottle and poured himself a portion of Scotch.

"But, I thought this was your suite." B.J. glanced around the luxurious room again.

"It is."

"But you just said…" She faltered, as her color rose. "Surely you don't think I'm going to—to…"

"What did you have in mind?" Taylor inquired with infuriating amusement.

"You said you wanted me to see how one of your other hotels was run, you never said anything about…about…"

"You really must learn to complete a sentence, B.J."

"I'm not sleeping with you," she stated very positively, her eyes like two summer storm clouds.

"I don't believe I asked you to," he said lazily before he took an easy sip of Scotch. "There are two very adequate bedrooms in this suite. I'm sure you'll find yours comfortable."

Embarrassment flooded her cheeks. "I'm not staying in here with you. Everyone will think that I'm…that we're…"

"I've never known you to be quite so coherent." His mockery increased her wrath, and her eyes narrowed to dangerous slits. "In any case," he continued unperturbed, "the purity of your reputation is already in question. As you're traveling with me, it will naturally be assumed that we're lovers. As we know differently," he went on as her mouth dropped open, "that hardly matters. Of course, if you'd like to make rumor fact, I might be persuaded."

"Oh, you insufferable, egotistical, conceited…"

"Name calling can hardly be considered persuasion," Taylor admonished, patting her head in an infuriating manner. "I assume, therefore, you'll want your own bedroom?"

"As this is off season," B.J. began, gaining a tenuous grip on her temper, "I'm sure there are a surplus of available rooms."

Smiling, he ran a finger down her arm. "Afraid you won't be able to resist temptation, B.J.?"

"Of course not," she said though her senses tingled at his touch.

"Then that's settled," he said, finishing off his drink. "If you're harboring the notion that I'll be overcome by lust, there's a perfectly sturdy lock on your bedroom door. I'm going down to see Bailey; why don't you change and grab some time at the beach? Your room's the second door on your left down the hall." He pointed as he moved to the door and slipped through before she had time to frame a response.

Before lifting her case and beginning to unpack, B.J. thought of at least a half a dozen withering remarks she should have made. However, she soon regained her sense of proportion.

After all, it wasn't every day that she had the opportunity to indulge in such luxury. She might as well enjoy it. Besides, the suite was certainly large enough for both of them.

Slipping into brief tan shorts and a lime green halter, B.J. decided to finish her unpacking later and head for the beach.

* * *

Taylor had certainly made the most of nature's gift, offering a luxury playground with an ocean and sky backdrop. B.J. had seen the huge mosaic tiled pool for those who preferred its filtered water to the sea. On her way to the beach, she glimpsed at the expanse of tennis courts with palms and flowering shrubs skirting about the entrance gate. She had seen enough of the hotel's interior to be certain that Taylor left his guests wanting for nothing.

From the beach B.J. shaded her eyes and studied again the perfection of the imposing resort. It was, she admitted with a sigh, elegantly appealing. As far out of her realm as its owner. *Egg noodles and caviar,* she thought ruefully, reflecting both on the comparison between inn and resort and Taylor and herself. They simply don't belong on the same plate.

"Hello."

Startled, B.J. turned, blinked against the brilliant sun and stared at an even white smile in a bronzed face.

"Hello." Returning the smile with a bit more caution, B.J. studied the attractive face surrounded by thick masses of light, sun bleached hair.

"Aren't you going to give the ocean a try?"

"Not today."

"That's very unusual." He fell into step beside her as she began to cross the sand. "Usually everyone spends their first day roasting and splashing."

"How did you know it was my first day?" B.J. asked.

"Because I haven't noticed you here before, and I would have." He gave her an encompassing and intensely male survey. "And because you're still peaches and cream instead of parboiled."

"Hardly the time of year," B.J. commented, admiring the deep, even tan as he shrugged on his shirt. "I'd say you've been here for some time."

"Two years," he returned, with an appealing grin. "I'm the tennis pro, Chad Hardy."

"B.J. Clark." She paused on the tiled walkway which led to the hotel's beach entrance. "How come you're on the beach instead of the courts?"

"My day off," he explained and surprised her by winding the tips of her hair around his finger. "But if you'd like a private lesson, it could be arranged."

"No, thanks," she declined lightly and turned again toward the door.

"How about dinner?" Chad captured her hand, gently but insistently bringing her back to face him.

"I don't think so."

"A drink?"

She smiled at his persistence. "No, sorry, it's a bit early."

"I'll wait."

Laughing, she shook her head and disengaged her

hand. ''No, but I appreciate the offer. Goodbye, Mr. Hardy.''

''Chad.'' He moved with her through the archway into the hotel's coolness. ''What about tomorrow? Breakfast, lunch, a weekend in Vegas?''

B.J. laughed; such ingenuous charm was hard to resist. ''I don't think you'll have any trouble finding a companion.''

''I'm having a great deal of trouble securing the one I want,'' he countered. ''If you had any compassion, you'd take pity on me.''

With a rueful smile, B.J. surrendered. ''All right, I wouldn't mind an orange juice.''

In short order, B.J. found herself seated at an umbrella table beside the pool.

''It's not really that early,'' Chad objected when she adhered to her choice of fruit juice. ''Most of the crowd is straggling in to wash off the sand and change for dinner.''

''This hits the spot.'' She sipped from the frosted glass. Then, gesturing with one slender hand, she glanced around at green fan palms and scarlet blooms. ''You must find it easy to work here.''

''It suits me,'' Chad agreed, swirling his own drink. ''I like the work, the sun.'' He lifted his glass and smiled with the half toast. ''And the benefits.'' His smile widened. Before she had the opportunity to draw them away, his hand captured her fingers. "How long will you be here?"

"A couple of days." She let her hand lie limp, feeling a struggle would make her appear foolish. "This was actually a spur-of-the-moment trip rather than a vacation."

"Then I'll drink to spur-of-the-moment trip," said Chad.

The friendly, polished charm was potent, and B.J. could not resist beaming him a smile. "Is that your best serve?"

"Just a warm-up." Returning the smile, his grip on her hand tightened slightly. "Watch out for my ace."

"B.J."

Twisting her head, she stared up at Taylor, frowning above her. "Hello, Taylor. Are you finished with Mr. Bailey?"

"For the moment." His glance shifted to Chad, drifted over their joined hands and returned to her face. "I've been looking for you."

"Oh?" Feeling unaccountably guilty, B.J. nibbled her lip in a tell-tale sign of agitation. "I'm sorry, this is Chad Hardy," she began.

"Yes, I know. Hello, Hardy."

"Mr. Reynolds," Chad returned with a polite nod. "I didn't know you were in the hotel."

"For a day or two. When you've finished," he

continued, giving B.J. the full benefit of a cold disapproving stare, ''I suggest you come up and change for dinner. I don't think that outfit's suitable for the dining room.'' With a curt nod, he turned on his heel and stalked away.

''Well, well.'' Releasing her hand, Chad leaned back in his chair and studied B.J. with new interest. ''You might have told me you were the big man's lady. I'm rather fond of my job here.''

Her mouth opened and closed twice. ''I am not Taylor's lady,'' B.J. spurted on her third try.

Chad's lips twisted in a wry grin. ''You'd better tell him that. A pity.'' He sighed with exaggerated regret. ''I was working on some interesting fantasies, but I steer clear of treading on dangerous ground.''

Standing, he lifted her chin and gave her a rather wistful smile. ''If you find yourself down here again without complications, look me up.''

Chapter Ten

The emphatic slamming of the suite's door gave B.J. small satisfaction. Advancing with purpose on Taylor's bedroom, she pounded on his door.

"Looking for me?" The voice was dry.

She whirled around. For a moment, she could only gape at the sight of Taylor leaning against the bathroom door, clad only in a dark green towel tied low over lean hips. His hair fell in tendrils over the lean planes of his face.

"Yes, I..." She faltered and swallowed. "Yes," she repeated with more firmness as she recalled Chad's comments. "That was an uncalled for exhibition out there. You deliberately left Chad with the impression that I was your..." She hesitated, eyes darkening with outraged impotence, as she searched for the right word.

''Mistress?'' Taylor suggested amiably.

B.J.'s pupils dilated with fury. ''He at least used the term lady.'' Forgetting the corded arms and dark mat of hair covering his chest, she stalked forward until she stood toe to toe. ''You did it on purpose, and I won't tolerate it.''

''Oh really?'' Had she not been so involved venting her own anger, B.J. might have recognized the dangerous pitch of his voice. ''It appears by the speed with which Hardy lured you into his corner, you're remarkably easy prey. I feel it's my obligation to look out for you.''

''Find someone else to protect,'' she retorted. ''I'm not putting up with it.''

''Just what do you intend to do about it?'' The simple arrogance of the question was accompanied by a like smile which robbed B.J. of all coherency. ''If giving Hardy and others of his type the impression that you're my property keeps you from making a fool of yourself, that's precisely what I'll do. Actually,'' he continued, ''you should be grateful.''

''Grateful?'' B.J. repeated, her voice rising. ''Your property? *A fool of myself?* Of all the arrogant, unspeakable gall!''

Her arm pulled back with the intention of connecting her fist with his midsection, but she found it twisted behind her back with astonishing speed. Her body was crushed against the hard undraped lines of his.

"I wouldn't try that again." The warning was soft. "You wouldn't like the consequences." His free hand lowered to her hip, bringing her closer as she tried to back away. "Don't do that," he ordered, holding her still and trapped against him. "You'll just hurt yourself. It seems we've broken our truce." His words were light, though she saw the signs of lingering temper in his eyes.

"You started it." Her declaration was half-defiant, half-defensive. She kept her eyes level with sheer determination.

"Did I?" he murmured before he took her mouth.

She was washed by the familiar flood of need. Offering no struggle, she went willingly into the uncharted world where only the senses ruled. His hand released her arm in order to roam over the bareness of her back, and she circled his neck, wanting only to remain in the drifting heat and velvet darkness.

Abruptly, he set her free. She stumbled back against the wall, thrown off balance by the swiftness of her liberation.

"Go change." He turned and gripped the knob of his door.

B.J. reached out to touch his arm.

"Taylor..."

“Go change!” he shouted. She stumbled back again, eyes round and wide at the swift flare of violence. He slammed the door behind him.

B.J. retreated to her room to sort out her feelings. Was it injured pride? Or was it rage? She could not for the life of her tell.

The early sky lightened slowly from black to misty blue. The stars faded, then died as the sun still lay hidden beneath the horizon. B.J. rose, grateful the restless night was behind her.

She had shared an uncomfortably polite dinner with Taylor, the elegance of the dining room only adding to the sensation that she had stood aside and watched two strangers go through the motions of dining. Taylor’s solicitous and unfamiliar formality had disturbed her more than his sudden seething fury. Her own responses had been stilted and cool. Immediately after dinner she pleaded fatigue and crept off unescorted to pass the evening hours alone and miserably awake in her room.

It had been late when she had heard Taylor’s key in the lock, his footsteps striding down the hall to pause outside her room. She had held her breath as if he might sense her wakefulness through the panel. Not until she had heard the muffled sound of his door closing had she let it out again.

* * *

B.J. felt no better the next morning. The events of the day before had left her with a lingering sense of loss and sorrow. Though she knew that there was little hope, she had finally acknowledged to herself that she was in love with Taylor. But there was no point thinking about it.

She slipped on her bikini, grabbed a terry robe, and tiptoed from her room.

The view from the wide window in the living room drew her. With a sigh of pleasure, she moved closer to watch the birth of day. The sun had tinted the edge of sea and sky with rose-gold streaks. Pinks and mauves shot through the dawning sky.

"Quite a view."

With a gasp, B.J. spun around, nearly colliding with Taylor whose footsteps had been hidden by the thickness of carpet. "Yes," she returned as their hands lifted simultaneously to brush back the fall of her hair which tumbled to her cheek. "There's nothing so beautiful as a sunrise." Disturbed by his closeness, she found her own words silly.

He was clad only in short denim cut-offs, frayed at the cuffs.

"How did you sleep?" His voice was politely concerned.

She shrugged off his question, evading a direct lie. "I thought I'd take an early swim before the beach gets crowded."

Deliberately, he turned her to face him, while he searched her face with habitual thoroughness. "Your eyes are shadowed." His finger traced the mauve smudges as a frown deepened the angles of his face. "I don't believe I've ever seen you look tired before. You seem to have some inner vitality that continually feeds itself. You look pale and fragile, quite unlike the pigtailed brat I watched sliding into home plate."

His touch was radiating the weakness through her so she stepped back in defense. "I…It's just the first night in a strange bed."

"Is it?" His brow lifted. "You're a generous creature, B.J. You don't even expect an apology, do you?"

Charmed by his smile, her weariness evaporated. "Taylor, I want…I'd like it if we could be friends." She finished in an impulsive rush.

"Friends?" he repeated as the sudden boyish grin split his face. "Oh, B.J., you're sweet, if a bit slow." Taking both hands in his, he lifted them to his lips before speaking again. "All right, friend, let's go for a swim."

But for gulls, the beach was deserted, a stretch of white pure and welcoming. The air already glowed with the promise of heat and light. B.J. stopped and gazed around, pleased with the quiet and the solitude.

"It's like everyone went away."

"You're not much for crowds, are you, B.J.?"

"No, I suppose not." She turned to him with a lift of bare shoulders. "I enjoy people, but more on a one to one level. When I'm around people, I like to know who they are, what they need. I'm good with small problems. I can shore up a brick here, hammer a nail there. I don't think I'm equipped to construct an entire building the way you are."

"One can't keep a building standing without someone shoring up bricks and hammering nails."

She smiled, so obviously pleased and surprised by his observation that he laughed and tousled her hair. "I'll race you to the water."

Giving him a considering look, B.J. shook her head in reluctance. "You're a lot taller than I am. You have an advantage."

"You forget, I've seen you run. And—" His eyes dropped to the length of shapely legs. "For a small woman, you have amazingly long legs."

"Well." She drew the word out, lips pursed. "O.K." Without waiting for his assent, she streaked across the sand and plunged into the sea, striking out with long strokes.

She was brought up short by hands on her waist.

Laughing, she struggled away, only to be caught and submerged in the ensuing tussle.

''Taylor, you're going to drown me,'' she protested as her legs tangled with his.

''That is not my intention,'' he informed her as he drew her closer. ''Hold still a minute or you'll take yourself under again.''

Relaxing in his hold, B.J. allowed him to keep them both afloat. She permitted herself a few moments of ecstasy cradled in his arms as the water pooled around them like a cool satin blanket. The change began like a gradual drizzle as she became more aware of his shoulder beneath her cheek, the possessive hold of the arm which banded her bare waist. Powerless to resist, she floated with him as his lips descended to the sleek cap of her hair, then wandered to tease the lobe of her ear with tongue and teeth before moving to the curve of her neck. His fingers traced the low line of the bikini snug at her hips as his mouth roamed her cheek in its journey to hers.

Her lips parted before he requested it, but his kiss remained gentle, the passion simmering just below the surface. His hand touched and fondled, slipping easily under the barrier of her brief top to trail over the curve of her breast. The water sighed gently as flesh met flesh.

What with gentle caresses, the drifting buoyancy

of the sea, and the growing heat of the ascending sun B.J. fell into a trancelike state. Perhaps, she thought, mind and limbs lethargic, she was meant to float forever in his arms. She shivered with pleasure.

"You're getting cold," Taylor murmured, drawing her away to study her face. "Come on." He released her, leaving her without support in the sighing sea. The magic shattered. "We'll sit in the sun."

B.J. started for the shore with Taylor swimming easily beside her.

On the beach, she fanned her hair in the sun while Taylor stretched negligently beside her. She tried not to look at the strong planes of his face, his bronzed, glistening skin.

He told me how it would be, she reminded herself. Right from the beginning. I don't seem to be able to do anything about it and if I don't, I'll end up being just another Darla in his life. Bringing her knees to her chest, she rested her chin on them and stared at the distant horizon. He's attracted to me for some reason, perhaps because I'm different from other women in his life. I haven't their sophistication or experience and I suppose he finds that appealing and amusing. I don't know how to fight both loving him and wanting him. If it were just physical, I could avoid being hurt. If it were only an attraction, I could resist him.

She recalled suddenly his quick violence of the

previous day and realized he was a man capable of employing whatever means necessary to gain an objective. At the moment, she knew he was playing her like a patient fisherman casting his line into calm waters. But ultimately, they both knew she would be captured in his net. Though it might be silk, it would still lead to eventual disaster.

"You're very far away." Sitting up, Taylor tangled his fingers in her damp hair and turned her to face him.

Silently, she studied every plane and angle of his face, engraving them on both heart and mind. *There is too much strength there,* she thought, rocked by a surge of love. Too much virility, too much knowledge. She scrambled to her feet, needing to postpone the inevitable.

"I'm starving," she claimed. "Are you going to spring for breakfast? After all, I did win the race."

"Did you?" He rose as she pulled the short robe over the briefness of her bikini.

"Yes," she said, "positively." Picking up Taylor's light blue pullover, she held it out. "I was the undisputed winner." She watched as he dragged the snug, crew necked shirt over his head then bent to retrieve the towels.

"Then you should buy my breakfast." Smiling, he held out his hand. After a brief hesitation, she accepted.

"How do you feel about corn flakes?"

"Unenthusiastic."

"Well." Her shoulders moved in regret. "I'm afraid my funds are rather limited as I was hauled to Florida without ceremony."

"Your credit's good." He released her hand and swung a friendly arm around her shoulders. They moved away from the sea.

By mid afternoon, B.J. felt euphoric. There was a new, charming friendliness about Taylor that made her realize she liked him every bit as much as she loved him.

She was given a thorough if belated tour of the hotel, allowed to wander through the silver and cobalt lounge, linger in the two elegantly stocked boutiques and examine the enormous expanse of the steel and white kitchen. In the game room, she was provided with an endless supply of change as Taylor watched her reckless enthusiasm with tolerance.

Leaning against a machine, he looked on as she steered her computer car to another horrendous wreck. "You know," he commented as she held her hand for another quarter, "by the time you've finished, you'll have spent every bit as much as that dress in the boutique cost. Why is it, you'll take the money for these noisy machines, but you refuse to let me buy you that very appealing dress?"

''This is different,'' she said vaguely, maneuvering the car around obstructions.

''How?'' He grimaced as she narrowly missed an unwary pedestrian and skidded around a corner.

''You never said if you worked out the problem,'' B.J. murmured as she twisted the wheel to avoid a slow moving vehicle.

''Problem?''

''Yes, the one you came down here to see to.''

''Oh, yes.'' He smiled and brushed an insistent wisp from her cheek. ''It's working out nicely.''

''Oh, blast!'' B.J. frowned as her car careened into a telephone pole, flipped through the air and landed with an impressive show of computer color and sound.

''Come on.'' Taylor grabbed her hand as she looked up hopefully. ''Let's have some lunch before I go bankrupt.''

On the sundeck above the pool, they enjoyed quiche Lorraine and Chablis. A handful of people splashed and romped in the pale blue water. Toying with the remains of her meal, B.J. stared down at the swimmers and sun bathers. Her gaze swept to include the curve of beach before returning to Taylor. He was watching her, a small secret smile on his lips and in his eyes. She blinked in confused embarrassment.

''Is something wrong?'' Battling the urge to wipe

her cheek to see if it was smudged, she lifted her glass and sipped the cool wine.

"No, I just enjoy looking at you. Your eyes are constantly changing hues. One minute they're like peat smoke, and the next clear as a lake. You'll never be able to keep secrets; they say too much." His smile spread as her color rose. Her eyes shifted to the golden lights in her glass. "You're an incredibly beautiful creature, B.J."

She lifted her head, her eyes wide in surprise.

With a light chuckle, he captured her hand and brought it to his lips. "I don't suppose I should tell you that too often. You'll begin to see how true it is and lose that appealing air of innocence."

Rising, he maintained possession of her hand, pulling her to her feet. "I'm going to take you to the Health Club. You can get a first hand impression of how this place works."

"All right, but…"

"I'm leaving instructions that you're to have the complete routine," he interrupted. "And when I meet you at seven for dinner, I don't want to see any shadows under your eyes."

Transferred from Taylor's authority to a perfectly shaped brunette, B.J. was whirlpooled, saunaed, pummeled and massaged. For three hours, she was alternately steamed and sprayed, plied with iced fruit juice and submerged in churning water. Her first instinct was to retrieve her clothes and quietly slip out. After finding they had been conveniently cached out of sight, she submitted, and soon found tensions she had been unaware of possessing seeping out of her.

Stomach down on a high table, she sighed under the magic hands of the masseuse and allowed her mind to float in the twilight world of half sleep. Dimly, the conversation of two women enjoying the same wonder drifted across to her.

"I happened to be staying here two years ago…so incredibly handsome…what a marvelous catch…All that lovely money as well…The Reynolds empire."

At Taylor's name, B.J.'s eyes opened and her inadvertent eavesdropping became deliberate.

"It's a wonder some smart woman hasn't snagged him yet." An auburn haired woman tucked a bright strand behind her ear and folded her arms under her chin.

"Darling, you can be sure scores have tried." Her brunette companion stifled a yawn and smiled with wry humor. "I don't imagine he's averse to the chase. A man like that thrives on feminine adulation."

"He's got mine."

"Did you see his companion? I caught a glimpse last night and again today by the pool."

"Mmm, I saw them when they arrived, but I was

too busy looking at him to take much notice. A blonde, wasn't she?''

''Um-hum, though I don't think that pale wheat shade was a gift of nature.''

B.J.'s first surge of outrage was almost immediately replaced by amusement. So, she decided, if I'm to be Taylor's temporary, if fictional mistress, I might as well hear the opinion of the masses.

''Do you think this one will get her hooks in? Who is she anyway?''

''That's precisely what I attempted to find out.'' The brunette grimaced and mirrored her companion's position of chin on arms. ''It cost me twenty dollars to learn her name is B.J. Clark of all things. Beyond that, not even dear Paul Bailey knows anything. She just popped up out of the blue. She's never been here before. As for getting her hooks in.'' Elegantly tanned shoulders shrugged. ''I wouldn't bet either way. His eyes simply devour her; it's enough to make you drool with envy.''

B.J. raised a skeptical eyebrow.

''I suppose,'' the brunette went on, ''huge gray eyes and masses of blond hair are appealing. And she is rather attractive in a wholesome, peaches and cream sort of way.''

B.J. rose on her elbows and smiled across the room. ''Thank you,'' she said simply, then lowered her head and grinned into the ensuing silence.

Chapter Eleven

Refreshed and pleased with herself, B.J. entered Taylor's suite, carrying a dress box under her arm. Though she had lost the minor tussle with the sales clerk in the boutique, she remained in high spirits. After her session in the spa, she had returned to the shop. Pointing to the gown of silver silk which Taylor had admired, she was prepared to surrender a large hunk of her bank account only to be told Mr. Reynolds had left instructions that any purchases she made were to be billed to him.

Annoyed by his arrogance, however generous, B.J. had argued with the implacable salesgirl. Ultimately, she had left the shop with the dress in hand vowing to see to the monetary details later.

If, she decided, pouring a substantial stream of bath salts under the rushing water of the tub, she was to portray the image of the mysterious lady from nowhere she was going to dress the part. She lowered herself into hot, frothy water and had just begun to relax when the door swung open.

"So, you're back," Taylor said easily, leaning against the door, "Did you enjoy yourself?"

"Taylor!" B.J. slid down in the tub, attempting to cover herself with the blanket of bubbles. "I'm having a bath!"

"Yes. I can see that, and little else. There's no need to drown yourself. Would you like a drink?" The question was pleasant and impersonal.

Recalling the overheard conversation in the spa, B.J.'s pride rallied. It's time, she decided, to give him back a bit of his own.

"That would be lovely." Fluttering her lashes, she hoped her expression was unconcerned. "Some sherry would be nice, if it's no bother."

Watching his brow lift in surprise, B.J. felt decidedly smug. "It's no trouble," he said as he retreated, leaving the door ajar. She prayed fervently the bubbles would not burst until she had a chance to leave the tub and slip into her robe.

"Here you are." Reentering, Taylor handed her a small glass shimmering with golden liquid.

B.J. gave him a smile and sipped. "Thanks. I'll be finished soon if you want the bath."

"Don't rush," he returned, delighted to see her coolness had somewhat rattled him, "I'll use the other."

"Suit yourself," she said agreeably, making sure her shrug was mild and did little to disturb her peaceful waters. Relieved that the door closed behind him, B.J. expelled a long breath and set the remains of her drink on the edge of the tub.

For a full five minutes, B.J. stared at her reflection in the full-length mirror. Silver silk draped crossways over the curve of each breast, narrowing to thin straps over her shoulders before continuing down her sides to leave her back bare to the waist. The skirt fell straight over her slender hips and legs, one side slit to mid-thigh. She had piled her hair in a loose knot on top of her head, allowing a few curling tendrils to escape and frame her face.

B.J. found the stranger in the mirror intimidating. With a flash of intuition, she knew B.J. Clark could not live up to the promises hinted at by the woman in the glass.

"Almost ready?" Taylor's knock and question jolted her out of her reverie.

"Yes, just coming." Shaking her head, she gave the reflection a reassuring smile. "It's just a dress," she reminded both B.J. Clarks and turned from the mirror.

Taylor's hand paused midway in the action of pouring pre-dinner drinks. He lifted his cigarette to his lips, inhaling slowly as he surveyed B.J.'s entrance. "Well," he said as she hesitated, "I see you bought it after all."

"Yes." With a surge of confidence, she crossed the room to join him. "As a woman of ill fame I felt my wardrobe inadequate."

"Care to elaborate?" He handed B.J. a delicate glass.

She accepted automatically. "Just a conversation I overheard in the spa." Her eyes lit with amusement, she set her glass on the bar. "Oh, Taylor, it was funny. I'm sure you have no idea how ardently your…ah…affairs are monitored." Describing her afternoon at the spa, she was unable to suppress her giggles.

"I can't tell you how it boosts the ego to be envied and touted as a woman of mystery! I certainly hope it's not discovered that I'm a hotel manager from Lakeside, Vermont. It would spoil it."

"No one would believe it anyway." He did not appear to be amused by her story as, frowning, he sipped at his drink.

Confused by his expression, B.J. asked, "Don't you like the dress after all?"

"I like it." He took her hand, the smile at last taking command of his mouth. "Obviously, we'll have to have champagne. You look much too elegant for anything else."

They began their meal with oysters Rockefeller and champagne. Their table sat high in the double level dining room, in front of a wide wall aquarium. As the London broil was served, B.J. sipped her wine and glanced around the room.

"This is a lovely place, Taylor." She gestured with a fine-boned hand to encompass the entire resort.

"It does the job." He spoke with the smooth confidence of one who knew the worth of his possessions.

"Yes, it certainly does. It runs beautifully. The staff is efficient and discreet, almost to the point of being invisible. You hardly know they're there, yet everything's perfect. I suppose it's elbow to elbow in here during the winter."

With a movement of his shoulders, he followed her gaze. "I try to avoid hitting the resorts during the heavy season."

"Our summer season will begin in a few weeks," she began, only to find her hand captured and her glass replenished with champagne.

"I've managed to keep you from bringing up the

inn all day; let's see if we can finish the evening without it. When we get back tomorrow, we can talk about vacancies and cancellations. I don't discuss business when I'm having dinner with a beautiful woman.''

B.J. smiled and surrendered. If only one evening remained of the interlude, she wanted to savor each moment.

''What do you discuss over dinner with a beautiful woman?'' she countered, buoyed by the wine.

''More personal matters.'' His finger traced the back of her hand. ''The way her voice flows like an easy river, the way her smile touches her eyes before it moves her mouth, the way her skin warms under my hand.'' With a low laugh, he lifted her hand, lips brushing the inside of her wrist.

Glancing up warily, B.J. asked, ''Taylor, are you making fun of me?''

''No.'' His voice was gentle. ''I have no intention of making fun of you, B.J.''

Satisfied with his answer, she smiled and allowed him to lead the conversation into a lighter vein.

Flickering candles, the muted chink of crystal and silver, the low murmur of voices, Taylor's eyes meeting hers—it was an evening B.J. knew she would always remember.

''Let's go for a walk.'' Taylor rose and pulled back her chair. ''Before you fall asleep in your champagne.'' Hand in hand they walked to the beach.

They walked in silence, enjoying each other and the night. Merging with the aroma of the sea and the night was the tenuous scent of orange blossoms. B.J. knew the fragrance would be forever melded with her memory of the man whose hand lay warm and firm over hers. Would she ever look at the moon again without thinking of him? Ever walk beneath the stars without remembering? Ever draw a breath without longing for him?

Tomorrow, she reflected, it would be business as usual, and a handful of days after, he would be gone. Only a name on a letterhead. Still, she would have the inn, she reminded herself. He'd said no more about changes. She'd have her home and her work and her memories, and that was much more than some ever had.

''Cold?'' Taylor asked, and she shivered, afraid he had read her mind. ''You're trembling.'' His arm slipped around her shoulders, bringing aching warmth. ''We'd better go back.''

Mutely, she nodded and forced tomorrows out of her mind. Relaxing, she felt the remnants of champagne mist pleasurably in her head.

''Oh, Taylor,'' she whispered as they crossed the lobby. ''That's one of the women from the spa this afternoon.'' She inclined her head toward the brunette watching them with avid interest.

''Hmm.'' Taylor pushed the button for the glass enclosed elevator.

''Do you think I should wave?'' B.J. asked before Taylor pulled her inside.

''No, I've a better idea.''

Before she realized his intent, he had her gathered into his arms, silencing her protest with a mind-spinning kiss. Releasing her, he grinned down at the openly staring brunette.

B.J. turned to Taylor as the door of the suite shut behind him. ''Really, Taylor, it's a crime I haven't a lurid past she could dig up.''

''It's perfectly all right, she'll invent one for you. Want a brandy?'' He moved to the bar and released the concealing panel.

''No, my nose is already numb.''

''I see; is that a congenial condition?''

''It is,'' she stated, sliding onto a bar stool, ''my gauge for the cautious consumption of liquor. When my nose gets numb, I've already had one more than my limit.''

''I see.'' Turning, he poured amber liquid into a solitary snifter. ''Obviously, my plans to ply you with liquor is doomed to fail.''

''I'm afraid so.''

"What's your weakness, B.J.?" The question was so unexpected she was caught unaware. *You,* she almost answered but caught herself in time. "I'm a pushover for soft lights and quiet music."

"Is that so?"

Magically, the lights lowered and music whispered through the room.

"How did you do that?"

He rounded the bar and stood in front of her. "There's a panel in back of the bar."

"The wonders of technology." Nerves prickling, she tensed like a cornered cat when his hand took her arm.

"I want to dance with you." He drew her to her feet. "Take the pins out of your hair. It smells like wildflowers; I want to feel it in my hands."

"Taylor, I..."

"Ssh." Slowly, he took out the pins until her hair tumbled free over her shoulders. Then, his fingers combed through the length of it before he gathered her close in his arms.

He moved gently to the music, keeping her molded against him. Her tension flowed away, replaced by a sleepy excitement. Her cheek rested naturally in the curve of his shoulder, as if they had danced countless times before, would dance countless times again.

"Are you going to tell me what B.J. stands for?" he murmured against her ear.

"No one knows," she responded hazily as his fingers followed the tingling delight along her bare skin. "Even the F.B.I. is baffled."

"I suppose I'll have to get it from your mother."

"She doesn't remember." She sighed and snuggled closer.

"How do you sign official papers?" His hand caressed the small of her back.

"Just B.J., I always use B.J."

"On a passport?"

She shrugged, her lips unconsciously brushing his neck, her cheek nuzzling the masculine roughness of his chin. "I haven't got one. I've never needed one."

"You need one to fly to Rome."

"Yes, I'll make sure I have one the next time I do. But I'd sign it Bea Jay." She grinned, knowing he would not realize she had just answered his question. She lifted her face to smile at him and found her lips captured in a gentle, teasing kiss.

"B.J.," he murmured and drew her away before her lips were satisfied. "I want…"

"Kiss me again, Taylor." Sweet and heavy, love lay on her. "Really kiss me," she whispered, shutting out the voice of reason. Her eyes fluttered closed as she urged his mouth back to hers.

He said her name again, the words soft on the lips which clung to his in silent request. With a low groan, he crushed her against him.

He swept her feet off the floor as his mouth took hers with unbridled hunger. In dizzying circles, the room whirled as she felt herself lowered to the thick plush of carpet. Unrestrained, his mouth savaged the yielding softness of hers, tongue claiming the sweet moistness. His hand pushed aside the thin silk of her bodice, seeking and finding the smooth promise for more, his mouth and hands roaming over her, finding heat beneath the cool silk, fingers trailing up the slit of her skirt until they captured the firm flesh of her thigh.

Tossed on the turbulent waves of love and need, B.J. responded with a burst of fire. His possession of her mouth and flesh was desperate. She answered by instinct, moving with a woman's hidden knowledge as he took with insatiable appetite the fruits she offered. Her own hands, no longer shy, found their way under his jacket to explore the hard ripple of muscles of his back and shoulders, half-terrified, half-delighting in their strength. From the swell and valley of her breasts, his mouth traveled, burning, tantalizing, to burrow against her neck. Her own lips sought to discover his taste and texture, to assuage her new and throbbing hunger.

His loving had lost all gentleness, his mouth and

hands now bringing painful excitement. Her fragile innocence began to dissolve with the ancient cravings of womanhood. B.J. began to tremble with fear and anticipation.

Taylor's mouth lifted from the curve of her neck, and he stared into the eyes cloudy with desire and uncertainty. Abruptly he rose and pulled her to her feet. "Go to bed," he commanded shortly. Turning to the bar, he poured himself another brandy.

Dazed by the abruptness of the rejection, B.J. stood frozen.

"Didn't you hear me? I said go to bed." Downing half his brandy, Taylor pulled out a cigarette.

"Taylor, I don't understand. I thought..." A hand lifted to push at her hair, her eyes liquid and pleading. "I thought you wanted me."

"I do." He drew deep on his cigarette. "Now, go to bed."

"Taylor." The fury in his eyes caused her to flinch.

"Just get out of here before I forget all the rules."

B.J. straightened her shoulders and swallowed her tears. "You're the boss." She ignored the swift flame of temper in his eyes and plunged on. "But I want you to know, what I offered you tonight was a one-time deal. I'll never willingly go into your arms again. From now on, the only thing between you and me is the Lakeside Inn."

''We'll leave it at that for now,'' he said in curt agreement as he turned away and poured another drink. ''Just go to bed.''

B.J. ran from the room and turned the lock on her door with an audible click.

Chapter Twelve

B.J. threw herself into the inn's routine like a bruised child returning to a mother's arms. She and Taylor had flown from Florida to Vermont in almost total silence, he working on his papers while she had buried herself in a magazine. Avoiding Taylor for the next two days was easy. He made no effort to see her. Annoyance made hurt more tolerable. B.J. worked with dedication to construct a wall of resentment to shield the emptiness she would experience when he left both the inn and her.

Furthering her resentment was the stubborn presence of Darla Trainor. Although B.J. observed Taylor was not often in her company, her mere existence rubbed the sore of wounded pride. Seeing Darla was a constant reminder of B.J.'s uncomfortable and confusing relationship with Taylor.

B.J. knew she could not have mistaken the desire he had felt for her the last night in Florida. She concluded, watching Darla's sensuous elegance, that he had ultimately been disappointed in her lack of experience in the physical demands of love.

Wanting to avoid any unnecessary contact with Taylor, B.J. established her office in her room for the duration of his stay. Buried to her elbows in paperwork one afternoon, she jumped and scattered receipts as the quiet afternoon was shattered by screams and scrambling feet above her head. Racing to the third floor, B.J. followed the sounds into 314. For a moment she could only stand in the doorway and gape at the tableau. In the center of the braid rug, Darla Trainor was engaged in a major battle with one of the housemaids. A helpless Eddie was caught in the middle, his pleas for peace ignored.

"Ladies, ladies, please." Taking her life in her hands, B.J. plunged into the thick of battle and attempted to restore order. Hands and mixed accusations flew. "Louise, Miss Trainor is a guest! What's gotten into you?" She tugged, without success, on the housemaid's arm, then switched her attention to Darla. "Please, stop shouting, I can't understand." Frustrated because she was shouting herself, B.J. lowered her voice and tried to pull Darla away.

''Please, Miss Trainor, she's half your size and twice your age. You'll hurt her.''

''Take your hands off me!'' Darla flung out an arm, and by accident or design, her fist connected, sending B.J. sprawling against the bedpost. The light shattered into fragments, then smothered with darkness as she slid gently to the floor.

''B.J.'' A voice called from down a long tunnel. B.J. responded with a moan and allowed her eyes to open into slits. ''Lie still,'' Taylor ordered. Gingerly, she permitted her eyes to open further and focused on his lean features. He was leaning over her, his face lined with concern while he stroked the hair away from her forehead.

''What happened?'' She ignored his command and attempted to sit up. Taylor pushed her back against the pillow.

''That's precisely what I want to know.'' As he glanced around, B.J. followed his gaze. Eddie sat on a small settee with his arm around a sniffling Louise. Darla stood by the window, her profile etched in indignation.

''Oh.'' Memory clearing, B.J. let out a long breath and shut her eyes. Unconsciousness, she decided, had its advantages. ''The three of them were wrestling in the middle of the room. I'm afraid I got in the path of Miss Trainor's left hook.''

The hand stroking her cheek stopped as Taylor's fingers tensed against her skin. ''She hit you?''

''It was an accident, Taylor.'' Darla interrupted B.J.'s response, her eyes shining with regret and persecution. ''I was simply trying to take these tacky curtains down when this…this maid—'' she gestured regally toward Louise ''—this maid comes in and begins shouting and pulling on me. Then he's shouting—'' She fluttered a hand toward Eddie before passing it across her eyes. ''Then Miss Clark appears from nowhere, and she begins pulling and shouting. It was a dreadful experience.'' With a long, shuddering sigh, Darla appeared to collect herself. ''I only tried to push her away. She had no business coming into my room in the first place. None of these people belong in my room.''

''She had no business trying to take down those curtains,'' Louise chimed in, wringing Eddie's handkerchief. She waved the soggy linen until all eyes shifted to the window in question. The white chintz hung drunkenly against the frame. ''She said they were out-of-date and impractical like everything else in this place. I washed those curtains myself two weeks ago.'' Louise placed a hand on her trembling bosom. ''I was not going to have her soiling them. I asked her very nicely to stop.''

''Nicely?'' Darla exploded. ''You attacked me.''

''I only attacked her,'' Louise countered with dignity, ''when she wouldn't come down. B.J., she was standing on the Bentwood chair. Standing on it!'' Louise buried her face in Eddie's shoulder, unable to go on.

''Taylor.'' Tucking an errant lock behind her ear, Darla moved toward him, blinking moist eyes. ''You aren't going to allow her to speak to me that way, are you? I want her fired. She might have injured me. She's unstable.'' Darla placed a hand on his arm as the first tear trembled on her lashes.

Infuriated by the display of helpless femininity, B.J. rose. She ignored both Taylor's restraining hand and the throbbing in her head. ''Mr. Reynolds, am I still manager of this inn?''

''Yes, Miss Clark.''

B.J. heard the annoyance in his voice and added it to her list of things to ignore. ''Very well. Miss Trainor, it falls under my jurisdiction as manager of the inn to oversee all hirings and firings. If you wish to lodge a formal complaint, please do so in writing to my attention. In the meantime, I should warn you that you will be held responsible for any damages done to the furnishings of your room. You should know, as well, that the inn will stand behind Louise in this matter.''

''Taylor.'' Nearly sputtering with anger, Darla turned back to him. ''You're not going to allow this?''

''Mr. Reynolds,'' B.J. interrupted, wishing for a bottle of aspirin and oblivion. ''Perhaps you'll take Miss Trainor to the lounge for a drink, and we can discuss this matter later.''

After a brief study, Taylor nodded. ''All right, we'll talk later. Rest in your room for the remainder of the day. I'll see you're not disturbed.''

B.J. accepted the display of gratitude and sympathy by both Eddie and Louise before trudging down to her room. Stepping over scattered papers, she secured much needed aspirin then curled up on the quilt of her bed. Dimly, she heard the door open and felt a hand brush through her hair. The grip of sleep was too strong, and she could not tell if the elusive kiss on her mouth was dream or reality.

When she woke up the throbbing had decreased to a negligible ache. Sitting up, B.J. stared at the neat stack of papers on her desk. Maybe it was a dream, she mused, confused by the lack of disorder on her floor. She touched the back of her head and winced as her fingers contacted with a small lump. Maybe I picked them up and don't remember. It's always the mediator who gets clobbered, she thought in disgust, and prepared to go downstairs to confront Taylor. In the lobby, she came upon Eddie, Maggie and Louise in a heated, low-voiced debate. With a sigh, she moved toward them to restore order.

"Oh, B.J." Maggie started with comical guilt. "Mr. Reynolds said you weren't to be disturbed. How are you feeling? Louise said that Miss Trainor gave you a nasty lump."

"It's nothing." She glanced from one solemn face to the next. She moved her shoulders in resignation. "All right, what's the problem?"

The question produced a jumble of words from three different tongues. Pampering her still aching head, B.J. held up a hand for silence. "Eddie," she decided, choosing at random.

"It's about the architect," he began, and she raised her brows in puzzlement.

"What architect?"

"The one who was here when you were in Florida. Only we didn't know he was an architect. Dot thought he was an artist because he was always walking around with a pad and pencil and making drawings."

Resigning herself to a partially coherent story, B.J. prompted, "Drawings of what?"

"Of the inn," Eddie announced with a flourish. "But he wasn't an artist."

"He was an architect," Maggie interrupted, unable to maintain her silence. Eddie shot her a narrow-eyed frown.

"And how do you know he was an architect?" After asking, B.J. wondered why it mattered. Her wandering attention was soon drawn back with a jolt.

"Because Louise heard Mr. Reynolds talking to him on the phone."

B.J.'s gaze shifted to the housemaid as a hollow feeling grew in the pit of her stomach. "How did you hear, Louise?"

"I wasn't eavesdropping," she claimed with dignity, then amended as B.J. raised her brows. "Well, not really, until I heard him talking about the inn. I was going to dust the office, and since Mr. Reynolds was on the phone, I waited outside. When I heard him say something about a new building, and he said the man's name, Fletcher, I remembered Dot talking about this man named Fletcher making sketches of the inn." She gave the group a small smile in self-reward for her memory. "Anyway, they talked awhile, technical sort of things about dimensions and timber. Then Mr. Reynolds said how he appreciated the Fletcher person not letting on he was an architect until he had everything settled."

"B.J.," Eddie began urgently, grabbing her arm. "Do you think he's going to remodel the inn after all? Do you think he's going to let us all go?"

"No." Feeling her head increase its throbbing, B.J. repeated more emphatically, "No, it's just some mix up, I'll see about it. Now, you all go back to work and don't spread this around anymore."

"It's no mix up." Darla glided over to the group.

"I told you three to go back to work," B.J. ordered in a voice which they recognized as indisputable. They dispersed, waiting until a safe distance before murmuring among themselves. "If you'll pardon me, Miss Trainor, I'm busy."

"Yes, Taylor's quite anxious to see you."

Cursing herself, B.J. nibbled at the bait. "Is he?"

"Oh, yes. He's ready to tell you about his plans for this little place. It's quite a challenge." She surveyed the lobby with the air of one planning a siege.

"What exactly do you know of his plans?" B.J. demanded.

"You didn't really think he intended to leave this place in this condition simply because you want him to?" With a light laugh, Darla brushed away a fictional speck of dust from her vivid blue blouse. "Taylor is much too practical for grand gestures. Though, he might keep you on in some minor capacity once the alterations are complete. You're hardly qualified to manage one of his resorts, but he does seem to think you have some ability. Of course, if I were you, I'd pack up and bow out now to spare myself the humiliation."

"Are you saying," B.J. began, spacing words with great care, "that Taylor has made definite plans to convert the inn into a resort?"

"Well, of course." Darla smiled indulgently.

''He'd hardly need me and an architect otherwise, would he? I wouldn't worry. I'm sure he'll keep the bulk of your staff on, at least temporarily.''

With a final smile, Darla turned and left B.J. staring at her retreating back.

After the first flow of despair, fury bubbled. She took the steps two at a time and slammed into her room. Minutes later, she sped out again, taking stairs in a headlong flight and stomping into the office unannounced.

''B.J.'' Rising from the desk, Taylor studied her furious face. ''What are you doing out of bed?''

For an answer, she slammed the paper on his desk. He lifted it, scanning her resignation. ''It seems we've been through this before.''

''You gave me your word.'' Her voice trembled at the breach of trust but she lifted her chin. ''You can tear that one up too, but it won't change anything. Find yourself a new patsy, Mr. Reynolds. I quit!''

Streaking from the room, she collided bodily with Eddie, brushed him aside and rushed up the stairs. In her room, she pulled out her cases and began to toss articles in them at random. Clothing, cosmetics, knick-knacks, whatever was close at hand was dumped, until the first case overflowed.

She stopped her frantic activities to whirl around

at the metallic click of the lock. The door opened to admit Taylor.

"Get out!" she commanded, wishing fleetingly she was big enough to toss him out. "This is my room until I leave."

"You're making one beautiful mess," he observed calmly. "You might as well stop that, you're not going anywhere."

"Yes, I am." She caught herself before she tossed her asparagus fern among her lingerie. "I'm leaving just as fast as I can pack. Not only is working for you intolerable, but being under the same roof is more than I can stand. You promised!" She spun to face him, cursing the mist which clouded her eyes. "I believed you. I trusted you. How could I have been so stupid! There's no way I could have prevented you once you'd made your decision, and I would have adjusted somehow. You could have been honest with me."

Tears were spilling over with more speed than she could blink them away, and impatiently she brushed at them with the back of her hand. "Oh!" She spun away to pull pictures from the wall. "I wish I were a man!"

"If you were a man, we'd have had no problem to begin with. If you don't stop tearing up the room, I'll have to stop you. I think you've been battered enough for one day."

She heard it in his voice, the calm control, the half-amused exasperation. Despair for her abiding love merged with fury at his betrayal.

"Just leave me alone!"

"Lie down, B.J., and we'll talk later."

"No, don't you touch me," she ordered as he made to take her arm. "I mean it, Taylor, don't touch me!"

At the desperation in her voice, he dropped his hand to his side. "All right then." The first warning signals of anger touched his face. In the cool precision of his voice, she could hear the danger. "Suppose you tell me what exactly it is I've done?"

"You know very well."

"Spell it out for me," he interrupted, moving away and lighting a cigarette.

"That architect you brought here while we were in Florida."

"Fletcher?" Taylor cut her off again, but this time he gave her his full attention. "What about him?"

"What about him?" B.J. repeated incredulously. "You brought him here behind my back, making all his little drawings and plans. You probably took me to Florida just to get me out of the way while he was here."

"That was a consideration."

His easy admission left her speechless. A wave of pain washed over her, reflecting in her eyes.

"B.J." Taylor's expression became more curious than angry. "Suppose you tell me precisely what you know."

"Darla was only too happy to enlighten me." Turning away, she assuaged the hurt with more furious packing. "Go talk to her."

"She's gone by now. I told her to leave, B.J., did you think I'd let her stay after she hit you?" The soft texture of his voice caused her hands to falter a moment. Quickly, she forced them to move again. "What did she say to you?"

"She told me everything. How you'd brought in the architect to draw up plans for turning the inn into a resort. That you're going to bring in someone to manage it, how…" Her voice broke. "It's bad enough you've been lying to me, Taylor, bad enough you broke your word, but that's personal. What is more important is that you're going to change the whole structure of this community, alter dozens of lives for a few more dollars you don't even need. Your resort in Palm Beach is beautiful and perfect for where and what it is, but the inn…"

"Be quiet, B.J." He crushed out his cigarette then thrust his hands in his pockets. "I told you before, I make my own decisions. I called Fletcher in for two reasons." A swift gesture of his hand haltered her furious retort. ‘‘One, to design a house for a piece of property my agent picked up for me last week. It’s about ten miles outside of town, five acres on a hill overlooking the lake. You probably know it.’’

‘‘Why do you need…’’

‘‘The second purpose,’’ he continued, ignoring her, ‘‘was to design an addition to the inn, adhering to its present architecture. The office space is just too limited. Since I plan to move my base from New York to the inn after we’re married, I require larger accommodations.’’

‘‘I don’t see…’’ Her words stumbled to a halt, as she stared into calm brown eyes. A medley of emotions played through her, eradicating the ache in her head. ‘‘I never agreed to marry you,’’ she managed at length.

‘‘But you will,’’ he countered and leaned against her desk. ‘‘In the meantime, you can ease the various minds downstairs that the inn will remain as is, and you’ll remain in the position of manager with some adjustments.’’

‘‘Adjustments?’’ She could only parrot his last word and sink into a chair.

‘‘I have no problem basing my business in Vermont, but I won’t base my marriage in a hotel. Therefore, we’ll live in the house when it’s completed, and Eddie can take over some of your duties.

You'll also have to be free to travel from time to time. We leave for Rome in three weeks."

"Rome?" she echoed him again, dimly remembering his speaking of Rome and passports.

"Yes, your mother's sending your birth certificate so you can see to getting a passport."

"My mother?" Unable to sit, B.J. rose and paced to the window, trying to clear the fog which covered her brain. "You seem to have everything worked out very neatly." She struggled for control. "I don't suppose it occurred to you to ask my feelings on the matter?"

"I know your feelings." His hands descended to her shoulders, and she stiffened. "I told you once, you can't keep secrets with those eyes."

"I guess it's very convenient for you that I happen to be in love with you." She swallowed, focusing on the gleam of the sun as it filtered through the pines on the hillside.

"It makes things less complicated." His fingers worked at the tension in her shoulders but she held herself rigid.

"Why do you want to marry me, Taylor?"

"Why do you think?" She felt his lips in her hair and squeezed her eyes shut.

"You don't have to marry me for that, and we both know it." Taking a deep breath, she gripped the windowsill tighter. ‘‘That first night you came to my room, you’d already won.’’

‘‘It wasn’t enough.’’ His arms circled her waist and brought her back against him. She struggled to keep her mind clear. ‘‘The minute you swaggered into the office with invisible six guns at your hips, I made up my mind to marry you. I knew I could make you want me, I’d felt that the first time I held you, but the night in your room, you looked up at me, and I knew making you want me wasn’t enough. I wanted you to love me.’’

‘‘So—’’ she moved her shoulders as if it was of little consequence ‘‘—you comforted yourself with Darla in the meantime.’’

She was spun around so quickly, her hair flew out to fall over her face, obscuring vision. ‘‘I never touched Darla or anyone from the first minute I saw you. That little charade in the nightgown was strictly for your benefit, and you were stupid enough to fall for it. Do you think I could touch another woman when I had you on my mind?’’

Without giving her time to answer, his mouth closed over hers, commanding and possessive. His arms banded her waist, dragging her against him. ‘‘You’ve been driving me crazy for nearly two weeks.’’ Allowing her time to draw a quick breath, his mouth crushed hers again. Slowly, the kiss altered in texture, softening, sweetening, his hand moving with a tender lightness which drugged her reason.

''B.J.,'' he murmured, resting his chin on her hair. ''It would be less intimidating if you owned a few more pounds and inches. I've had a devil of a time fighting my natural instincts. I don't want to hurt you, and you're too small and much too innocent.'' Lifting her chin, he framed her face with his hands. ''Have I told you yet that I love you?''

Her eyes grew wide, her mouth opening, but powerless to form sound. She shook her head briskly and swallowed the obstruction in her throat.

''I didn't think I had. Actually, I think I was hit the minute you stood up from home plate, turned those eyes on me and claimed you were absolutely safe.'' He bent down and brushed her lips.

She threw her arms around his neck as though he might vanish in a puff of smoke. ''Taylor, why have you waited so long?''

Drawing her away, he lifted a brow in amusement, reminding her of the brevity of their relationship.

''It's been years,'' she claimed, burying her face in his shoulder as joy washed over her. ''Decades, centuries.''

''And during the millennium,'' he replied, stroking fingers through her hair, ''you've been more exasperating than receptive. The day I came into the lounge and found you ticking off bourbon bottles, I had hoped to start things along a smooth road, but you turned on the ice very effectively. The next day in your room, when you switched to fire, it was very illuminating. The things you said made a great deal of sense, so I decided a change of setting and attitude were in order. Providentially, Bailey called from Florida.''

``You said you had to go to Palm Beach to help him with a problem.''

``I lied,'' he said simply, then laughed with great enjoyment at her astonishment. ``I had planned,'' he began, dropping into a chair and pulling her into his lap, ``to get you away from the inn for a couple of days. More important to have you to myself. I wanted you relaxed and perhaps a bit off guard.'' He laughed again and nuzzled her ear. ``Of course, then I had to see you sitting with Hardy and looking like a fresh peach ripe for picking.''

``You were jealous.'' Indescribably pleased, she sighed and burrowed closer.

``That's a mild word for it.''

They spent the next few minutes in mutually agreeable silence. Taylor lingered over the taste of her mouth, his hand sliding beneath the barrier of her shirt. ``I was quite determined to do things properly, hence the dinner and wine and soft music. I had fully intended to tell you I loved you and ask you to marry me that last night in Florida.''

''Why didn't you?''

''You distracted me.'' His lips trailed along her cheek, reminding her of the power of their last night together. ''I had no intention of allowing things to progress the way they did, but you have a habit of stretching my willpower. That night it snapped. Then, I felt you trembling, and your eyes were so young.'' He sighed and rested his cheek on her hair. ''I was furious with myself for losing control of the situation.''

''I thought you were furious with me.''

''It was better that you did. If I had told you then how I felt about you, nothing would have stopped me from taking you. I was in no frame of mind to introduce you gently to the ways of love. I've never needed anyone so much in my life as I needed you that night.''

Round and liquid with love, her eyes lifted to his. ''Do you need me, Taylor?''

His hand lifted to brush back her hair. The arm cradling her shifted her closer. ''You look like a child,'' he murmured, tracing her lips with his finger. ''A child's mouth, and I can't seem to do without the taste of it. Yes, B.J., I need you.''

His mouth lowered, featherlight, but her arm circled his neck and demanded more. The pressure increased, and the door opened to the world of heat and passion. She felt his hand on her breast, never aware that the buttons of her shirt had been loosened. Her fingers tightened in his hair, willing him to prolong the ecstasy.

His mouth moved to her brow, then rested on her hair, his fingers tracing lightly over her bare skin. "You can see why I've been keeping away from you the last day or so."

With a soft sound of agreement, she buried her face against his shoulder.

"I wanted to get everything set up before I got near you again. I could have done with one more day; we still need a marriage license."

"I'll talk to Judge Walker," she murmured, "if you want one quickly. He's Eddie's uncle."

"Small towns are the backbone of America," Taylor decided. He pulled her close to cover her mouth again when a frantic knock sounded on the door.

"B.J." Eddie's voice drifted through the panel. "Mrs. Frank wants to feed Julius, and I can't find his dinner. And the Bodwin sisters are out of sunflower seeds for Horatio."

"Who's Horatio?" Taylor demanded.

"The Bodwin's parakeet."

"Tell him to feed Horatio to Julius," he suggested, giving the door a scowl.

''It's a thought.'' Lingering on it briefly, B.J. cast it aside. ''Julius's dinner is on the third shelf right hand side of the fridge,'' she called out. ''Send someone into town for a package of sunflower seeds. Now, go away, Eddie, I'm very busy. Mr. Reynolds and I are in conference.'' With a smile, she circled Taylor's neck again. ''Now, Mr. Reynolds, perhaps you'd like my views on the construction of this house you're planning as well as my educated opinion on the structure of your office space.''

''Be quiet, B.J.''

''You're the boss,'' she agreed the moment before their lips met.

* * * * *

Dear Reader,

We are delighted to offer you this classic novel from the incomparable Nora Roberts.

As many of Nora's fans know, Nora began her career writing category romance for Harlequin Books. These hard-to-find novels from Nora's early days as a writer are first and foremost romantic novels, featuring strong characterisations, sparkling dialogue and the kind of happy ending Nora's category readers have always cherished. We hope you'll enjoy this treasured romance, too.

Sincerely,

The Editors
Harlequin Mills & Boon.

NORA ROBERTS

The Law Is A Lady

First Published 1984
Third Australian Paperback Edition 2004
ISBN 0 733 55160 2

Published by
Harlequin Mills & Boon
3 Gibbes Street
CHATSWOOD NSW 2067
AUSTRALIA

Printed and bound in Australia by
McPherson's Printing Group

To all the experts at R&R Lighting Company

Chapter 1

Merle T. Johnson sat on the ripped vinyl seat of a stool in Annie's Cafe, five miles north of Friendly. He lingered over a lukewarm root beer, half listening to the scratchy country number piping out from Annie's portable radio. "*A woman was born to be hurt*" was the lament of Nashville's latest hopeful. Merle didn't know enough about women to disagree.

He was on his way back to Friendly after checking out a complaint on one of the neighboring ranches. Sheep-stealing, he thought as he chugged down more root beer. Might've been exciting if there'd been anything to it. Potts was getting too old to know how many sheep he had in the first place. Sheriff knew there was nothing to it, Merle thought glumly. Sitting in the dingy little cafe with the smell of fried hamburgers and onions clinging to the air, Merle bemoaned the injustice of it.

There was nothing more exciting in Friendly, New Mexico, than hauling in old Silas when he got drunk and disorderly on Saturday nights. Merle T. Johnson had been born too late. If it had been the 1880s instead of the 1980s, he'd have had a chance to face desperados, ride in a posse, face off a gunslinger—the things deputies were supposed to do. And here he was, he told himself fatalistically, nearly twenty-four years old, and the biggest arrest he had made was pulling in the Kramer twins for busting up the local pool hall.

Merle scratched his upper lip where he was trying, without much success, to grow a respectable mustache. The best part of his life was behind him, he decided, and he'd never be more than a deputy in a forgotten little town, chasing imaginary sheep thieves.

If just *once* somebody'd rob the bank. He dreamed over this a minute, picturing himself in a high-speed chase and shootout. That would be something, yessiree. He'd have his picture in the paper, maybe a flesh wound in the shoulder. The idea became more appealing. He could wear a sling for a few days. Now, if the sheriff would only let him carry a gun…

"Merle T., you gonna pay for that drink or sit there dreaming all day?"

Merle snapped back to reality and got hastily to his feet. Annie stood watching him with her hands on her ample hips. She had small, dark eyes, florid skin and an amazing thatch of strawberry-colored hair. Merle was never at his best with women.

"Gotta get back," he muttered, fumbling for his wallet. "Sheriff needs my report."

Annie gave a quick snort and held out her hand, damp palm up. After she snatched the crumpled bill, Merle headed out without asking for his change.

The sun was blinding and brilliant. Merle automatically narrowed his eyes against it. It bounced off the road surface in waves that shimmered almost like liquid. But the day was hot and dusty. On both sides of the ribbon of road stretched nothing but rock and sand and a few tough patches of grass. There was no cloud to break the strong, hard blue of the sky or filter the streaming white light of the sun. He pulled the rim of his hat down over his brow as he headed for his car, wishing he'd had the nerve to ask Annie for his change. His shirt was damp and sticky before he reached for the door handle.

Merle saw the sun radiate off the windshield and chrome of an oncoming car. It was still a mile away, he judged idly as he watched it tool up the long, straight road. He continued to watch its progress with absent-minded interest, digging in his pocket for his keys. As it drew closer his hand remained in his pocket. His eyes grew wide.

That's some car! he thought in stunned admiration.

One of the fancy foreign jobs, all red and flashy. It whizzed by without pausing, and Merle's head whipped around to stare after it. *Oo-wee!* he thought with a grin. *Some* car. Must have been doing seventy easy. Probably has one of those fancy dashboards with— Seventy!

Springing into his car, Merle managed to get the keys out of his pocket and into the ignition. He flipped on his siren and peeled out, spitting gravel and smoking rubber. He was in heaven.

* * *

Phil had been driving more than eighty miles nonstop. During the early part of the journey, he'd held an involved conversation on the car phone with his producer in L.A. He was annoyed and tired. The dust-colored scenery and endless flat road only annoyed him further. Thus far, the trip had been a total waste. He'd checked out five different towns in southwest New Mexico, and none of them had suited his needs. If his luck didn't change, they were going to have to use a set after all. It wasn't his style. When Phillip Kincaid directed a film, he was a stickler for authenticity. Now he was looking for a tough, dusty little town that showed wear around the edges. He wanted peeling paint and some grime. He was looking for the kind of place everyone planned to leave and no one much wanted to come back to.

Phil had spent three long hot days looking, and nothing had satisfied him. True, he'd found a couple of sand-colored towns, a little faded, a little worse for wear, but they hadn't had the right feel. As a director—a highly successful director of American films—Phillip Kincaid relied on gut reaction before he settled down to refining angles. He needed a town that gave him a kick in the stomach. And he was running short on time.

Already Huffman, the producer, was getting antsy, pushing to start the studio scenes. Phil was cursing himself again for not producing the film himself when he cruised by Annie's Cafe. He had stalled Huffman for another week, but if he didn't find the right town to represent New Chance, he would have to trust his location manager to find it. Phil scowled down the endless stretch of road. He didn't trust details to anyone but himself. That, and his undeniable talent, were the reasons for his success at the age of thirty-four. He was tough, critical and volatile, but he treated each of his films as though it were a child requiring endless care and patience. He wasn't always so understanding with his actors.

He heard the wail of the siren with mild curiosity. Glancing in the mirror, Phil saw a dirty, dented police car that might have been white at one time. It was bearing down on him enthusiastically. Phil swore, gave momentary consideration to hitting the gas and leaving the annoyance with his dust, then resignedly pulled over. The blast of heat that greeted him when he let down the window did nothing to improve his mood. Filthy place, he thought, cutting the engine. Grimy dust hole. He wished for his own lagoonlike pool and a long, cold drink.

Elated, Merle climbed out of his car, ticket book in hand. Yessiree, he thought again, this was some machine. About the fanciest piece he'd seen outside the TV. Mercedes, he noted, turning the sound of it over in his mind. French, he decided with admiration. Holy cow, he'd stopped himself a French car not two miles out of town. He'd have a story to tell over a beer that night.

The driver disappointed him a bit at first. He didn't look foreign or even rich. Merle's glance passed ignorantly over the gold Swiss watch to take in the T-shirt and jeans. Must be one of those eccentrics, he concluded. Or maybe the car was stolen. Merle's blood began to pound excitedly. He looked at the man's face.

It was lean and faintly aristocratic, with well-defined bones and a long, straight nose. The mouth was unsmiling, even bored. He was clean shaven with the suggestion of creases in his cheeks. His hair seemed a modest brown; it was a bit long and curled over his ears. In the tanned face the eyes were an arresting clear water blue. They were both bored and annoyed and, if Merle had been able to latch on the word, aloof. He wasn't Merle's image of a desperate foreign-car thief.

"Yes?"

The single frosty syllable brought Merle back to business. "In a hurry?" he asked, adopting what the sheriff would have called his tough-cop stance.

"Yes."

The answer made Merle shift his feet. "License and registration," he said briskly, then leaned closer to the window as Phil reached in the glove compartment. "Glory be, look at the dash! It's got everything and then some. A phone, a phone right there in the car. Those French guys are something."

Phil sent him a mild glance. "German," he corrected, handing Merle the registration.

"German?" Merle frowned doubtfully. "You sure?"

"Yes." Slipping his license out of his wallet, Phil passed it through the open window. The heat was pouring in.

Merle accepted the registration. He was downright sure Mercedes was a French name. "This your car?" he asked suspiciously.

"As you can see by the name on the registration," Phil returned coolly, a sure sign that his temper was frayed around the edges.

Merle was reading the registration at his usual plodding speed. "You streaked by Annie's like a bat out of—" He broke off, remembering that the sheriff didn't hold with swearing on the job. "I stopped you for excessive speed. Clocked you at seventy-two. I bet this baby rides so smooth you never noticed."

"As a matter of fact, I didn't." Perhaps if he hadn't been angry to begin with, perhaps if the heat hadn't been rolling unmercifully into the car, Phil might have played his hand differently. As Merle began to write up the ticket Phil narrowed his eyes. "Just how do I know you clocked me at all?"

"I was just coming out of Annie's when you breezed by," Merle said genially. His forehead creased as he formed the letters. "If I'd waited for my change, I wouldn't have seen you." He grinned, pleased with the hand of fate. "You just sign this," he said as he ripped the ticket from the pad. "You can stop off in town and pay the fine."

Slowly, Phil climbed out of the car. When the sun hit his hair, deep streaks of red shot through it. Merle was reminded of his mother's mahogany server. For a moment they stood eye to eye, both tall men. But one was lanky and tended to slouch, the other lean, muscular and erect.

"No," Phil said flatly.

"No?" Merle blinked against the direct blue gaze. "No what?"

"No, I'm not signing it."

"Not signing?" Merle looked down at the ticket still in his hand. "But you have to."

"No, I don't." Phil felt a trickle of sweat roll down his back. Inexplicably it infuriated him. "I'm not signing, and

I'm not paying a penny to some two-bit judge who's feeding his bank account from this speed trap.''

''Speed trap!'' Merle was more astonished than insulted. ''Mister, you were doing better'n seventy, and the road's marked clear: fifty-five. Everybody knows you can't do more than fifty-five.''

''Who says I was?''

''I clocked you.''

''Your word against mine,'' Phil returned coolly. ''Got a witness?''

Merle's mouth fell open. ''Well, no, but...'' He pushed back his hat. ''Look, I don't need no witness, I'm the deputy. Just sign the ticket.''

It was pure perversity. Phil hadn't the least idea how fast he'd been going and didn't particularly care. The road had been long and deserted; his mind had been in L.A. But knowing this wasn't going to make him take the cracked ballpoint the deputy offered him.

''No.''

''Look, mister, I already wrote up the ticket.'' Merle read refusal in Phil's face and set his chin. After all, he was the law. ''Then I'm going to have to take you in,'' he said dangerously. ''The sheriff's not going to like it.''

Phil gave him a quick smirk and held out his hands, wrists close. Merle stared at them a moment, then looked helplessly from car to car. Beneath the anger, Phil felt a stir of sympathy.

''You'll have to follow me in,'' Merle told him as he pocketed Phil's license.

''And if I refuse?''

Merle wasn't a complete fool. ''Well, then,'' he said

amiably, "I'll have to take you in and leave this fancy car sitting here. It might be all in one piece when the tow truck gets here; then again..."

Phil acknowledged the point with a slight nod, then climbed back into his car. Merle sauntered to his, thinking how fine he was going to look bringing in that fancy red machine.

They drove into Friendly at a sedate pace. Merle nodded occasionally to people who stopped their business to eye the small procession. He stuck his hand out the window to signal a halt, then braked in front of the sheriff's office.

"Okay, inside." Abruptly official, Merle stood straight. "The sheriff'll want to talk to you." But the icy gleam in the man's eye kept Merle from taking his arm. Instead he opened the door and waited for his prisoner to walk through.

Phil glimpsed a small room with two cells, a bulletin board, a couple of spindly chairs and a battered desk. An overhead fan churned the steamy air and whined. On the floor lay a large mound of mud-colored fur that turned out to be a dog. The desk was covered with books and papers and two half-filled cups of coffee. A dark-haired woman bent over all this, scratching industriously on a yellow legal pad. She glanced up as they entered.

Phil forgot his annoyance long enough to cast her in three different films. Her face was classically oval, with a hint of cheekbone under honey-toned skin. Her nose was small and delicate, her mouth just short of wide, with a fullness that was instantly sensual. Her hair was black, left to fall loosely past her shoulders in carelessly sweeping waves. Her brows arched in question. Beneath them her eyes were thickly lashed, darkly green and faintly amused.

"Merle?"

The single syllable was full throated, as lazy and sexy as black silk. Phil knew actresses who would kill for a voice like that one. If she didn't stiffen up in front of a camera, he thought, and if the rest of her went with the face... He let his eyes sweep down. Pinned to her left breast was a small tin badge. Fascinated, Phil stared at it.

"Excess of speed on Seventeen, Sheriff."

"Oh?" With a slight smile on her face, she waited for Phil's eyes to come back to hers. She had recognized the appraisal when he had first walked in, just as she recognized the suspicion now. "Didn't you have a pen, Merle?"

"A pen?" Baffled, he checked his pockets.

"I wouldn't sign the ticket." Phil walked to the desk to get a closer look at her face. "Sheriff," he added. She could be shot from any imaginable angle, he concluded, and still look wonderful. He wanted to hear her speak again.

She met his assessing stare straight on. "I see. What was his speed, Merle?"

"Seventy-two. Tory, you should see his car!" Merle exclaimed, forgetting himself.

"I imagine I will," she murmured. She held out her hand, her eyes still on Phil's. Quickly, Merle gave her the paperwork.

Phil noted that her hands were long, narrow and elegant. The tips were painted in shell pink. What the hell is she doing here? he wondered, more easily visualizing her in Beverly Hills.

"Well, everything seems to be in order, Mr.... Kincaid." Her eyes came back to his. A little mascara, he noticed, a touch of eyeliner. The color's hers. No powder, no lipstick. He wished fleetingly for a camera and a couple of hand-held lights. "The fine's forty dollars," she said lazily. "Cash."

"I'm not paying it."

Her lips pursed briefly, causing him to speculate on their taste. "Or forty days," she said without batting an eye. "I think you'd find it less...inconvenient to pay the fine. Our accommodations won't suit you."

The cool amusement in her tone irritated him. "I'm not paying any fine." Placing his palms on the desk, he leaned toward her, catching the faint drift of a subtle, sophisticated scent. "Do you really expect me to believe you're the sheriff? What kind of scam are you and this character running?"

Merle opened his mouth to speak, glanced at Tory, then shut it again. She rose slowly. Phil found himself surprised that she was tall and as lean as a whippet. A model's body, he thought, long and willowy—the kind that made you wonder what was underneath those clothes. This one made jeans and a plaid shirt look like a million dollars.

"I never argue with beliefs, Mr. Kincaid. You'll have to empty your pockets."

"I will not," he began furiously.

"Resisting arrest." Tory lifted a brow. "We'll have to make it sixty days." Phil said something quick and rude.

Instead of being offended, Tory smiled. ''Lock him up, Merle.''

''Now, just a damn minute—''

''You don't want to make her mad,'' Merle whispered, urging Phil back toward the cells. ''She can be mean as a cat.''

''Unless you want us to tow your car…and charge you for that as well,'' she added, ''you'll give Merle your keys.'' She flicked her eyes over his furious face. ''Read him his rights, Merle.''

''I know my rights, damn it.'' Contemptuously he shrugged off Merle's hand. ''I want to make a phone call.''

''Of course.'' Tory sent him another charming smile. ''As soon as you give Merle your keys.''

''Now, look…'' Phil glanced down at her badge again—''Sheriff,'' he added curtly, ''you don't expect me to fall for an old game. This one''—he jerked a thumb at Merle—''waits for an out-of-towner to come by, then tries to hustle him out of a quick forty bucks. There's a law against speed traps.''

Tory listened with apparent interest. ''Are you going to sign the ticket, Mr. Kincaid?''

Phil narrowed his eyes. ''No.''

''Then you'll be our guest for a while.''

''You can't sentence me,'' Phil began heatedly. ''A judge—''

''Justice of the peace,'' Tory interrupted, then tapped a tinted nail against a small framed certificate. Phil saw the name Victoria L. Ashton.

He gave her a long, dry look. ''You?''

"Yes, handy, isn't it?" She cocked her head to the side. "Sixty days, Mr. Kincaid, or two hundred and fifty dollars."

"Two-fifty!"

"Bail's set at five hundred. Would you care to post it?"

"The phone call," he said through clenched teeth.

"The keys," she countered affably.

Swearing under his breath, Phil pulled the keys from his pocket and tossed them to her. Tory caught them neatly. "You're entitled to one local call, Mr. Kincaid."

"It's long distance," he muttered. "I'll use my credit card."

After indicating the phone on her desk, Tory took the keys to Merle. "Two-fifty!" he said in an avid whisper. "Aren't you being a little rough on him?"

Tory gave a quick, unladylike snort. "Mr. Hollywood Kincaid needs a good kick in the ego," she mumbled. "It'll do him a world of good to stew in a cell for a while. Take the car to Bestler's Garage, Merle."

"Me? *Drive* it?" He looked down at the keys in his hand.

"Lock it up and bring back the keys," Tory added. "And don't play with any of the buttons."

"Aw, Tory."

"Aw, Merle," she responded, then sent him on his way with an affectionate look.

Phil waited impatiently as the phone rang. Someone picked up. "Answering for Sherman, Miller and Stein." He swore.

"Where the hell's Lou?" he demanded.

"Mr. Sherman is out of the office until Monday," the

operator told him primly. ''Would you care to leave your name?''

''This is Phillip Kincaid. You get Lou now, tell him I'm in—'' He turned to cast a dark look at Tory.

''Welcome to Friendly, New Mexico,'' she said obligingly.

Phil's opinion was a concise four-letter word. ''Friendly, New Mexico. In jail, damn it, on some trumped-up charge. Tell him to get his briefcase on a plane, pronto.''

''Yes, Mr. Kincaid, I'll try to reach him.''

''You reach him,'' he said tightly and hung up. When he started to dial again, Tory walked over and calmly disconnected him.

''One call,'' she reminded him.

''I got a damn answering service.''

''Tough break.'' She gave him the dashing smile that both attracted and infuriated him. ''Your room's ready, Mr. Kincaid.''

Phil hung up the phone to face her squarely. ''You're not putting me in that cell.''

She looked up with a guileless flutter of lashes. ''No?''

''No.''

Tory looked confused for a moment. Her sigh was an appealingly feminine sound as she wandered around the desk. ''You're making this difficult for me, Mr. Kincaid. You must know I can't manhandle you into a cell. You're bigger than I am.''

Her abrupt change of tone caused him to feel more reasonable. ''Ms. Ashton…'' he began.

''Sheriff Ashton,'' Tory corrected and drew a .45 out

of the desk drawer. Her smile never wavered as Phil gaped at the large gun in her elegant hand. "Now, unless you want another count of resisting arrest on your record, you'll go quietly into that first cell over there. The linen's just been changed."

Phil wavered between astonishment and amusement. "You don't expect me to believe you'd use that thing."

"I told you I don't argue with beliefs." Though she kept the barrel lowered, Tory quite deliberately cocked the gun.

He studied her for one full minute. Her eyes were too direct and entirely too calm. Phil had no doubt she'd put a hole in him—in some part of his anatomy that she considered unimportant. He had a healthy respect for his body.

"I'll get you for this," he muttered as he headed for the cell.

Her laugh was rich and attractive enough to make him turn in front of the bars. Good God, he thought, he'd like to tangle with her when she didn't have a pistol in her hand. Furious with himself, Phil stalked into the cell.

"Doesn't that line go something like: 'When I break outta this joint, you're gonna get yours'?" Tory pulled the keys from a peg, then locked the cell door with a jingle and snap. Struggling not to smile, Phil paced the cell. "Would you like a harmonica and a tin cup?"

He grinned, but luckily his back was to her. Dropping onto the bunk, he sent her a fulminating glance. "I'll take the tin cup if it has coffee in it."

"Comes with the service, Kincaid. You've got free room and board in Friendly." He watched her walk back to the desk to replace the pistol. Something in the lazy, leggy gait affected his blood pressure pleasantly. "Cream and sugar?" she asked politely.

"Black."

Tory poured the coffee, aware that his eyes were on her. She was partly amused by him, partly intrigued. She knew exactly who he was. Over her basic disdain for what she considered a spoiled, tinsel-town playboy was a trace of respect. He hadn't attempted to influence her with his name or his reputation. He'd relied on his temper. And it was his temper, she knew, that had landed him in the cell in the first place.

Too rich, she decided, too successful, too attractive. And perhaps, she mused as she poured herself a cup, too talented. His movies were undeniably brilliant. She wondered what made him tick. His movies seemed to state one image, the glossies another. With a quiet laugh she thought she might find out for herself while he was her "guest."

"Black," she stated, carrying both cups across the room. "Made to order."

He was watching the way she moved; fluidly, with just a hint of hip. It was those long legs, he decided, and some innate confidence. Under different circumstances he would have considered her quite a woman. At the moment he considered her an outrageous annoyance. Silently he unfolded himself from the bunk and went to accept the coffee she held between the bars. Their fingers brushed briefly.

"You're a beautiful woman, Victoria L. Ashton," he muttered. "And a pain in the neck."

She smiled. "Yes."

That drew a laugh from him. "What the hell are you doing here, playing sheriff?"

"What the hell are you doing here, playing criminal?"

Merle burst in the door, grinning from ear to ear. "Holy cow, Mr. Kincaid, that's *some* car!" He dropped the keys in Tory's hand, then leaned against the bars. "I swear, I could've just sat in it all day. Bestler's eyes just about popped out when I drove it in."

Making a low sound in his throat, Phil turned away to stare through the small barred window at the rear of the cell. He scowled at his view of the town. Look at this place! he thought in frustration. Dusty little nowhere. Looks like all the color was washed away twenty years ago. Baked away, he corrected himself as sweat ran uncomfortably down his back. There seemed to be nothing but brown—dry, sparse mesa in the distance and parched sand. All the buildings, such as they were, were different dull shades of brown, all stripped bare by the unrelenting sun. Damn place still had wooden sidewalks, he mused, sipping at the strong coffee. There wasn't a coat of paint on a storefront that wasn't cracked and peeling. The whole town looked as though it had drawn one long, tired communal breath and settled down to wait until it was all over.

It was a gritty, hopeless-looking place with a sad sort of character under a film of dust and lethargy. People stayed in a town like this when they had no place else to go or nothing to do. Came back when they'd lost hope for anything better. And here he was, stuck in some steamy little cell....

His mind sharpened.

Staring at the tired storefronts and sagging wood, Phil saw it all through the lens of a camera. His fingers wrapped around a window bar as he began to plot out scene after scene. If he hadn't been furious, he'd have seen it from the first moment.

This was Next Chance.

Chapter 2

For the next twenty minutes Tory paid little attention to her prisoner. He seemed content to stare out of the window with the coffee growing cold in his hand. After dispatching Merle, Tory settled down to work.

She was blessed with a sharp, practical and stubborn mind. These traits had made her education extensive. Academically she'd excelled, but she hadn't always endeared herself to her instructors. *Why?* had always been her favorite question. In addition her temperament, which ranged from placid to explosive, had made her a difficult student. Some of her associates called her a tedious annoyance—usually when they were on the opposing side. At twenty-seven Victoria L. Ashton was a very shrewd, very accomplished attorney.

In Albuquerque she kept a small, unpretentious office in an enormous old house with bad plumbing. She shared it with an accountant, a real-estate broker and a private investigator. For nearly five years she had lived on the third floor in two barnlike rooms while keeping her office below. It was a comfortable arrangement that Tory had had no inclination to alter even when she'd been able to afford to.

Professionally she liked challenges and dealing with finite details. In her personal life she was more lackadaisical. No one would call her lazy, but she saw more virtue in a nap than a brisk jog. Her energies poured out in the office or courtroom—and temporarily in her position as sheriff of Friendly, New Mexico.

She had grown up in Friendly and had been content with its yawning pace. The sense of justice she had inherited from her father had driven her to law school. Still, she had had no desire to join a swank firm on either coast, or in any big city in between. Her independence had caused her to risk starting her own practice. Fat fees were no motivation for Tory. She'd learned early how to stretch a dollar when it suited her—an ability she got from her mother. People, and the way the law could be made to work to their advantage or disadvantage, interested her.

Now Tory settled behind her desk and continued drafting out a partnership agreement for a pair of fledgling songwriters. It wasn't always simple to handle cases long distance, but she'd given her word. Absentmindedly she sipped her coffee. By fall she would be back in Albuquerque, filling her caseload again and trading her badge for a briefcase. In the meantime the weekend was looming. Payday. Tory smiled a little as she wrote. Friendly livened up a bit on Saturday nights. People tended to have an extra beer. And there was a poker game scheduled at Bestler's Garage that she wasn't supposed to know about. Tory knew when it was advantageous to look the other way. Her father would have said people need their little entertainments.

Leaning back to study what she had written, Tory propped one booted foot on the desk and twirled a raven lock around her finger. Abruptly coming out of his reverie, Phil whirled to the door of the cell.

"I have to make a phone call!" His tone was urgent and excited. Everything he had seen from the cell window had convinced him that fate had brought him to Friendly.

Tory finished reading a paragraph, then looked up languidly. "You've had your phone call, Mr. Kincaid. Why don't you relax? Take a tip from Dynamite there," she suggested, wiggling her fingers toward the mound of dog. "Take a nap."

Phil curled his hands around the bars and shook them. "Woman, I have to use the phone. It's important."

"It always is," Tory murmured before she lowered her eyes to the paper again.

Ready to sacrifice principle for expediency, Phil growled at her. "Look, I'll sign the ticket. Just let me out of here."

"You're welcome to sign the ticket," she returned pleasantly, "but it won't get you out. There's also the charge of resisting arrest."

"Of all the phony, trumped-up—"

"I could add creating a public nuisance," she considered, then glanced over the top of her papers with a smile. He was furious. It showed in the rigid stance of his hard body, in the grim mouth and fiery eyes. Tory felt a small twinge in the nether regions of her stomach. Oh, yes, she could clearly see why his name was linked with dozens of attractive women. He was easily the most beautiful male animal she'd ever seen. It was that trace of aristocratic aloofness, she mused, coupled with the really extraordinary physique and explosive temper. He was like some sleek, undomesticated cat.

Their eyes warred with each other for a long, silent moment. His were stony; hers were calm.

"All right," he muttered, "how much?"

Tory lifted a brow. "A bribe, Kincaid?"

He knew his quarry too well by this time. "No. How much is my fine...Sheriff?"

"Two hundred and fifty dollars." She sent her hair over her shoulder with a quick toss of her head. "Or you can post bail for five hundred."

Scowling at her, Phil reached for his wallet. When I get out of here, he thought dangerously, I'm going to make that tasty little morsel pay for this. A glance in his wallet found him more than a hundred dollars short of bond. Phil swore, then looked back at Tory. She still had the gently patient smile on her face. He could cheerfully strangle her. Instead he tried another tack. Charm had always brought him success with women.

"I lost my temper before, Sheriff," he began, sending her the slightly off-center smile for which he was known. "I apologize. I've been on the road for several days and your deputy got under my skin." Tory went on smiling. "If I said anything out of line to you, it was because you just don't fit the image of small-town peace officer." He grinned and became boyishly appealing—Tom Sawyer caught with his hand in the sugar bowl.

Tory lifted one long, slim leg and crossed it over the other on the desk. "A little short, are you, Kincaid?"

Phil clenched his teeth on a furious retort. "I don't like to carry a lot of cash on the road."

"Very wise," she agreed with a nod. "But we don't accept credit cards."

"Damn it, I have to get out of here!"

Tory studied him dispassionately. "I can't buy claustrophobia," she said. "Not when I read you crawled into a two-foot pipe to check camera angles on *Night of Desperation.*"

"It's not—" Phil broke off. His eyes narrowed. "You know who I am?"

"Oh, I make it to the movies a couple of times a year," she said blithely.

The narrowed eyes grew hard. "If this is some kind of shakedown—"

Her throaty laughter cut him off. "Your self-importance is showing." His expression grew so incredulous, she laughed again before she rose. "Kincaid, I don't care who you are or what you do for a living, you're a bad-tempered man who refused to accept the law and got obnoxious." She sauntered over to the cell. Again he caught the hint of a subtle perfume that suited French silk, more than faded denim. "I'm obliged to rehabilitate you."

He forgot his anger in simple appreciation of blatant beauty. "God, you've got a face," he muttered. "I could work a whole damn film around that face."

The words surprised her. Tory was perfectly aware that

she was physically attractive. She would have been a fool to think otherwise, and she'd heard men offer countless homages to her looks. This was hardly a homage. But something in his tone, in his eyes, made a tremor skip up her spine. She made no protest when he reached a hand through the bars to touch her hair. He let it fall through his fingers while his eyes stayed on hers.

Tory felt a heat to which she had thought herself immune. It flashed through her as though she had stepped into the sun from out of a cool, dim room. It was the kind of heat that buckled your knees and made you gasp out loud in astonished wonder. She stood straight and absorbed it.

A dangerous man, she concluded, surprised. A very dangerous man. She saw a flicker of desire in his eyes, then a flash of amusement. As she watched, his mouth curved up at the corners.

"Baby," he said, then grinned, "I could make you a star."

The purposely trite words dissolved the tension and made her laugh. "Oh, Mr. Kincaid," she said in a breathy whisper, "can I really have a screen test?" A startled Phil could only watch as she flung herself against the bars of the cell dramatically. "I'll wait for you, Johnny," she said huskily as tears shimmered in her eyes and her soft lips trembled. "No matter how long it takes." Reaching through the bars, she clutched at him. "I'll write you every day," she promised brokenly. "And dream of you every night. Oh, Johnny..." her lashes fluttered down—"kiss me goodbye!"

Fascinated, Phil moved to oblige her, but just before his

lips brushed hers, she stepped back, laughing. ''How'd I do, Hollywood? Do I get the part?''

Phil studied her in amused annoyance. It was a pity, he thought, that he hadn't at least gotten a taste of that beautiful mouth. ''A little overdone,'' he stated with more asperity than truth. ''But not bad for an amateur.''

Tory chuckled and leaned companionably against the bars. ''You're just mad.''

''Mad?'' he tossed back in exasperation. ''Have you ever spent any time in one of these cages?''

''As a matter of fact I have.'' She gave him an easy grin. ''Under less auspicious circumstances. Relax, Kincaid, your friend will come bail you out.''

''The mayor,'' Phil said on sudden inspiration. ''I want to see the mayor. I have a business proposition,'' he added.

''Oh.'' Tory mulled this over. ''Well, I doubt I can oblige you on a Saturday. The mayor mostly fishes on Saturday. Want to tell me about it?''

''No.''

''Okay. By the way, your last film should've taken the Oscar. It was the most beautiful movie I've ever seen.''

Her sudden change of attitude disconcerted him. Cautiously, Phil studied her face but saw nothing but simple sincerity. ''Thanks.''

''You don't look like the type who could make a film with intelligence, integrity and emotion.''

With a half laugh he dragged a hand through his hair. ''Am I supposed to thank you for that too?''

''Not necessarily. It's just that you really do look like

the type who squires all those busty celebrities around. When do you find time to work?''

He shook his head. ''I...manage,'' he said grimly.

''Takes a lot of stamina,'' Tory agreed.

He grinned. ''Which? The work or the busty celebrities?''

''I guess you know the answer to that. By the way,'' she continued before he could formulate a reasonable response, ''don't tell Merle T. you make movies.'' Tory gave him the swift, dashing grin. ''He'll start walking like John Wayne and drive us both crazy.''

When he smiled back at her, both of them studied each other in wary silence. There was an attraction on both sides that pleased neither of them.

''Sheriff,'' Phil said in a friendly tone, ''a phone call. Remember the line about the quality of mercy?''

Her lips curved, but before she could agree, the door to the office burst in.

''Sheriff!''

''Right here, Mr. Hollister,'' she said mildly. Tory glanced from the burly, irate man to the skinny, terrified teenager he pulled in with him. ''What's the problem?'' Without hurry she crossed back to her desk, stepping over the dog automatically.

''Those punks,'' he began, puffing with the exertion of running. ''I warned you about them!''

''The Kramer twins?'' Tory sat on the corner of her desk. Her eyes flickered down to the beefy hand that gripped a skinny arm. ''Why don't you sit down, Mr. Hollister. You''—she looked directly at the boy—''it's Tod, isn't it?''

He swallowed rapidly. "Yes, ma'am—Sheriff. Tod Swanson."

"Get Mr. Hollister a glass of water, Tod. Right through there."

"He'll be out the back door before you can spit," Hollister began, then took a plaid handkerchief out of his pocket to wipe at his brow.

"No, he won't," Tory said calmly. She jerked her head at the boy as she pulled up a chair for Hollister. "Sit down, now, you'll make yourself sick."

"Sick!" Hollister dropped into a chair as the boy scrambled off. "I'm already sick. Those—those punks."

"Yes, the Kramer twins."

She waited patiently while he completed a lengthy, sometimes incoherent dissertation on the youth of today. Phil had the opportunity to do what he did best: watch and absorb.

Hollister, he noticed, was a hotheaded old bigot with a trace of fear for the younger generation. He was sweating profusely, dabbing at his brow and the back of his neck with the checkered handkerchief. His shirt was wilted and patched with dark splotches. He was flushed, overweight and tiresome. Tory listened to him with every appearance of respect, but Phil noticed the gentle tap of her forefinger against her knee as she sat on the edge of the desk.

The boy came in with the water, two high spots of color on his cheeks. Phil concluded he'd had a difficult time not slipping out the back door. He judged the boy to be about thirteen and scared right down to the bone. He had a smooth, attractive face, with a mop of dark hair and huge brown eyes that wanted to look everywhere at once. He was too thin; his jeans and grubby shirt were nearly in tatters. He handed Tory the water with a hand that shook. Phil saw that when she took it from him, she gave his hand a quick, reassuring squeeze. Phillip began to like her.

"Here." Tory handed Hollister the glass. "Drink this, then tell me what happened."

Hollister drained the glass in two huge gulps. "Those punks, messing around out back of my store. I've chased 'em off a dozen times. They come in and steal anything they can get their hands on. I've told you."

"Yes, Mr. Hollister. What happened this time?"

"Heaved a rock through the window." He reddened alarmingly again. "This one was with 'em. Didn't run fast enough."

"I see." She glanced at Tod, whose eyes were glued to the toes of his sneakers. "Which one threw the rock?"

"Didn't see which one, but I caught this one." Hollister rose, stuffing his damp handkerchief back in his pocket. "I'm going to press charges."

Phil saw the boy blanch. Though Tory continued to look at Hollister, she laid a hand on Tod's arm. "Go sit down in the back room, Tod." She waited until he was out of earshot. "You did the right thing to bring him in, Mr. Hollister." She smiled. "And to scare the pants off him."

"He should be locked up," the man began.

"Oh, that won't get your window fixed," she said reasonably. "And it would only make the boy look like a hero to the twins."

"In my day—"

"I guess you and my father never broke a window,"

she mused, smiling at him with wide eyes. Hollister blustered, then snorted.

"Now, look here, Tory..."

"Let me handle it, Mr. Hollister. This kid must be three years younger than the Kramer twins." She lowered her voice so that Phil strained to hear. "He could have gotten away."

Hollister shifted from foot to foot. "He didn't try," he mumbled. "Just stood there. But my window—"

"How much to replace it?"

He lowered his brows and puffed for a minute. "Twenty-five dollars should cover it."

Tory walked around the desk and opened a drawer. After counting out bills, she handed them over. "You have my word, I'll deal with him—and with the twins."

"Just like your old man," he muttered, then awkwardly patted her head. "I don't want those Kramers hanging around my store."

"I'll see to it."

With a nod he left.

Tory sat on her desk again and frowned at her left boot. She wasn't just like her old man, she thought. He'd always been sure and she was guessing. Phil heard her quiet, troubled sigh and wondered at it.

"Tod," she called, then waited for him to come to her. As he walked in his eyes darted in search of Hollister before they focused, terrified, on Tory. When he stood in front of her, she studied his white, strained face. Her heart melted, but her voice was brisk.

"I won't ask you who threw the rock." Tod opened his

mouth, closed it resolutely and shook his head. "Why didn't you run?"

"I didn't—I couldn't...." He bit his lip. "I guess I was too scared."

"How old are you, Tod?" She wanted to brush at the hair that tumbled over his forehead. Instead she kept her hands loosely folded in her lap.

"Fourteen, Sheriff. Honest." His eyes darted up to hers, then flew away like a small, frightened bird. "Just last month."

"The Kramer twins are sixteen," she pointed out gently. "Don't you have friends your own age?"

He gave a shrug of his shoulders that could have meant anything.

"I'll have to take you home and talk to your father, Tod."

He'd been frightened before, but now he looked up at her with naked terror in his eyes. It wiped the lecture she had intended to give him out of her mind. "Please." It came out in a whisper, as though he could say nothing more. Even the whisper was hopeless.

"Tod, are you afraid of your father?" He swallowed and said nothing. "Does he hurt you?" He moistened his lips as his breath began to shake. "Tod," Tory's voice became very soft, "you can tell me. I'm here to help you."

"He..." Tod choked, then shook his head swiftly. "No, ma'am."

Frustrated, Tory looked at the plea in his eyes. "Well, then, perhaps since this is a first offense, we can keep it between us."

"M-ma'am?"

"Tod Swanson, you were detained for malicious mischief. Do you understand the charge?"

"Yes, Sheriff." His Adam's apple began to tremble.

"You owe the court twenty-five dollars in damages, which you'll work off after school and on weekends at a rate of two dollars an hour. You're sentenced to six months probation, during which time you're to keep away from loose women, hard liquor and the Kramer twins. Once a week you're to file a report with me, as I'll be serving as your probation officer."

Tod stared at her as he tried to take it in. "You're not...you're not going to tell my father?"

Slowly, Tory rose. He was a few inches shorter, so that he looked up at her with his eyes full of confused hope. "No." She placed her hands on his shoulders. "Don't let me down."

His eyes brimmed with tears, which he blinked back furiously. Tory wanted badly to hold him, but knew better. "Be here tomorrow morning. I'll have some work for you."

"Yes, yes, ma'am—Sheriff." He backed away warily, waiting for her to change her mind. "I'll be here, Sheriff." He was fumbling for the doorknob, still watching her. "Thank you." Like a shot, he was out of the office, leaving Tory staring at the closed door.

"Well, Sheriff," Phil said quietly, "you're quite a lady."

Tory whirled to see Phil eyeing her oddly. For the first time she felt the full impact of the clear blue gaze. Disconcerted, she went back to her desk. "Did you enjoy seeing the wheels of justice turn, Kincaid?" she asked.

"As a matter of fact, I did." His tone was grave enough to cause her to look back at him. "You did the right thing by that boy."

Tory studied him a moment, then let out a long sigh. "Did I? We'll see, won't we? Ever seen an abused kid, Kincaid? I'd bet that fifteen-hundred-dollar watch you're wearing one just walked out of here. There isn't a damn thing I can do about it."

"There are laws," he said, fretting against the bars. Quite suddenly he wanted to touch her.

"And laws," she murmured. When the door swung open, she glanced up. "Merle. Good. Take over here. I have to run out to the Kramer place."

"The twins?"

"Who else?" Tory shot back as she plucked a black flat-brimmed hat from a peg. "I'll grab dinner while I'm out and pick up something for our guest. How do you feel about stew, Kincaid?"

"Steak, medium rare," he tossed back. "Chef's salad, oil and vinegar and a good Bordeaux."

"Don't let him intimidate you, Merle," Tory warned as she headed for the door. "He's a cream puff."

"Sheriff, the phone call!" Phil shouted after her as she started to close the door.

With a heavy sigh Tory stuck her head back in. "Merle T., let the poor guy use the phone. Once," she added firmly, then shut the door.

Ninety minutes later Tory sauntered back in with a wicker hamper over her arm. Phil was sitting on his bunk, smoking quietly. Merle sat at the desk, his feet propped up, his hat over his face. He was snoring gently.

"Is the party over?" Tory asked. Phil shot her a silent glare. Chuckling, she went to Merle and gave him a jab in the shoulder. He scrambled up like a shot, scraping his boot heels over the desk surface.

"Aw, Tory," he muttered, bending to retrieve his hat from the floor.

"Any trouble with the desperate character?" she wanted to know.

Merle gave her a blank look, then grinned sheepishly. "Come on, Tory."

"Go get something to eat. You can wander down to Hernandez's Bar and the pool hall before you go off duty."

Merle placed his hat back on his head. "Want me to check Bestler's Garage?"

"No," she said, remembering the poker game. Merle would figure it his bound duty to break it up if he happened in on it. "I checked in earlier."

"Well, okay..." He shuffled his feet and cast a sidelong glance at Phil. "One of us should stay here tonight."

"I'm staying." Plucking up the keys, she headed for the cell. "I've got some extra clothes in the back room."

"Yeah, but, Tory..." He wanted to point out that she was a woman, after all, and the prisoner had given her a couple of long looks.

"Yes?" Tory paused in front of Phil's cell.

"Nothin'," he muttered, reminded that Tory could handle herself and always had. He blushed before he headed for the door.

"Wasn't that sweet?" she murmured. "He was worried about my virtue." At Phil's snort of laughter she lifted a wry brow.

"Doesn't he know about the large gun in the desk drawer?"

"Of course he does." Tory unlocked the cell. "I told him if he played with it, I'd break all his fingers. Hungry?"

Phil gave the hamper a dubious smile. "Maybe."

"Oh, come on, cheer up," Tory ordered. "Didn't you get to make your phone call?"

She spoke as though appeasing a little boy. It drew a reluctant grin from Phil. "Yes, I made my phone call." Because the discussion with his producer had gone well, Phil was willing to be marginally friendly. Besides, he was starving. "What's in there?"

"T-bone, medium rare, salad, roasted potato—"

"You're kidding!" He was up and dipping into the basket himself.

"I don't kid a man about food, Kincaid, I'm a humanitarian."

"I'll tell you exactly what I think you are—after I've eaten." Phil pulled foil off a plate and uncovered the steak. The scent went straight to his stomach. Dragging over a shaky wooden chair, he settled down to devour his free meal.

"You didn't specify dessert, so I went for apple pie." Tory drew a thick slice out of the hamper.

"I might just modify my opinion of you," Phil told her over a mouthful of steak.

"Don't do anything hasty," she suggested.

"Tell me something, Sheriff." He swallowed, then indicated the still-sleeping dog with his fork. "Doesn't that thing ever move?"

"Not if he can help it."

"Is it alive?"

"The last time I looked," she muttered. "Sorry about the Bordeaux," she continued. "Against regulations. I got you a Dr Pepper."

"A what?"

Tory pulled out a bottle of soda. "Take it or leave it."

After a moment's consideration Phil held out his hand. "What about the mayor?"

"I left him a message. He'll probably see you tomorrow."

Phil unscrewed the top off the bottle, frowning at her. "You're not actually going to make me sleep in this place."

Cocking her head, Tory met his glance. "You have a strange view of the law, Kincaid. Do you think I should book you a room at the hotel?"

He washed down the steak with the soda, then grimaced. "You're a tough guy, Sheriff."

"Yeah." Grinning, she perched on the edge of the bunk. "How's your dinner?"

"It's good. Want some?"

"No. I've eaten." They studied each other with the same wary speculation. Tory spoke first. "What is Phillip C. Kincaid, boy wonder, doing in Friendly, New Mexico?"

"I was passing through," he said warily. He wasn't

going to discuss his plans with her. Something warned him he would meet solid opposition.

"At seventy-two miles per hour," she reminded him.

"Maybe."

With a laugh she leaned back against the brick wall. He watched the way her hair settled lazily over her breasts. A man would be crazy to tangle with that lady, he told himself. Phillip Kincaid was perfectly sane.

"And what is Victoria L. Ashton doing wearing a badge in Friendly, New Mexico?"

She gazed past him for a moment with an odd look in her eyes. "Fulfilling an obligation," she said softly.

"You don't fit the part," Phil contemplated her over another swig from the bottle. "I'm an expert on who fits and who doesn't."

"Why not?" Lifting her knee, Tory laced her fingers around it.

"Your hands are too soft." Thoughtfully, Phil cut another bite of steak. "Not as soft as I expected when I saw that face, but too soft. You don't pamper them, but you don't work with them either."

"A sheriff doesn't work with her hands," Tory pointed out.

"A sheriff doesn't wear perfume that costs a hundred and fifty an ounce that was designed to drive men wild either."

Both brows shot up. Her full bottom lip pushed forward in thought. "Is that what it was designed for?"

"A sheriff," he went on, "doesn't usually look like she just walked off the cover of *Harper's Bazaar,* treat her deputy like he was her kid brother or pay some boy's fine out of her own pocket.''

''My, my,'' Tory said slowly, ''you are observant.'' He shrugged, continuing with his meal. ''Well, then, what part would you cast me in?''

''I had several in mind the minute I saw you.'' Phil shook his head as he finished off his steak. ''Now I'm not so sure. You're no fragile desert blossom.'' When her smile widened, he went on. ''You could be if you wanted to, but you don't. You're no glossy sophisticate either. But that's a choice too.'' Taking the pie, he rose to join her on the bunk. ''You know, there are a number of people out in this strange world who would love to have me as a captive audience while they recited their life's story.''

''At least three of four,'' Tory agreed dryly.

''You're rough on my ego, Sheriff.'' He tasted the pie, approved, then offered her the next bite. Tory opened her mouth, allowing herself to be fed. It was tangy, spicy and still warm.

''What do you want to know?'' she asked, then swallowed.

''Why you're tossing men in jail instead of breaking their hearts.''

Her laugh was full of appreciation as she leaned her head back against the wall. Still, she wavered a moment. It had been so long, she mused, since she'd been able just to talk to someone—to a man. He was interesting and, she thought, at the moment harmless.

''I grew up here,'' she said simply.

''But you didn't stay.'' When she sent him a quizzical look, he fed her another bite of pie. It occurred to him that it had been a long time since he'd been with a woman who didn't want or even expect anything from him. "You've got too much polish, Victoria," he said, finding her name flowed well on his tongue. "You didn't acquire it in Friendly."

"Harvard," she told him, rounding her tones. "Law."

"Ah." Phil sent her an approving nod. "That fits. I can see you with a leather briefcase and a pin-striped suit. Why aren't you practicing?"

"I am. I have an office in Albuquerque." Her brows drew together. "A pin-striped suit?"

"Gray, very discreet. How can you practice law in Albuquerque and uphold it in Friendly?" He pushed the hair from her shoulder in a casual gesture that neither of them noticed.

"I'm not taking any new cases for a while, so my work load's fairly light." She shrugged it off. "I handle what I can on paper and make a quick trip back when I have to."

"Are you a good lawyer?"

Tory grinned. "I'm a terrific lawyer, Kincaid, but I can't represent you—unethical."

He shoved another bite of pie at her. "So what are you doing back in Friendly?"

"You really are nosy, aren't you?"

"Yes."

She laughed. "My father was sheriff here for years and years." A sadness flickered briefly into her eyes and was controlled. "I suppose in his own quiet way he held the town together—such as it is. When he died, nobody knew just what to do. It sounds strange, but in a town this size, one person can make quite a difference, and he was…a special kind of man."

The wound hasn't healed yet, he thought, watching her steadily. He wondered, but didn't ask, how long ago her father had died.

"Anyway, the mayor asked me to fill in until things settled down again, and since I had to stay around to straighten a few things out anyway, I agreed. Nobody wanted the job except Merle, and he's…" She gave a quick, warm laugh. "Well, he's not ready. I know the law, I know the town. In a few months they'll hold an election. My name won't be on the ballot." She shot him a look. "Did I satisfy your curiosity?"

Under the harsh overhead lights, her skin was flawless, her eyes sharply green. Phil found himself reaching for her hair again. "No," he murmured. Though his eyes never left hers, Tory felt as though he looked at all of her—slowly and with great care. Quite unexpectedly her mouth went dry. She rose.

"It should have," she said lightly as she began to pack up the dirty dishes. "Next time we have dinner, I'll expect your life story." When she felt his hand on her arm, she stopped. Tory glanced down at the fingers curled around her arm, then slowly lifted her eyes to his. "Kincaid," she said softly, "you're in enough trouble."

"I'm already in jail," he pointed out as he turned her to face him.

"The term of your stay can easily be lengthened."

Knowing he should resist and that he couldn't, Phil drew her into his arms. "How much time can I get for making love to the sheriff?"

"What you're going to get is a broken rib if you don't let me go." *Miscalculation,* her mind stated bluntly. This man is never harmless. On the tail of that came the thought of how wonderful it felt to be held against him. His mouth was very close and very tempting. And it simply wasn't possible to forget their positions.

"Tory," he murmured. "I like the way that sounds." Running his fingers up her spine, he caught them in her hair. With her pressed tight against him, he could feel her faint quiver of response. "I think I'm going to have to have you."

A struggle wasn't going to work, she decided, any more than threats. As her own blood began to heat, Tory knew she had to act quickly. Tilting her head back slightly, she lifted a disdainful brow. "Hasn't a woman ever turned you down before, Kincaid?"

She saw his eyes flash in anger, felt the fingers in her hair tighten. Tory forced herself to remain still and relaxed. Excitement shivered through her, and resolutely she ignored it. His thighs were pressed hard against hers; the arms wrapped around her waist were tense with muscle. The firm male feel of him appealed to her, while the temper in his eyes warned her not to miscalculate again. They remained close for one long throbbing moment.

Phil's fingers relaxed before he stepped back to measure her. "There'll be another time," he said quietly. "Another place."

With apparent calm, Tory began gathering the dishes again. Her heart was thudding at the base of her throat. "You'll get the same answer."

"The hell I will."

Annoyed, she turned to see him watching her. With his hands in his pockets he rocked back gently on his heels. His eyes belied the casual stance. ‘‘Stick with your bubble-headed blondes,’’ she advised coolly. ‘‘They photograph so well, clinging to your arm.’’

She was angry, he realized suddenly, and much more moved by him than she had pretended. Seeing his advantage, Phil approached her again. ‘‘You ever take off that badge, Sheriff?’’

Tory kept her eyes level. ‘‘Occasionally.’’

Phil lowered his gaze, letting it linger on the small star. ‘‘When?’’

Sensing that she was being outmaneuvered, Tory answered cautiously. ‘‘That's irrelevant.’’

When he lifted his eyes back to hers, he was smiling. ‘‘It won't be.’’ He touched a finger to her full bottom lip. ‘‘I'm going to spend a lot of time tasting that beautiful mouth of yours.’’

Disturbed, Tory stepped back. ‘‘I'm afraid you won't have the opportunity or the time.’’

‘‘I'm going to find the opportunity and the time to make love with you several times—’’ He sent her a mocking grin. ‘‘—Sheriff.’’

As he had anticipated, her eyes lit with fury. ‘‘You conceited fool,’’ she said in a low voice. ‘‘You really think you're irresistible.’’

‘‘Sure I do.’’ He continued to grin maddeningly. ‘‘Don't you?’’

‘‘I think you're a spoiled, egotistical ass.’’

His temper rose, but Phil controlled it. If he lost it, he'd lose his advantage. He stepped closer, keeping a bland smile on his face. "Do you? Is that a legal opinion or a personal one?"

Tory tossed back her head, fuming. "My personal opinion is—"

He cut her off with a hard, bruising kiss.

Taken completely by surprise, Tory didn't struggle. By the time she had gathered her wits, she was too involved to attempt it. His mouth seduced hers expertly, parting her lips so that he could explore deeply and at his leisure. She responded out of pure pleasure. His mouth was hard, then soft—gentle, then demanding. He took her on a brisk roller coaster of sensation. Before she could recover from the first breathtaking plunge, they were climbing again. She held on to him, waiting for the next burst of speed.

He took his tongue lightly over hers, then withdrew it, tempting her to follow. Recklessly, she did, learning the secrets and dark tastes of his mouth. For a moment he allowed her to take the lead; then, cupping the back of her head in his hand, he crushed her lips with one last driving force. He wanted her weak and limp and totally conquered.

When he released her, Tory stood perfectly still, trying to remember what had happened. The confusion in her eyes gave him enormous pleasure. "I plead guilty, Your Honor," he drawled as he dropped back onto the bunk. "And it was worth it."

Hot, raging fury replaced every other emotion. Storming over to him, she grabbed him by the shirt front. Phil didn't resist, but grinned.

"Police brutality," he reminded her. She cursed him fluently, and with such effortless style, he was unable to conceal his admiration. "Did you learn that at Harvard?" he asked when she paused for breath.

Tory released him with a jerk and whirled to scoop up the hamper. The cell door shut behind her with a furious clang. Without pausing, she stormed out of the office.

Still grinning, Phil lay back on the bunk and pulled out a cigarette. She'd won round one, he told himself. But he'd taken round two. Blowing out a lazy stream of smoke, he began to speculate on the rematch.

Chapter 3

When the alarm shrilled, Tory knocked it off the small table impatiently. It clattered to the floor and continued to shrill. She buried her head under the pillow. She wasn't at her best in the morning. The noisy alarm vibrated against the floor until she reached down in disgust and slammed it off. After a good night's sleep she was inclined to be cranky. After a poor one she was dangerous.

Most of the past night had been spent tossing and turning. The scene with Phil had infuriated her, not only because he had won, but because she had fully enjoyed that one moment of mindless pleasure. Rolling onto her back, Tory kept the pillow over her face to block out the sunlight. The worst part was, she mused, he was going to get away with it. She couldn't in all conscience use the law to punish him for something that had been strictly personal. It had been her own fault for lowering her guard and inviting the consequences. And she had enjoyed talking with him, sparring with someone quick with words. She missed matching wits with a man.

But that was no excuse, she reminded herself. He'd made her forget her duty…and he'd enjoyed it. Disgusted, Tory tossed the pillow aside, then winced at the brilliant sunlight. She'd learned how to evade an advance as a teenager. What had caused her to slip up this time? She didn't want to dwell on it. Grumpily she dragged herself from the cot and prepared to dress.

Every muscle in his body ached. Phil stretched out his legs to their full length and gave a low groan. He was willing to swear Tory had put the lumps in the mattress for his benefit. Cautiously opening one eye, he stared at the man in the next cell. The man slept on, as he had from the moment Tory had dumped him on the bunk the night before. He snored outrageously. When she had dragged him in, Phil had been amused. The man was twice her weight and had been blissfully drunk. He'd called her "good old Tory," and she had cursed him halfheartedly as she had maneuvered him into the cell. Thirty minutes after hearing the steady snoring, Phil had lost his sense of humor.

She hadn't spoken a word to him. With a detached interest Phil had watched her struggle with the drunk. It had pleased him to observe that she was still fuming. She'd been in and out of the office several times before midnight, then had locked up in the same frigid silence. He'd enjoyed that, but then had made a fatal error: When she had gone into the back room to bed, he had tortured himself by watching her shadow play on the wall as she had undressed. That, combined with an impossible mattress and a snoring drunk-and-disorderly, had led to an uneasy night. He hadn't awakened in the best of moods.

Sitting up with a wince, he glared at the unconscious man in the next cell. His wide, flushed face was cherubic, ringed with a curling blond circle of hair. Ruefully, Phil rubbed a hand over his own chin and felt the rough stubble. A fastidious man, he was annoyed at not having a razor, a hot shower or a fresh set of clothes. Rising, he determined to gain access to all three immediately.

"Tory!" His voice was curt, one of a man accustomed to being listened to. He received no response. "Damn it, Tory, get out here!" He rattled the bars, wishing belligerently that he'd kept the tin cup. He could have made enough noise with it to wake even the stuporous man in the next cell. "Tory, get out of that bed and come here." He swore, promising himself he'd never allow anyone to lock him in anything again. "When I get out..." he began.

Tory came shuffling in, carrying a pot of water. "Button up, Kincaid."

"You listen to me," he retorted. "I want a shower and a razor and my clothes. And if—"

"If you don't shut up until I've had my coffee, you're going to take your shower where you stand." She lifted the pot of water meaningfully. "You can get cleaned up as soon as Merle gets in." She went to the coffeepot and began to clatter.

"You're an arrogant wretch when you've got a man caged," he said darkly.

"I'm an arrogant wretch anyway. Do yourself a favor,

Kincaid, don't start a fight until I've had two cups. I'm not a nice person in the morning.''

''I'm warning you.'' His voice was as low and dangerous as his mood. ''You're going to regret locking me in here.''

Turning, she looked at him for the first time that morning. His clothes and hair were disheveled. The clean lines of his aristocratic face were shadowed by the night's growth of beard. Fury was in his stance and in the cool water-blue of his eyes. He looked outrageously attractive.

''I think I'm going to regret letting you out,'' she muttered before she turned back to the coffee. ''Do you want some of this, or are you just going to throw it at me?''

The idea was tempting, but so was the scent of the coffee. ''Black,'' he reminded her shortly.

Tory drained half a cup, ignoring her scalded tongue before she went to Phil. ''What do you want for breakfast?'' she asked as she passed the cup through the bars.

He scowled at her. ''A shower, and a sledgehammer for your friend over there.''

Tory cast an eye in the next cell. ''Silas'll wake up in an hour, fresh as a daisy.'' She swallowed more coffee. ''Keep you up?''

''Him and the feather bed you provided.''

She shrugged. ''Crime doesn't pay.''

''I'm going to strangle you when I get out of here,'' he promised over the rim of his cup. ''Slowly and with great pleasure.''

''That isn't the way to get your shower.'' She turned as the door opened and Tod came in. He stood hesitantly at the door, jamming his hands in his pockets. ''Good morning.'' She smiled and beckoned him in. ''You're early.''

''You didn't say what time.'' He came warily, shifting his eyes from Phil to Silas and back to Phil again. ''You got prisoners.''

''Yes, I do.'' Catching her tongue between her teeth, she jerked a thumb at Phil. ''This one's a nasty character.''

''What's he in for?''

''Insufferable arrogance.''

''He didn't kill anybody, did he?''

''Not yet,'' Phil muttered, then added, unable to resist the eager gleam in the boy's eyes, ''I was framed.''

''They all say that, don't they, Sheriff?''

''Absolutely.'' She lifted a hand to ruffle the boy's hair. Startled, he jerked and stared at her. Ignoring his reaction, she left her hand on his shoulder. ''Well, I'll put you to work, then. There's a broom in the back room. You can start sweeping up. Have you had breakfast?''

''No, but—''

''I'll bring you something when I take care of this guy. Think you can keep an eye on things for me for a few minutes?''

His mouth fell open in astonishment. ''Yes, ma'am!''

''Okay, you're in charge.'' She headed for the door, grabbing her hat on the way. ''If Silas wakes up, you can let him out. The other guy stays where he is. Got it?''

''Sure thing, Sheriff.'' He sent Phil a cool look. ''He won't pull nothing on me.''

Stiffling a laugh, Tory walked outside.

Resigned to the wait, Phil leaned against the bars and

drank his coffee while the boy went to work with the broom. He worked industriously, casting furtive glances over his shoulder at Phil from time to time. He's a good-looking boy, Phil mused. He brooded over his reaction to Tory's friendly gesture, wondering how he would react to a man.

"Live in town?" Phil ventured.

Tod paused, eyeing him warily. "Outside."

"On a ranch?"

He began to sweep again, but more slowly. "Yeah."

"Got any horses?"

The boy shrugged. "Couple." He was working his way cautiously over to the cell. "You're not from around here," he said.

"No, I'm from California."

"No, kidding?" Impressed, Tod sized him up again. "You don't look like such a bad guy," he decided.

"Thanks." Phil grinned into his cup.

"How come you're in jail, then?"

Phil pondered over the answer and settled for the unvarnished truth. "I lost my temper."

Tod gave a snort of laughter and continued sweeping. "You can't go to jail for that. My pa loses his all the time."

"Sometimes you can." He studied the boy's profile. "Especially if you hurt someone."

The boy passed the broom over the floor without much regard for dust. "Did you?"

"Just myself," Phil admitted ruefully. "I got the sheriff mad at me."

"Zac Kramer said he don't hold with no woman sheriff."

Phil laughed at that, recalling how easily a woman sheriff had gotten him locked in a cell. "Zac Kramer doesn't sound very smart to me."

Tod sent Phil a swift, appealing grin. "I heard she went to their place yesterday. The twins have to wash all Old Man Hollister's windows, inside and out. For free."

Tory breezed back in with two covered plates. "Breakfast," she announced. "He give you any trouble?" she asked Tod as she set a plate on her desk.

"No, ma'am." The scent of food made his mouth water, but he bent back to his task.

"Okay, sit down and eat."

He shot her a doubtful look. "Me?"

"Yes, you." Carrying the other plate, she walked over to get the keys. "When you and Mr. Kincaid have finished, run the dishes back to the hotel." Without waiting for a response, she unlocked Phil's cell. But Phil watched the expression on Tod's face as he started at his breakfast.

"Sheriff," Phil murmured, taking her hand, rather than the plate she held out to him, "you're a very classy lady." Lifting her hand, he kissed her fingers lightly.

Unable to resist, she allowed her hand to rest in his a moment. "Phil," she said on a sigh, "don't be disarming; you'll complicate things."

His brow lifted in surprise as he studied her. "You know," he said slowly, "I think it's already too late."

Tory shook her head, denying it. "Eat your breakfast," she ordered briskly. "Merle will be coming by with your clothes soon."

When she turned to leave, he held her hand another moment. ''Tory,'' he said quietly, ''you and I aren't finished yet.''

Carefully she took her hand from his. ''You and I never started,'' she corrected, then closed the door of the cell with a resolute clang. As she headed back to the coffeepot she glanced at Tod. The boy was making his way through bacon and eggs without any trouble.

''Aren't you eating?'' Phil asked her as he settled down to his own breakfast.

''I'll never understand how anyone can eat at this hour,'' Tory muttered, fortifying herself on coffee. ''Tod, the sheriff's car could use a wash. Can you handle it?''

''Sure thing, Sheriff.'' He was half out of the chair before Tory put a restraining hand on his shoulder.

''Eat first,'' she told him with a chuckle. ''If you finish up the sweeping and the car, that should do it for today.'' She sat on the corner of the desk, enjoying his appetite. ''Your parents know where you are?'' she asked casually.

''I finished my chores before I left,'' he mumbled with a full mouth.

''Hmmm.'' She said nothing more, sipping instead at her coffee. When the door opened, she glanced over, expecting to see Merle. Instead she was struck dumb.

''Lou!'' Phil was up and holding on to the bars. ''It's about time.''

''Well, Phil, you look very natural.''

Lou Sherman, Tory thought, sincerely awed. One of the top attorneys in the country. She'd followed his cases, studied his style, used his precedents. He looked just as commanding in person as in any newspaper or magazine picture she'd ever seen of him. He was a huge man, six foot four, with a stocky frame and a wild thatch of white hair. His voice had resonated in courtrooms for more than forty years. He was tenacious, flamboyant and feared. For the moment Tory could only stare at the figure striding into her office in a magnificent pearl-gray suit and baby-pink shirt.

Phil called him an uncomplimentary name, which made him laugh loudly. "You'd better have some respect if you want me to get you out of there, son." His eyes slid to Phil's half-eaten breakfast. "Finish eating," he advised, "while I talk to the sheriff." Turning, he gazed solemnly from Tory to Tod. "One of you the sheriff?"

Tory hadn't found her voice yet. Tod jerked his head at her. "She is," he stated with his mouth still full.

Lou let his eyes drift down to her badge. "Well, so she is," he said genially. "Best-looking law person I've seen… No offense," he added with a wide grin.

Remembering herself, Tory rose and extended her hand. "Victoria Ashton, Mr. Sherman. It's a pleasure to meet you."

"My pleasure, Sheriff Ashton," he corrected with a great deal of charm. "Tell me, what's the kid done now?"

"Lou—" Phil began, and got an absent wave of the hand from his attorney.

"Finish your eggs," he ordered. "I gave up a perfectly good golf date to fly over here. Sheriff?" he added with a questioning lift of brow.

"Mr. Kincaid was stopped for speeding on Highway Seventeen," Tory began. "When he refused to sign the ticket, my deputy brought him in." After Lou's heavy sigh she continued. ''I'm afraid Mr. Kincaid wasn't cooperative.''

''Never is,'' Lou agreed apologetically.

''Damn it, Lou, would you just get me out of here?''

''All in good time,'' he promised without looking at him. ''Are there any other charges, Sheriff?''

''Resisting arrest,'' she stated, not quite disguising a grin. ''The fine is two hundred and fifty, bail set at five hundred. Mr. Kincaid, when he decided to...cooperate, was a bit short of funds.''

Lou rubbed a hand over his chin. The large ruby on his pinky glinted dully. ''Wouldn't be the first time,'' he mused.

Incensed at being ignored and defamed at the same time, Phil interrupted tersely. ''She pulled a gun on me.''

This information was met with another burst of loud laughter from his attorney. ''Damn, I wish I'd been here to see his face.''

''It was worth the price of a ticket,'' Tory admitted.

Phil started to launch into a stream of curses, remembered the boy—who was listening avidly—and ground his teeth instead. ''Lou,'' he said slowly, ''are you going to get me out or stand around exchanging small talk all day? I haven't had a shower since yesterday.''

''Very fastidious,'' Lou told Tory. ''Gets it from his father. I got him out of a tight squeeze or two as I recall. There was this little town in New Jersey... Ah, well, that's another story. I'd like to consult with my client, Sheriff Ashton.''

''Of course.'' Tory retrieved the keys.

''Ashton,'' Lou murmured, closing his eyes for a moment. "Victoria Ashton. There's something about that name." He stroked his chin. "Been sheriff here long?"

Tory shook her head as she started to unlock Phil's cell. "No, actually I'm just filling in for a while."

"She's a lawyer," Phil said disgustedly.

"That's it!" Lou gave her a pleased look. "I knew the name was familiar. The Dunbarton case. You did a remarkable job."

"Thank you."

"Had your troubles with Judge Withers," he recalled, flipping through his memory file. "Contempt of court. What was it you called him?"

"A supercilious humbug," Tory said with a wince.

Lou chuckled delightedly. "Wonderful choice of words."

"It cost me a night in jail," she recalled.

"Still, you won the case."

"Luckily the judge didn't hold a grudge."

"Skill and hard work won you that one," Lou disagreed. "Where did you study?"

"Harvard."

"Look," Phil interrupted testily. "You two can discuss this over drinks later."

"Manners, Phil, you've always had a problem with manners." Lou smiled at Tory again. "Excuse me, Sheriff. Well, Phil, give me one of those corn muffins there and tell me your troubles."

Tory left them in privacy just as Merle walked in, carrying Phil's suitcase. Dynamite wandered in behind him, found his spot on the floor and instantly went to sleep. "Just leave that by the desk," Tory told Merle. "After

Kincaid's taken care of, I'm going out to the house for a while. You won't be able to reach me for two hours.''

''Okay.'' He glanced at the still-snoring Silas. ''Should I kick him out?''

''When he wakes up.'' She looked over at Tod. ''Tod's going to wash my car.''

Stuffing in the last bite, Tod scrambled up. ''I'll do it now.'' He dashed out the front door.

Tory frowned after him. ''Merle, what do you know about Tod's father?''

He shrugged and scratched at his mustache. ''Swanson keeps to himself, raises some cattle couple miles north of town. Been in a couple of brawls, but nothing important.''

''His mother?''

''Quiet lady. Does some cleaning work over at the hotel now and again. You remember the older brother, don't you? He lit out a couple years ago. Never heard from him since.''

Tory absorbed this with a thoughtful nod. ''Keep an eye out for the boy when I'm not around, okay?''

''Sure. He in trouble?''

''I'm not certain.'' She frowned a moment, then her expression relaxed again. ''Just keep your eyes open, Merle T.,'' she said, smiling at him affectionately. ''Why don't you go see if the kid's found a bucket? I don't think it would take much persuasion to get him to wash your car too.''

Pleased with the notion, Merle strode out again.

''Sheriff''—Tory turned back to the cell as Lou came out—''my client tells me you also serve as justice of the peace?''

"That's right, Mr. Sherman."

"In that case, I'd like to plead temporary insanity on the part of my client."

"You're cute, Lou," Phil muttered from the cell door. "Can I take that shower now?" he demanded, indicating his suitcase.

"In the back," Tory told him. "You need a shave," she added sweetly.

He picked up the case, giving her a long look. "Sheriff, when this is all over, you and I have some personal business."

Tory lifted her half-finished coffee. "Don't cut your throat, Kincaid."

Lou waited until Phil had disappeared into the back room. "He's a good boy," he said with a paternal sigh. Tory burst out laughing.

"Oh, no," she said definitely, "he's not."

"Well, it was worth a try." He shrugged it off and settled his enormous bulk into a chair. "About the charge of resisting arrest," he began. "I'd really hate for it to go on his record. A night in jail was quite a culture shock for our Phillip, Victoria."

"Agreed." She smiled. "I believe that charge could be dropped if Mr. Kincaid pays the speeding fine."

"I've advised him to do so," Lou told her, pulling out a thick cigar. "He doesn't like it, but I'm..." He studied the cigar like a lover. "...persuasive," he decided. He shot her an admiring look. "So are you. What kind of a gun?"

Tory folded her hands primly. "A .45."

Lou laughed heartily as he lit his cigar. "Now, tell me about the Dunbarton case, Victoria."

* * *

The horse kicked up a cloud of brown dust. Responding to Tory's command, he broke into an easy gallop. Air, as dry as the land around them, whipped by them in a warm rush. The hat Tory had worn to shield herself from the sun lay on the back of her neck, forgotten. Her movements were so attuned to the horse, she was barely conscious of his movements beneath her. Tory wanted to think, but first she wanted to clear her mind. Since childhood, riding had been her one sure way of doing so.

Sports had no appeal for her. She saw no sense in hitting or chasing a ball around some court or course. It took too much energy. She might swim a few laps now and again, but found it much more agreeable to float on a raft. Sweating in a gym was laughable. But riding was a different category. Tory didn't consider it exercise or effort. She used it now, as she had over the years, as a way to escape from her thoughts for a short time.

For thirty minutes she rode without any thought of destination. Gradually she slowed the horse to a walk, letting her hands relax on the reins. He would turn, she knew, and head back to the ranch.

Phillip Kincaid. He shot back into her brain. A nuisance, Tory decided. One that should be over. At the moment he should already be back on his way to L.A. Tory dearly hoped so. She didn't like to admit that he had gotten to her. It was unfortunate that despite their clash, despite his undeniable arrogance, she had liked him. He was interesting and funny and sharp. It was difficult to dislike someone who could laugh at himself. There would be no problem if it ended there.

Feeling the insistent beat of the sun on her head, Tory

absently replaced her hat. It hadn't ended there because there had been that persistent attraction. That was strictly man to woman, and she hadn't counted on it when she had tossed him in jail. He'd outmaneuvered her once. That was annoying, but the result had been much deeper. When was the last time she had completely forgotten herself in a man's arms? When was the last time she had spent most of the night thinking about a man? Had she ever? Tory let out a deep breath, then frowned at the barren, stone-colored landscape.

No, her reaction had been too strong for comfort—and the fact that she was still thinking about him disturbed her. A woman her age didn't dwell on one kiss that way. Yet, she could still remember exactly how his mouth had molded to hers, how the dark, male taste of him had seeped into her. With no effort at all, she could feel the way his body had fit against hers, strong and hard. It didn't please her.

There were enough problems to be dealt with during her stay in Friendly, Tory reminded herself, without dwelling on a chance encounter with some bad-tempered Hollywood type. She'd promised to ease the town through its transition to a new sheriff; there was the boy, Tod, on her mind. And her mother. Tory closed her eyes for a moment. She had yet to come to terms with her mother.

So many things had been said after her father's death. So many things had been left unsaid. For a woman who was rarely confused, Tory found herself in a turmoil whenever she dealt with her mother. As long as her father had been alive, he'd been the buffer between them. Now, with him gone, they were faced with each other. With a wry laugh Tory decided her mother was just as baffled as she was. The strain between them wasn't lessening, and the distance was growing. With a shake of her head she decided to let it lie. In a few months Tory would be back in Albuquerque and that would be that. She had her life to live, her mother had hers.

The wise thing to do, she mused, was to develop the same attitude toward Phil Kincaid. Their paths weren't likely to cross again. She had purposely absented herself from town for a few hours to avoid him. Tory made a face at the admission. No, she didn't want to see him again. He was trouble. It was entirely too easy for him to be charming when he put his mind to it. And she was wise enough to recognize determination when she saw it. For whatever reason—pique or attraction—he wanted her. He wouldn't be an easy man to handle. Under most circumstances Tory might have enjoyed pitting her will against his, but something warned her not to press her luck.

"The sooner he's back in Tinsel Town, the better," she muttered, then pressed her heels against the horse's sides. They were off at a full gallop.

Phil pulled his car to a halt beside the corral and glanced around. A short distance to the right was a small white-framed house. It was a very simple structure, two stories high, with a wide wooden porch. On the side was a clothesline with a few things baking dry in the sun. There were a few spots of color from flowers in pottery pots on either side of the steps. The grass was short and parched. One of the window screens was torn. In the background he could see a few outbuildings and what appeared to be the beginnings of a vegetable garden. Tory's sheriff's car was parked in front, freshly washed but already coated with a thin film of dust.

Something about the place appealed to him. It was isolated and quiet. Without the car in front, it might fit into any time frame in the past century. There had been some efforts to keep it neat, but it would never be prosperous. He would consider it more a homestead than a ranch. With the right lighting, he mused, it could be very effective. Climbing out of the car, Phil moved to the right to study it from a different angle. When he heard the low drum of hoofs, he turned and watched Tory approach.

He forgot the house immediately and swore at his lack of a camera. She was perfect. Under the merciless sun she rode a palamino the shade of new gold. Nothing could have been a better contrast for a woman of her coloring. With her hat again at her back, her hair flew freely. She sat straight, her movements in perfect timing with the horse's. Phil narrowed his eyes and saw them in slow motion. That was how he would film it—with her hair lifting, holding for a moment before it fell again. The dust would hang in the air behind them. The horse's strong legs would fold and unfold so that the viewer could see each muscle work. This was strength and beauty and a mastery of rider over horse. He wished he could see her hands holding the reins.

He knew the moment she became aware of him. The rhythm never faltered, but there was a sudden tension in the set of her shoulders. It made him smile. No, we're not through yet, he thought to himself. Not nearly through. Leaning against the corral fence, he waited for her.

Tory brought the palamino to a stop with a quick tug of reins. Remaining in the saddle, she gave Phil a long, silent look. Casually he took sunglasses out of his pocket and slipped them on. The gesture annoyed her. ''Kincaid,'' she said coolly.

''Sheriff,'' he returned.

''Is there a problem?''

He smiled slowly. ''I don't think so.''

Tory tossed her hair behind her shoulder, trying to disguise the annoyance she felt at finding him there. ''I thought you'd be halfway to L.A. by now.''

''Did you?''

With a sound of impatience she dismounted. The saddle creaked with the movement as she brought one slim leg over it, then vaulted lightly to the ground. Keeping the reins in her hand, she studied him a moment. ''I assume your fine's been paid. You know the other charges were dropped.''

''Yes.''

She tilted her head. ''Well?''

''Well,'' he returned amiably, amused at the temper that shot into her eyes. Yes, I'm getting to you, Victoria, he thought, and I haven't even started yet.

Deliberately she turned away to uncinch the saddle. ''Has Mr. Sherman gone?''

''No, he's discussing flies and lures with the mayor.'' Phil grinned. ''Lou found a fishing soulmate.''

''I see.'' Tory hefted the saddle from the palamino, then set it on the fence. ''Then you discussed your business with the mayor this morning.''

''We came to an amicable agreement,'' Phil replied,

watching as she slipped the bit from the horse's mouth. "He'll give you the details."

Without speaking, Tory gave the horse a slap on the flank, sending him inside the corral. The gate gave a long creak as she shut it. She turned then to face Phil directly. "Why should he?"

"You'll want to know the schedule and so forth before the filming starts."

Her brows drew together. "I beg your pardon."

"I came to New Mexico scouting out a location for my new movie. I needed a tired little town in the middle of nowhere."

Tory studied him for a full ten seconds. "And you found it," she said flatly.

"Thanks to you." He smiled, appreciating the irony. "We'll start next month."

Sticking her hands in her back pockets, Tory turned to walk a short distance away. "Wouldn't it be simpler to shoot in a studio or in a lot?"

"No."

At his flat answer she turned back again. "I don't like it."

"I didn't think you would." He moved over to join her. "But you're going to live with it for the better part of the summer."

"You're going to bring your cameras and your people and your confusion into town," she began angrily. "Friendly runs at its own pace; now you want to bring in a life-style most of these people can't even imagine."

"We'll give very sedate orgies, Sheriff," he promised with a grin. He laughed at the fury that leaped to her eyes.

"Tory, you're not a fool. We're not coming to party; we're coming to work. Keep an actor out in this sun for ten takes, he's not going to be disturbing the peace at night: He's going to be unconscious." He caught a strand of her hair and twisted it around his finger. "Or do you believe everything you read in *Inside Scoop?*"

She swiped his hand away in an irritated gesture. "I know more about Hollywood than you know about Friendly," she retorted. "I've spent some time in L.A., represented a screenwriter in an assault case. Got him off," she added wryly. "A few years ago I dated an actor, went to a few parties when I was on the coast." She shook her head. "The gossip magazines might exaggerate, Phil, but the values and life-style come through loud and clear."

He lifted a brow. "Judgmental, Tory?"

"Maybe," she agreed. "But this is my town. I'm responsible for the people and for the peace. If you go ahead with this, I warn you, one of your people gets out of line, he goes to jail."

His eyes narrowed. "We have our own security."

"Your security answers to me in my town," she tossed back. "Remember it."

"Not going to cooperate, are you?"

"Not any more than I have to."

For a moment they stood measuring each other in silence. Behind them the palamino paced restlessly around the corral. A fleeting, precious breeze came up to stir the heat and dust. "All right," Phil said at length, "let's say you stay out of my way, I'll stay out of yours."

''Perfect,'' Tory agreed, and started to walk away. Phil caught her arm.

''That's professionally,'' he added.

As she had in his cell, Tory gave the hand on her arm a long look before she raised her eyes to his. This time Phil smiled.

''You're not wearing your badge now, Tory.'' Reaching up, he drew off his sunglasses, then hooked them over the corral fence. ''And we're not finished.''

''Kincaid—''

''Phil,'' he corrected, drawing her deliberately into his arms. ''I thought of you last night when I was lying in that damned cell. I promised myself something.''

Tory stiffened. Her palms pressed against his chest, but she didn't struggle. Physically he was stronger, she reasoned. She had to rely on her wits. ''Your thoughts and your promises aren't my problem,'' she replied coolly. ''Whether I'm wearing my badge or not, I'm still sheriff, and you're annoying me. I can be mean when I'm annoyed.''

''I'll just bet you can be,'' he murmured. Even had he wanted to, he couldn't prevent his eyes from lingering on her mouth. ''I'm going to have you, Victoria,'' he said softly. ''Sooner or later.'' Slowly he brought his eyes back to hers. ''I always keep my promises.''

''I believe I have something to say about this one.''

His smile was confident. ''Say no,'' he whispered before his mouth touched hers. She started to jerk back, but he was quick. His hand cupped the back of her head and kept her still. His mouth was soft and persuasive. Long before the stiffness left her, he felt the pounding of her heart against his. Patiently he rubbed his lips over hers, teasing, nibbling. Tory let out an unsteady breath as her fingers curled into his shirt.

He smelled of soap, a fragrance that was clean and sharp. Unconsciously she breathed it in as he drew her closer. Her arms had found their way around his neck. Her body was straining against his, no longer stiff but eager. The mindless pleasure was back, and she surrendered to it. She heard his quiet moan before his lips left hers, but before she could protest, he pressed them to her throat. He was murmuring something neither of them understood as his mouth began to explore. The desperation came suddenly, as if it had been waiting to take them both unaware. His mouth was back on hers with a quick savageness that she anticipated.

She felt the scrape of his teeth and answered by nipping into his bottom lip. The hands at her hips dragged her closer, tormenting both of them. Passion flowed between them so acutely that avid, seeking lips weren't enough. He ran his hands up her sides, letting his thumbs find their way between their clinging bodies to stroke her breasts. She responded by diving deep into his mouth and demanding more.

Tory felt everything with impossible clarity: the soft, thin material of her shirt rubbing against the straining points of her breasts as his thumbs pressed against her; the heat of his mouth as it roamed wildly over her face, then back to hers; the vibration of two heartbeats.

He hadn't expected to feel this degree of need. Attraction and challenge, but not pain. It wasn't what he had planned—it wasn't what he wanted, and yet, he couldn't stop. She was filling his mind, crowding his senses. Her hair was too soft, her scent too alluring. And her taste…her taste too exotic. Greedily, he devoured her while her passion drove him further into her.

He knew he had to back away, but he lingered a moment longer. Her body was so sleek and lean, her mouth so incredibly agile. Phil allowed himself to stroke her once more, one last bruising contact of lips before he dragged himself away.

They were both shaken and both equally determined not to admit it. Tory felt her pulse hammering at every point in her body. Because her knees were trembling, she stood very straight. Phil waited a moment, wanting to be certain he could speak. Reaching over, he retrieved his sunglasses and put them back on. They were some defense; a better one was to put some distance between them until he found his control.

"You didn't say no," he commented.

Tory stared at him, warning herself not to think until later. "I didn't say yes," she countered.

He smiled. "Oh, yes," he corrected, "you did. I'll be back," he added before he strode to his car.

Driving away, he glanced in his rearview mirror to see her standing where he had left her. As he punched in his cigarette lighter he saw his hand was shaking. Round three, he thought on a long breath, was a draw.

Chapter 4

Tory stood exactly where she was until even the dust kicked up by Phil's tires had settled. She had thought she knew the meaning of passion, need, excitement. Suddenly the words had taken on a new meaning. For the first time in her life she had been seized by something that her mind couldn't control. The hunger had been so acute, so unexpected. It throbbed through her still, like an ache, as she stared down the long flat road, which was now deserted. How was it possible to need so badly, so quickly? And how was it, she wondered, that a woman who had always handled men with such casual ease could be completely undone by a kiss?

Tory shook her head and made herself turn away from the road Phil had taken. None of it was characteristic. It was almost as if she had been someone else for a moment—someone whose strength and weakness could be drawn out and manipulated. And yet, even now, when she had herself under control, there was something inside her fighting to be recognized. She was going to have to take some time and think about this carefully.

Hoisting the saddle, Tory carried it toward the barn. *I'll be back.* Phil's last words echoed in her ears and sent an odd thrill over her skin. Scowling, Tory pushed open the barn door. It was cooler inside, permeated with the pungent scent of animals and hay. It was a scent of her childhood, one she barely noticed even when returning after months away from it. It never occurred to her to puzzle over why she was as completely at home there as she was in a tense courtroom or at a sophisticated party. After replacing the tack, she paced the concrete floor a moment and began to dissect the problem.

Phil Kincaid was the problem; the offshoots were her strong attraction to him, his effect on her and the fact that he was coming back. The attraction, Tory decided, was unprecedented but not astonishing. He was appealing, intelligent, fun. Even his faults had a certain charm. If they had met under different circumstances, she could imagine them getting to know each other slowly, dating perhaps, enjoying a congenial relationship. Part of the spark, she mused, was due to the way they had met, and the fact that each was determined not to be outdone by the other. That made sense, she concluded, feeling better.

And if that made sense, she went on, it followed that his effect on her was intensified by circumstances. Logic was comfortable, so Tory pursued it. There was something undeniably attractive about a man who wouldn't take no for an answer. It might be annoying, even infuriating, but it was still exciting. Beneath the sheriff's badge and behind the Harvard diploma, Tory was a woman first and last. It didn't hurt when a man knew how to kiss the way Phil Kincaid knew how to kiss, she added wryly. Unable to resist, Tory ran the tip of her tongue over her lips. Oh, yes, she thought with a quick smile, the man was some terrific kisser.

Vaguely annoyed with herself, Tory wandered from the barn. The sun made her wince in defense as she headed for the house. Unconsciously killing time, she poked inside the hen house. The hens were sleeping in the heat of the afternoon, their heads tucked under their wings. Tory left them alone, knowing her mother had gathered the eggs that morning.

The problem now was that he was coming back. She was going to have to deal with him—and with his own little slice of Hollywood, she added with a frown. At the moment Tory wasn't certain which disturbed her more. Damn, but she wished she'd known of Phil's plans. If she could have gotten to the mayor first… Tory stopped herself with a self-depreciating laugh. She would have changed absolutely nothing. As mayor, Bud Toomey would eat up the prestige of having a major film shot in his town. And as the owner of the one and only hotel, he must have heard the dollars clinking in his cash register.

Who could blame him? Tory asked herself. Her objections were probably more personal than professional in any case. The actor she had dated had been successful and slick, an experienced womanizer and hedonist. She knew too many of her prejudices lay at his feet. She'd been very young when he'd shown her Hollywood from his vantage point. But even without that, she reasoned, there was the disruption the filming would bring to Friendly, the effect on the townspeople and the very real possibility of property damage. As sheriff, all of it fell to her jurisdiction.

What would her father have done? she wondered as she stepped into the house. As always, the moment she was inside, memories of him assailed her—his big, booming voice, his laughter, his simple, man-of-the-earth logic. To Tory his presence was an intimate part of everything in the house, down to the hassock where he had habitually rested his feet after a long day.

The house was her mother's doing. There were the clean white walls in the living room, the sofa that had been re-covered again and again—this time it wore a tidy floral print. The rugs were straight and clean, the pictures carefully aligned. Even they had been chosen to blend in rather than to accent. Her mother's collection of cacti sat on the windowsill. The fragrance of a potpourri, her mother's mixture, wafted comfortably in the air. The floors and furniture were painstakingly clean, magazines neatly tucked away. A single geranium stood in a slender vase on a crocheted doily. All her mother's doing; yet, it was her father Tory thought of when she entered her childhood home. It always was.

But her father wouldn't come striding down the steps again. He wouldn't catch her to him for one of his bear hugs and noisy kisses. He'd been too young to die, Tory thought as she gazed around the room as though she were a stranger. Strokes were for old men, feeble men, not strapping men in their prime. There was no justice to it, she thought with the same impotent fury that hit her each time she came back. No justice for a man who had dedicated his life to justice. He should have had more time, might have had more time, if... Her thoughts broke off as she heard the quiet sounds coming from the kitchen.

Tory pushed away the pain. It was difficult enough to see her mother without remembering that last night in the hospital. She gave herself an extra moment to settle before she crossed to the kitchen.

Standing in the doorway, she watched as Helen re-lined the shelves in the kitchen cabinets. Her mother's consistent tidiness had been a sore point between them since Tory had been a girl. The woman she watched was tiny and blond, a youthful-looking fifty, with ladylike hands and a trim pink housedress. Tory knew the dress had been pressed and lightly starched. Her mother would smell faintly of soap and nothing else. Even physically Tory felt remote from her. Her looks, her temperament, had all come from her father. Tory could see nothing of herself in the woman who patiently lined shelves with dainty striped paper. They'd never been more than careful strangers to each other, more careful as the years passed. Tory kept a room at the hotel rather than at home for the same reason she kept her visits with her mother brief. Invariably their encounters ended badly.

"Mother."

Surprised, Helen turned. She didn't gasp or whirl at the intrusion, but simply faced Tory with one brow slightly lifted. "Tory. I thought I heard a car drive away."

"It was someone else."

"I saw you ride out." Helen straightened the paper meticulously. "There's lemonade in the refrigerator. It's a dry day." Without speaking, Tory fetched two glasses and added ice. "How are you, Tory?"

"Very well." She hated the stiffness but could do nothing about it. So much stood between them. Even as she poured the fresh lemonade from her mother's marigold-trimmed glass pitcher, she could remember the night of her father's death, the ugly words she had spoken, the ugly feelings she had not quite put to rest. They had never understood each other, never been close, but that night had brought a gap between them that neither knew how to bridge. It only seemed to grow wider with time.

Needing to break the silence, Tory spoke as she replaced the pitcher in the refrigerator. "Do you know anything about the Swansons?"

"The Swansons?" The question in Helen's voice was mild. She would never have asked directly. "They've lived outside of town for twenty years. They keep to themselves, though she's come to church a few times. I believe he has a difficult time making his ranch pay. The oldest son was a good-looking boy, about sixteen when he left." Helen replaced her everyday dishes on the shelf in tidy stacks, then closed the cupboard door. "That would have been about four years ago. The younger one seems rather sweet and painfully shy."

"Tod," Tory murmured.

"Yes." Helen read the concern but knew nothing about drawing people out, particularly her daughter. "I heard about Mr. Hollister's window."

Tory lifted her eyes briefly. Her mother's were a calm, deep brown. "The Kramer twins."

A suggestion of a smile flickered on her mother's lips. "Yes, of course."

"Do you know why the older Swanson boy left home?"

Helen picked up the drink Tory had poured her. But she didn't sit. "Rumor is that Mr. Swanson has a temper. Gossip is never reliable," she added before she drank.

"And often based in fact," Tory countered.

They fell into one of the stretches of silence that characteristically occurred during their visits. The refrigerator gave a loud click and began to hum. Helen carefully wiped away the ring of moisture her glass had made on the countertop.

"It seems Friendly is about to be immortalized on film," Tory began. At her mother's puzzled look she continued. "I had Phillip C. Kincaid in a cell overnight. Now it appears he's going to use Friendly as one of the location shoots for his latest film."

"Kincaid," Helen repeated, searching her mind slowly. "Oh, Marshall Kincaid's son."

Tory grinned despite herself. She didn't think Phil would appreciate that sort of recognition; it occurred to her simultaneously that it was a tag he must have fought all of his professional career. "Yes," she agreed thoughtfully. "He's a very successful director," she found herself saying, almost in defense, "with an impressive string of hits. He's been nominated for an Oscar three times."

Though Helen digested this, her thoughts were still on Tory's original statement. "Did you say you had him in jail?"

Tory shook off the mood and smiled a little. "Yes, I

did. Traffic violation,'' she added with a shrug. ''It got a little complicated....'' Her voice trailed off as she remembered that stunning moment in his cell when his mouth had taken hers. ''He's coming back,'' she murmured.

''To make a film?'' Helen prompted, puzzled by her daughter's bemused expression.

''What? Yes,'' Tory said quickly. ''Yes, he's going to do some filming here, I don't have the details yet. It seems he cleared it with the mayor this morning.''

But not with you, Helen thought, but didn't say so. ''How interesting.''

''We'll see,'' Tory muttered. Suddenly restless, she rose to pace to the sink. The view from the window was simply a long stretch of barren ground that was somehow fascinating. Her father had loved it for what it was—stark and desolate.

Watching her daughter, Helen could remember her husband standing exactly the same way, looking out with exactly the same expression. She felt an intolerable wave of grief and controlled it. ''Friendly will be buzzing about this for quite some time,'' she said briskly.

''It'll buzz all right,'' Tory muttered. But no one will think of the complications, she added to herself.

''Do you expect trouble?'' her mother asked.

''I'll handle it.''

''Always so sure of yourself, Tory.''

Tory's shoulders stiffened automatically. ''Am I, Mother?'' Turning, she found her mother's eyes, calm and direct, on her. They had been just that calm, and just that direct, when she had told Tory she had requested her father's regulator be unplugged. Tory had seen no sorrow, no regret or indecision. There had been only the passive face and the matter-of-fact words. For that, more than anything else, Tory had never forgiven her.

As they watched each other in the sun-washed kitchen, each remembered clearly the garishly lit waiting room that smelled of old cigarettes and sweat. Each remembered the monotonous hum of the air conditioner and the click of feet on tile in the corridor outside....

"No!" Tory had whispered the word, then shouted it. "No, you can't! You can't just let him die!"

"He's already gone, Tory," Helen had said flatly. "You have to accept it."

"No!" After weeks of seeing her father lying motionless with a machine pumping oxygen into his body, Tory had been crazy with grief and fear. She had been a long, long way from acceptance. She'd watched her mother sit calmly while she had paced—watched her sip tea while her own stomach had revolted at the thought of food. *Brain-dead.* The phrase had made her violently ill. It was she who had wept uncontrollably at her father's bedside while Helen had stood dry-eyed.

"You don't care," Tory had accused. "It's easier for you this way. You can go back to your precious routine and not be disturbed."

Helen had looked at her daughter's ravaged face and nodded. "It is easier this way."

"I won't let you." Desperate, Tory had pushed her hands through her hair and tried to think. "There are ways to stop you. I'll get a court order, and—"

"It's already done," Helen had told her quietly.

All the color had drained from Tory's face, just as she

had felt all the strength drain from her body. Her father was dead. At the flick of a switch he was dead. Her mother had flicked the switch. "You killed him."

Helen hadn't winced or shrunk from the words. "You know better than that, Tory."

"If you'd loved him—if you'd loved him, you couldn't have done this."

"And your kind of love would have him strapped to that machine, helpless and empty."

"Alive!" Tory had tossed back, letting hate wash over the unbearable grief. "Damn you, he was still alive."

"Gone," Helen had countered, never raising her voice. "He'd been gone for days. For weeks, really. It's time you dealt with it."

"It's so easy for you, isn't it?" Tory had forced back the tears because she had wanted—needed—to meet her mother on her own terms. "Nothing—no one—has ever managed to make you *feel.* Not even him."

"There are different kinds of love, Tory," Helen returned stiffly. "You've never understood anything but your own way."

"Love?" Tory had gripped her hands tightly together to keep from striking out. "I've never seen you show anyone love. Now Dad's gone, but you don't cry. You don't mourn. You'll go home and hang out the wash because nothing—by God, nothing—can interfere with your precious routine."

Helen's shoulders had been very straight as she faced her daughter. "I won't apologize for being what I am," she had said. "Any more than I expect you to defend yourself to me. But I do say you loved your father too much, Victoria. For that I'm sorry.''

Tory had wrapped her arms around herself tightly, unconsciously rocking. ''Oh, you're so cold,'' she had whispered. ''So cold. You have no feelings.'' She had badly needed comfort then, a word, an arm around her. But Helen was unable to offer, Tory unable to ask. ''You did this,'' she had said in a strained, husky voice. ''You took him from me. I'll never forgive you for it.''

''No.'' Helen had nodded slightly. ''I don't expect you will. You're always so sure of yourself, Tory.''

Now the two women watched each other across a new grave: dry-eyed, expressionless. A man who had been husband and father stood between them still. Words threatened to pour out again—harsh, bitter words. Each swallowed them.

''I have to get back to town,'' Tory told her. She walked from the room and from the house. After standing in the silence a moment, Helen turned back to her shelves.

The pool was shaped like a crescent and its water was deep, deep blue. There were palm trees swaying gently in the night air. The scent of flowers was strong, almost tropical. It was a cool spot, secluded by trees, banked with blossoming bushes. A narrow terrace outlined the pool with mosaic tile that glimmered in the moonlight. Speakers had been craftily camouflaged so that the strains of Debussy seemed to float out of the air. A tall iced drink laced with Jamaican rum sat on a glass-topped patio table beside a telephone.

Still wet from his swim, Phil lounged on a chaise. Once

again he tried to discipline his mind. He'd spent the entire day filming two key scenes in the studio. He'd had a little trouble with Sam Dressler, the leading man. It wasn't surprising. Dressler didn't have a reputation for being congenial or cooperative, just for being good. Phil wasn't looking to make a lifelong friendship, just a film. Still, when the clashes began this early in a production, it wasn't a good omen of things to come. He was going to have to use some strategy in handling Dressler.

At least, Phil mused as he absently picked up his drink, he'd have no trouble with the crew. He'd handpicked them and had worked with each and every one of them before. Bicks, his cinematographer, was the best in the business—creative enough to be innovative and practical enough not to insist on making a statement with each frame. His assistant director was a workhorse who knew the way Phil's mind worked. Phil knew his crew down to the last gaffer and grip. When they went on location…

Phil's thoughts drifted back to Tory, as they had insisted on doing for days. She was going to be pretty stiff-necked about having her town invaded, he reflected. She'd hang over his shoulder with that tin badge pinned to her shirt. Phil hated to admit that the idea appealed to him. With a little pre-planning, he could find a number of ways to put himself in her path. Oh, yes, he intended to spend quite a bit of time getting under Sheriff Ashton's skin.

Soft, smooth skin, Phil remembered, that smelled faintly of something that a man might find in a harem. Dark, dusky and titillating. He could picture her in silk, something chic and vivid, with nothing underneath but that long, lean body of hers.

The quick flash of desire annoyed him enough to cause him to toss back half his drink. He intended to get under her skin, but he didn't intend for it to work the other way around. He knew women, how to please them, charm them. He also knew how to avoid the complication of *one* woman. There was safety in numbers; using that maxim, Phil had enjoyed his share of women.

He liked them not only sexually but as companions. A great many of the women whose names he had been romantically linked with were simply friends. The number of women he had been credited with conquering amused him. He could hardly have worked the kind of schedule he imposed on himself if he spent all his time in the bedroom. Still, he had enjoyed perhaps a bit more than his share of romances, always careful to keep the tone light and the rules plain. He intended to do exactly the same thing with Tory.

It might be true that she was on his mind a great deal more often than any other woman in his memory. It might be true that he had been affected more deeply by her than anyone else. But…

Phil frowned over the *but* a moment. But, he reaffirmed, it was just because their meeting had been unique. The memory of his night in the steamy little cell caused him to grimace. He hadn't paid her back for that yet, and he was determined to. He hadn't cared for being under someone else's control. He'd grown used to deference in his life, a respect that had come first through his parents and then through his own talent. He never thought much about money. The fact that he hadn't been able to buy himself out of the cell was infuriating. Though more often than not he did for himself, he was accustomed to servants—perhaps more to having his word obeyed. Tory hadn't done what he ordered, and had done what he asked only when it had suited her.

It didn't matter that Phil was annoyed when people fawned over him or catered to him. That was what he was used to. Instead of fawning, Tory had been lightly disdainful, had tossed out a compliment on his work, then laughed at him. And had made him laugh, he remembered.

He wanted to know more about her. For days he had toyed with the notion of having someone check into Victoria L. Ashton, Attorney. What had stopped him had not been a respect for privacy so much as a desire to make the discoveries himself. Who was a woman who had a face like a madonna, a voice like whiskey and honey and handled a .45? Phil was going to find out if it took all of the dry, dusty summer. He'd find the time, he mused, although the shooting schedule was back-breaking.

Leaning back against the cushion of the chaise, Phil looked up at the sky. He'd refused the invitation to a party on the excuse that he had work and a scene to shoot early in the morning. Now he was thinking of Tory instead of the film, and he no longer had any sense of time. He knew he should work her out of his system so that he could give the film his full attention, without distractions. He knew he wouldn't. Since he'd returned from Friendly, he hadn't had the least inclination to pick up the phone and call any of the women he knew. He could pacify friends and acquaintances by using the excuse of his work schedule, but he knew. There was only one companion he wanted at the moment, one woman. One lover.

He wanted to kiss her again to be certain he hadn't imagined the emotions he had felt. And the sense of *rightness.* Oddly, he found he didn't want to dilute the sensation with the taste or feel of another woman. It worried him but he brushed it off, telling himself that the obsession would fade once he had Tory where he wanted her. What worried him more was the fact that he wanted to talk to her. Just talk.

Vaguely disturbed, Phil rose. He was tired, that was all. And there was that new script to read before he went to bed. The house was silent when he entered through the glass terrace doors. Even the music had stopped without his noticing. He stepped down into the sunken living room, the glass still in his hand.

The room smelled very faintly of the lemon oil the maid had used that morning. The maroon floor tiles shone. On the deep, plump cushions of the sofa a dozen pillows were tossed with a carelessness that was both inviting and lush. He himself had chosen the tones of blue and green and ivory that dominated the room, as well as the Impressionist painting on the wall, the only artwork in the room. There were mirrors and large expanses of windows that gave the room openness. It held nothing of the opulence of the houses he had grown up in, yet maintained the same ambience of money and success. Phil was easy with it, as he was with his life, himself and his views on his future.

Crossing the room, he walked toward the curving open staircase that led to the second floor. The treads were uncarpeted. His bare feet slapped the wood gently. He was thinking that he had been pleased with the rushes. He and Huffman had watched them together. Now that the filming was progressing, his producer was more amiable. There were fewer mutterings about guarantors and cost overruns. And Huffman had been pleased with the idea of shooting the bulk of the film on location. Financially the deal with Friendly had been advantageous. Nothing put a smile on a producer's face quicker, Phil thought wryly. He went to shower.

The bath was enormous. Even more than the secluded location, it had been Phil's main incentive for buying the house high in the hills. The shower ran along one wall, with the spray shooting from both sides. He switched it on, stripping out of his trunks while the bathroom grew steamy. Even as he stepped inside, he remembered the cramped little stall he had showered in that stifling morning in Friendly.

The soap had still been wet, he recalled, from Tory. It had been a curiously intimate feeling to rub the small cake along his own skin and imagine it sliding over hers. Then he had run out of hot water while he was still covered with lather. He'd cursed her fluently and wanted her outrageously. Standing between the hot crisscrossing sprays, Phil knew he still did. On impulse he reached out and grabbed the phone that hung on the wall beside the shower.

"I want to place a call to Friendly, New Mexico," he told the operator. Ignoring the time, he decided to take a chance. "The sheriff's office." Phil waited while steam rose from the shower. The phone clicked and hummed then rang.

"Sheriff's office."

The sound of her voice made him grin. "Sheriff."

Tory frowned, setting down the coffee that was keeping her awake over the brief she was drafting. "Yes?"

"Phil Kincaid."

There was complete silence as Tory's mouth opened and closed. She felt a thrill she considered ridiculously juvenile and straightened at her desk. "Well," she said lightly, "did you forget your toothbrush?"

"No." He was at a loss for a moment, struggling to formulate a reasonable excuse for the call. He wasn't a love-struck teenager who called his girl just to hear her voice. "The shooting's on schedule," he told her, thinking fast. "We'll be in Friendly next week. I wanted to be certain there were no problems."

Tory glanced over at the cell, remembering how he had looked standing there. "Your location manager has been in touch with me and the mayor," she said, deliberately turning her eyes away from the cell. "You have all the necessary permits. The hotel's booked for you. I had to fight to keep my own room. Several people are making arrangements to rent out rooms in their homes to accommodate you." She didn't have to add that the idea didn't appeal to her. Her tone told him everything. Again he found himself grinning.

"Still afraid we're going to corrupt your town, Sheriff?"

"You and your people will stay in line, Kincaid," she returned, "or you'll have your old room back."

"It's comforting to know you have it waiting for me. Are you?"

"Waiting for you?" She gave a quick snort of laughter. "Just like the Egyptians waited for the next plague."

"Ah, Victoria, you've a unique way of putting things."

Tory frowned, listening to the odd hissing on the line. "What's that noise?"

"Noise?"

"It sounds like water running."

"It is," he told her. "I'm in the shower."

For a full ten seconds Tory said nothing, then she burst out laughing. "Phil, why did you call me from the shower?"

Something about her laughter and the way she said his name had him struggling against a fresh torrent of needs. "Because it reminded me of you."

Tory propped her feet on the desk, forgetting her brief. Something in her was softening. "Oh?" was all she said.

"I remembered running out of hot water halfway through my shower in your guest room." He pushed wet hair out of his eyes. "At the time I wasn't in the mood to lodge a formal complaint."

"I'll take it up with the management." She caught her tongue between her teeth for a moment. "I wouldn't expect deluxe accommodations in the hotel, Kincaid. There's no room service or phones in the bathroom."

"We'll survive."

"That's yet to be seen," she said dryly. "Your group may undergo culture shock when they find themselves without a Jacuzzi."

"You really think we're a soft bunch, don't you?" Annoyed, Phil switched the phone to his other hand. It nearly slid out of his wet palm. "You may learn a few things about the people in the business this summer, Victoria. I'm going to enjoy teaching you."

''There's nothing I want to learn from you,'' she said quietly.

''*Want* and *need* are entirely different words,'' he pointed out. He could almost see the flash of temper leap into her eyes. It gave him a curious pleasure.

''As long as you play by the rules, there won't be any trouble.''

''There'll be a time, Tory,'' he murmured into the receiver, ''that you and I will play by my rules. I still have a promise to keep.''

Tory pulled her legs from the desk so that her boots hit the floor with a clatter. ''Don't forget to wash behind your ears,'' she ordered, then hung up with a bang.

Chapter 5

Tory was in her office when they arrived. The rumble of cars outside could mean only one thing. She forced herself to complete the form she was filling out before she rose from her desk. Of course she wasn't in any hurry to see him again, but it was her duty to be certain the town remained orderly during the arrival of the people from Hollywood. Still, she hesitated a moment, absently fingering her badge. She hadn't yet resolved how she was going to handle Phil. She knew the law clearly enough, but the law wouldn't help when she had to deal with him without her badge. Tod burst through the door, his eyes wide, his face flushed.

"Tory, they're here! A whole bunch of them in front of the hotel. There're vans and cars and everything!"

Though she felt more like swearing, she had to smile at him. He only forgot himself and called her Tory when he was desperately excited. And he was such a sweet boy, she mused, so full of dreams. Crossing to him, she dropped an arm over his shoulder. He no longer cringed.

"Let's go see," she said simply.

"Tory—Sheriff," Tod corrected himself, although the words all but tumbled over each other, "do you think that guy'll let me watch him make the movie? You know, the guy you had in jail."

"I know," Tory murmured as they stepped outside. "I imagine so," she answered absentmindedly.

The scene outside was so out of place in Friendly, it almost made Tory laugh. There were several vehicles in front of the hotel, and crowds of people. The mayor stood on the sidewalk, talking to everyone at once. Several of the people from California were looking around the town with expressions of curiosity and astonishment. They were being looked over with the same expressions by people from Friendly.

Different planets, Tory mused with a slight smile. Take me to your leader. When she spotted Phil, the smile faded.

He was dressed casually, as he had been on his first visit to town—no different than the members of his crew. And yet, there was a difference. He held the authority; there was no mistaking it. Even while apparently listening to the mayor, he was giving orders. And, Tory added thoughtfully, being obeyed. There seemed to be a certain friendliness between him and his crew, as well as an underlying respect. There was some laughter and a couple of shouts as equipment was unloaded, but the procedure was meticulously orderly. He watched over every detail.

"Wow," Tod said under his breath. "Look at all that

stuff. I bet they've got cameras in those boxes. Maybe I'll get a chance to look through one.''

''Mmm.'' Tory saw Phil laugh and heard the sound of it drift to her across the street. Then he saw her.

His smile didn't fade but altered subtly. They assessed each other while his people milled and hers whispered. The assessment became a challenge with no words spoken. She stood very straight, her arm still casually draped around the boy's shoulders. Phil noticed the gesture even as he felt a stir that wasn't wholly pleasant. He ached, he discovered, baffled. Just looking at her made him ache. She looked cool, even remote, but her eyes were directed at his. He could see the small badge pinned to the gentle sweep of her breast. On the dry, sweltering day she was wine, potent and irresistible—and perhaps unwise. One of his crew addressed him twice before Phil heard him.

''What?'' His eyes never left Tory's.

''Huffman's on the phone.''

''I'll get back to him.'' Phil started across the street.

When Tory's arm stiffened, Tod glanced up at her in question. He saw that her eyes were fixed on the man walking toward them. He frowned, but when Tory's arm relaxed, so did he.

Phil stopped just short of the sidewalk so that their eyes were at the same level. ''Sheriff.''

''Kincaid,'' she said coolly.

Briefly he turned to the boy and smiled. ''Hello, Tod. How are you?''

''Fine.'' The boy stared at him from under a thatch of tumbled hair. The fact that Phil had spoken to him, and remembered his name, made something move inside Tory.

She pushed it away, reminding herself she couldn't afford too many good feelings toward Phil Kincaid. "Can I..." Tod began. He shifted nervously, then drew up his courage. "Do you think I could see some of that stuff?"

A grin flashed on Phil's face. "Sure. Go over and ask for Bicks. Tell him I said to show you a camera."

"Yeah?" Thrilled, he stared at Phil for a moment, then glanced up at Tory in question. When she smiled down at him, Phil watched the boy's heart leap to his eyes.

Uh-oh, he thought, seeing the slight flush creep into the boy's cheeks. Tory gave him a quick squeeze and the color deepened.

"Go ahead," she told him.

Phil watched the boy dash across the street before he turned his gaze back to Tory. "It seems you have another conquest. I have to admire his taste." When she stared at him blankly, he shook his head. "Good God, Tory, the kid's in love with you."

"Don't be ridiculous," she retorted. "He's a child."

"Not quite," he countered. "And certainly old enough to be infatuated with a beautiful woman." He grinned again, seeing her distress as her eyes darted after Tod. "I was a fourteen-year-old boy once myself."

Annoyed that he had pointed out something she'd been oblivious to, Tory glared at him. "But never as innocent as that one."

"No," he agreed easily, and stepped up on the sidewalk. She had to shift the angle of her chin to keep her eyes in line with his. "It's good to see you, Sheriff."

"Is it?" she returned lazily as she studied his face.

"Yes, I wondered if I'd imagined just how beautiful you were."

"You've brought quite a group with you," she commented, ignoring his statement. "There'll be more, I imagine."

"Some. I need some footage of the town, the countryside. The actors will be here in a couple of days."

Nodding, she leaned against a post. "You'll have to store your vehicles at Bestler's. If you have any plans to use a private residence or a store for filming, you'll have to make the arrangements individually. Hernandez's Bar is open until eleven on weeknights, one on Saturday. Consumption of alcohol on the streets is subject to a fifty-dollar fine. You're liable for any damage to private property. Whatever alterations you make for the filming will again have to be cleared individually. Anyone causing a disturbance in the hotel or on the streets after midnight will be fined and sentenced. As this is your show, Kincaid, I'll hold you personally responsible for keeping your people in line."

He listened to her rundown of the rules with the appearance of careful interest. "Have dinner with me."

She very nearly smiled. "Forget it." When she started to walk by him, he took her arm.

"Neither of us is likely to do that, are we?"

Tory didn't shake off his arm. It felt too good to be touched by him again. She did, however, give him a long, lazy look. "Phil, both of us have a job to do. Let's keep it simple."

"By all means." He wondered what would happen if he kissed her right then and there. It was what he wanted, he discovered, more than anything he had wanted in quite some time. It would also be unwise. "What if we call it a business dinner?"

Tory laughed. "Why don't we call it what it is?"

"Because then you wouldn't come, and I do want to talk to you."

The simplicity of his answer disconcerted her. "About what?"

"Several things." His fingers itched to move to her face, to feel the soft, satiny texture of her skin. He kept them loosely hooked around her arm. "Among them, my show and your town. Wouldn't it simplify matters for both of us if we understood each other and came to a few basic agreements?"

"Maybe."

"Have dinner with me in my room." When her brow arched, he continued lazily. "It's also my office for the time being," he reminded her. "I'd like to clear the air regarding my film. If we're going to argue, Sheriff, let's do it privately."

The *Sheriff* did it. It was both her title and her job. "All right," she agreed. "Seven o'clock."

"Fine." When she started to walk away, he stopped her. "Sheriff," he said with a quick grin, "leave the gun in the desk, okay? It'll kill my appetite."

She gave a snort of laughter. "I can handle you without it, Kincaid."

Tory frowned at the clothes hanging inside her closet. Even while she had been showering, she had considered putting on work clothes—and her badge—for her dinner with Phil. But that would have been petty, and pettiness wasn't her style. She ran a fingertip over an emerald-green silk dress. It was very simply cut, narrow, with a high neck that buttoned to the waist. Serviceable and attractive, she decided, slipping it off the hanger. Laying it across the bed, she shrugged out of her robe.

Outside, the streets were quiet. She hoped they stayed that way, as she'd put Merle in charge for the evening. People would be gathered in their homes, at the drugstore, at the bar, discussing the filming. That had been the main topic of the town for weeks, overriding the heat, the lack of rain and the Kramer twins. Tory smiled as she laced the front of her teddy. Yes, people needed their little entertainments, and this was the biggest thing to happen in Friendly in years. She was going to have to roll with it. To a point.

She slipped the dress over her head, feeling the silk slither on her skin. It had been a long time, she realized, since she had bothered about clothes. In Albuquerque she took a great deal of care about her appearance. A courtroom image was as important as an opening statement, particularly in a jury trial. People judged. Still, she was a woman who knew how to incorporate style with comfort.

The dress flattered her figure while giving her complete freedom of movement. Tory looked in the bureau-top mirror to study her appearance. The mirror cut her off at just above the waist. She rose on her toes and turned to the side but was still frustrated with a partial view of herself. Well, she decided, letting her feet go flat again, it would just have to do.

She sprayed on her scent automatically, remembering

too late Phil's comment on it. Tory frowned at the delicate bottle as she replaced it on the dresser. She could hardly go and scrub the perfume off now. With a shrug she sat on the bed to put on her shoes. The mattress creaked alarmingly. Handling Phil Kincaid was no problem, she told herself. That was half the reason she had agreed to have dinner with him. It was a matter of principle. She wasn't a woman to be seduced or charmed into submission, particularly by a man of Kincaid's reputation. Spoiled, she thought again, but with a tad too much affection for her liking. He'd grown up privileged, in a world of glitter and glamour. He expected everything to come his way, women included.

Tory had grown up respecting the value of a dollar in a world of ordinary people and day-to-day struggles. She, too, expected everything to come her way—after she'd arranged it. She left the room determined to come out on top in the anticipated encounter. She even began to look forward to it.

Phil's room was right next door. Though she knew he had seen to that small detail himself, Tory planned to make no mention of it. She gave a brisk knock and waited.

When he opened the door, the glib remark Phil had intended to make vanished from his brain. He remembered his own thoughts about seeing her in something silk and vivid and could only stare. *Exquisite.* It was the word that hammered inside his brain, but even that wouldn't come through his lips. He knew at that moment he'd have to have her or go through his life obsessed with the need to.

"Victoria," he managed after a long moment.

Though her pulse had begun to pound at the look in his

eyes, at the husky way he had said her name, she gave him a brisk smile. "Phillip," she said very formally. "Shall I come in or eat out here?"

Phil snapped back. Stammering and staring wasn't going to get him very far. He took her hand to draw her inside, then locked the door, uncertain whether he was locking her in or the world out.

Tory glanced around the small, haphazardly furnished room. Phil had already managed to leave his mark on it. The bureau was stacked with papers. There was a note pad, scrawled in from margin to margin, a few stubby pencils and a two-way radio. The shades were drawn and the room was lit with candles. Tory lifted her brows at this, glancing toward the folding card table covered with the hotel's best linen. Two dishes were covered to keep in the heat while a bottle of wine was open. Strolling over, Tory lifted it to study the label.

"*Château Haut-Brion Blanc,*" she murmured with a perfect accent. Still holding the bottle, she sent Phil a look. "You didn't pick this up at Mendleson's Liquors."

"I always take a few...amenities when I go on location."

Tilting her head, Tory set down the bottle. "And the candles?"

"Local drugstore," he told her blandly.

"Wine and candlelight," she mused. "For a business dinner?"

"Humor the director," he suggested, crossing over to pour out two glasses of wine. "We're always setting scenes. It's uncontrollable." Handing her a glass, he touched it with the rim of his own. ''Sheriff, to a comfortable relationship.''

''Association,'' she corrected, then drank. ''Very nice,'' she approved. She let her eyes skim over him briefly. He wore casual slacks, impeccably tailored, with an open-collared cream-colored shirt that accented his lean torso. The candlelight picked up the deep tones of red in his hair. ''You look more suited to your profession than when I first saw you,'' she commented.

''And you less to yours,'' he countered.

''Really?'' Turning away, she wandered the tiny room. The small throw rug was worn thin in patches, the headboard of the bed scarred, the nightstand a bit unsteady. ''How do you like the accommodations, Kincaid?''

''They'll do.''

She laughed into her wine. ''Wait until it gets hot.''

''Isn't it?''

''Do the immortal words 'You ain't seen nothing yet' mean anything to you?''

He forced himself to keep his eyes from the movements of her body under the silk. ''Want to see all the Hollywood riffraff melt away, Tory?''

Turning, she disconcerted him by giving him her dashing smile. ''No, I'll wish you luck instead. After all, I invariably admire your finished product.''

''If not what goes into making it.''

''Perhaps not,'' she agreed. ''What are you feeding me?''

He was silent for a moment, studying the eyes that laughed at him over the rim of a wineglass. ''The menu is rather limited.''

"Meat loaf?" she asked dubiously, knowing it was the hotel's specialty.

"God forbid. Chicken and dumplings."

Tory walked back to him. "In that case I'll stay." They sat, facing each other across the folding table. "Shall we get business out of the way, Kincaid, or will it interfere with your digestion?"

He laughed, then surprised her by reaching out to take one of her hands in both of his. "You're a hell of a woman, Tory. Why are you afraid to use my first name?"

She faltered a moment, but let her hand lay unresisting in his. Because it's too personal, she thought. "Afraid?" she countered.

"Reluctant?" he suggested, allowing his fingertip to trace the back of her hand.

"Immaterial." Gently she removed her hand from his. "I was told you'd be shooting here for about six weeks." She lifted the cover from her plate and set it aside. "Is that firm?"

"According to the guarantors," Phil muttered, taking another sip of wine.

"Guarantors?"

"Tyco, Inc., completion-bond company."

"Oh, yes." Tory toyed with her chicken. "I'd heard that was a new wave in Hollywood. They guarantee that the movie will be completed on time and within budget—or else they pay the overbudget costs. They can fire you, can't they?"

"Me, the producer, the stars, anyone," Phil agreed.

"Practical."

"Stifling," he returned, and stabbed into his chicken.

"From your viewpoint, I imagine," Tory reflected. "Still, as a business, it makes sense. Creative people often have to be shown certain…boundaries. Such as," she continued, "the ones I outlined this morning."

"And boundaries often have to be flexible. Such as," he said with a smile, "some night scenes we'll be shooting: I'm going to need your cooperation. The townspeople are welcome to watch any phase of the shoot, as long as they don't interfere, interrupt or get in the way. Also, some of the equipment being brought in is very expensive and very sensitive. We have security, but as sheriff, you may want to spread the word that it's off limits."

"Your equipment is your responsibility," she reminded him. "But I will issue a statement. Before you shoot your night scenes, you'll have to clear it through my office."

He gave her a long, hard look. "Why?"

"If you're planning on working in the middle of the night in the middle of town, I'll need prior confirmation. In that way I can keep disorder to a minimum."

"There'll be times I'll need the streets blocked off and cleared."

"Send me a memo," she said. "Dates, times. Friendly can't come to a stop to accommodate you."

"It's nearly there in any case."

"We don't have a fast lane." Irresistibly she sent him a grin. "As you discovered."

He gave her a mild glance. "I'd also like to use some of the locals for extras and walk-ons."

Tory rolled her eyes. "God, you are looking for trouble. Go ahead," she said with a shrug, "send out your casting call, but you'd better use everyone that answers it, one way or another.''

As he'd already figured that one out for himself, Phil was unperturbed. ''Interested?'' he asked casually.

''Hmm?''

''Are you interested?''

Tory laughed as she held out her glass for more wine. ''No.''

Phil let the bottle hover a moment. ''I'm serious, Tory. I'd like to put you on film.''

''I haven't got the time or the inclination.''

''You've got the looks and, I think, the talent.''

She smiled, more amused than flattered. ''Phil, I'm a lawyer. That's exactly what I want to be.''

''Why?''

He saw immediately that the question had thrown her off balance. She stared at him a moment with the glass to her lips. ''Because the law fascinates me,'' she said after a pause. ''Because I respect it. Because I like to think that occasionally I have something to do with the process of justice. I worked hard to get into Harvard, and harder when I got there. It means something to me.''

''Yet, you've given it up for six months.''

''Not completely.'' She frowned at the steady flame of the candle. ''Regardless, it's necessary. There'll still be cases to try when I go back.''

''I'd like to see you in the courtroom,'' he murmured, watching the quiet light flicker in her eyes. ''I bet you're fabulous.''

''Outstanding,'' she agreed, smiling again. ''The assistant D.A. hates me.'' She took another bite of chicken. ''What about you? Why directing instead of acting?''

''It never appealed to me.'' Leaning back, Phil found himself curiously relaxed and stimulated. He felt he could look at her forever. Her fragrance, mixed with the scent of hot wax, was erotic, her voice soothing. ''And I suppose I liked the idea of giving orders rather than taking them. With directing you can alter a scene, change a tone, set the pace for an entire story. An actor can only work with one character, no matter how complex it may be.''

''You've never directed either of your parents.'' Tory let the words hang so that he could take them either as a statement or a question. When he smiled, the creases in his cheeks deepened so that she wondered how it would feel to run her fingers along them.

''No.'' He tipped more wine into his glass. ''It might make quite a splash, don't you think? The three of us together on one film. Even though they've been divorced for over twenty-five years, they'd send the glossies into a frenzy.''

''You could do two separate films,'' she pointed out.

''True.'' He pondered over it a moment. ''If the right scripts came along...'' Abruptly he shook his head. ''I've thought of it, even been approached a couple of times, but I'm not sure it would be a wise move professionally or personally. They're quite a pair,'' he stated with a grin. ''Temperamental, explosive and probably two of the best dramatic actors in the last fifty years. Both of them wring the last drop of blood from a character.''

''I've always admired them,'' Tory agreed. ''Especially

in the movies they made together. They put a lot of chemistry on the screen."

"And off it," Phil murmured. "It always amazed me that they managed to stay together for almost ten years. Neither of them had that kind of longevity in their other marriages. The problem was that they never stopped competing. It gave them the spark on the screen and a lot of problems at home. It's difficult to live with someone when you're afraid he or she might be just a little better than you are."

"But you're very fond of them, aren't you?" She watched his mobile brow lift in question. "It shows," she told him. "It's rather nice."

"Fond," he agreed. "Maybe a little wary. They're formidable people, together or separately. I grew up listening to lines being cued over breakfast and hearing producers torn to shreds at dinner. My father lived each role. If he was playing a psychotic, I could expect to find a crazed man in the bathroom."

"*Obsession,*" Tory recalled, delighted. "1957."

"Very good," Phil approved. "Are you a fan?"

"Naturally. I got my first kiss watching Marshall Kincaid in *Endless Journey.*" She gave a throaty laugh. "The movie was the more memorable of the two."

"You were in diapers when that movie was made," Phil calculated.

"Ever heard of the late show?"

"Young girls," he stated, "should be in bed at that hour."

Tory suppressed a laugh. Resting her elbows on the

table, she set her chin on cupped hands. "And young boys?"

"Would stay out of trouble," he finished.

"The hell they would," Tory countered, chuckling. "As I recall, your…exploits started at a tender age. What was the name of that actress you were involved with when you were sixteen? She was in her twenties as I remember, and—"

"More wine?" Phil interrupted, filling her glass before she could answer.

"Then there was the daughter of that comedian."

"We were like cousins."

"Really?" Tory drew out the word with a doubtful look. "And the dancer…ah, Nicki Clark."

"Great moves," Phil remembered, then grinned at her. "You seem to be more up on my…exploits than I am. Did you spend all your free time at Harvard reading movie magazines?"

"My roommate did," Tory confessed. "She was a drama major. I see her on a commercial now and again. And then I knew someone in the business. Your name's dropped quite a bit at parties."

"The actor you dated."

"Total recall," Tory murmured, a bit uncomfortable. "You amaze me."

"Tool of the trade. What was his name?"

Tory picked up her wine, studying it for a moment. "Chad Billings."

"Billings?" Surprised and not altogether pleased, Phil frowned at her. "A second-rate leech, Tory. I wouldn't think him your style."

''No?'' She shot him a direct look. ''He was diverting and...educational.''

''And married.''

''Judgmental, Phil?'' she countered, then gave a shrug. ''He was in between victims at the time.''

''Aptly put,'' Phil murmured. ''If you got your view of the industry through him, I'm surprised you didn't put up roadblocks to keep us out.''

''It was a thought,'' she told him, but smiled again. ''I'm not a complete fool, you know.''

But Phil continued to frown at her, studying her intensely. He was more upset at thinking of her with Billings than he should have been. ''Did he hurt you?'' he demanded abruptly.

Surprised, Tory stared at him. ''No,'' she said slowly. ''Although I suppose he might have if I'd allowed it. We didn't see each other exclusively or for very long. I was in L.A. on a case at the time.''

''Why Albuquerque?'' Phil wondered aloud. ''Lou was impressed with you, and he's not easily impressed. Why aren't you in some glass and leather office in New York?''

''I hate traffic,'' Tory sat back now, swirling the wine and relaxing. ''And I don't rush.''

''L.A.?''

''I don't play tennis.''

He laughed, appreciating her more each moment. ''I love the way you boil things down, Tory. What do you do when you're not upholding the law?''

''As I please, mostly. Sports and hobbies are too demanding.'' She tossed back her hair. ''I like to sleep.''

''You forget, I've seen you ride.''

"That's different." The wine had mellowed her mood. She didn't notice that the candles were growing low and the hour late. "It relaxes me. Clears my head."

"Why do you live in a room in the hotel when you have a house right outside of town?" Her fingers tightened on the stem of the wineglass only slightly: He was an observant man.

"It's simpler."

Leave this one alone for a while, he warned himself. It's a very tender spot.

"And what do you do when you're not making a major statement on film?" she asked, forcing her hand to relax.

Phil accepted her change of subject without question. "Read scripts…watch movies."

"Go to parties," Tory added sagely.

"That too. It's all part of the game."

"Isn't it difficult sometimes, living in a town where so much is pretense? Even considering the business end of your profession, you have to deal with the lunacy, the make-believe, even the desperation. How do you separate the truth from the fantasy?"

"How do you in your profession?" he countered.

Tory thought for a moment, then nodded. "Touché." Rising, she wandered to the window. She pushed aside the shade, surprised to see that the sun had gone down. A few red streaks hovered over the horizon, but in the east the sky was dark. A few early stars were already out. Phil sat where he was, watched her and wanted her.

"There's Merle making his rounds," Tory said with a smile in her voice. "He's got his official expression on. I imagine he's hoping to be discovered. If he can't be a tough lawman from the nineteenth century, he'd settle for playing one.'' A car pulled into town, stopping in front of the pool hall with a sharp squeal of brakes. ''Oh, God, it's the twins.'' She sighed, watching Merle turn and stride in their direction. ''There's been no peace in town since that pair got their licenses. I suppose I'd better go down and see that they stay in line.''

''Can't Merle handle a couple of kids?''

Tory's laugh was full of wicked appreciation. ''You don't know the Kramers. There's Merle,'' she went on, ''giving them basic lecture number twenty-two.''

''Did they wash all of Hollister's windows?'' Phil asked as he rose to join her.

Tory turned her head, surprised. ''How did you know about that?''

''Tod told me.'' He peeked through the window, finding he wanted a look at the infamous twins. They seemed harmless enough from a distance, and disconcertingly alike. ''Which one's Zac?''

''Ah…on the right, I think. Maybe,'' she added with a shake of her head. ''Why?''

'''Zac Kramer don't hold with no woman sheriff,''' he quoted.

Tory grinned up at him. ''Is that so?''

''Just so.'' Hardly aware he did so, Phil reached for her hair. ''Obviously he's not a very perceptive boy.''

''Perceptive enough to wash Mr. Hollister's windows,'' Tory corrected, amused by the memory. ''And to call me a foxy chick only under his breath when he thought I couldn't hear. Of course, that could have been Zeke.''

'''Foxy chick'?'' Phil repeated.

"Yes," Tory returned with mock hauteur. "'A *very* foxy chick.' It was his ultimate compliment."

"Your head's easily turned," he decided. "What if I told you that you had a face that belongs in a Raphael painting?"

Tory's eyes lit with humor. "I'd say you're reaching."

"And hair," he said with a subtle change in his voice. "Hair that reminds me of night…a hot summer night that keeps you awake, and thinking, and wanting." He plunged both hands into it, letting his fingers tangle. The shade snapped back into place, cutting them off from the outside.

"Phil," Tory began, unprepared for the suddenness of desire that rose in both of them.

"And skin," he murmured, not even hearing her, "that makes me think of satin sheets and tastes like something forbidden." He touched his mouth to her cheek, allowing the tip of his tongue to brush over her. "Tory." She felt her name whisper along her skin and thrilled to it. She had her hands curled tightly around his arms, but not in protest. "Do you know how often I've thought of you these past weeks?"

"No." She didn't want to resist. She wanted to feel that wild sweep of pleasure that came from the press of his mouth on hers. "No," she said again, and slid her arms around his neck.

"Too much," he murmured, then swore. "Too damn much." And his mouth took her waiting one.

The passion was immediate, frenetic. It ruled both of them. Each of them sought the mindless excitement they had known briefly weeks before. Tory had thought she had intensified the sensation in her mind as the days had passed. Now she realized she had lessened it. This sort of fervor couldn't be imagined or described. It had to be experienced. Everything inside her seemed to speed up—her blood, her heart, her brain. And all sensation, all emotion, seemed to be centered in her mouth. The taste of him exploded on her tongue, shooting through her until she was so full of him, she could no longer separate herself. With a moan she tilted her head back, inviting him to plunge deeper into her mouth. But he wanted more.

Her hair fell straight behind her, leaving her neck vulnerable. Surrendering to a desperate hunger, he savaged it with kisses. Tory made a sound that was mixed pain and pleasure. Her scent seemed focused there, heated by the pulse at her throat. It drove him nearer the edge. He dragged at the silk-covered buttons, impatient to find the hidden skin, the secret skin that had preyed on his mind. The groan sounded in his throat as he slipped his hand beneath the thin teddy and found her.

She was firm, and slender enough to fit his palm. Her heartbeat pounded against it. Tory turned her head, but only to urge him to give the neglected side of her neck attention. With her hands in his hair she pulled him back to her. His hands searched everywhere with a sort of wild reverence, exploring, lingering, possessing. She could feel his murmurs as his lips played over her skin, although she could barely hear them and understood them not at all. The room seemed to grow closer and hotter, so that she longed to be rid of her clothes and find relief…and delight.

Then he pulled her close so that their bodies pressed urgently. Their mouths met with fiery demand. It seemed the storm had just begun. Again and again they drew from each other until they were both breathless. Though he had fully intended to end the evening with Tory in his bed, Phil hadn't expected to be desperate. He hadn't known that all control could be so easily lost. The warm curves of a woman should bring easy pleasure, not this trembling pain. A kiss was a prelude, not an all-consuming force. He knew only that all of him, much more than his body, was crying out for her. Whatever was happening to him was beyond his power to stop. And she was the only answer he had.

"God, Tory." He took his mouth on a wild journey of her face, then returned to her lips. "Come to bed. For God's sake, come to bed. I want you."

She felt as though she were standing on the edge of a cliff. The plunge had never seemed more tempting—or more dangerous. It would be so easy, so easy, just to lean forward and fly. But the fall… She fought for sanity through a brain clouded with the knowledge of one man. It was much too soon to take the step.

"Phil." Shaken, she drew away from him to lean against the windowsill. "I…no," she managed, lifting both hands to her temples. He drew her back against him.

"Yes," he corrected, then crushed his lips to hers again. Her mouth yielded irresistibly. "You can't pretend you don't want me as much as I want you."

"No." She let her head rest on his shoulder a moment before she pushed out of his arms. "I can't," she agreed in a voice thickened with passion. "But I don't do everything I want. That's one of the basic differences between us."

His eyes flicked briefly down to the unbuttoned dress.

"We also seem to have something important in common. This doesn't happen every time—between every man and woman."

"No." Carefully she began to do up her buttons. "It shouldn't have happened between us. I didn't intend it to."

"I did," he admitted. "But not quite this way."

Her eyes lifted to his. She understood perfectly. This had been more intense than either of them had bargained for. "It's going to be a long summer, Phil," she murmured.

"We're going to be together sooner or later, Tory. We both know it." He needed something to balance him. Going to the table, he poured out another glass of wine. He drank, drank again, then looked at her. "I have no intention of backing off."

She nodded, accepting. But she didn't like the way her hands were shaking. "I'm not ready."

"I can be a patient man when necessary." He wanted nothing more than to pull her to the bed and take what they both needed. Instead he took out a cigarette and reminded himself he was a civilized man.

Tory drew herself up straight. "Let's both concentrate on our jobs, shall we?" she said coolly. She wanted to get out, but she didn't want to retreat. "I'll see you around, Kincaid."

"Damn right you will," he murmured as she headed for the door.

She flicked the lock off, then turned to him with a half smile. "Keep out of trouble," she ordered, closing the door behind her.

Chapter 6

Phil sat beside the cameraman on the Tulip crane. "Boom up." At his order the crane operator took them seventeen feet above the town of Friendly. It was just dawn. He'd arranged to have everyone off the streets, although there was a crowd of onlookers behind the crane and equipment. All entrances to town had been blocked off on the off chance that someone might drive through. He wanted desolation and the tired beginning of a new day.

Glancing down, he saw that Bicks was checking the lighting and angles. Brutes, the big spotlights, were set to give daylight balance. He knew, to an inch, where he wanted the shadows to fall. For this shot Phil would act as assistant cameraman, pulling the focus himself.

Phil turned his attention back to the street. He knew what he wanted, and he wanted to capture it as the sun rose, with as much natural light as possible. He looked through the lens and set the shot himself. The crane was set on tracks. He would have the cameraman begin with a wide shot of the horizon and the rising sun, then dolly back to take in the entire main street of Friendly. No soft focus there, just harsh reality. He wanted to pick up the dust on the storefront windows. Satisfied with what he saw through the camera lens, Phil marked the angle with tape, then nodded to his assistant director.

"Quiet on the set."

"New Chance, scene three, take one."

"Roll it," Phil ordered, then waited. With his eyes narrowed, he could visualize what his cameraman saw through the lens. The light was good. Perfect. They'd have to get it in three takes or less or else they'd have to beef it up with gels and filters. That wasn't what he wanted here. He felt the crane roll backward slowly on cue. A straight shot, no panning right to left. They'd take in the heart of the town in one long shot. Chipped paint, sagging wood, torn screens. Later they'd cut in the scene of the leading man walking in from the train station. He was coming home, Phil mused, because there was no place else to go. And he found it, exactly as he had left it twenty years before.

"Cut." The noise on the ground started immediately. "I want another take. Same speed."

At the back of the crowd Tory watched. She wasn't thrilled with being up at dawn. Both her sense of duty and her curiosity had brought her. Phil had been perfectly clear about anyone peeking through windows during this shot. He wanted emptiness. She told herself she'd come to keep her people out of mischief, but when it was all said and done, she had wanted to see Phil at work.

He was very commanding and totally at ease with it, but, she reasoned as she stuck her hands in her back pockets, it didn't seem so hard. Moving a little to the side, she tried to see the scene she was imagining. The town looked tired, she decided, and a little reluctant to face the new day. Though the horizon was touched with golds and pinks, a gray haze lay over the street and buildings.

It was the first time he had shot anything there. For the past week he had been filming landscapes. Tory had stayed in Friendly, sending Merle out occasionally to check on things. It had kept him happy and had given Tory the distance she wanted. As her deputy came back brimming with reports and enthusiasm, she was kept abreast in any case.

But today the urge to see for herself had been too strong to resist. It had been several days—and several long nights—since their evening together. She had managed to keep herself busier than necessary in order to avoid him. But Tory wasn't a woman to avoid a problem for long. Phil Kincaid was still a problem.

Apparently satisfied, Phil ordered the operator to lower the crane. People buzzed around Tory like bees. A few children complained about being sent off to school. Spotting Tod, Tory smiled and waved him over.

''Isn't it neat?'' he demanded the moment he was beside her. ''I wanted to go up in it,'' he continued, indicating the crane, ''but Mr. Kincaid said something about insurance. Steve let me see his camera though, even let me take some pictures. It's a thirty-five millimeter with all kinds of lenses.''

''Steve?''

''The guy who was sitting next to Mr. Kincaid. He's the cameraman.'' Tod glanced over, watching Phil in a discussion with his cameraman and several members of the crew. ''Isn't he something?''

''Steve?'' Tory repeated, smiling at Tod's pleasure.

''Well, yeah, but I meant Mr. Kincaid.'' Shaking his head, he let out a long breath. ''He's awful smart. You should hear some of the words he uses. And boy, when he says so, everybody jumps.''

''Do they?'' Tory murmured, frowning over at the man under discussion.

''You bet,'' Tod confirmed. ''And I heard Mr. Bicks say to Steve that he'd rather work with Mr. Kincaid than anybody. He's a tough sonofa—'' Catching himself, Tod broke off and flushed. ''I mean, he said he was tough, but the best there was.''

As she watched, Phil was pointing, using one hand and then the other as he outlined his needs for the next shot. It was very clear that he knew what he wanted and that he'd get it. She could study him now. He was too involved to notice her or the crowd of people who stared and mumbled behind the barrier of equipment.

He wore jeans and a pale blue T-shirt with scuffed sneakers. Hanging from his belt was a case that held sunglasses and another for a two-way radio. He was very intense, she noted, when working. There was none of the careless humor in his eyes. He talked quickly, punctuating the words with hand gestures. Once or twice he interrupted what he was saying to call out another order to the grips who were setting up light stands.

A perfectionist, she concluded, and realized it shouldn't surprise her. His movies projected the intimate care she was now seeing firsthand. A stocky man in a fielder's cap lumbered up to him, talking over an enormous wad of gum.

"That's Mr. Bicks," Tod murmured reverently. "The cinematographer. He's got two Oscars and owns part of a boxer."

Whatever he was saying, Phil listened carefully, then simply shook his head. Bicks argued another moment, shrugged, then gave Phil what appeared to be a solid punch on the shoulder before he walked away. A tough sonofabitch, Tory mused. Apparently so.

Turning to Tod, she mussed his hair absently. "You'd better get to school."

"Aw, but..."

She lifted her brow, effectively cutting off his excuse. "It's nearly time for summer vacation. They'll still be here."

He mumbled a protest, but she caught the look in his eye as he gazed up at her. Uh-oh, she thought, just as Phil had. Why hadn't she seen this coming? She was going to have to be careful to be gentle while pointing the boy in another direction. A teenage crush was nothing to smile at and brush away.

"I'll come by after school," he said, beaming up at her. Before she could respond, he was dashing off, leaving her gnawing on her bottom lip and worrying about him.

"Sheriff."

Tory whirled sharply and found herself facing Phil. He smiled slowly, setting the sunglasses in front of his eyes. It annoyed her that she had to strain to see his expression through the tinted glass. "Kincaid," she responded. "How's it going?"

"Good. Your people are very cooperative."

"And yours," she said. "So far."

He grinned at that. "We're expecting the cast this afternoon. The location manager's cleared it with you about parking the trailers and so forth?"

"She's very efficient," Tory agreed. "Are you getting what you want?"

He took a moment to answer. "With regard to the film, yes, so far." Casually he reached down to run a finger over her badge. "You've been busy the last few days."

"So have you."

"Not that busy. I've left messages for you."

"I know."

"When are you going to see me?"

She lifted both brows. "I'm seeing you right now." He took a step closer and cupped the back of her neck in his hand. "Phil—"

"Soon," he said quietly.

Though she could feel the texture of each of his fingers on the back of her neck, she gave him a cool look. "Kincaid, create your scenes on the other side of the camera. Accosting a peace officer will land you back in that cell. You'll find it difficult to direct from there."

"Oh, I'm going to accost you," he warned under his breath. "With or without that damn badge, Victoria. Think about it."

She didn't step back or remove his hand, although she knew several pair of curious eyes were on them. "I'll give it a few minutes," she promised dryly.

Only the tensing of his fingers on her neck revealed his annoyance. She thought he was about to release her and relaxed. His mouth was on hers so quickly, she could only stand in shock. Before she could think to push him away, he set her free. Her eyes were sharply green and furious when he grinned down at her.

"See you, Sheriff," he said cheerfully, and sauntered back to his crew.

For the better part of the day Tory stayed in her office and fumed. Now and again Phil's voice carried through her open window as he called out instructions. She knew they were doing pans of the town and stayed away from the window. She had work to do, she reminded herself. And in any case she had no interest in the filming. It was understandable that the townspeople would stand around and gawk, but she had better things to do.

I should have hauled him in, she thought, scowling down at her legal pad. I should have hauled him in then and there. And she would have if it wouldn't have given him too much importance. He'd better watch his step, Tory decided. One wrong move and she was going to come down on him hard. She picked up her coffee and gulped it down with a grimace. It was cold. Swearing, she rose to pour a fresh cup.

Through the screen in the window she could see quite a bit of activity and hear a flood of conversation interrupted when the filming was in progress. It was past noon and hot as the devil. Phil had been working straight through for hours. With a grudging respect she admitted that he didn't take his job lightly. Going back to her desk, Tory concentrated on her own.

She hardly noticed that two hours had passed when Merle came bursting into the office. Hot, tired and annoyed with having her concentration broken, she opened her mouth to snap at him, but he exploded with enthusiasm before she had the chance.

"Tory, they're here!"

"Terrific," she mumbled, turning to her notes again. "Who?"

"The actors. Came from the airport in limousines. Long, black limousines. There are a half dozen of those Winnebagos set up outside of town for dressing rooms and stuff. You should see inside them. They've got telephones and TVs and everything."

She lifted her head. "Been busy, Merle T.?" she asked languidly, but he was too excited to notice.

"Sam Dressler," he went on, pacing back and forth with a clatter of boots. "Sam Dressler, right here in Friendly. I guess I've seen every movie he's ever made. He shook my hand," he added, staring down at his own palm, awed. "Thought I was the sheriff." He sent Tory a quick look. "'Course I told him I was the deputy."

"Of course," she agreed, amused now. It was never possible for her to stay annoyed with Merle. "How'd he look?"

"Just like you'd think," he told her with a puzzled shake of his head. "All tanned and tough, with a diamond on his finger fit to blind you. Signed autographs for everybody who wanted one."

Unable to resist, Tory asked, ''Did you get one?''

''Sure I did.'' He grinned and pulled out his ticket book. ''It was the only thing I had handy.''

''Very resourceful.'' She glanced at the bold signature Merle held out for her. At the other end of the page were some elegant looping lines. ''Marlie Summers,'' Tory read. She recalled a film from the year before, and the actress's pouting sexuality.

''She's about the prettiest thing I ever saw,'' Merle murmured.

Coming from anyone else, Tory would have given the remark no notice. In this case, however, her eyes shot up and locked on Merle's. What she saw evoked in her a feeling of distress similar to what she had experienced with Tod. ''Really?'' she said carefully.

''She's just a little thing,'' Merle continued, gazing down at the autograph. ''All pink and blond. Just like something in a store window. She's got big blue eyes and the longest lashes...'' He trailed off, tucking the book back in his pocket.

Growing more disturbed, Tory told herself not to be silly. No Hollywood princess was going to look twice at Merle T. Johnson. ''Well,'' she began casually, ''I wonder what her part is.''

''She's going to tell me all about it tonight,'' Merle stated, adjusting the brim of his hat.

''What?'' It came out in a quick squeak.

Grinning, Merle gave his hat a final pat, then stroked his struggling mustache. ''We've got a date.'' He strode out jauntily, leaving Tory staring with her mouth open.

''A date?'' she asked the empty office. Before she could

react, the phone beside her shrilled. Picking it up, she barked into it, "What is it?"

A bit flustered by the greeting, the mayor stammered. "Tory—Sheriff Ashton, this is Mayor Toomey."

"Yes, Bud." Her tone was still brisk as she stared at the door Merle had shut behind him.

"I'd like you to come over to the office, Sheriff. I have several members of the cast here." His voice rang with importance again. "Mr. Kincaid thought it might be a good idea for you to meet them."

"Members of the cast," she repeated, thinking of Marlie Summers. "I'd love to," she said dangerously, then hung up on the mayor's reply.

Her thoughts were dark as she crossed the street. No Hollywood tootsie was going to break Merle's heart while she was around. She was going to make that clear as soon as possible. She breezed into the hotel, giving several members of Phil's crew a potent stare as they loitered in the lobby. Bicks doffed his fielder's cap and grinned at her.

"Sheriff."

Tory sent him a mild glance and a nod as she sauntered through to the office. Behind her back he rolled his eyes to the ceiling, placing the cap over his heart. A few remarks were made about the advantages of breaking the law in Friendly while Tory disappeared into a side door.

The tiny office was packed, the window air-conditioning unit spitting hopefully. Eyes turned to her. Tory gave the group a brief scan. Marlie was sitting on the arm of Phil's chair, dressed in pink slacks and a frilled halter. Her enviable curves were displayed to perfection.

Her hair was tousled appealingly around a piquant face accented with mink lashes and candy-pink lipstick. She looked younger than Tory had expected, almost like a high school girl ready to be taken out for an ice-cream soda. Tory met the baby-blue eyes directly, and with an expression that made Phil grin. He thought mistakenly that she might be a bit jealous.

"Sheriff." The mayor bustled over to her, prepared to act as host. "This is quite an honor for Friendly," he began, in his best politician's voice. "I'm sure you recognize Mr. Dressler."

Tory extended her hand to the man who approached her. "Sheriff." Her voice was rich, the cadence mellow as he clasped her hand in both of his. She was a bit surprised to find them callused. "This is unexpected," he murmured while his eyes roamed her face thoroughly. "And delightful."

"Mr. Dressler, I admire your work." The smile was easy because the words were true.

"Sam, please." His brandy voice had only darkened attractively with age, losing none of its resonance. "We get to be a close little family on location shoots. Victoria, isn't it?"

"Yes." She found herself inclined to like him and gave him another smile.

"Bud, here, is making us all quite comfortable," he went on, clapping the mayor on the shoulder. "Will you join us in a drink."

"Ginger ale's fine, Bud."

"The sheriff's on duty." Hearing Phil's voice, Tory turned, her head only, and glanced at him. "You'll find she takes her work very seriously.'' He touched Marlie's creamy bare shoulder. ''Victoria Ashton, Marlie Summers.''

''Sheriff.'' Marlie smiled her dazzling smile. The tiniest hint of a dimple peeked at the corner of her mouth. ''Phil said you were unusual. It looks like he's right again.''

''Really?'' Accepting the cold drink Bud handed her, Tory assessed the actress over the rim. Marlie, accustomed to long looks and feminine coolness, met the stare straight on.

''Really,'' Marlie agreed. ''I met your deputy a little while ago.''

''So I heard.''

So the wind blows in that direction, Marlie mused as she sipped from her own iced sangria. Sensing tension and wanting to keep things smooth, Bud hurried on with the rest of the introductions.

The cast ranged from ingenues to veterans—a girl Tory recognized from a few commercials; an ancient-looking man she remembered from the vague black-and-white movies on late-night television; a glitzy actor in his twenties, suited for heart throbs and posters. Tory managed to be pleasant, stayed long enough to satisfy the mayor, then slipped away. She'd no more than stepped outside when she felt an arm on her shoulder.

''Don't you like parties, Sheriff?''

Taking her time, she turned to face Phil. ''Not when I'm on duty.'' Though she knew he'd worked in the sun all day, he didn't look tired but exhilarated. His shirt was streaked with sweat, his hair curling damply over his ears, but there was no sign of fatigue on his face. It's the pressure that feeds him, she realized. Again she was drawn to him, no less than when they had been alone in his room. "You've put in a long day," she murmured.

He caught her hair in his hand. "So have you. Why don't we go for a drive?"

Tory shook her head. "No, I have things to do." Wanting to steer away from the subject, she turned to what had been uppermost on her mind. "Your Marlie made quite an impression on Merle."

Phil gave a quick laugh. "Marlie usually does."

"Not on Merle," Tory said so seriously that he sobered.

"He's a big boy, Tory."

"A boy," she agreed significantly. "He's never seen anything like your friend in there. I won't let him get hurt."

Phil let out a deep breath. "Your duties as sheriff include advice to the lovelorn? Leave him alone," he ordered before she could retort. "You treat him as though he were a silly puppy who doesn't respond to training."

She took a step back at that. "No, I don't," she disagreed, sincerely shaken by the idea. "He's a sweet boy who—"

"Man," Phil corrected quietly. "He's a man, Tory. Cut the apron strings."

"I don't know what you're talking about," she snapped.

"You damn well do," he corrected. "You can't keep him under your wing the way you do with Tod."

"I've known Merle all my life," she said in a low voice. "Just keep Cotton Candy in line, Kincaid."

"Always so sure of yourself, aren't you?"

Her color drained instantly, alarmingly. For a moment Phil stared at her in speechless wonder. He'd never expected to see that kind of pain in her eyes. Instinctively he reached out for her. "Tory?"

"No." She lifted a hand to ward him off. "Just—leave me alone." Turning away, she walked across the street and climbed into her car. With an oath Phil started to go back into the hotel, then swore again and backtracked. Tory was already on her way north.

Her thoughts were in turmoil as she drove. Too much was happening. She squeezed her eyes shut briefly. Why should that throw her now, she wondered. She'd always been able to take things in stride, handle them at her own pace. Now she had a deep-seated urge just to keep driving, just to keep going. So many people wanted things from her, expected things. Including, she admitted, herself. It was all closing in suddenly. She needed someone to talk to. But the only one who had ever fit that job was gone.

God, she wasn't sure of herself. Why did everyone say so? Sometimes it was so hard to be responsible, to *feel* responsible. Tod, Merle, the mayor, the Kramers, Mr. Hollister. Her mother. She just wanted peace—enough time to work out what was happening in her own life. Her feelings for Phil were closing in on her. Pulling the car to a halt, Tory realized it was those feelings that were causing her—a woman who had always considered herself calm—to be tense. Piled on top of it were problems that had to come first. She'd learned that from her father.

Glancing up, she saw she had driven to the cemetery without even being aware of it. She let out a long breath, resting her forehead against the steering wheel. It was time she went there, time she came to terms with what she had closed her mind to since that night in the hospital. Climbing out of the car, Tory walked across the dry grass to her father's grave.

Odd that there'd been a breeze here, she mused, looking at the sky, the distant mountains, the long stretches of nothing. She looked at anything but what was at her feet. There should be some shade, she thought, and cupped her elbows in her palms. Someone should plant some trees. I should have brought some flowers, she thought suddenly, then looked down.

WILLIAM H. ASHTON

She hadn't seen the gravestone before—hadn't been back to the cemetery since the day of the funeral. Now a quiet moan slipped through her lips. "Oh, Dad."

It isn't right, she thought with a furious shake of her head. It just isn't right. How can he be down there in the dark when he always loved the sun? "Oh, no," she murmured again, I don't know what to do, she thought silently, pleading with him. I don't know how to deal with it all. I still need you. Pressing a palm on her forehead, she fought back tears.

Phil pulled up behind her car, then got out quietly. She looked very alone and lost standing among the headstones. His first instinct was to go to her, but he suppressed it. This was private for her. Her father, he thought, looking toward the grave at which Tory stared. He stood by a low wrought-iron gate at the edge of the cemetery and waited.

There was so much she needed to talk about, so much she still needed to say. But there was no more time. He'd been taken too suddenly. Unfair, she thought again on a wave of desolate fury. He had been so young and so good.

"I miss you so much," she whispered. "All those long talks and quiet evenings on the porch. You'd smoke those awful cigars outside so that the smell wouldn't get in the curtains and irritate Mother. I was always so proud of you. This badge doesn't suit me," she continued softly, lifting her hand to it. "It's the law books and the courtroom that I understand. I don't want to make a mistake while I'm wearing it, because it's yours." Her fingers tightened around it. All at once she felt painfully alone, helpless, empty. Even the anger had slipped away unnoticed. And yet the acceptance she tried to feel was blocked behind a grief she refused to release. If she cried, didn't it mean she'd taken the first step away?

Wearily she stared down at the name carved into the granite. "I don't want you to be dead," she whispered. "And I hate it because I can't change it."

When she turned away from the grave, her face was grim. She walked slowly but was halfway across the small cemetery before she saw Phil. Tory stopped and stared at him. Her mind went blank, leaving her with only feelings. He went to her.

For a moment they stood face-to-face. He saw her lips tremble open as if she were about to speak, but she only shook her head helplessly. Without a word he gathered her close. The shock of grief that hit her was stronger than anything that had come before. She trembled first, then clutched at him.

''Oh, Phil, I can't bear it.'' Burying her face against his shoulder, Tory wept for the first time since her father's death.

In silence he held her, overwhelmed with a tenderness he'd felt for no one before. Her sobbing was raw and passionate. He stroked her hair, offering comfort without words. Her grief poured out in waves that seemed to stagger her and made him hurt for her to a degree that was oddly intimate. He thought he could feel what she felt, and held her tighter, waiting for the first throes to pass.

At length her weeping quieted, lessening to trembles that were somehow more poignant than the passion. She kept her face pressed against his shoulder, relying on his strength when her own evaporated. Light-headed and curiously relieved, she allowed him to lead her to a small stone bench. He kept her close to his side when they sat, his arm protectively around her.

''Can you talk about it?'' he asked softly.

Tory let out a long, shuddering sigh. From where they sat she could see the headstone clearly. ''I loved him,'' she murmured. ''My mother says too much.'' Her throat felt dry and abused when she swallowed. ''He was everything good. He taught me not just right and wrong but all the shades in between.'' Closing her eyes, she let her head rest on Phil's shoulder. ''He always knew the right thing. It was something innate and effortless. People knew they could depend on him, that he'd make it right. I depended on him, even in college, in Albuquerque—I knew he was there if I needed him.''

He kissed her temple in a gesture of simple understanding. ''How did he die?''

Feeling a shudder run through her, Phil drew her closer still. ‘‘He had a massive stroke. There was no warning. He’d never even been sick that I can remember. When I got here, he was in a coma. Everything...’’ She faltered, searching for the strength to continue. With his free hand Phil covered hers. ‘‘Everything seemed to go wrong at once. His heart just...stopped.’’ She ended in a whisper, lacing her fingers through his. ‘‘They put him on a respirator. For weeks there was nothing but that damn machine. Then my mother told them to turn it off.’’

Phil let the silence grow, following her gaze toward the headstone. ‘‘It must have been hard for her.’’

‘‘No.’’ The word was low and flat. ‘‘She never wavered, never cried. My mother’s a very decisive woman,’’ she added bitterly. ‘‘And she made the decision alone. She told me after it was already done.’’

‘‘Tory.’’ Phil turned her to face him. She looked pale, bright-eyed and achingly weary. Something seemed to tear inside him. ‘‘I can’t tell you the right or wrong of it, because there really isn’t any. But I do know there comes a time when everyone has to face something that seems impossible to accept.’’

‘‘If only I could have seen it was done for love and not...expediency.’’ Shutting her eyes, she shook her head. ‘‘Hold me again.’’ He drew her gently into his arms. ‘‘That last night at the hospital was so ugly between my mother and me. He would have hated that. I couldn’t stop it,’’ she said with a sigh. ‘‘I still can’t.’’

‘‘Time.’’ He kissed the top of her head. ‘‘I know how trite that sounds, but there’s nothing else but time.’’

She remained silent, accepting his comfort, drawing

strength from it. If she had been able to think logically, Tory would have found it inconsistent with their relationship thus far that she could share her intimate feelings with him. At the moment she trusted Phil implicitly.

"Once in a while, back there," she murmured. "I panic."

It surprised him enough to draw her back and study her face again. "You?"

"Everyone thinks because I'm Will Ashton's daughter, I'll take care of whatever comes up. There're so many variables to right and wrong."

"You're very good at your job."

"I'm a good lawyer," she began.

"And a good sheriff," he interrupted. Tilting her chin up, he smiled at her. "That's from someone who's been on the wrong side of your bars." Gently he brushed the hair from her cheeks. They were warm and still damp. "And don't expect to hear me say it in public."

Laughing, she pressed her cheek to his. "Phil, you can be a very nice man."

"Surprised?"

"Maybe," she murmured. With a sigh she gave him one last squeeze, then drew away. "I've got work to do."

He stopped her from rising by taking her hands again. "Tory, do you know how little space you give yourself?"

"Yes." She disconcerted him by bringing his hand to her lips. "These six months are for him. It's very important to me."

Standing as she did, Phil cupped her face in his hands. She seemed to him very fragile, very vulnerable, suddenly.

His need to look out for her was strong. "Let me drive you back. We can send someone for your car."

"No, I'm all right. Better." She brushed her lips over his. "I appreciate this. There hasn't been anyone I could talk to."

His eyes became very intense. "Would you come to me if you needed me?"

She didn't answer immediately, knowing the question was more complex than the simple words. "I don't know," she said at length.

Phil let her go, then watched her walk away.

Chapter 7

The camera came in tight on Sam and Marlie. Phil wanted the contrast of youth and age, of dissatisfaction and acceptance. It was a key scene, loaded with tension and restrained sexuality. They were using Hernandez's Bar, where the character Marlie portrayed worked as a waitress. Phil had made almost no alterations in the room. The bar was scarred, the mirror behind it cracked near the bottom. It smelled of sweat and stale liquor. He intended to transmit the scent itself onto film.

The windows were covered with neutral-density paper to block off the stream of the sun. It trapped the stale air in the room. The lights were almost unbearably hot, so that he needed no assistance from makeup to add beads of sweat to Sam's face. It was the sixth take, and the mood was growing edgy.

Sam blew his lines and swore ripely.

"Cut." Struggling with his temper, Phil wiped his forearm over his brow. With some actors a few furious words worked wonders. With Dressler, Phil knew, they would only cause more delays.

"Look, Phil"—Sam tore off the battered Stetson he wore and tossed it aside—"this isn't working."

"I know. Cut the lights," he ordered. "Get Mr. Dressler a beer." He addressed this to the man he had hired to see to Sam's needs on the location shoot. The individual attention had been Phil's way of handling Dressler and thus far had had its benefits. "Sit down for a while, Sam," he suggested. "We'll cool off." He waited until Sam was seated at a rear table with a portable fan and a beer before he plucked a can from the cooler himself.

"Hot work," Marlie commented, leaning against the bar.

Glancing over, Phil noted the line of sweat that ran down the front of her snug blouse. He passed her the can of beer. "You're doing fine."

"It's a hell of a part," she said before she took a deep drink. "I've been waiting for one like this for a long time."

"The next take," Phil began, narrowing his eyes, "when you say the bit about sweat and dust, I want you to grab his shirt and pull him to you."

Marlie thought it over, then set the can on the bar. "Like this?...*There's nothing,*" she spat out, grabbing Phil's damp shirt, "*nothing in this town but sweat and dust.*" She put her other hand to his shirt and pulled him closer. "*Even the dreams have dust on them.*"

"Good."

Marlie flashed a smile before she picked up the beer again. ''Better warn Sam,'' she suggested, offering Phil the can. ''He doesn't like improvising.''

''Hey, Phil.'' Phil glanced over to see Steve with his hand on the doorknob. ''That kid's outside with the sheriff. Wants to know if they can watch.''

Phil took a long, slow drink. ''They can sit in the back of the room.'' His eyes met Tory's as she entered. It had been two days since their meeting in the cemetery. Since then there had been no opportunity—or she'd seen to it that there'd been none—for any private conversation. She met the look, nodded to him, then urged Tod back to a rear table.

''The law of the land,'' Marlie murmured, causing Phil to look at her in question. ''She's quite a woman, isn't she?''

''Yes.''

Marlie grinned before she commandeered the beer again. ''Merle thinks she's the greatest thing to come along since sliced bread.''

Phil pulled out a cigarette. ''You're seeing quite a bit of the deputy, aren't you? Doesn't seem your style.''

''He's a nice guy,'' she said simply, then laughed. ''His boss would like me run out of town on a rail.''

''She's protective.''

With an unintelligible murmur that could have meant anything, Marlie ran her fingers through her disordered cap of curls. ''At first I thought she had something going with him.'' In response to Phil's quick laugh she lifted a thin, penciled brow. ''Of course, that was before I saw the way you looked at her.'' It was her turn to laugh when

Phil's expression became aloof. "Damn, Phil, you can look like your father sometimes." After handing him the empty can of beer, she turned away. "Makeup!" she demanded.

"Those are 4Ks," Tod was telling Tory, pointing to lights. "They have to put that stuff over the windows so the sun doesn't screw things up. On an inside shoot like this, they have to have something like 175-foot candles."

"You're getting pretty technical, aren't you?"

Tod shifted a bit in his chair, but his eyes were excited when they met Tory's. "Mr. Kincaid had them develop the film I shot in the portable lab. He said it was good. He said there were schools I could go to to learn about cinematography."

She cast a look in Phil's direction, watching him discuss something in undertones with Steve. "You're spending quite a lot of time with him," she commented.

"Well, when he's not busy... He doesn't mind."

"No, I'm sure he doesn't." She gave his hand a squeeze.

Tod returned the pressure boldly. "I'd rather spend time with you," he murmured.

Tory glanced down at their joined hands, wishing she knew how to begin. "Tod..."

"Quiet on the set!"

With a sigh Tory turned her attention to the scene in front of the bar. She'd come because Tod had been so pitifully eager that she share his enthusiasm. And she felt it was good for him to take such an avid interest in the technical aspects of the production. Unobtrusively she had kept her eye on him over the past days, watching him with members of the film crew. Thus far, no one appeared to object to his presence or his questions. In fact, Tory mused, he was becoming a kind of mascot. More and more his conversations were accented with the jargon of the industry. His mind seemed to soak up the terms, and his understanding was almost intuitive. He didn't appear to be interested in the glamorous end of it.

And what was so glamorous about it? she asked herself. The room was airless and steaming. It smelled, none too pleasantly, of old beer. The lights had the already unmerciful temperature rising. The two people in position by the bar were circled by equipment. How could they be so intense with each other, she wondered, when lights and cameras were all but on top of them? Yet, despite herself, Tory became engrossed with the drama of the scene.

Marlie's character was tormenting Sam's, ridiculing him for coming back a loser, taunting him. But somehow a rather abrasive strength came through in her character. She seemed a woman trapped by circumstances who was determined to fight her way out. Somehow she made the differences in their ages inconsequential. As the scene unfolded, an objective viewer would develop a respect for her, perhaps a cautious sympathy. Before long the viewer would be rooting for her. Tory wondered if Dressler realized, for all his reputation and skill, who would be the real star of this scene.

She's very good, Tory admitted silently. Marlie Summers wasn't the pampered, glittery Tinsel Town cutie Tory had been ready to believe her to be. Tory recognized strength when she saw it. Marlie infused both a grit and a vulnerability into the character that was instantly admirable. And the sweat, Tory continued, was her own.

"Cut!" Phil's voice jolted her in her chair. "That's it." Tory saw Marlie exhale a long breath. She wondered if there was some similarity in finishing a tense scene such as that one and winding up a difficult cross-examination. She decided that the emotion might be very much the same.

"Let's get some reaction shots, Marlie." Painstakingly he arranged for the change in angles and lighting. When the camera was in position, he checked through the lens himself, repositioned Marlie, then checked again. "Roll it.... Cue."

They worked for another thirty minutes, perfecting the shot. It was more than creativity, more than talent. The nuts and bolts end of the filming were tough, technical and wearily repetitious. No one complained, no one questioned, when told to change or to do over. There was an unspoken bond: the film. Perhaps, she reflected, it was because they knew it would outlast all of them. Their small slice of immortality. Tory found herself developing a respect for these people who took such an intense pride in their work.

"Cut. That's a wrap." Tory could almost feel the communal sigh of relief. "Set up for scene fifty-three in..." Phil checked his watch—"two hours." The moment the lights shut down, the temperature dropped.

"I'm going to see what Mr. Bicks is doing," Tod announced, scrambling up. Tory remained sitting where she was a moment, watching Phil answer questions and give instructions. He never stops, she realized. One might be an actor, another a lighting expert or a cinematographer, but he touches every aspect. Rich and privileged, yes, she reflected, but not afraid of hard work.

"Sheriff."

Tory turned her head to see Marlie standing beside her. "Ms. Summers. You were very impressive."

"Thanks." Without waiting for an invitation, Marlie took a chair. "What I need now is a three-hour shower." She took a long pull from the glass of ice water she held in her hand as the two women studied each other in silence. "You've got an incredible face," Marlie said at length. "If I'd had one like that, I wouldn't have had to fight for a part with some meat on it. Mine's like a sugarplum."

Tory found herself laughing. Leaning back, she hooked her arm over the back of her chair. "Ms. Summers, as sheriff, I should warn you that stealing's a crime. You stole that scene from Sam very smoothly."

Tilting her head, Marlie studied her from a new angle. "You're very sharp."

"On occasion."

"I can see why Merle thinks you hold the answer to the mysteries of the universe."

Tory sent her a long, cool look. "Merle is a very naive, very vulnerable young man."

"Yes." Marlie set down her glass. "I like him." They gave each other another measuring look. "Look, let me ask you something, from one attractive woman to another. Did you ever find it pleasant to be with a man who liked to talk to you, to listen to you?"

"Yes, of course." Tory frowned. "Perhaps it's that I can't imagine what Merle would say to interest you."

Marlie gave a quick laugh, then cupped her chin on her palm. "You're too used to him. I've been scrambling my way up the ladder since I was eighteen. There's nothing I want more than to be on top. Along the way, I've met a lot of men. Merle's different."

"If he falls in love with you, he'll be hurt," Tory pointed out. "I've looked out for him on and off since we were kids."

Marlie paused a moment. Idly she drew patterns through the condensation on the outside of her water glass. "He's not going to fall in love with me," she said slowly. "Not really. We're just giving each other a bit of the other's world for a few weeks. When it's over, we'll both have something nice to remember." She glanced over her shoulder and spotted Phil. "We all need someone now and again, don't we, Sheriff?"

Tory followed the direction of Marlie's gaze. At that moment Phil's eyes lifted to hers. "Yes," she murmured, watching him steadily. "I suppose we do."

"I'm going to get that shower now." Marlie rose. "He's a good man," she added. Tory looked back at her, knowing who she referred to now.

"Yes, I think you're right." Deep in thought, Tory sat a moment longer. Then, standing, she glanced around for Tod.

"Tory." Phil laid a hand on her arm. "How are you?"

"Fine." She smiled, letting him know she hadn't forgotten the last time they had been together. "You're tougher than I thought, Kincaid, working in this oven all day.''

He grinned. ''That, assuredly, is a compliment.''

''Don't let it go to your head. You're sweating like a pig.''

''Really,'' he said dryly. ''I hadn't noticed.''

She spotted a towel hung over the back of a chair and plucked it up. ''You know,'' she said as she wiped off his face, ''I imagined directors would do more delegating than you do.''

''My film,'' he said simply, stirred by the way she brushed the cloth over his face. ''Tory.'' He captured her free hand. ''I want to see you—alone.''

She dropped the towel back on the table. ''Your film,'' she reminded him. ''And there's something I have to do.'' Her eyes darted past him, again in search of Tod.

''Tonight,'' he insisted. He'd gone beyond the point of patience. ''Take the evening off, Tory.''

She brought her eyes back to his. She'd gone beyond the point of excuses. ''If I can,'' she agreed. ''There's a place I know,'' she added with a slow smile. ''South of town, about a mile. We used it as a swimming hole when I was a kid. You can't miss it; it's the only water around.''

''Sunset?'' He would have lifted her hand to his lips, but she drew it away.

''I can't promise.'' Before he could say anything else, she stepped past him, then called for Tod.

Even as she drew the boy back outside, he was expounding. ''Tory, it's great, isn't it? About the greatest thing to happen in town in forever! If I could, I'd go with them when they leave.'' He sent her a look from under his tumbled hair. ''Wouldn't you like to go, Tory?''

''To Hollywood?'' she replied lightly. ''Oh, I don't think it's my style. Besides, I'll be going back to Albuquerque soon.''

''I want to come with you,'' he blurted out.

They were just outside her office door. Tory turned and looked down at him. Unable to resist, she placed her hand on his cheek. ''Tod,'' she said softly.

''I love you, Tory,'' he began quickly. ''I could—''

''Tod, come inside.'' For days she had been working out what she would say to him and how to say it. Now, as they walked together into her office, she felt completely inadequate. Carefully she sat on the edge of her desk and faced him. ''Tod—'' She broke off and shook her head. ''Oh, I wish I were smarter.''

''You're the smartest person I know,'' he said swiftly. ''And so beautiful, and I love you, Tory, more than anything.''

Her heart reached out for him even as she took his hands. ''I love you, too, Tod.'' As he started to speak she shook her head again. ''But there are different kinds of love, different ways of feeling.''

''I only know how I feel about you.'' His eyes were very intense and just above hers as she sat on the desk. Phil had been right, she realized. He wasn't quite a child.

''Tod, I know this won't be easy for you to understand. Sometimes people aren't right for each other.''

''Just because I'm younger,'' he began heatedly.

''That's part of it,'' Tory agreed, keeping her voice quiet. ''It's hard to accept, when you feel like a man, that you're still a boy. There's so much you have to experience yet, and to learn."

"But when I do..." he began.

"When you do," she interrupted, "you won't feel the same way about me."

"Yes, I will!" he insisted. He surprised both of them by grabbing her arms. "It won't change because I don't want it to. And I'll wait if I have to. I love you, Tory."

"I know you do. I know it's very real." She lifted her hands to cover his. "Age doesn't mean anything to the heart, Tod. You're very special to me, a very important part of my life."

"But you don't love me." The words trembled out with anger and frustration.

"Not in the way you mean." She kept her hands firm on his when he would have jerked away.

"You think it's funny."

"No," she said sharply, rising. "No, I think it's lovely. And I wish things could be different because I know the kind of man you'll be. It hurts—for me too."

He was breathing quickly, struggling with tears and a sharp sense of betrayal. "You don't understand," he accused, pulling away from her. "You don't care."

"I do. Tod, please—"

"No." He stopped her with one ravaged look. "You don't." With a dignity that tore at Tory's heart, he walked out of the office.

She leaned back against the desk, overcome by a sense of failure.

The sun was just setting when Tory dropped down on the short, prickly grass by the water. Pulling her knees to her chest, she watched the flaming globe sink toward the horizon. There was an intensity of color against the darkening blue of the sky. Nothing soft or mellow. It was a vivid and demanding prelude to night.

Tory watched the sky with mixed emotions. The day as a whole was the kind she would have liked to wrap up and ship off to oblivion. The situation with Tod had left her emotionally wrung out and edgy. As a result she had handled a couple of routine calls with less finesse than was her habit. She'd even managed to snarl at Merle before she had gone off duty. Glancing down at the badge on her breast, she considered tossing it into the water.

A beautiful mess you've made of things, Sheriff, she told herself. Ah, the hell with it, she decided, resting her chin on her knees. She was taking the night off. Tomorrow she would straighten everything out, one disaster at a time.

The trouble was, she thought with a half smile, she'd forgotten the art of relaxation over the past few weeks. It was time to reacquaint herself with laziness. Laying back, Tory shut her eyes and went instantly to sleep.

Drifting slowly awake with the feather-light touch of fingers on her cheek. Tory gave a sleepy sigh and debated whether she should open her eyes. There was another touch—a tracing of her lips this time. Enjoying the sensation, she made a quiet sound of pleasure and let her lashes flutter up.

The light was dim, deep, deep dusk. Her eyes focused gradually on the sky above her. No clouds, no stars, just a mellow expanse of blue. Taking a deep breath, she lifted her arms to stretch. Her hand was captured and kissed. Tory turned her head and saw Phil sitting beside her.

"Hello."

"Watching you wake up is enough to drive a man crazy," he murmured, keeping her hand in his. "You're sexier sleeping than most women are wide awake."

She gave a lazy laugh. "Sleeping's always been one of my best things. Have you been here long?"

"Not long. The filming ran a bit over schedule." He flexed his back muscles, then smiled down at her. "How was your day?"

"Rotten." Tory blew out a breath and struggled to sit up. "I talked with Tod this afternoon. I didn't handle it well. Damn." Tory rested her forehead on her knees again. "I didn't want to hurt that boy."

"Tory"—Phil stroked a hand down her hair—"there was no way he wouldn't be hurt some. Kids are resilient; he'll bounce back."

"I know." She turned her head to look at him, keeping her cheeks on her knees. "But he's so fragile. Love's fragile, isn't it? So easily shattered. I suppose it's best that he hate me for a while."

"He won't." Phil disagreed. "You mean too much to him. After a while his feelings will slip into perspective. I imagine he'll always think of you as his first real love."

"It makes me feel very special, but I don't think I made him believe that. Anyway," she continued, "after I'd made a mess out of that, I snarled at one of the town fathers, bit off the head of a rancher and took a few swipes at Merle." She swore with the expertise he had admired before. "Sitting here, I knew I was in danger of having a major pity party, so I went to sleep instead."

"Wise choice. I came near to choking my overseer."

"Overseer? Oh, the guarantor." Tory laughed, shaking back her hair. "So we both had a lovely day."

"Let's drink to it." Phil picked up a bottle of champagne from beside him.

"Well, how about that." Tory glanced at the label and pursed her lips. "You always go first class, Kincaid."

"Absolutely," he agreed, opening the bottle with a pop and fizz. He poured the brimming wine into a glass. Tory took it, watching the bubbles explode as he filled his own. "To the end of the day."

"To the end of the day!" she agreed, clinking her glass against his. The ice-cold champagne ran excitedly over her tongue. "Nice," she murmured, shutting her eyes and savoring. "Very nice."

They drank in companionable silence as the darkness deepened. Overhead a few stars flickered hesitantly while the moon started its slow rise. The night was as hot and dry as the afternoon and completely still. There wasn't even a whisper of breeze to ripple the water. Phil leaned back on an elbow, studying Tory's profile.

"What are you thinking?"

"That I'm glad I took the night off." Smiling, she turned her head so she faced him fully. The pale light of the moon fell over her features, accenting them.

"Good God, Tory," he breathed. "I've got to get that face on film."

She threw back her head and laughed with a freedom she hadn't felt in days. "So take a home movie, Kincaid."

"Would you let me?" he countered immediately.

She merely filled both glasses again. "You're obsessed," she told him.

"More than's comfortable, yes," he murmured. He sipped, enjoying the taste, but thinking of her. "I wasn't sure you'd come."

"Neither was I." She studied the wine in her glass with apparent concentration. "Another glass of this and I might admit I enjoy being with you."

"We've half a bottle left."

Tory lifted one shoulder in a shrug before she drank again. "One step at a time," she told him. "But then," she murmured, "I suppose we've come a few steps already, haven't we?"

"A few." His fingers ran over the back of her hand. "Does it worry you?"

She gave a quick, rueful laugh. "More than's comfortable, yes."

Sitting up, he draped a casual arm around her shoulders. "I like the night best. I have the chance to think." He sensed her complete relaxation, feeling a pleasant stir as she let her head rest on his shoulder. "During the day, with all the pressure, the demands, when I think, I think on my feet."

"That's funny." She lifted a hand across her body to lace her fingers with his. "In Albuquerque I did some of my best planning in bed the night before a court date. It's easier to let things come and go in your head at night." Tilting her face, Tory brushed his lips with hers. "I do enjoy being with you."

He returned the kiss, but with equal lightness. "I didn't need the champagne?"

"Well...it didn't hurt." When he chuckled, she settled her head in the crook of his shoulder again. It felt right there, as if it belonged. "I've always loved this spot," Tory said quietly. "Water's precious around here, and this has always been like a little mirage. It's not very big, but it's pretty deep in places. The townspeople enjoy calling it a lake." She laughed suddenly. "When we were kids, we'd troop out here sometimes on an unbearably hot day. We'd strip and jump in. Of course, it was frowned on when we were teenagers, but we still managed."

"Our decadent youth."

"Good, clean fun, Kincaid," she disagreed.

"Oh, yeah? Why don't you show me?"

Tory turned to him with a half smile. When he only lifted a brow in challenge, she grinned. A small pulse of excitement beat deep inside her. "You're on." Pushing him away, she tugged off her shoes. "The name of the game is to get in first."

As he stripped off his shirt it occurred to him that he'd never seen her move quickly before. He was still pulling off his shoes when she was naked and racing for the water. The moonlight danced over her skin, over the hair that streamed behind her back, causing him to stop and stare after her. She was even more exquisite than he had imagined. Then she was splashing up to her waist and diving under. Shaking himself out of the trance, Phil stripped and followed her.

The water was beautifully cool. It shocked his heated skin on contact, then caressed it. Phil gave a moan of pure pleasure as he sank to his shoulders. The small swimming hole in the middle of nowhere gave him just as much relief as his custom-made pool. More, he realized, glancing around for Tory. She surfaced, face lifted, hair slicked back. The moonlight caught the glisten of water on her face. A naiad, he thought. She opened her eyes. They glimmered green, like a cat's.

"You're slow, Kincaid."

He struggled against an almost painful flood of desire. This wasn't the moment to rush. They both knew this was their time, and there were hours yet to fill. "I've never seen you move fast before," he commented, treading water.

"I save it up." The bottom was just below her toes. Tory kicked lazily to keep afloat. "Conserving energy is one of my personal campaigns."

"I guess that means you don't want to race."

She gave him a long look. "You've got to be kidding."

"Guess you wouldn't be too hard to beat," he considered. "Skinny," he added.

"I am not." Tory put the heel of her hand into the water, sending a spray into his face.

"Couple of months in a good gym might build you up a bit." He smiled, calmly wiping the water from his eyes.

"I'm built up just fine," she returned. "Is this amateur psychology, Kincaid?"

"Did it work?" he countered.

In answer she twisted and struck out, kicking up a curtain of water into his face as she headed for the far side of the pool. Phil grinned, observing that she could move like lightning when she put her mind to it, then started after her.

She beat him by two full strokes, then waited, laughing, while she shook back her hair. "Better keep up your membership to that gym, Kincaid."

"You cheated," he pointed out.

"I won. That's what counts."

He lifted a brow, amused and intrigued that she wasn't even winded. Apparently her statement about strong energy was perfectly true. "And that from an officer of the law."

"I'm not wearing my badge."

"I noticed."

Tory laughed again, moving out in a gentle sidestroke toward the middle of the pool. "I guess you're in pretty good shape…for a Hollywood director."

"Is that so?" He swam alongside of her, matching her languid movements.

"You don't have a paunch—yet," she added, grinning. Gently but firmly, Phil pushed her head under. "So you want to play dirty," she murmured when she surfaced. In a quick move she had his legs scissored between hers, then gave his chest a firm shove. Off guard, Phil went over backward and submerged. He came up, giving his head a toss to free his eyes of dripping hair. Tory was already a few yards away, treading water and chuckling.

"Basic Self-Defense 101," she informed him. "Though you have to make allowances for buoyancy in the water."

This time Phil put more effort into his strokes. Before Tory had reached the other side, he had a firm grip on her ankle. With a tug he took her under the water and back to him. Sputtering, she found herself caught in his arms.

"Want to try a few free throws?" he invited.

A cautious woman, Tory measured her opponent and the odds. "I'll pass. Water isn't my element."

Her arms were trapped between their bodies, but when she tried to free them, he only brought her closer. His smile faded into a look of understanding. She felt her heart begin a slow, dull thud.

He took her mouth with infinite care, wanting to savor the moment. Her lips were wet and cool. With no hesitation her tongue sought his. The kiss deepened slowly, luxuriously while he supported her, keeping her feet just above the sandy bottom. The feeling of weightlessness aroused her and she allowed herself to float, holding on to him as though he were an anchor. Their lips warmed from an intimate heat before they began to search for new tastes.

Without hurry they roamed each other's faces, running moist kisses over moist skin. With quiet whispers the water lapped around them as they shifted and searched.

Finding her arms free at last, Tory wrapped them about his neck, pressing her body against his. She heard Phil suck in his breath at the contact, felt the shudder race through him before his mouth crushed down on hers. The time had passed for slow loving. Passion too long suppressed exploded as mouth sought eager mouth. Keeping one arm firm at her waist, he began to explore her as he had longed to do. His fingers slid over her wet skin.

Tory moved against him, weakening them both so that they submerged, locked together. Streaming wet, they surfaced with their lips still fused, then gasped for air. Her hands ran over him, drawing him closer, then away, to seek more of him. Unable to bear the hunger, she thrust her fingers into his hair and pulled his lips back to hers. With a sudden violence he bent her back until her hair streamed behind her on the surface of the water. His mouth rushed over her face, refusing her efforts to halt it with hers while he found her breast with his palm.

The throaty moan that wrenched from her evoked a new wave of passion. Phil lifted her so he could draw her hot, wet nipple into his mouth. His tongue tormented them both until her hands fell into the pool in a submission he hadn't expected. Drunk on power, he took his mouth over her trembling skin, down to where the water separated him from her. Frustrated with the barrier, he let his mouth race up again to her breast until Tory clutched at his shoulders, shuddering.

Her head fell back as he lowered her so that her neck was vulnerable and glistening in the moonlight. He kissed it hungrily, hearing her cry with anguished delight.

Cool, cool water, but she was so hot that his legs nearly buckled at the feel of her. Tory was beyond all but dark, vivid sensations. To her the water felt steamy, heated by her own body. Her breathing seemed to echo in the empty night, then shudder back to her. She would have shouted for him to take her, but his name would only come as a gasp through her lips. She couldn't bear it; the need was unreasonable. With a strength conceived in passion she locked her legs tightly around his waist and lowered herself to him.

They swayed for a moment, equally stunned. Then he

gripped her legs, letting her take him on a wild, impossible journey. There was a rushing, like the sound of the wind inside her head. Trembling, they slid down into the water.

With some vague recollection of where they were, Phil caught Tory against him again. ''We'd better get out of here,'' he managed. ''We'll drown.''

Tory let her head fall on his shoulder. ''I don't mind.''

With a low, shaky laugh, Phil lifted her into his arms and carried her from the pond.

Chapter 8

He laid her down, then dropped on his back on the grass beside her. For some time the only sound in the night was their mixed breathing. The stars were brilliant now, the moon nearly full. Both of them stared up.

"You were saying something," Phil began in a voice that still wasn't steady, "about water not being your element."

Tory gave a choke of laughter that turned into a bubble, then a burst of pure appreciation. "I guess I could be wrong."

Phil closed his eyes, the better to enjoy the heavy weakness that flowed through his system.

Tory sighed and stretched. "That was wonderful."

He drew her closer against his side. "Cold?"

"No."

"This grass—"

"Terrible, isn't it?" With another laugh Tory twisted so that she lay over his chest. Her wet skin slid over his. Lazily he ran a hand down the length of her back as she smiled back at him. Her hair was slicked close to her head, her skin as pale and exquisite as marble in the moonlight. A few small drops of water clung to her lashes.

"You're beautiful when you're wet," he told her, drawing her down for a slow, lingering kiss.

"So are you." When he grinned, she ran both thumbs from his jaw to his cheekbones. "I like your face," she decided, tilting her head as she studied it. "That aristocratic bone structure you get from your father. It's no wonder he was so effective playing those swashbuckling roles early in his career." She narrowed her eyes as if seeking a different perspective. "Of course," she continued thoughtfully, "I rather like it when yours takes on that aloof expression."

"Aloof?" He shifted a bit as the grass scratched his bare skin.

"You do it very well. Your eyes have a terrific way of saying 'I beg your pardon' and meaning 'Go to hell.' I've noticed it, especially when you talk to that short man with the little glasses."

"Tremaine," Phil muttered. "Associate producer and general pain in the neck."

Tory chuckled and kissed his chin. "Don't like anyone else's hands on your movie, do you?"

"I'm very selfish with what belongs to me." He took her mouth again with more fervor than he had intended. As the kiss lengthened and deepened he gave a quick sound of pleasure and pressed her closer. When their lips parted, their eyes met. Both of them knew they were heading for dangerous ground. Both of them treaded carefully. Tory lowered her head to his chest, trying to think logically.

"I suppose we knew this was going to happen sooner or later."

"I suppose we did."

She caught her bottom lip between her teeth a moment. "The important thing is not to let it get complicated."

"No." He frowned up at the stars. "We both want to avoid complications."

"In a few weeks we'll both be leaving town." They were unaware that they had tightened their holds on the other. "I have to pick up my case load again."

"I have to finish the studio scenes," he murmured.

"It's a good thing we understand each other right from the beginning." She closed her eyes, drawing in his scent as though she were afraid she might forget it. "We can be together like this, knowing no one will be hurt when it's over."

"Yeah."

They lay in silence, dealing with a mutual and unstated sense of depression and loss. We're adults, Tory thought, struggling against the mood. Attracted to each other. It isn't any more than that. Can't be any more than that. But she wasn't as sure of herself as she wanted to be.

"Well," she said brightly, lifting her head again. "So tell me how the filming's going? That scene today seemed to click perfectly."

Phil forced himself to match her mood, ignoring the

doubts forming in his own head. "You came in on the last take," he said dryly. "It was like pulling teeth."

Tory reached across him for the bottle of champagne. The glass was covered with beads of sweat. "It looked to me like Marlie Summers came out on top," she commented as she poured.

"She's very good."

Resting her arm on his chest, Tory drank. The wine still fizzled cold. "Yes, I thought so, too, but I wish she'd steer away from Merle."

"Worried about his virtue, Tory?" he asked dryly.

She shot him an annoyed look. "He's going to get hurt."

"Why?" he countered. "Because a beautiful woman's interested enough to spend some time with him? Now, look," he continued before she could retort, "you have your own view of him; it's possible someone else might have another."

Frowning, she drank again. "How's he going to feel when she leaves?"

"That's something he'll have to deal with," Phil said quietly. "He already knows she's going to."

Again their eyes met in quick, almost frightened recognition. Tory looked away to study the remaining wine in her glass. It was different, she told herself. She and Phil both had certain priorities. When they parted, it would be without regret or pain. It had to be.

"It might not be easy to accept," she murmured, wanting to believe she still spoke of Merle.

"On either side," he replied after a long pause.

Tory turned her head to find his eyes on hers, light and

clear and very intense. The ground was getting shaky again. ‘‘I suppose it’ll work out for the best...for everyone.’’ Determined to lighten the mood, she smiled down at him. ‘‘You know, the whole town’s excited about those scenes you’re shooting with them as extras. The Kramer twins haven’t gotten out of line for an entire week.’’

‘‘One of them asked me if he could have a close-up.’’

‘‘Which one?’’

‘‘Who the hell can tell?’’ Phil demanded. ‘‘This one tried to hustle a date with Marlie.’’

Tory laughed, pressing the back of her wrist to her mouth to hold in a swallow of champagne. ‘‘Had to be Zac. He’s impossible. Are you going to give him his close-up?’’

‘‘I’ll give him a swift kick in the pants if he messes around the crane again,’’ Phil returned.

‘‘Uh-oh, I didn’t hear about that.’’

Phil shrugged. ‘‘It didn’t seem necessary to call the law on him.’’

‘‘Tempting as it might be,’’ she returned. ‘‘I wouldn’t have thrown him in the penitentiary. Handling the Kramers has become an art.’’

‘‘I had one of my security guards put the fear of God into him,’’ Phil told her easily. ‘‘It seemed to do the trick.’’

‘‘Listen, Phil, if any of my people need restraining, I expect to be informed.’’

With a sigh, he plucked the glass from her hand, tossed it aside, then rolled on top of her. ‘‘You’ve got the night off, Sheriff. We’re not going to talk about it.’’

"Really." Her arms were already linked around his neck. "Just what are we going to talk about, then?"

"Not a damn thing," he muttered and pressed his mouth to hers.

Her response was a muffled sound of agreement. He could taste the champagne on her tongue and lingered over it. The heat of the night had already dried their skin, but he ran his hands through the cool dampness of her hair. He could feel her nipples harden against the pressure of his chest. This time, he thought, there would be no desperation. He could enjoy her slowly—the long, lean lines of her body, the silken texture of her skin, the varied, heady tastes of her.

From the wine-flavored lips he took an unhurried journey to the warmer taste of her throat. But his hands were already roaming demandingly. Tory moved under him with uncontrollable urgency as his thumb found the peak of her breast, intensifying her pleasure. To his amazement Phil found he could have taken her immediately. He banked the need. There was still so much of her to learn of, so much to experience. Allowing the tip of his tongue to skim along her skin, he moved down to her breast.

Tory arched, pressing him down. His slow, teasing kisses made her moan in delighted frustration. Beneath the swell of her breast, his mouth lingered to send shivers and more shivers of pleasure through her. His tongue flicked lazily over her nipple, then retreated to soft flesh. She moaned his name, urging him back. He circled slowly, mouth on one breast, palm on the other, thrilling to her mindless murmurs and convulsive movements beneath him. Taking exquisite care, he captured a straining peak between his teeth. Leaving it moist and wanting, he journeyed to her other breast to savor, to linger, then to devour.

His hands had moved lower, so that desire throbbed over her at so many points, she was delirious for fulfillment. Anxious to discover all she could about his body, Tory ran her fingertips over the taut muscles of his shoulders, down the strong back. Through a haze of sensation she felt him shudder at her touch. With delicious slowness she skimmed her fingers up his rib cage. She heard him groan before his teeth nipped into her tender flesh. Open and hungry, his mouth came swiftly back to hers.

When she reached for him, he drew in a sharp breath at the contact. Burying his face in her neck, Phil felt himself drowning in pleasure. The need grew huge, but again he refused it.

''Not yet,'' he murmured to himself and to her. ''Not yet.''

He passed down the valley between her breasts, wallowing in the hot scent that clung to her skin. Her stomach quivered under his lips. Tory no longer felt the rough carpet of grass under her back, only Phil's seeking mouth and caressing hands. His mouth slipped lower and she moaned, arching—willing, wanting. His tongue was quick and greedy, shooting pleasure from the core of her out even to her fingertips. Her body was heavy with it, her head light. He brought her to a shuddering crest, but relentlessly allowed no time for recovery. His fingers sought her even as his mouth found fresh delight in the taste of her thigh.

She shook her head, unable to believe she could be so

helpless. Her fingers clutched at the dry grass while her lips responded to the dizzying pace he set. Her skin was damp again, quivering in the hot night air. Again and again he drove her up, never letting her settle, never allowing her complete release.

''Phil,'' she moaned between harsh, shallow breaths. ''I need...''

He'd driven himself to the verge of madness. His body throbbed in one solid ache for her. Wildly he took his mouth on a frantic journey up her body. ''What?'' he demanded. ''What do you need?''

''You,'' she breathed, no longer aware of words or meanings. ''You.''

With a groan of triumph he thrust into her, catapulting them both closer to what they insisted on denying.

She'd warned him about the heat. Still, Phil found himself cursing the unrelenting sun as he set up for another outdoor shot. The grips had set up stands with butterflies—long black pieces of cloth—to give shade between takes. The cameraman stood under a huge orange and white umbrella and sweated profusely. The actors at least could spend a few moments in the shade provided while Phil worked almost exclusively in the streaming sun, checking angles, lighting, shadows. Reflectors were used to bounce the sunlight and carbon arcs balanced the back lighting. A gaffer, stripped to the waist, adjusted a final piece of blue gel over a bulb. The harsh, glaring day was precisely what Phil wanted, but it didn't make the work any more pleasant.

Forcing down more salt tablets, he ordered the next

take. Oddly, Dressler seemed to have adjusted to the heat more easily than the younger members of the cast and crew. Or, Phil mused as he watched him come slowly down the street with the fledgling actor who played his alter ego, he's determined not to be outdone. As time went on, he became more competitive—and the more competitive he became, particularly with Marlie, the more Phil was able to draw out of him.

Yeah, Phil thought as Dressler turned to the younger actor with a look of world-weariness. He ran through his dialogue slowly, keeping the pace just short of dragging. He was a man giving advice reluctantly, without any confidence that it was viable or would be listened to in any case. He talked almost to himself. For a moment Phil forgot his own discomfort in simple admiration for a pro who had found the heart of his character. He was growing old and didn't give a damn—wanted to be left alone, but had no hope that his wishes would be respected. Once he had found his moment of glory, then had lost it. He saw himself in the younger man and felt a bitter pity. Ultimately he turned and walked slowly away. The camera stayed on him for a silent thirty seconds.

"Cut. Perfect," Phil announced in a rare show of unconditional approval. "Lunch," he said dropping a hand on the younger actor's shoulder. "Get out of the sun for a while; I'll need you for reaction shots in thirty minutes." He walked over to meet Sam. "That was a hell of a job."

Grinning, Sam swiped at his brow. "Somebody's got to show these kids how it's done. That love scene with Marlie's going to be interesting," he added a bit ruefully. "I keep remembering she's my daughter's age."

"That should keep you in character."

Sam laughed, running his fingers through his thick salt-and-pepper hair. "Well, the girl's a pro," he said after a moment. "This movie's going to shoot her into the fast lane quick." He sent Phil a long, steady look. "And you and I," he added, "are going to win each other an Oscar." When Phil only lifted a brow, Sam slapped him on the back. "Don't give me that look, boy," he said, amused. "You're talking to one who's been passed over a few times himself. You can be lofty and say awards don't mean a damn…but they do." Again his eyes met Phil's. "I want this one just as much as you do." He ran a hand over his stomach. "Now I'm going to get myself a beer and put my feet up."

He sauntered off, leaving Phil looking after him. He didn't want to admit, even to himself, that he desired his profession's ultimate accolade. In a few short words Dressler had boiled it all down. Yes, he wanted to direct outstanding films—critically and financially successful, lasting, important. But he wanted that little gold statue. With a wry grin Phil swiped at his brow with his forearm. It seemed that the need to win, and to be acknowledged, didn't fade with years. Dressler had been in the business longer than Phil had been alive; yet, he was still waiting for the pot at the end of the rainbow. Phil adjusted his sunglasses, admitting he wasn't willing to wait thirty-five years.

"Hey, Phil." Bicks lumbered over to him, mopping his face. "Look, you've got to do something about that woman."

Phil pulled out a cigarette. "Which?"

"That sheriff." Bicks popped another piece of gum into his mouth. "Great looker," he added. "Got a way of walking that makes a man home right in on her..." He trailed off, observing the look in Phil's eyes. "Just an observation," he muttered.

"What do you expect me to do about the way Sheriff Ashton walks, Bicks?"

Catching the amusement in Phil's tone, Bicks grinned. "Nothing, please. A man's got to have something pleasant to look at in this place. But damn it, Phil, she gave me a ticket and slapped a two-hundred-and-fifty-dollar fine on me."

Phil pushed his glasses up on his head with a weary sigh. He'd wanted to catch a quick shower before resuming the shoot. "What for?"

"Littering."

"Littering?" Phil repeated over a snort of laughter.

"Two hundred and fifty bucks for dropping gum wrappers in the street," Bicks returned, not seeing the humor. "Wouldn't listen to reason either. I'd have picked 'em up and apologized. Two hundred and fifty bucks for a gum wrapper, Phil. Jeez."

"All right, all right, I'll talk to her." After checking his watch, Phil started up the street. "Set up for the next scene in twenty minutes."

Tory sat with her feet propped up on the desk as she struggled to decipher Merle's report on a feud between two neighboring ranches. It seemed that a dispute over a line of fence was becoming more heated. It was going to require her attention. So was the letter she had just received from one of her clients in Albuquerque. When Phil walked in, she glanced up from the scrawled pad and smiled.

"You look hot," she commented.

"Am hot," he countered, giving the squeaking fan above their heads a glance. "Why don't you get that thing fixed?"

"And spoil the atmosphere?"

Phil stepped over the sleeping dog, taking a seat on the corner of her desk. "We're going to be shooting one of the scenes with the townspeople milling around later. Are you going to watch?"

"Sure."

"Want to do a cameo?" he asked with a grin.

"No, thanks."

Leaning over, he pressed his lips to hers. "Dinner in my room tonight?"

Tory smiled. "You still have those candles?"

"All you want," he agreed.

"You talked me into it," she murmured, drawing his face back for a second kiss.

"Tory, if I brought a camera out to your ranch one day, would you let me film you riding that palomino?"

"Phil, for heaven's sake—"

"Home movies?" he interrupted, twirling her hair around his finger.

She gave a capitulating sigh. "If it's important to you."

"It is." He straightened, checked his watch, then pulled out a cigarette. "Listen, Tory, Bicks tells me you fined him for littering."

"That's right." The phone rang, and Phil waited while she took the call. After a moment he realized her tone was slightly different. With interest he listened to the legal jargon roll off her tongue. It must be Albuquerque, he realized. He watched her carefully, discovering this was a part of her life he knew nothing of. She'd be tough in court, he mused. There was an intensity under that languid exterior that slipped out at unexpected moments. And what did she do after a day in court or a day in the office?

There'd be men, he thought, instantly disliking the image. A woman like Tory would only spend evenings alone, nights alone, if she chose to. He looked away, taking a deep drag on his cigarette. He couldn't start thinking along those lines, he reminded himself. They were both free agents. That was the first rule.

"Phil?"

He turned back to see that she had replaced the receiver. "What?"

"You were saying?"

"Ah…" He struggled to remember the point of his visit. "Bicks," he continued.

"Yes, what about him?"

"A two-hundred-and-fifty-dollar fine for littering," Phil stated, not quite erasing the frown that had formed between his brows.

"Yes, that's the amount of the fine."

"Tory, be reasonable."

Her brow lifted. "Reasonable, Kincaid?"

Her use of his surname told him what level they were dealing on. "It's certainly extreme for a gum wrapper."

"We don't vary the fine according to the style of trash," she replied with an easy shrug. "A tin of caviar would have cost him the same amount."

Goaded, Phil rose. ''Listen, Sheriff—''

''And while we're on the subject,'' she interrupted, ''you can tell your people that if they don't start picking up after themselves more carefully, they're all going to be slapped with fines.'' She gave him a mild smile. ''Let's keep Friendly clean, Kincaid.''

He took a slow drag. ''You're not going to hassle my people.''

''You're not going to litter my town.''

He swore, coming around the desk when the door opened. Pleased to see Tod, Tory swung her legs to the floor and started to stand. It was then that she saw the dull bruise on the side of his face. Fury swept through her so quickly, she was forced to clench her hands into fists to control it. Slowly she walked to him and took his face in her hands.

''How did you get this?''

He shrugged, avoiding her eyes. ''It's nothing.''

Fighting for calm. Tory lifted his hands, examining the knuckles carefully. There was no sign that he'd been fighting. ''Your father?''

He shook his head briskly. ''I came to do the sweeping up,'' he told her, and tried to move away.

Tory took him firmly by the shoulders. ''Tod, look at me.''

Reluctantly he lifted his eyes. ''I've still got five dollars to work off,'' he said tightly.

''Did your father put this bruise on your face?'' she demanded. When he started to drop his eyes again, she gave him a quick shake. ''You answer me.''

''He was just mad because—'' He broke off, observing

the rage that lit her face. Instinctively he cringed away from it. Tory set him aside and started for the door.

"Where are you going?" Moving quickly, Phil was at the door with her, his hand over hers on the knob.

"To see Swanson."

"*No!*" They both turned to see Tod standing rigid in the center of the room. "No, you can't. He won't like it. He'll get awful mad at you."

"I'm going to talk to your father, Tod," Tory said in a careful voice, "to explain to him why it's wrong for him to hurt you this way."

"Only when he loses his temper." Tod dashed across the room to grab her free hand. "He's not a bad man. I don't want you to put him in jail."

Though her anger was lethal, Tory gave Tod's hand a reassuring squeeze. "I'm just going to talk to him, Tod."

"He'll be crazy mad if you do, Tory. I don't want him to hurt you either."

"He won't, don't worry." She smiled, seeing by the expression in Tod's eyes that she'd already been forgiven. "Go get the broom now. I'll be back soon."

"Tory, please..."

"Go on," she said firmly.

Phil waited until the boy had disappeared into the back room. "You're not going."

Tory sent him a long look, then pulled open the door. Phil spun her around as she stepped outside. "I said you're not going."

"You're interfering with the law, Kincaid."

"The hell with that!" Infuriated, Phil pushed her back

against the wall. "You're crazy if you think I'm going to let you go out there."

"You don't *let* me do anything," she reminded him. "I'm sworn to protect the people under my jurisdiction. Tod Swanson is one of my people."

"A man who punches a kid isn't going to hesitate to take a swing at you just because you've got that little piece of tin on your shirt."

Because her anger was racing, Tory forced herself to speak calmly. "What do you suggest I do? Ignore what I just saw?"

Frustrated by the image of Tod's thin face, Phil swore. "I'll go."

"You have no right." She met his eyes squarely. "You're not the law, and what's more, you're an outsider."

"Send Merle."

"Don't you hold with no woman sheriff, Kincaid?"

"Damn it, Tory." He shook her, half in fear, half in frustration. "This isn't a joke."

"No, it's not," she said seriously. "It's my job. Now, let go of me, Phil."

Furious, Phil complied, then watched her stride to her car. "Tory," he called after her, "if he puts a hand on you, I'll kill him."

She slipped into the car, driving off without looking back.

Tory took the short drive slowly, wanting to get her emotions under control before she confronted Swanson. She had to be objective, she thought, as her knuckles whitened on the steering wheel. But first she had to be calm. It wasn't possible to do what she needed to do in anger, or to let Phil's feelings upset her. To live up to the badge on her shirt, she had to set all that aside.

She wasn't physically afraid, not because she was foolishly brave, but because when she saw a blatant injustice, Tory forgot everything but the necessity of making it right. As she took the left fork toward the Swanson ranch, however, she had her first stirring of self-doubt.

What if she mishandled the situation? she thought in sudden panic. What if her meeting with Swanson only made more trouble for the boy? The memory of Tod's terrified face brought on a quick queasiness that she fought down. No, she wasn't going to mishandle it, she told herself firmly as the house came into view. She was going to confront Swanson and at the very least set the wheels in motion for making things right. Tory's belief that all things could be set right with patience, through the law, had been indoctrinated in childhood. She knew and accepted no other way.

She pulled up behind Swanson's battered pickup, then climbed out of the sheriff's car. Instantly a dog who had been sleeping on the porch sent out angry, warning barks. Tory eyed him a moment, wary, then saw that he came no farther than the edge of the sagging porch. He looked as old and unkempt as the house itself.

Taking a quick look around, Tory felt a stir of pity for Tod. This was borderline poverty. She, too, had grown up where a tightened belt was often a rule, but between her mother's penchant for neatness and the hard work of both her parents, their small ranch had always had a homey charm. This place, on the other hand, looked desolate and hopeless. The grass grew wild, long overdue for trimming. There were no brightening spots of color from flowers or potted plants. The house itself was frame, the paint faded down to the wood in places. There was no chair on the porch, no sign that anyone had the time or inclination to sit and appreciate the view.

No one came to the door in response to the dog's barking. Tory debated calling out from where she stood or taking a chance with the mangy mutt. A shout came from the rear of the house with a curse and an order to shut up. The dog obeyed, satisfying himself with low growls as Tory headed in the direction of the voice.

She spotted Swanson working on the fence of an empty corral. The back of his shirt was wet with sweat, while his hat was pulled low to shade his face. He was a short, stocky man with the strong shoulders of a laborer. Thinking of Tod's build, Tory decided he had inherited it, and perhaps his temperament, from his mother.

"Mr. Swanson?"

His head jerked up. He had been replacing a board on the fence; the hand that swung the hammer paused on the downswing. Seeing his face, Tory decided he had the rough, lined face of a man constantly fighting the odds of the elements. He narrowed his eyes; they passed briefly over her badge.

"Sheriff," he said briefly, then gave the nail a final whack. He cared little for women who interfered in a man's work.

"I'd like to talk to you, Mr. Swanson."

"Yeah?" He pulled another nail out of an old coffee can. "What about?"

"Tod." Tory waited until he had hammered the nail into the warped board.

"That boy in trouble?"

"Apparently," she said mildly. She told herself to overlook his rudeness as he turned his back to take out another nail.

"I handle my own," he said briefly. "What's he done?"

"He hasn't done anything, Mr. Swanson."

"Either he's in trouble or he's not." Swanson placed another nail in position and beat it into the wood. The sound echoed in the still air. From somewhere to the right, Tory heard the lazy moo of a cow. "I ain't got time for conversation, Sheriff."

"He's in trouble, Mr. Swanson," she returned levelly. "And you'll talk to me here or in my office."

The tone had him taking another look and measuring her again. "What do you want?"

"I want to talk to you about the bruise on your son's face." She glanced down at the meaty hands, noting that the knuckles around the hammer whitened.

"You've got no business with my boy."

"Tod's a minor," she countered. "He's very much my business."

"I'm his father."

"And as such, you are not entitled to physically or emotionally abuse your child."

"I don't know what the hell you're talking about." The

color in his sun reddened face deepened angrily. Tory's eyes remained calm and direct.

"I'm well aware that you've beaten the boy before," she said coolly. "There are very strict laws to protect a child against this kind of treatment. If they're unknown to you, you might want to consult an attorney."

"I don't need no damn lawyer," he began, gesturing at Tory with the hammer as his voice rose.

"You will if you point that thing at me again," she told him quietly. "Attempted assault on a peace officer is a very serious crime."

Swanson looked down at the hammer, then dropped it disgustedly to the ground. "I don't assault women," he muttered.

"Just children?"

He sent her a furious glance from eyes that watered against the sun. "I got a right to discipline my own. I got a ranch to run here." A gesture with his muscular arm took in his pitiful plot of land. "Every time I turn around, that boy's off somewheres."

"Your reasons don't concern me. The results do."

With rage burning on his face, he took a step toward her. Tory held her ground. "You just get back in your car and get out. I don't need nobody coming out here telling me how to raise my boy."

Tory kept her eyes on his, although she was well aware his hands had clenched into fists. "I can start proceedings to make Tod a ward of the court."

"You can't take my boy from me."

Tory lifted a brow. "Can't I?"

"I got rights," he blustered.

"So does Tod."

He swallowed, then turned back to pick up his hammer and nails. "You ain't taking my boy."

Something in his eyes before he had turned made Tory pause. Justice, she reminded herself, was individual. "He wouldn't want me to," she said in a quieter tone. "He told me you were a good man and asked me not to put you in jail. You bruise his face, but he doesn't stop loving you."

She watched Swanson's back muscles tighten. Abruptly he flung the hammer and the can away. Nails scattered in the wild grass. "I didn't mean to hit him like that," he said with a wrench in his voice that kept Tory silent. "Damn boy should've fixed this fence like I told him." He ran his hands over his face. "I didn't mean to hit him like that. Look at this place," he muttered, gripping the top rail of the fence. "Takes every minute just to keep it up and scrape by, never amount to anything. But it's all I got. All I hear from Tod is how he wants to go off to school, how he wants this and that, just like—"

"His brother?" Tory ventured.

Swanson turned his head slowly, and his face was set. "I ain't going to talk about that."

"Mr. Swanson, I know something about what it takes to keep up a place like this. But your frustrations and your anger are no excuse for misusing your boy."

He turned away again, the muscles in his jaw tightening. "He's gotta learn."

"And your way of teaching him is to use your fists?"

"I tell you I didn't mean to hit him." Furious, he whirled back to her. "I don't mean to take a fist to him the way my father done to me. I know it ain't right, but when he pushes me—'' He broke off again, angry with himself for telling his business to an outsider. ''I ain't going to hit him anymore,'' he muttered.

''But you've told yourself that before, haven't you?'' Tory countered. ''And meant it, I'm sure.'' She took a deep breath, as he only stared at her. ''Mr. Swanson, you're not the only parent who has a problem with control. There are groups and organizations designed to help you and your family.''

''I'm not talking to any psychiatrists and do-gooders.''

''There are ordinary people, exactly like yourself, who talk and help each other.''

''I ain't telling strangers my business. I can handle my own.''

''No, Mr. Sawnson, you can't.'' For a moment Tory wished helplessly that there was an easy answer. ''You don't have too many choices. You can drive Tod away, like you did your first boy.'' Tory stood firm as he whirled like a bull. ''Or,'' she continued calmly, ''you can seek help, the kind of help that will justify your son's love for you. Perhaps your first decision is what comes first, your pride or your boy.''

Swanson stared out over the empty corral. ''It would kill his mother if he took off too.''

''I have a number you can call, Mr. Swanson. Someone who'll talk to you, who'll listen. I'll give it to Tod.''

His only acknowledgment was a shrug. She waited a moment, praying her judgment was right. ''I don't like ultimatums,'' she continued. ''But I'll expect to see Tod daily. If he doesn't come to town, I'll come here. Mr.

Swanson, if there's a mark on that boy, I'll slap a warrant on you and take Tod into custody."

He twisted his head to look at her again. Slowly, measuringly, he nodded. "You've got a lot of your father in you, Sheriff."

Automatically Tory's hand rose to her badge. She smiled for the first time. "Thanks." Turning, she walked away. Not until she was out of sight did she allow herself the luxury of wiping her sweaty palms on the thighs of her jeans.

Chapter 9

Tory was stopped at the edge of town by a barricade. Killing the engine, she stepped out of the car as one of Phil's security men approached her.

"Sorry, Sheriff, you can't use the main street. They're filming."

With a shrug Tory leaned back on the hood of her car. "It's all right. I'll wait."

The anger that had driven her out to the Swanson ranch was gone. Now Tory appreciated the time to rest and think. From her vantage point she could see the film crew and the townspeople who were making their debut as extras. She watched Hollister walk across the street in back of two actors exchanging lines in the scene. It made Tory smile, thinking how Hollister would brag about this moment of glory for years to come. There were a dozen people she knew, milling on the streets or waiting for their opportunity to mill. Phil cut the filming, running through take after take. Even with the distance Tory could sense he was frustrated. She frowned, wondering if their next encounter would turn into a battle. She couldn't back down, knowing that she had done the right thing—essentially the only thing.

Their time together was to be very brief, she mused. She didn't want it plagued by arguments and tension. But until he accepted the demands and responsibilities of her job, tension was inevitable. It had already become very important to Tory that the weeks ahead be unmarred. Perhaps, she admitted thoughtfully, too important. It was becoming more difficult for her to be perfectly logical when she thought of Phil. And since the night before, the future had become blurred and distant. There seemed to be only the overwhelming present.

She couldn't afford that, Tory reminded herself. That wasn't what either one of them had bargained for. She shifted her shoulders as her shirt grew hot and damp against her back. There was the summer, and just the summer, before they both went their separate ways. It was, of course, what each of them wanted.

"Sheriff…ah, Sheriff Ashton?"

Disoriented, Tory shook her head and stared at the man beside her. "What—? Yes?"

The security guard held out a chilled can of soda. "Thought you could use this."

"Oh, yeah, thanks." She pulled the tab, letting the air out in a hiss. "Do you think they'll be much longer?"

"Nah." He lifted his own can to drink half of it down

without a breath. ''They've been working on this one scene over an hour now.''

Gratefully, Tory let the icy drink slide down her dry throat. ''Tell me, Mr.—''

''Benson, Chuck Benson, ma'am.''

''Mr. Benson,'' Tory continued, giving him an easy smile. ''Have you had any trouble with any of the townspeople?''

''Nothing to speak of,'' he said as he settled beside her against the hood. ''Couple of kids—those twins.''

''Oh, yes,'' Tory murmured knowingly.

''Only tried to con me into letting them on the crane.'' He gave an indulgent laugh, rubbing the cold can over his forehead to cool it. ''I've got a couple teenagers of my own,'' he explained.

''I'm sure you handled them, Mr. Benson.'' Tory flashed him a dashing smile that lifted his blood pressure a few degrees. ''Still, I'd appreciate hearing about it if anyone in town gets out of line—particularly the Kramer twins.''

Benson chuckled. ''I guess those two keep you busy.''

''Sometimes they're a full-time job all by themselves.'' Tory rested a foot on the bumper and settled herself more comfortably. ''So tell me, how old are your kids?''

By the time Phil had finished shooting the scene, he'd had his fill of amateurs for the day. He'd managed, with a good deal of self-control, to hold on to his patience and speak to each one of his extras before he dismissed them. He wanted to shoot one more scene before they wrapped up for the day, so he issued instructions immediately. It would take an hour to set up, and with luck they'd have the film in the can before they lost the light.

The beeper at his hip sounded, distracting him. Impatiently, Phil drew out the walkie-talkie. ''Yeah, Kincaid.''

''Benson. I've got the sheriff here. All right to let her through now?''

Automatically, Phil looked toward the edge of town. He spotted Tory leaning lazily against the hood, drinking from a can. He felt twin surges of relief and annoyance. ''Let her in,'' he ordered briefly, then shoved the radio back in place. Now that he knew she was perfectly safe, Phil had a perverse desire to strangle her. He waited until she had parked in front of the sheriff's office and walked up the street to meet her. Before he was halfway there, Tod burst out of the door.

''Sheriff!'' He teetered at the edge of the sidewalk, as if unsure of whether to advance any farther.

Tory stepped up and ran a fingertip down the bruise on his cheek. ''Everything's fine, Tod.''

''You didn't...'' He moistened his lips. ''You didn't arrest him?''

She rested her arms on his shoulders. ''No.'' Tory felt his shuddering sigh.

''He didn't get mad at you or...'' He trailed off again and looked at her helplessly.

''No, we just talked. He knows he's wrong to hurt you, Tod. He wants to stop.''

''I was scared when you went, but Mr. Kincaid said you knew what you were doing and that everything would be all right.''

''Did he?'' Tory turned her head as Phil stepped beside

her. The look held a long and not quite comfortable moment. "Well, he was right." Turning back to Tod, she gave his shoulders a quick squeeze. "Come inside a minute. There's a number I want you to give to your father. Want a cup of coffee, Kincaid?"

"All right."

Together, they walked into Tory's office. She went directly to her desk, pulling out a smart leather-bound address book that looked absurdly out of place. After flipping through it, she wrote a name and phone number on a pad, then ripped off the sheet. "This number is for your whole family," she said as she handed Tod the paper. "Go home and talk to your father, Tod. He needs to understand that you love him."

He folded the sheet before slipping it into his back pocket. Shifting from foot to foot, he stared down at the cluttered surface of her desk. "Thanks. Ah…I'm sorry about the things I said before." Coloring a bit, he glanced at Phil. "You know," he murmured, lowering his gaze to the desk again.

"Don't be sorry, Tod." She laid a hand over his until he met her eyes. "Okay?" she said, and smiled.

"Yeah, okay." He blushed again, but drew up his courage. Giving Tory a swift kiss on the cheek, he darted for the door.

With a low laugh she touched the spot where his lips had brushed. "I swear," she murmured, "if he were fifteen years older…" Phil grabbed both her arms.

"Are you really all right?"

"Don't I look all right?" she countered.

"Damn it, Tory!"

"Phil." Taking his face in her hands, she gave him a hard, brief kiss. "You had no reason to worry. Didn't you tell Tod that I knew what I was doing?"

"The kid was terrified." And so was I, he thought as he pulled her into his arms. "What happened out there?" he demanded.

"We talked," Tory said simply. "He's a very troubled man. I wanted to hate him and couldn't. I'm counting on him calling that number."

"What would you have done if he'd gotten violent?"

"I would have handled it," she told him, drawing away a bit. "It's my job."

"You can't—"

"Phil"—Tory cut him off quickly and firmly—"I don't tell you how to set a scene; don't tell me how to run my town."

"It's not the same thing and you know it." He gave her an angry shake. "Nobody takes a swing at me when I do a retake."

"How about a frustrated actor?"

His eyes darkened. "Tory, you can't make a joke out of this."

"Better a joke than an argument," she countered. "I don't want to fight with you. Phil, don't focus on something like this. It isn't good for us."

He bit off a furious retort, then strode away to stare out the window. Nothing seemed as simple as it had been since the first time he'd walked into that cramped little room. "It's hard," he murmured. "I care."

Tory stared at his back while a range of emotions swept through her. Her heart wasn't listening to the strict common sense she had imposed on it. No longer sure what she wanted, she suppressed the urge to go to him and be held again. "I know," she said at length. "I care too."

He turned slowly. They looked at each other as they had once before, when there were bars between them—a bit warily. For a long moment there was only the sound of the whining fan and the mumble of conversation outside. "I have to get back," he told her, carefully slipping his hands in his pockets. The need to touch her was too strong. "Dinner?"

"Sure." She smiled, but found it wasn't as easy to tilt her lips up as it should have been. "It'll have to be a little later—around eight?"

"That's fine. I'll see you then."

"Okay." She waited until the door had closed behind him before she sat at her desk. Her legs were weak. Leaning her head on her hand, she let out a long breath.

Oh, boy, she thought. Oh, boy. The ground was a lot shakier than she had anticipated. But she couldn't be falling in love with him, she reassured herself. Not that. Everything was intensified because of the emotional whirlwind of the past couple of days. She wasn't ready for the commitments and obligations of being in love, and that was all there was to it. Rising, she plugged in the coffeepot. She'd feel more like herself if she had a cup of coffee and got down to work.

Phil spent more time than he should have in the shower. It had been a very long, very rough twelve-hour day. He was accustomed to impossible hours and impossible demands in his job. Characteristically he took them in stride. Not this time.

The hot water and steam weren't drawing out the tension in his body. It had been there from the moment when Tory had driven off to the Swanson ranch, then had inexplicably increased during their brief conversation in her office. Because he was a man who always dealt well with tension, he was annoyed that he wasn't doing so this time.

He shut his eyes, letting the water flood over his head. She'd been perfectly right, he mused, about his having no say in her work. For that matter he had no say in any aspect of her life. There were no strings on their relationship. And he didn't want them any more than Tory did. He'd never had this problem in a relationship before. Problem? he mused, pushing wet hair out of his eyes. A perspective problem, he decided. What was necessary was to put his relationship with Tory back in perspective.

And who better to do that than a director? he thought wryly, then switched off the shower with a jerk of the wrist. He was simply letting too much emotion leak into the scene. Take two, he decided, grabbing a towel. Somehow he'd forgotten a very few basic, very vital rules. Keep it simple, keep it light, he reminded himself. Certainly someone with his background and experience was too smart to look for complications. What was between him and Tory was completely elemental and without strain, because they both wanted to keep it that way.

That was one of the things that had attracted him to her in the first place, Phil remembered. Hooking a towel loosely around his waist, he grabbed another to rub his hair dry. She wasn't a woman who expected a commitment, who looked for a permanent bond like love or marriage. Those were two things they were both definitely too smart to get mixed up with. In the steam-hazed mirror Phil caught the flicker of doubt in his own eyes.

Oh, no, he told himself, absolutely not. He wasn't in love with her. It was out of the question. He cared, naturally: She was a very special woman—strong, beautiful, intelligent, independent. And she had a great deal of simple sweetness that surfaced unexpectedly. It was that one quality that kept a man constantly off-balance. So he cared about her, Phil mused, letting the second towel fall to the floor. He could even admit that he felt closer to her than to many people he'd known for years. There was nothing unusual about that. They had something in common that clicked—an odd sort of friendship, he decided. That was safe enough. It was only because he'd been worried about her that he'd allowed things to get out of proportion for a time.

But he was frowning abstractedly at his reflection when he heard the knock on the door.

"Who is it?"

"Room service."

The frown turned into a grin instantly as he recognized Tory's voice.

"Well, hi." Tory gave him a look that was both encompassing and lazy when he opened the door. "You're a little late for your reservation, Kincaid."

He stepped aside to allow her to enter with a large tray. "I lost track of time in the shower. Is that our dinner?"

"Bud phoned me." Tory set the tray on the card table they'd used before. "He said you'd ordered dinner for eight but didn't answer your phone. Since I was starving, I decided to expedite matters.'' Slipping her arms around his waist, she ran her hands up his warm, damp back. ''Ummm, you're tense,'' she murmured, enjoying the way his hair curled chaotically around his face. ''Rough day?''

''And then some,'' he agreed before he kissed her.

He smelled clean—of soap and shampoo—yet, Tory found the scent as arousing as the darker musky fragrance she associated with him. Her hunger for food faded as quickly as her hunger for him rose. Pressing closer, she demanded more. His arms tightened; his muscles grew taut. He was losing himself in her again, and found no power to control it.

''You really are tense,'' Tory said against his mouth. ''Lie down.''

He gave a half chuckle, nibbling on her bottom lip. ''You work fast.''

''I'll rub your back,'' she informed him as she drew away. ''You can tell me all the frustrating things those nasty actors did today while you were striving to be brilliant.''

''Let me show you how we deal with smart alecks on the coast,'' Phil suggested.

''On the bed, Kincaid.''

''Well...'' He grinned. ''If you insist.''

''On your stomach,'' she stated when he started to pull her with him.

Deciding that being pampered might have its advantages, he complied. ''I've got a bottle of wine in the cooler.'' He sighed as he stretched out full length. ''It's a hell of a place to keep a fifty-year-old Burgundy.''

"Don't be a snob," Tory warned, sitting beside him. "You must have worked ten or twelve hours today," she began. "Did you get much accomplished?"

"Not as much as we should have." He gave a quiet groan of pleasure as she began to knead the muscles in his shoulders. "That's wonderful."

"The guys in the massage parlor always asked for Tory."

His head came up. "What?"

"Just wanted to see if you were paying attention. Down, Kincaid." She chuckled softly, working down his arms. "Were there technical problems or temperament ones?"

"Both," he answered, settling again. He found closing his eyes was a sensuous luxury. "Had some damaged diachorics. With luck the new ones'll get here tomorrow. Most of the foul-ups came during the crowd scene. Your people like to grin into the camera," he said dryly. "I expected one of them to wave any minute."

"That's show biz," Tory concluded as she shifted to her knees. She hiked her dress up a bit for more freedom. Opening his eyes, Phil was treated to a view of thigh. "I wouldn't be surprised if the town council elected to build a theater in Friendly just to show your movie. Think of the boon to the industry."

"Merle walked across the street like he's sat on a horse for three weeks." Because her fingers were working miracles over his back muscles, Phil shut his eyes again.

"Merle's still seeing Marlie Summers."

"Tory."

"Just making conversation," she said lightly, but dug a bit harder than necessary into his shoulder blades.

"Ouch!"

"Toughen up, Kincaid." With a laugh she placed a loud, smacking kiss in the center of his back. "You're not behind schedule, are you?"

"No. With all the hazards of shooting on location, we're doing very well. Another four weeks should wrap it up."

They were both silent for a moment, unexpectedly depressed. "Well, then," Tory said briskly, "you shouldn't have to worry about the guarantor."

"He'll be hanging over my shoulder until the film's in the can," Phil muttered. "There's a spot just to the right…oh, yeah," he murmured as her fingers zeroed in on it.

"Too bad you don't have any of those nifty oils and lotions," she commented. In a fluid movement Tory straddled him, the better to apply pressure. "You're a disappointment, Kincaid. I'd have thought all you Hollywood types would carry a supply of that kind of thing."

"Mmmm." He would have retorted in kind, but his mind was beginning to float. Her fingers were cool and sure as they pressed on the small of his back just above the line of the towel. Her legs, clad in thin stockings, brushed his sides, arousing him with each time she flexed. The scent of her shampoo tickled his nostrils as she leaned up to knead his shoulders again. Though the sheet was warm—almost too warm—beneath him, he couldn't summon the energy to move. As the sun was setting, the light shifted, dimming. The room was filled with a golden haze that suited his mood. He could hear the rumble of a car on the street below, then only the sound of Tory's light, even breathing above him. His muscles were relaxed and limber, but he didn't consider telling her to stop. He'd forgotten completely about the dinner growing cold on the table behind them.

Tory continued to run her hands along his back, thinking him asleep. He had a beautiful body, she mused, hard and tanned and disciplined. The muscles in his back were supple and strong. For a moment she simply enjoyed exploring him. When she shifted lower, the skirt of her dress rode up high on her thighs. With a little sound of annoyance she unzipped the dress and pulled it over her head. She could move with more freedom in her sheer teddy.

His waist was trim. She allowed her hands to slide over it, approving its firmness. Before their lovemaking had been so urgent, and she had been completely under his command. Now she enjoyed learning the lines and planes of his body. Down the narrow hips, over the brief swatch of towel, to his thighs. There were muscles there, too, she discovered, hardened by hours of standing, tennis, swimming. The light mat of hair over his skin made her feel intensely feminine. She massaged his calves, then couldn't resist the urge to place a light kiss on the back of his knee. Phil's blood began to heat in a body too drugged with pleasure to move. It gave her a curiously warm feeling to rub his feet.

He worked much harder than she'd initially given him credit for, she mused as she roamed slowly back up his legs. He spent hours in the sun, on his feet, going over and over the same shot until he'd reached the perfection he strove for. And she had come to know that the film was never far from his thoughts, even during his free hours. Phillip Kincaid, she thought with a gentle smile, was a very impressive man—with much more depth than the glossy playboy the press loved to tattle on. He'd earned her respect during the time he'd been in Friendly, and she was growing uncomfortably certain he'd earned something more complex. She wouldn't think of it now. Perhaps she would have no choice but to think of it after he'd gone. But for now, he was here. That was enough.

With a sigh she bent low over his back to lay her cheek on his shoulder. The need for him had crept into her while she was unaware. Her pulse was pounding, and a thick warmth, like heated honey, seemed to flow through her veins.

"Phil." She moved her mouth to his ear. Her tongue traced it, slipping inside to arouse him to wakefulness. She heard his quiet groan as her heart began to beat jerkily. With her teeth she pulled and tugged on the lobe, then moved to experiment with the sensitive area just below. "I want you," she murmured. Quickly she began to take her lips over him with the same thorough care as her fingers.

He seemed so pliant as she roamed over him that when a strong arm reached out to pull her down, it took her breath away. Before she could recover it, his mouth was on hers. His lips were soft and warm, but the kiss was bruisingly potent. His tongue went deep to make an avid search of moist recesses as his weight pressed her into the mattress. He took a quick, hungry journey across her face before he looked down at her. There was nothing sleepy in his expression. The look alone had her breath trembling.

"My turn," he whispered.

With nimble fingers he loosened the range of tiny buttons down the front of her teddy. His lips followed, to send a trail of fire along the newly exposed skin. The plunge of the V stopped just below her navel. He lingered there, savoring the soft, honey-hued flesh. Tory felt herself swept through a hurricane of sensation to the heavy, waiting air of the storm's eye. Phil's hands cupped her upper thighs, his thumbs pressing insistently where the thin silk rose high. Expertly he unhooked her stockings, drawing them off slowly, his mouth hurrying to taste. Tory moaned, bending her leg to help him as torment and pleasure tangled.

For one heady moment his tongue lingered at the top of her thigh. With his tongue he gently slipped beneath the silk, making her arch in anticipation. His breath shot through the material into the core of her. But he left her moist and aching to come greedily back to her mouth. Tory met the kiss ardently, dragging him closer. She felt his body pound and pulse against hers with a need no greater than her own. He found her full bottom lip irresistible and nibbled and sucked gently. Tory knew a passion so concentrated and volatile, she struggled under him to find the ultimate release.

"Here," he whispered, moving down to the spot on her neck that always drew him. "You taste like no one else," he murmured. Her flavor seemed to tremble on the tip of his tongue. With a groan he let his voracious appetite take over.

Her breasts were hard, waiting for him. Slowly he moistened the tips with his tongue, listening to her shuddering breathing as he journeyed from one to the other—teasing, circling, nibbling, until her movements beneath him were abandoned and desperate. Passion built to a delicious peak until he drew her, hot and moist, into his mouth to suckle ravenously. She wasn't aware when he slipped the teddy down her shoulders, down her body, until she was naked to the waist. The last lights of the sun poured into the room like a dark red mist. It gave her skin an exotic cast that aroused him further. He drew the silk lower and still lower, until it was lost in the tangle of sheets.

Desperate, Tory reached for him. She heard Phil's sharp intake of breath as she touched him, felt the sudden, convulsive shudder. She wanted him now with an intensity too strong to deny.

"More," he breathed, but was unable to resist as she drew him closer.

"Now," she murmured, arching her hips to receive him.

Exhausted, they lay in silence as the first fingers of moonlight flickered into the room. He knew he should move—his full weight pushed Tory deep into the mattress. But they felt so right, flesh to flesh, his mouth nestled comfortably against her breast. Her fingers were in his hair, tangling and stroking with a sleepy gentleness. Time crept by easily—seconds to minutes without words or the need for them. He could hear her heartbeat gradually slow and level. Lazily he flicked his tongue over a still-erect nipple and felt it harden even more.

"Phil," she moaned in weak protest.

He laughed quietly, enormously pleased that he could move her so effortlessly. "Tired?" he asked, nibbling a moment longer.

"Yes." She gave a low groan as he began to toy with her other breast. "Phil, I can't."

Ignoring her, he brought his mouth to hers for long, slow kisses while his hands continued to stroke. He had intended only to kiss her before taking his weight from her. Her lips were unbearably soft and giving. Her breath shuddered into him, rebuilding his passion with dizzying speed. Tory told herself it wasn't possible as sleepy desire became a torrent of fresh need.

Phil found new delight in the lines of her body, in the heady, just-loved flavor of her skin. A softly glowing spark rekindled a flame. "I want a retake," he murmured.

He took her swiftly, leaving them both staggered and damp and clinging in a room speckled with moonlight.

"How do you feel?" Phil murmured later. She was close to his side, one arm flung over his chest.

"Astonished."

He laughed, kissing her temple. "So do I. I guess our dinner got cold."

"Mmm. What was it?"

"I don't remember."

Tory yawned and snuggled against him. "That's always better cold anyway." She knew with very little effort she could sleep for a week.

"Not hungry?"

She considered a moment. "Is it something you have to chew?"

He grinned into the darkness. "Probably."

"Uh-uh." She arched like a contented cat when he ran a hand down her back. "Do you have to get up early?"

"Six."

Groaning, she shut her eyes firmly. "You're ruining your mystique," she told him. "Hollywood Casanovas don't get up at six."

He gave a snort of laughter. "They do if they've got a film to direct."

"I suppose when you leave, you'll still have a lot of work to do before the film's finished."

His frown mirrored hers, although neither was aware of it. "There's still a lot to be shot in the studio, then the editing…I wish there was more time."

She knew what he meant, and schooled her voice carefully. "We both knew. I'll only be in town a few weeks longer than you," she added. "I've got a lot of work to catch up on in Albuquerque."

"It's lucky we're both comfortable with the way things are." Phil stared up at the ceiling while his fingers continued to tangle in her hair. "If we'd fallen in love, it would be an impossible situation."

"Yes," Tory murmured, opening her eyes to the darkness. "Neither of us has the time for impossible situations."

Chapter 10

Tory pulled up in front of the ranch house. Her mother's geraniums were doing beautifully. White and pink plants had been systematically placed between the more common red. The result was an organized, well tended blanket of color. Tory noted that the tear in the window screen had been mended. As always, a few articles of clothing hung on the line at the side of the house. She dreaded going in.

It was an obligation she never shirked but never did easily. At least once a week she drove out to spend a strained half hour with her mother. Only twice since the film crew had come to Friendly had her mother made the trip into town. Both times she had dropped into Tory's office, but the visits had been brief and uncomfortable for both women. Time was not bridging the gap, only widening it.

Normally, Tory confined her trips to the ranch to Sunday afternoons. This time, however, she had driven out a day early in order to placate Phil. The thought caused her to smile. He'd finally pressured her into agreeing to his "home movies." When he had wound up the morning's shoot in town, he would bring out one of the backup video cameras. Though she could hardly see why it was so vital to him to put her on film, Tory decided it wouldn't do any harm. And, she thought wryly, he wasn't going to stop bringing it up until she agreed. So let him have his fun, she concluded as she slipped from the car. She'd enjoy the ride.

From the corral the palomino whinnied fussily. He pawed the ground and pranced as Tory watched him. He knew, seeing Tory, that there was a carrot or apple in it for him, as well as a bracing ride. They were both aware that he could jump the fence easily if he grew impatient enough. As he reared, showing off for her, Tory laughed.

"Simmer down, Justice. You're going to be in the movies." She hesitated a moment. It would be so easy to go to the horse, pamper him a bit in return for his unflagging affection. There were no complications or undercurrents there. Her eyes drifted back to the house. With a sigh she started up the walk.

Upon entering, Tory caught the faint whiff of bee's wax and lemon and knew her mother had recently polished the floors. She remembered the electric buffer her father had brought home one day. Helen had been as thrilled as if he'd brought her diamonds. The windows glittered in the sun without a streak or speck.

How does she do it? Tory wondered, gazing around the spick-and-span room. How does she stand spending each and every day chasing dust? Could it really be all she wants out of life?

As far back as she could remember, she could recall her mother wanting nothing more than to change slipcovers or curtains. It was difficult for a woman who always looked for angles and alternatives to understand such placid acceptance. Perhaps it would have been easier if the daughter had understood the mother, or the mother the daughter. With a frustrated shake of her head she wandered to the kitchen, expecting to find Helen fussing at the stove.

The room was empty. The appliances winked, white and gleaming, in the strong sunlight. The scent of fresh-baked bread hovered enticingly in the air. Whom did she bake it for? Tory demanded of herself, angry without knowing why. There was no one there to appreciate it now—no one to break off a hunk and grin as he was scolded. Damn it, didn't she know that everything was different now? Whirling away, Tory strode out of the room.

The house was too quiet, she realized. Helen was certainly there. The tired little compact was in its habitual place at the side of the house. It occurred to Tory that her mother might be in one of the outbuildings. But then, why hadn't she come out when she heard the car drive up? Vaguely disturbed, Tory glanced up the stairs. She opened her mouth to call, then stopped. Something impelled her to move quietly up the steps.

At the landing she paused, catching some faint sound coming from the end of the hall. Still moving softly, Tory walked down to the doorway of her parents' bedroom. The door was only half closed. Pushing it open, Tory stepped inside.

Helen sat on the bed in a crisp yellow housedress. Her blond hair was caught back in a matching kerchief. Held tight in her hands was one of Tory's father's work shirts. It was a faded blue, frayed at the cuffs. Tory remembered it as his favorite, one that Helen had claimed was fit only for a dust rag. Now she clutched it to her breast, rocking gently and weeping with such quiet despair that Tory could only stare.

She'd never seen her mother cry. It had been her father whose eyes had misted during her high school and college graduations. It had been he who had wept with her when the dog she had raised from a puppy had died. Her mother had faced joy and sadness with equal restraint. But there was no restraint in the woman Tory saw now. This was a woman in the depths of grief, blind and deaf to all but her own mourning.

All anger, all resentment, all sense of distance, vanished in one illuminating moment. Tory felt her heart fill with sympathy, her throat burn from her own grief.

"Mother."

Helen's head jerked up. Her eyes were glazed and confused as they focused on Tory. She shook her head as if in denial, then struggled to choke back the sobs.

"No, don't." Tory rushed to her, gathering her close. "Don't shut me out."

Helen went rigid in an attempt at composure, but Tory only held her tighter. Abruptly, Helen collapsed, dropping her head on her daughter's shoulder and weeping without restraint. "Oh, Tory, Tory, why couldn't it have been me?'' With the shirt caught between them, Helen accepted the comfort of her daughter's strong arms. ''Not Will, never Will. It should have been me.''

''No, don't say that.'' Hot tears coursed down her face. ''You mustn't think that way. Dad wouldn't want you to.''

''All those weeks, those horrible weeks, in the hospital I prayed and prayed for a miracle.'' She gripped Tory tighter, as if she needed something solid to hang on to. ''They said no hope. No hope. Oh, God, I wanted to scream. He couldn't die without me…not without me. That last night in the hospital before…I went into his room. I begged him to show them they were wrong, to come back. He was gone.'' She moaned and would have slid down if Tory hadn't held her close. ''He'd already left me. I couldn't leave him lying there with that machine. I couldn't do that, not to Will. Not to my Will.''

''Oh, Mother.'' They rocked together, heads on each other's shoulders. ''I'm so sorry. I didn't know—I didn't think…I'm so sorry.''

Helen breathed a long, shuddering sigh as her sobs quieted. ''I didn't know how to tell you or how to explain. I'm not good at letting my feelings out. I knew how much you loved your father,'' she continued. ''But I was too angry to reach out. I suppose I wanted you to lash out at me. It made it easier to be strong, even though I knew I hurt you more.''

''That doesn't matter now.''

''Tory—''

''No, it doesn't.'' Tory drew her mother back, looking into her tear-ravaged eyes. ''Neither of us tried to understand the other that night. We were both wrong. I think we've both paid for it enough now."

"I loved him so much." Helen swallowed the tremor in her voice and stared down at the crumpled shirt still in her hand. "It doesn't seem possible that he won't walk through the door again."

"I know. Every time I come in the house, I still look for him."

"You're so like him." Hesitantly, Helen reached up to touch her cheek. "There's been times it's been hard for me even to look at you. You were always his more than mine when you were growing up. My fault," she added before Tory could speak. "I was always a little awed by you."

"Awed?" Tory managed to smile.

"You were so smart, so quick, so demanding. I always wondered how much I had to do with the forming of you. Tory"—she took her hands, staring down at them a moment—"I never tried very hard to get close to you. It's not my way."

"I know."

"It didn't mean that I didn't love you."

She squeezed Helen's hands. "I know that too. But it was always him we looked at first."

"Yes." Helen ran a palm over the crumpled shirt. "I thought I was coping very well," she said softly. "I was going to clean out the closet. I found this, and… He loved it so. You can still see the little holes where he'd pin his badge."

"Mother, it's time you got out of the house a bit, starting seeing people again." When Helen started to shake her head, Tory gripped her hands tighter. "Living again."

Helen glanced around the tidy room with a baffled smile. "This is all I know how to do. All these years..."

"When I go back to Albuquerque, why don't you come stay with me a while? You've never been over."

"Oh, Tory, I don't know."

"Think about it," she suggested, not wanting to push. "You might enjoy watching your daughter rip a witness apart in cross-examination."

Helen laughed, brushing the lingering tears briskly away. "I might at that. Would you be offended if I said sometimes I worry about you being alone—not having someone like your father to come home to?"

"No." The sudden flash of loneliness disturbed her far more than the words. "Everyone needs something different."

"Everyone needs someone, Tory," Helen corrected gently. "Even you."

Tory's eyes locked on her mother's a moment, then dropped away. "Yes, I know. But sometimes the someone—" She broke off, distressed by the way her thoughts had centered on Phil. "There's time for that," she said briskly. "I still have a lot of obligations, a lot of things I want to do, before I commit myself...to anyone."

There was enough anxiety in Tory's voice to tell Helen that "anyone" had a name. Feeling it was too soon to offer advice, she merely patted Tory's hand. "Don't wait too long," she said simply. "Life has a habit of moving quickly." Rising, she went to the closet again. The need to be busy was too ingrained to allow her to sit for long. "I didn't expect you today. Are you going to ride?"

"Yes." Tory pressed a hand down on her father's shirt before she stood. "Actually I'm humoring the director of the film being shot in town." Wandering to the window, she looked down to see Justice pacing the corral restlessly. "He has this obsession with getting me on film. I flatly refused to be an extra in his production, but I finally agreed to let him shoot some while I rode Justice."

"He must be very persuasive," Helen commented.

Tory gave a quick laugh. "Oh, he's that all right."

"That's Marshall Kincaid's son," Helen stated, remembering. "Does he favor his father?"

With a smile Tory thought that her mother would be more interested in the actor than the director. "Yes, actually he does. The same rather aristocratic bone structure and cool blue eyes." Tory saw the car kicking up dust on the road leading to the ranch. "He's coming now, if you'd like to meet him."

"Oh, I..." Helen pressed her fingers under her eyes. "I don't think I'm really presentable right now, Tory."

"All right," she said as she started toward the door. In the doorway she hesitated a moment. "Will you be all right now?"

"Yes, yes, I'm fine. Tory..." She crossed the room to give her daughter's cheek a brief kiss. Tory's eyes widened in surprise at the uncharacteristic gesture. "I'm glad we talked. Really very glad."

Phil again stopped his car beside the corral. The horse pranced over to hang his head over the fence, waiting for attention. Leaving the camera in the backseat, Phil walked over to pat the strong golden neck. He found the palomino avidly nuzzling at his pockets.

"Hey!" With a half laugh he stepped out of range.

"He's looking for this." Holding a carrot in her hand, Tory came down the steps.

"Your friend should be arrested for pickpocketing," Phil commented as Tory drew closer. His smile of greeting faded instantly. "Tory..." He took her shoulders, studying her face. "You've been crying," he said in an odd voice.

"I'm fine." Turning, she held out the carrot, letting the horse pluck in from her hand.

"What's wrong?" he insisted, pulling her back to him again. "What happened?"

"It was my mother."

"Is she ill?" he demanded quickly.

"No." Touched by the concern in his voice, Tory smiled. "We talked," she told him, then let out a long sigh. "We really talked, probably for the first time in twenty-seven years."

There was something fragile in the look as she lifted her eyes to his. He felt much as he had the day in the cemetery—protective and strong. Wordlessly he drew her into the circle of his arms. "Are you okay?"

"Yes, I'm fine." She closed her eyes as her head rested against his shoulder. "Really fine. It's going to be so much easier now."

"I'm glad." Tilting her face to his, he kissed her softly. "If you don't feel like doing this today—"

"No you don't, Kincaid," she said with a quick grin.

"You claimed you were going to immortalize me, so get on with it."

"Go fix your face first, then." He pinched her chin. "I'll set things up."

She turned away to comply, but called back over her shoulder. "There's not going to be any of that 'Take two' business. You'll have to get it right the first time."

He enjoyed her hoot of laughter before he reached into the car for the camera and recorder.

Later, Tory scowled at the apparatus. "You said film," she reminded him. "You didn't say anything about sound."

"It's tape," he corrected, expertly framing her. "Just saddle the horse."

"You're arrogant as hell when you play movies, Kincaid." Without fuss Tory slipped the bit into the palomino's mouth. Her movements were competent as she hefted the saddle onto the horse's back. She was a natural, he decided. No nerves, no exaggerated gestures for the benefit of the camera. He wanted her to talk again. Slowly he circled around for a new angle. "Going to have dinner with me tonight?"

"I don't know." Tory considered as she tightened the cinches. "That cold steak you fed me last night wasn't very appetizing."

"Tonight I'll order cold cuts and beer," he suggested. "That way it won't matter when we get to it."

Tory sent him a grin over her shoulder. "It's a deal."

"You're a cheap date, Sheriff."

"Uh-uh," she disagreed, turning to him while she wrapped a companionable arm around the horse's neck.

"I'm expecting another bottle of that French champagne very soon. Why don't you let me play with the camera now and you can stand next to the horse?"

"Mount up."

Tory lifted a brow. "You're one tough cookie, Kincaid." Grasping the saddle horn, Tory swung into the saddle in one lazy movement. "And now?"

"Head out, the direction you took the first time I saw you ride. Not too far," he added. "When you come back, keep it at a gallop. Don't pay any attention to the camera. Just ride."

"You're the boss," she said agreeably. "For the moment." With a kick of her heels Tory sent the palomino west at a run.

She felt the exhilaration instantly. The horse wanted speed, so Tory let him have his head as the hot air whipped at her face and hair. As before, she headed toward the mountains. There was no need to escape this time, but only a pleasure in moving fast. The power and strength below her tested her skill.

Zooming in on her, Phil thought she rode with understated flare. No flash, just confidence. Her body hardly seemed to move as the horse pounded up dust. It almost seemed as though the horse led her, but something in the way she sat, in the way her face was lifted, showed her complete control.

When she turned, the horse danced in place a moment, still anxious to run. He tossed his head, lifting his front feet off the ground in challenge. Over the still, silent air, Phil heard Tory laugh. The sound of it sent shivers down his spine.

Magnificent, he thought, zooming in on her as close as the lens would allow. She was absolutely magnificent. She wasn't looking toward him. Obviously she had no thoughts about the camera focused on her. Her face was lifted to the sun and the sky as she controlled the feisty horse with apparent ease. When she headed back, she started at a loping gallop that built in speed.

The palomino's legs gathered and stretched, sending up a plume of dirt in their wake. Behind them was a barren land of little more than rock and earth with the mountains harsh in the distance. She was Eve, Phil thought. The only woman. And if this Eve's paradise was hard and desolate, she ruled it in her own style.

Once, as if remembering he was there, Tory looked over, full into the camera. With her face nearly filling the lens, she smiled. Phil felt his palms go damp. If a man had a woman like that, he realized abruptly, he'd need nothing and no one else. The only woman, he thought again, then shook his head as if to clear it.

With a quick command and a tug on the reins, Tory brought the horse to a stop. Automatically she leaned forward to pat his neck. "Well, Hollywood?" she said lazily.

Knowing he wasn't yet in complete control, Phil kept the camera trained on her. "Is that the best you can do?"

She tossed her hair behind her head. "What did you have in mind?"

"No fancy tricks?" he asked, moving around the horse to vary the angle.

Tory looked down on him with tolerant amusement. "If you want to see someone stand on one foot in the saddle, go to the circus."

"We could set up a couple of small jumps—if you can handle it."

As she ruffled the palomino's blond mane, she gave a snort of laughter. "I thought you wanted me to ride, not win a blue ribbon." Grinning, she turned the horse around. "But okay," she said obligingly. At an easy lope she went for the corral fence. The horse took the four feet in a long, powerful glide. "Will that do?" she asked as she doubled back and rode past.

"Again," Phil demanded, going down on one knee. With a shrug Tory took the horse over the fence again. Lowering his camera for the first time, Phil shaded his eyes and looked up at her. "If he can do that, how do you keep him in?"

"He knows a good thing when he's got it," Tory stated, letting the palomino prance a bit while she rubbed his neck. "He's just showing off for the camera. Is that a wrap, Kincaid?"

Lifting the camera again, he aimed it at her. "Is that all you can do?"

"Well..." Tory considered a moment, then sent him a slow smile. "How about this?" Keeping one hand loosely on the reins, she started to unbutton her blouse.

"I like it."

After three buttons she paused, catching her tongue between her teeth. "I don't want you to lose your G rating," she decided. Swinging a leg over the saddle, she slid to the ground.

"This is a private film," he reminded her. "The censors'll never see it."

She laughed, but shook her head. "Fade out," she suggested, loosening the horse's girth. "Put your toy away, Kincaid," she told him as he circled around the horse, still taping.

"Look at me a minute." With a half smile Tory complied. "God, that face," he muttered. "One way or the other, I'm going to get it on the screen."

"Forget it." Tory lifted the saddle to balance it on the fence. "Unless you start videotaping court cases."

"I can be persistent."

"I can be stubborn," she countered. At her command the palomino trotted back into the corral.

After loading the equipment back in the car, Phil turned to gather Tory in his arms. Without a word their mouths met in long, mutual pleasure. "If there was a way," he murmured as he buried his face in her hair, "to have a few days away from here, alone..."

Tory shut her eyes, feeling the stir...and the ache. "Obligations, Phil," she said quietly. "We both have a job to do."

He wanted to say the hell with it, but knew he couldn't. Along with the obligations was the agreement they had made at the outset. "If I called you in Albuquerque, would you see me?"

She hesitated. It was something she wanted and feared. "Yes." She realized abruptly that she was suffering. For a moment she stood still, absorbing the unexpected sensation. "Phil, kiss me again."

She found his mouth quickly to let the heat and pleasure of the kiss dull the pain. There were still a few precious weeks left, she told herself as she wrapped her arms tighter around him. There was still time before...with a moan she pressed urgently against him, willing her mind to go blank. There was a sigh, then a tremble, before she rested her head against his shoulder. ''I have to put the tack away,'' she murmured. It was tempting to stay just as she was, held close, with her blood just beginning to swim. Taking a long breath, she drew away from him and smiled. ''Why don't you be macho and carry the saddle?''

''Directors don't haul equipment,'' he told her as he tried to pull her back to him.

''Heave it up, Kincaid.'' Tory swung the reins over her shoulder. ''You've got some great muscles.''

''Yeah?'' Grinning, he lifted the saddle and followed her toward the barn. Bicks was right, Phil mused, watching her walk. She had a way of moving that drove men mad.

The barn door creaked in protest when Tory pulled it open. ''Over here.'' She moved across the concrete floor to hang the reins on a peg.

Phil set down the saddle, then turned. The place was large, high-ceilinged and refreshingly cool. ''No animals?'' he asked, wandering to an empty stall.

''My mother keeps a few head of cattle,'' Tory explained as she joined him. ''They're grazing. We had more horses, but she doesn't ride much.'' Tory lifted a shoulder. ''Justice has the place mostly to himself.''

''I've never been in a barn.''

''A deprived child.''

He sent her a mild glance over his shoulder as he roamed. ''I don't think I expected it to be so clean.''

Tory's laugh echoed. ''My mother has a vendetta against dirt,'' she told him. Oddly, she felt amusement now rather than resentment. It was a clean feeling. "I think she'd have put curtains on the windows in the loft if my father had let her."

Phil found the ladder and tested its sturdiness. "What's up there?"

"Hay," Tory said dryly. "Ever seen hay?"

"Don't be smug," he warned before he started to climb. Finding his fascination rather sweet, Tory exerted the energy to go up with him. "The view's incredible." Standing beside the side opening, he could see for miles. The town of Friendly looked almost neat and tidy with the distance.

"I used to come up here a lot." Tucking her hands in her back pockets, Tory looked over his shoulder.

"What did you do?"

"Watch the world go by," she said, nodding toward Friendly. "Or sleep."

He laughed, turning back to her. "You're the only person I know who can turn sleeping into an art."

"I've dedicated quite a bit of my life to it." She took his hand to draw him away.

Instead he pulled her into a dim corner. "There's something I've always wanted to do in a hayloft."

With a laugh Tory stepped away. "Phil, my mother's in the house."

"She's not here," he pointed out. He hooked a hand in the low V where she had loosened her blouse. A hard tug had her stumbling against him.

"Phil—"

"It must have been carrying that saddle," he mused,

giving her a gentle push that had her falling backward into a pile of hay.

"Now, wait a minute..." she began, and struggled up on her elbows.

"And the primitive surroundings," he added as he pressed her body back with his own. "If I were directing this scene, it would start like this." He took her mouth in a hot, urgent kiss that turned her protest into a moan. "The lighting would be set so that it seemed one shaft of sunlight was slanting down across here." With a fingertip he traced from her right ear, across her throat, to the hollow between her breasts. "Everything else would be a dull gold, like your skin."

She had her hands pressed against his shoulders, holding him off, although her heart was beating thickly. "Phil, this isn't the time."

He placed two light kisses at either corner of her mouth. He found it curiously exciting to have to persuade her. Light as a breeze, his hand slipped under her blouse until his fingers found her breast. The peak was already taut. At his touch her eyes lost focus and darkened. The hands at his shoulders lost their resistance and clutched at him. "You're so sensitive," he murmured, watching the change in her face. "It drives me crazy to know when I touch you like this your bones turn to water and you're completely mine."

Letting his fingers fondle and stroke, he lowered his mouth to nibble gently at her yielding lips. *Strong, self-sufficient, decisive.* Those were words he would have used to describe her. Yet, he knew, when they were together like this, he had the power to mold her. Even now, as she lifted them to his face to urge him closer, he felt the weakness come over him in thick waves. It was both frightening and irresistible.

She could have asked anything of him, and he would have been unable to deny her. Even his thoughts could no longer be considered his own when she was so intimately entwined in them. The fingers that loosened the rest of her buttons weren't steady. He should have been used to her by now, he told himself as he sought the tender skin of her neck almost savagely. It shouldn't be so intense every time he began to make love to her. Each time he told himself the desperation would fade; yet, it only returned—doubled, tripled, until he was completely lost in her.

There was only her now, over the clean, country smell of hay. Her subtly alluring fragrance was a contrast too exciting to bear. She was murmuring to him as she drew his shirt over his head. The sound of her voice seemed to pulse through his system. The sun shot through the window to beat on his bare back, but he only felt the cool stroking of her fingers as she urged him down until they were flesh to flesh.

His mouth devoured hers as he tugged the jeans over her hips. Greedily he moved to her throat, her shoulders, her breasts, ravenous for each separate taste. His mouth ranged over her, his tongue moistening, savoring, as her skin heated. She was naked but for the brief swatch riding low on her hips. He hooked his fingers beneath it, tormenting them both by lowering it fraction by fraction while his lips followed the progress.

The pleasure grew unmanageable. He began the wild journey back up her body, his fingers fumbling with the snap of his jeans until Tory's brushed them impatiently away.

She undressed him swiftly, while her own mouth streaked over his skin. The sudden change from pliancy to command left him stunned. Then she was on top of him, straddling him while her lips and teeth performed dark magic at the pulse in his throat. Beyond reason, he grasped her hips, lifting her. Tory gave a quick cry as they joined. In delight her head flung back as she let this new exhilaration rule her. Her skin was shiny with dampness when she crested. Delirious, she started to slide toward him, but he rolled her over, crushing her beneath him as he took her to a second peak, higher than the first.

As they lay, damp flesh to damp flesh, their breaths shuddering, she knew a contentment so fulfilling, it brought the sting of tears to her eyes. Hurriedly blinking them away, Tory kissed the curve of his shoulder.

"I guess there's more to do in a hayloft than sleep."

Phil chuckled. Rolling onto his back, he drew her against his side to steal a few more moments alone with her.

Chapter 11

One of the final scenes to be filmed was a tense night sequence outside Hernandez's Bar. Phil had opted to shoot at night with a low light level rather than film during the day with filters. It would give the actors more of a sense of the ambience and keep the gritty realism in the finished product. It was a scene fraught with emotion that would lose everything if overplayed. From the beginning nothing seemed to go right.

Twice the sound equipment broke down, causing lengthy delays. A seasoned supporting actress blew her lines repeatedly and strode off the set, cursing herself. A defective bulb exploded, scattering shards of glass that had to be painstakingly picked up. For the first time since the shooting began, Phil had to deal with a keyed-up, uncooperative Marlie.

"Okay," he said, taking her by the arm to draw her away. "What the hell's wrong with you?"

"I can't get it right," she said furiously. With her hands on her hips she strode a few paces away and kicked at the dirt. "Damn it, Phil, it just doesn't *feel* right."

"Look, we've been at this over two hours. Everybody's a little fed up." His own patience was hanging on by a thread. In two days at the most, he'd have no choice but to head back to California. He should have been pleased that the bulk of the filming was done—that the rushes were excellent. Instead he was tense, irritable and looking for someone to vent his temper on. "Just pull yourself together," he told Marlie curtly. "And get it done."

"Now, just a damn minute!" Firing up instantly, Marlie let her own frustration pour out in temper. "I've put up with your countless retakes, with that stinking, sweaty bar and this godforsaken town because this script is gold. I've let you work me like a horse because I need you. This part is my ticket into the big leagues and I know it right down to the gut."

"You want the ticket," Phil tossed back, "You pay the price."

"I've paid my dues," she told him furiously. A couple of heads turned idly in their direction, but no one ventured over. "I don't have to take your lousy temper on the set because you've got personal problems."

He measured her with narrowed eyes. "You have to take exactly what I give you."

"I'll tell you something, Kincaid"—she poked a small finger into his chest—"I don't have to take anything, because I'm every bit as important to this movie as you are, and we both know it. It doesn't mean a damn who's getting top billing. Kate Lohman's the key to this picture, and I'm Kate Lohman. Don't you forget it, and don't throw your weight around with me.''

When she turned to stride off, Phil grabbed her arm, jerking her back. His eyes had iced. The fingers on her arm were hard. Looking down at her set face, he felt temper fade into admiration. ''Damn you, Marlie,'' he said quietly, ''you know how to stay in character, don't you?''

''I know this one inside out,'' she returned. The stiffness went out of her stance.

''Okay, what doesn't feel right?''

The corners of her mouth curved up. ''I wanted to work with you,'' she began, ''because you're the best out there these days. I didn't expect to like you. All right,'' she continued, abruptly professional, ''when Sam follows me out of the bar, grabs me, finally losing control, he's furious. Everything he's held in comes pouring out. His dialogue's hard.''

''You haven't been off his back since he came into town,'' Phil reminded her, running over the scene in his mind. ''Now he's had enough. After the scene he's going to take you back to your room and make love. You win.''

''Do I?'' Marlie countered. ''My character is a tough lady. She's got reason to be; she's got enough vulnerabilities to keep the audience from despising her, but she's no pushover.''

''So?''

''So he comes after me, he calls me a tramp—a cold,

money-grabbing whore, among other things—and my response is to take it—damp-eyed and shocked.''

Phil considered, a small smile growing. ''What would you do?''

''I'd punch the jerk in the mouth.''

His laugh echoed down the street. ''Yeah, I guess you would at that.''

''Tears, maybe,'' Marlie went on, tasting victory, ''but anger too. She's becoming very close to what he's accusing her of. And she hates it—and him, for making it matter.''

Phil nodded, his mind already plotting the changes and the angles. Frowning, he called Sam over and outlined the change.

''Can you pull this off without busting my caps?'' Sam demanded of Marlie.

She grinned. ''Maybe.''

''After she hits you,'' Phil interrupted, ''I want dead silence for a good ten seconds. You wipe your mouth with the back of your hand, slow, but don't break the eye contact. Let's set it up from where Marlie walks out of the bar. Bicks!'' He left the actors to give his cinematographer a rundown.

''Quiet.... Places.... Roll....'' Standing by the cameraman's shoulder, Phil watched the scene unfold. The adrenaline was pumping now. He could see it in Marlie's eyes, in the set of her body, as she burst out the door of the bar onto the sidewalk. When Sam grabbed her, instead of merely being whirled around, she turned on him. The mood seemed to fire into him as well, as his lines became

harsher, more emotional. Before there had been nothing in the scene but the man's anger; now there was the woman's too. Now the underlying sexuality was there. When she hit him, it seemed everyone on the set held their breath. The gesture was completely unexpected and, Phil mused as the silence trembled, completely in character. He could almost feel Sam's desire to strike her back, and his inability to do so. She challenged him to, while her throat moved gently with a nervous swallow. He wiped his mouth, never taking his eyes from hers.

"Cut!" Phil swore jubilantly as he walked over and grabbed Marlie by the shoulders. He kissed her, hard. "Fantastic," he said, then kissed her again. "Fantastic." Looking up, he grinned at Sam.

"Don't try that on me," Sam warned, nursing his lower lip. "She packs a hell of a punch." He gave her a rueful glance. "Ever heard about pulling right before you make contact?" he asked. "Show biz, you know."

"I got carried away."

"I nearly slugged you."

"I know." Laughing, she pushed her hair back with both hands.

"Okay, let's take it from there." Phil moved back to the cameraman. "Places."

"Can't we take it from right before the punch?" Marlie asked with a grin for Sam. "It would sort of give me a roll into the rest of the scene."

"Stand in!" Sam called.

In her office Tory read over with care a long, detailed letter from an opposing attorney. The tone was very clear through the legal terms and flowery style. The case was going through litigation, she thought with a frown. It might take two months or more, she mused, but this suit wasn't going to be settled out of court. Though normally she would have wanted to come to terms without a trial, she began to feel a tiny flutter of excitement. She'd been away from her own work for too long. She would be back in Albuquerque in a month. Tory discovered she wanted—needed—something complicated and time-consuming on her return.

Adjustments, she decided as she tried to concentrate on the words in the letter. There were going to be adjustments to be made when she left Friendly this time. When she left Phil. No, she corrected, catching the bridge of her nose between her thumb and forefinger. He was leaving first—tomorrow, the day after. It was uncomfortably easy to see the hole that was already taking shape in her life. Tory reminded herself that she wasn't allowed to think of it. The rules had been made plain at the outset—by both of them. If things had begun to change for her, she simply had to backpedal a bit and reaffirm her priorities. *Her* work, *her* career, *her* life. At that moment the singular possessive pronoun never sounded more empty. Shaking her head, Tory began to read the letter from the beginning a second time.

Merle paced the office, casting quick glances at Tory from time to time. He'd made arrangements for Marlie to meet him there after her work was finished. What he hadn't expected was for Tory to be glued to her desk all evening. No expert with subtleties, Merle had no idea how to move his boss along and have the office to himself. He peeked out the window, noting that the floodlights up the street were being shut off. Shuffling his feet and clearing his throat, he turned back to Tory.

"Guess you must be getting tired," he ventured.

"Hmmm."

"Things are pretty quiet tonight," he tried again, fussing with the buttons on his shirt.

"Um-hmm." Tory began to make notations on her yellow pad.

Merle lifted his eyes to the ceiling. Maybe the direct approach would do it, he decided. "Why don't you knock off and go home."

Tory continued to write. "Trying to get rid of me, Merle T.?"

"Well, no, ah..." He looked down at the dusty tips of his shoes. Women never got any easier to handle.

"Got a date?" she asked mildly as she continued to draft out her answer to the letter.

"Sort of...well, yeah," he said with more confidence.

"Go ahead, then."

"But—" He broke off, stuffing his hands in his pockets.

Tory looked up and studied him. The mustache, she noted, had grown in respectability. It wasn't exactly a prizewinner, but it added maturity to a face she'd always thought resembled a teddy bear's. He still slouched, and even as she studied at him, color seeped into his cheeks. But he didn't look away as he once would have done. His eyes stayed on hers so that she could easily read both frustration and embarrassment. The old affection stirred in her.

"Marlie?" she asked gently.

"Yeah." He straightened his shoulders a bit.

"How are you going to feel when she leaves?"

With a shrug Merle glanced toward the window again. "I guess I'll miss her. She's a terrific lady."

The tone caused Tory to give his profile a puzzled look. There was no misery in it, just casual acceptance. With a light laugh she stared back at her notes. Odd, she thought, it seemed their reactions had gotten reversed somewhere along the line. "You don't have to stay, Merle," she said lightly. "If you'd planned to have a late supper or—"

"We did," he interrupted. "Here."

Tory looked up again. "Oh, I see." She couldn't quite control the smile. "Looks like I'm in the way."

Uncomfortable, he shuffled again. "Aw, Tory."

"It's okay." Rising, she exaggerated her accommodating tone. "I know when I'm not wanted. I'll just go back to my room and work on this all by myself."

Merle struggled with loyalty and selfishness while Tory gathered her papers. "You could have supper with us," he suggested gallantly.

Letting the papers drop, Tory skirted the desk. With her hands on his shoulders, she kissed both of his cheeks. "Merle T.," she said softly, "you're a jewel."

Pleased, he grinned as the door opened behind them. "Just like I told you, Phil," Marlie stated as they entered. "Beautiful woman can't keep away from him. You'll have to stand in line, Sheriff,'' she continued, walking over to hook her arm through Merle's. ''I've got first dibs tonight.''

''Why don't I get her out of your way?'' Phil suggested. ''It's the least I can do after that last scene.''

''The man is totally unselfish,'' Marlie confided to Tory. ''No sacrifice is too great for his people.''

With a snort Tory turned back to her desk. ''I might let him buy me a drink,'' she considered while slipping her papers into a small leather case. When he sat on the corner of her desk, she cast him a look. ''And dinner,'' she added.

''I might be able to come up with some cold cuts,'' he murmured.

Tory's low, appreciative laugh was interrupted by the phone. ''Sheriff's office.'' Her sigh was automatic as she listened to the excited voice on the other end. ''Yes, Mr. Potts.'' Merle groaned, but she ignored him. ''I see. What kind of noise?'' Tory waited while the old man jabbered in her ear. ''Are your doors and windows locked? No, Mr. Potts, I don't want you going outside with your shotgun. Yes, I realize a man has to protect his property.'' A sarcastic sound from Merle earned him a mild glare. ''Let me handle it. I'll be there in ten minutes. No, I'll be quiet, just sit tight.''

''Sheep thieves,'' Merle muttered as Tory hung up.

''Burglars,'' she corrected, opening the top drawer of her desk.

''Just what do you think you're going to do with that?'' Phil demanded as he saw Tory pull out the gun.

''Absolutely nothing, I hope.'' Coolly she began to load it.

''Then why are you—? Wait a minute,'' he interrupted himself, rising. ''Do you mean that damn thing wasn't loaded?''

''Of course not.'' Tory slipped in the last bullet. ''Nobody with sense keeps a loaded gun in an unlocked drawer.''

''You got me into that cell with an empty gun?''

She sent him a lazy smile as she strapped on a holster. ''You were so cute, Kincaid.''

Ignoring amusement, he took a step toward her. ''What would you have done if I hadn't backed down.''

''The odds were in my favor,'' she reminded him. ''But I'd have thought of something. Merle, keep an eye on things until I get back.''

''Wasting your time.''

''Just part of the job.''

''If you're wasting your time,'' Phil began as he stopped her at the door, ''why are you taking that gun?''

''It looks so impressive,'' Tory told him as she walked outside.

''Tory, you're not going out to some sheep ranch with a gun at your hip like some modern-day Belle Starr.''

''She was on the wrong side,'' she reminded him.

''Tory, I mean it!'' Infuriated, Phil stepped in front of the car to block her way.

''Look, I said I'd be there in ten minutes; I'm going to have to drive like a maniac as it is.''

He didn't budge. ''What if there is someone out there?''

"That's exactly why I'm going."

When she reached for the door handle, he put his hand firmly over hers. "I'm going with you."

"Phil, I don't have time."

"I'm going."

Narrowing her eyes, she studied his face. There was no arguing with that expression, she concluded. "Okay, you're temporarily deputized. Get in and do what you're told."

Phil lifted a brow at her tone. The thought of her going out to some secluded ranch with only a gun for company had him swallowing his pride. He slid across to the passenger seat. "Don't I get a badge?" he asked as Tory started the engine.

"Use your imagination," she advised.

Tory's speed was sedate until they reached the town limits. Once the buildings were left behind, Phil watched the climbing speedometer with growing trepidation. Her hands were relaxed and competent on the wheel. The open window caused her hair to fly wildly, but her expression was calm.

She doesn't think there's anything to this, he decided as he watched the scenery whiz by. But if she did, his thoughts continued, she'd be doing exactly the same thing. The knowledge gave him a small thrill of fear. The neat black holster at her side hid an ugly, very real weapon. She had no business chasing burglars or carrying guns. She had no business taking the remotest chance with her own well-being. He cursed the phone call that had made it all too clear just how potentially dangerous her position in Friendly was. It had been simpler to think of her as a kind of figurehead, a referee for small-town squabbles. The late-night call and the gun changed everything.

"What will you do if you have to use that thing?" he demanded suddenly.

Without turning, Tory knew where his thoughts centered. "I'll deal with that when the time comes."

"When's your term up here?"

Tory took her eyes from the road for a brief two seconds. Phil was looking straight ahead. "Three weeks."

"You're better off in Albuquerque," he muttered. *Safer* was the word heard but not said. Tory recalled the time a client had nearly strangled her in his cell before the guards had pulled him off. She decided it was best unmentioned. Hardly slackening the car's speed, she took a right turn onto a narrow, rut-filled dirt road. Phil swore as the jolting threw him against the door.

"You should have strapped in," she told him carelessly.

His response was rude and brief.

The tiny ranch house had every light blazing. Tory pulled up in front of it with a quick squeal of brakes.

"Think you missed any?" Phil asked her mildly as he rubbed the shoulder that had collided with the door.

"I'll catch them on the way back." Before he could retort, Tory was out of the car and striding up the porch steps. She knocked briskly, calling out to identify herself. When Phil joined her on the porch, the door opened a crack. "Mr. Potts," she began.

"Who's he?" the old man demanded through the crack in the door.

"New deputy," Tory said glibly. "We'll check the grounds and the outside of the house now."

Potts opened the door a bit more, revealing an ancient, craggy face and a shiny black shotgun. "I heard them in the bushes."

"We'll take care of it, Mr. Potts." She put her hands on the butt of his gun. "Why don't you let me have this for now?"

Unwilling, Potts held firm. "I gotta have protection."

"Yes, but they're not in the house," she reminded him gently. "I could really use this out here."

He hesitated, then slackened his grip. "Both barrels," he told her, then slammed the door. Tory heard the triple locks click into place.

"That is not your average jolly old man," Phil commented.

Tory took the two shells out of the shotgun. "Alone too long," she said simply. "Let's take a look around."

"Go get 'em, big guy."

Tory barely controlled a laugh. "Just keep out of the way, Kincaid."

Whether she considered it a false alarm or not, Phil noted that Tory was very thorough. With the empty shotgun in one hand and a flashlight in the other, she checked every door and window on the dilapidated ranch house. Watching her, he walked into a pile of empty paint cans, sending them clattering. When he swore, Tory turned her head to look at him.

"You move like a cat, Kincaid," she said admiringly.

"The man's got junk piled everywhere," he retorted. "A burglar doesn't have a chance."

Tory smothered a chuckle and moved on. They circled the house, making their way through Potts's obstacle course of old car parts, warped lumber and rusted tools. Satisfied that no one had attempted to break into the house for at least twenty-five years, Tory widened her circle to check the ground.

"Waste of time," Phil muttered, echoing Merle.

"Then let's waste it properly." Tory shone her light on the uneven grass as they continued to walk. Resigned, Phil kept to her side. There were better ways, he was thinking, to spend a warm summer night. And the moon was full. Pure white, he observed as he gazed up at it. Cool and full and promising. He wanted to make love to her under it, in the still, hot air with nothing and no one around for miles. The desire came suddenly, intensely, washing over him with a wave of possession that left him baffled.

"Tory," he murmured, placing a hand on her shoulder.

"Ssh!"

The order was sharp. He felt her stiffen under his hand. Her eyes were trained on a dry, dying bush directly in front of them. Even as he opened his mouth to say something impatient, Phil saw the movement. His fingers tightened on Tory's shoulder as he automatically stepped forward. The protective gesture was instinctive, and so natural neither of them noticed it. He never thought: This is my woman, and I'll do anything to keep her from harm;

he simply reacted. With his body as a shield for hers, they watched the bush in silence.

There was a slight sound, hardly a whisper on the air, but Tory felt the back of her neck prickle. The dry leaves of the bush cracked quietly with some movement. She reached in her pocket for the two shells, then reloaded the shotgun. The moonlight bounced off the oiled metal. Her hands were rock steady. Phil was poised, ready to lunge as Tory aimed the gun at the moon and fired both barrels. The sound split the silence like an axe.

With a terrified bleat, the sheep that had been grazing lazily behind the bush scrambled for safety. Without a word Phil and Tory watched the dirty white blob run wildly into the night.

"Another desperate criminal on the run from the law," Tory said dryly.

Phil burst into relieved laughter. He felt each separate muscle in his body relax. "I'd say 'on the lamb.'"

"I was hoping you wouldn't." Because the hand holding the gun was shaking, Tory lowered it to her side. She swallowed; her throat was dry. "Well, let's go tell Potts his home and hearth are safe. Then we can go have that drink."

Phil laid his hands on her shoulders, looking down on her face in the moonlight. "Are you all right?"

"Sure."

"You're trembling."

"That's you," she countered, smiling at him.

Phil slid his hand down to her wrist to feel the race of her pulse. "Scared the hell out of you," he said softly.

Tory's eyes didn't waver. "Yeah." She was able to smile again, this time with more feeling. "How about you?"

"Me too." Laughing, he gave her a light kiss. "I'm not going to need that badge after all." And I'm not going to feel safe, he added silently, until you take yours off for the last time.

"Oh, I don't know, Kincaid." Tory led the way back with the beam of her flashlight. "First night on the job and you flushed out a sheep."

"Just give the crazy old man his gun and let's get out of here."

It took ten minutes of Tory's diplomacy to convince Potts that everything was under control. Mollified more by the fact that Tory had used his gun than the information that his intruder was one of his own flock, he locked himself in again. After contacting Merle on the radio, she headed back to town at an easy speed.

"I guess I could consider this a fitting climax to my sojourn to Friendly," Phil commented. "Danger and excitement on the last night in town."

Tory's fingers tightened on the wheel, but she managed to keep the speed steady. "You're leaving tomorrow."

He listened for regret in the statement but heard none. Striving to match her tone, he continued to stare out the window. "We finished up tonight, a day ahead of schedule. I'll head out with the film crew tomorrow. I want to be there when Huffman sees the film."

"Of course." The pain rammed into her, dazzlingly physical. It took concentrated control to keep from moaning with it. ‘‘You’ve still quite a lot of work to do before it’s finished, I suppose.’’

‘‘The studio scenes,’’ he agreed, struggling to ignore twin feelings of panic and desolation. ‘‘The editing, the mixing…I guess your schedule’s going to be pretty tight when you get back to Albuquerque.’’

‘‘It looks that way.’’ Tory stared at the beams of the headlights. A long straight road, no curves, no hills. No end. She bit the inside of her lip hard before she trusted herself to continue. ‘‘I’m thinking about hiring a new law clerk.’’

‘‘That’s probably a good idea.’’ He told himself that the crawling emptiness in his stomach was due to a lack of food. ‘‘I don’t imagine your case load’s going to get any smaller.’’

‘‘No, it should take me six months of concentrated work to get it under control again. You’ll probably start on a new film the minute this one’s finished.’’

‘‘It’s being cast now,’’ he murmured. ‘‘I’m going to produce it, too.’’

Tory smiled. ‘‘No guarantors?’’

Phil answered the smile. ‘‘We’ll see.’’

They drove for another half mile in silence. Slowing down, Tory pulled off onto a small dirt road and stopped. Phil took a quick glance around at nothing in particular, then turned to her. ‘‘What are we doing?’’

‘‘Parking.’’ She scooted from under the steering wheel, winding her arms around his neck.

‘‘Isn’t there some legality about using an official car for

illicit purposes?'' His mouth was already seeking hers, craving.

''I'll pay the fine in the morning.'' She silenced his chuckle with a deep, desperate kiss.

As if by mutual consent, they went slowly. All pleasure, all desire, was concentrated in tastes. Lips, teeth and tongues brought shuddering arousal, urging them to hurry. But they would satisfy needs with mouths only first. Her lips were silkily yielding even as they met and increased his demand. Wild, crazy desires whipped through him, but her mouth held him prisoner. He touched her nowhere else. This taste—spiced honey, this texture—heated satin—would live with him always.

Tory let her lips roam his face. She knew each crease, each angle, each slope, more intimately than she knew her own features. With her eyes closed she could see him perfectly, and knew she had only to close her eyes again, in a year, in ten years, to have the same vivid picture. The skin on his neck was damp, making the flavor intensify as her tongue glided over it. Without thinking, she ran her fingers down his shirt, nimbly loosening buttons. When his chest was vulnerable, she spread both palms over it to feel his quick shudder. Then she brought her mouth, lazily, invitingly, back to his.

Her fingertips sent a path of ice, a path of fire, over his naked skin. Her mouth was drawing him in until his head swam. His labored breathing whispered on the night air. Wanting her closer, he shifted, cursed the cramped confines of the car, then dragged her across his lap. Lifting her to him, he buried his face against the side of her neck.

He fed there, starving for her until she moaned and brought his hand to rest on her breast. With torturous slowness he undid the series of buttons, allowing his fingertips to trail along her skin as it was painstakingly exposed. He let the tips of his fingers bring her to desperation.

The insistent brush of his thumb over the point of her breast released a shaft of exquisite pain so sharp, she cried out with it, dragging him closer. Open and hungry, her mouth fixed on his while she fretted to touch more of him. Their position made it impossible, but her body was his. He ran his hands over it, feeling her skin jump as he roamed to the waistband of her jeans. Loosening them, he slid his hand down to warm, moist secrets. His mouth crushed hers as he drank in her moan.

Tory struggled, maddened by the restrictions, wild with desire, as his fingers aroused her beyond belief. He kept her trapped against him, knowing once she touched him that his control would shatter. This night, he thought, this final night, would last until there was no tomorrow.

When she crested, he rose with her, half delirious. No woman was so soft, no woman was so responsive. His heart pounded, one separate pain after another, as he drove her up again.

Her struggles ceased. Compliance replaced them. Tory lay shuddering in a cocoon of unrivaled sensations. She was his. Though her mind was unaware of the total gift of self, her body knew. She'd been his, perhaps from the first, perhaps only for that moment, but there would never be any turning back. Love swamped her; desire sated her.

There was nothing left but the need to possess, to be possessed, by one man. In that instant she conceded her privacy.

The change in her had something racing through him. Phil couldn't question, couldn't analyze. He knew only that they must come together now—now, while there was something magic shimmering. It had nothing to do with the moonlight beaming into the car or the eerie silence surrounding them. It concerned only them and the secret that had grown despite protests. He didn't think, he didn't deny. With a sudden madness he tugged on her clothes and his own. Speed was foremost in his mind. He had to hurry before whatever trembled in the tiny confines was lost. Then her body was beneath his, fused to his, eager, asking.

He took her on the seat of the car like a passionate teenager. He felt like a man who had been given something precious, and as yet unrecognizable.

Chapter 12

A long sleepy time. Moonlight on the back of closed lids…night air over naked skin. The deep, deep silence of solitude by the whispering breathing of intimacy.

Tory floated in that luxurious plane between sleep and wakefulness—on her side, on the narrow front seat, with her body fitted closely against Phil's. Their legs were tangled, their arms around each other, as much for support as need. With his mouth near her ear, his warm breath skipped along her skin.

There were two marginally comfortable beds back at the hotel. They could have chosen either of them for their last night together, but they had stayed where they were, on a rough vinyl seat, on a dark road, as the night grew older. There they were alone completely. Morning still seemed very far away.

A hawk cried out as it drove toward earth. Some small animal screamed in the brush. Tory's lids fluttered up to find Phil's eyes open and on hers. In the moonlight his irises were very pale. Needing no words, perhaps wanting none, Tory lifted her mouth to his. They made love again, quietly, slowly, with more tenderness than either was accustomed to.

So they dozed again, unwilling to admit that the night was slipping away from them. When Tory awoke, there was a faint lessening in the darkness—not light, but the texture that meant morning was close.

A few more hours, she thought, gazing at the sky through the far window as she lay beside him. When the sun came up, it would be over. Now his body was warm against hers. He slept lightly, she knew. She had only to shift or murmur his name and he would awaken. She remained still. For a few more precious moments she wanted the simple unity that came from having him sleep at her side. There would be no stopping the sun from rising in the east—or stopping her lover from going west. It was up to her to accept the second as easily as she accepted the first. Closing her eyes, she willed herself to be strong. Phil stirred, dreaming.

He walked through his house in the hills, purposely, from room to room, looking, searching, for what was vague to him; but time after time he turned away, frustrated. Room after room after room. Everything was familiar: the colors, the furniture, even small personal objects that identified his home, his belongings. Something was missing. Stolen, lost? The house echoed emptily around him as he continued to search for something vital and unknown. The emotions of the man in the dream communicated themselves to the man dreaming. He felt the helplessness, the anger and the panic.

Hearing him murmur her name, Tory shifted yet closer. Phil shot awake, disoriented. The dream slipped into some corner of his mind that he couldn't reach.

"It's nearly morning," she said quietly.

A bit dazed, struggling to remember what he had dreamed that had left him feeling so empty, Phil looked at the sky. It was lightening. The first pale pinks bloomed at the horizon. For a moment they watched in silence as the day crept closer, stealing their night.

"Make love to me again," Tory whispered. "Once more, before morning."

He could see the quiet need in her eyes, the dark smudges beneath that told of patchy sleep, the soft glow that spoke clearly of a night of loving. He held the picture in his mind a moment, wanting to be certain he wouldn't lose it when time had dimmed other memories. He lowered his mouth to hers in bittersweet goodbye.

The sky paled to blue. The horizon erupted with color. The gold grew molten and scarlet bled into it as dawn came up. They loved intensely one final time. As morning came they lost themselves in each other, pretending it was still night. Where he touched, she trembled. Where she kissed, his skin hummed until they could no longer deny the need. The sun had full claim when they came together, so that the light streamed without mercy. Saying little, they dressed, then drove back to town.

* * *

When Tory stopped in front of the hotel, she felt she was in complete control again. No regrets, she reminded herself, as she turned off the ignition. We've just come to the fork in the road. We knew it was there when we started. Turning, she smiled at Phil.

"We're liable to be a bit stiff today."

Grinning, he leaned over and kissed her chin. "It was worth it."

"Remember that when you're moaning for a hot bath on your way back to L.A." Tory slid from the car. When she stepped up on the sidewalk, Phil took her hand. The contact threatened her control before she snapped it back into place.

"I'm going to be thinking of you," he murmured as they stepped into the tiny lobby.

"You'll be busy." She let her hand slide on the banister as they mounted the stairs.

"Not that busy." Phil turned her to him when they reached the top landing. "Not that busy, Tory," he said again.

Her courtroom experience came to her aid. Trembling inside, Tory managed an easy smile. "I'm glad. I'll think of you too." *Too often, too much. Too painful.*

"If I call you—"

"I'm in the book," she interrupted. Play it light, she ordered herself. The way it was supposed to be, before... "Keep out of trouble, Kincaid," she told him as she slipped her room key into its lock.

"Tory."

He stepped closer, but she barred the way into the room.

"I'll say goodbye now." With another smile she rested a hand on his cheek. "It'll be simpler, and I think I'd better catch a couple hours sleep before I go into the office."

Phil took a long, thorough study of her face. Her eyes were direct, her smile easy. Apparently there was nothing left to say. "If that's what you want."

Tory nodded, not fully trusting herself. "Be happy, Phil," she managed before she disappeared into her room. Very carefully Tory turned the lock before she walked to the bed. Lying down, she curled into a ball and wept, and wept, and wept.

It was past noon when Tory awoke. Her head was pounding. Dragging herself to the bathroom, she studied herself objectively in the mirror over the sink. Terrible, she decided without emotion. The headache had taken the color from her cheeks, and her eyes were swollen and red from tears. Dispassionately, Tory ran the water until it was icy cold, then splashed her face with it. When her skin was numb, she stripped and stepped under the shower.

She decided against aspirin. The pills would dull the pain, and the pain made it difficult to think. Thinking was the last thing she felt she needed to do at the moment. Phil was gone, back to his own life. She would go on with hers. The fact that she had fallen in love with him over her own better judgment was simply her hard luck. In a few days she would be able to cope with it easily enough. Like hell you will, she berated herself as she dried her skin with a rough towel. You fell hard, and some bruises take years to heal…if ever.

Wasn't it ironic, she mused as she went back into the

bedroom to dress. Victoria L. Ashton, Attorney at Law, dedicated to straightening out other people's lives, had just made a beautiful mess of her own. And yet, there hadn't been any options. A deal was a deal.

Phil, she said silently, I've decided to change our contract. Circumstances have altered, and I'm in love with you. I propose we include certain things like commitment and reciprocal affection into our arrangement, with options for additions such as marriage and children, should both parties find it agreeable.

She gave a short laugh and pulled on a fresh shirt. Of course, she could merely have clung to him, tearfully begging him not to leave her. What man wouldn't love to find himself confronted with a hysterical woman who won't let go?

Better this way, she reminded herself, tugging on jeans. Much better to have a clean, civilized break. Aloud, she said something potent about being civilized as she pinned on her badge. The one thing she had firmly decided during her crying jag was that it was time for her to leave Friendly. Merle could handle the responsibilities of the office for the next few weeks without too much trouble. She had come to terms with her father's death, with her mother. She felt confident that she'd helped in Tod's family situation. Merle had grown up a bit. All in all, Tory felt she wasn't needed any longer. In Albuquerque she could put her own life in motion again. She needed that if she wasn't going to spend three weeks wallowing in self-pity and despair. At least, she decided, it was something she could start on. Naturally she would have to talk to the mayor and officially resign. There would be a visit to her mother. If she spent a day briefing Merle, she should be able to leave before the end of the week.

Her own rooms, Tory thought, trying to work up some excitement. The work she was trained for—a meaty court case that would take weeks of preparation and a furnace of energy. She felt suddenly that she had a surplus of it and nowhere to go. Back in the bath, she applied a careful layer of makeup to disguise the effects of tears, then brushed her hair dry. The first step was the mayor. There was no point putting it off.

It took thirty minutes for Tory to convince the mayor she was serious and another fifteen to assure him that Merle was capable of handling the job of acting sheriff until the election.

"You know, Tory," Bud said when he saw her mind was made up, "we're going to be sorry to lose you. I guess we all kept hoping you'd change your mind and run. You've been a good sheriff, I guess you come by it naturally."

"I appreciate that—really." Touched, Tory took the hand he offered her. "Pat Rowe and Nick Merriweather are both fair men. Whoever wins, the town's in good hands. In a few years Merle will make you a fine sheriff."

"If you ever change your mind..." Bud trailed off wanting to leave the door open.

"Thanks, but my niche in the law isn't in enforcement. I have to get back to my practice."

"I know, I know." He sighed, capitulating. "You've done more than we had a right to expect."

''I did what I wanted to do,'' she corrected.

''I guess things will be quiet for a while, especially with the movie people gone.'' He gave a regretful glance toward the window. Excitement, he mused, wasn't meant for Friendly. ''Come by and see me before you leave town.''

Outside, the first thing Tory noticed was the absence of the movie crew. There were no vans, no sets, no lights or packets of people. Friendly had settled back into its yawning pace as though there had never been a ripple. Someone had written some graffiti in the dust on the window of the post office. A car puttered into town and stopped in front of the hardware store. Tory started to cross the street, but stopped in the center when she was hailed. Shielding her eyes, she watched Tod race toward her.

''Sheriff, I've been looking for you.''

''Is something wrong?''

''No.'' He grinned the quick-spreading grin that transformed his thin face. ''It's real good, I wanted you to know. My dad...well, we've been talking, you know, and we even drove out to see those people you told us about.''

''How'd it go?''

''We're going to go back—my mom too.''

''I'm happy for you.'' Tory brushed her knuckles over his cheek. ''It's going to take time, Tod. You'll all have to work together.''

''I know, but...'' He looked up at her, his eyes wide and thrilled. ''He really loves me. I never thought he did. And my mom, she wondered if you could come out to the house sometime. She wants to thank you.''

"There isn't any need for that."

"She wants to."

"I'll try." Tory hesitated, finding that this goodbye would be more difficult than most. "I'm going away in a couple of days."

His elated expression faded. "For good?"

"My mother lives here," she reminded him. "My father's buried here. I'll come back from time to time."

"But not to stay."

"No," Tory said softly. "Not to stay."

Tod lowered his gaze to the ground. "I knew you'd leave. I guess I was pretty stupid that day in your office when I..." He trailed off with a shrug and continued to stare at the ground.

"I didn't think you were stupid. It meant a lot to me." Tory put out a hand to lift his face. "*Means* a lot to me."

Tod moistened his lips. "I guess I still love you—if you don't mind."

"Oh." Tory felt the tears spring to her eyes and pulled him into her arms. "I'm going to miss you like crazy. Would you think I was stupid if I said I wish I were a fourteen-year-old girl?"

Grinning, he drew away. Nothing she could have said could have pleased him more. "I guess if you were I could kiss you goodbye."

With a laugh Tory brushed a light kiss on his lips. "Go on, get out of here," she ordered unsteadily. "Nothing undermines the confidence of a town more than having its sheriff crying in the middle of the street."

Feeling incredibly mature, Tod dashed away. Turning,

he ran backward for a moment. ''Will you write sometime?''

''Yes, yes, I'll write.'' Tory watched him streak off at top speed. Her smile lost some of its sparkle. She was losing, she discovered, quite a bit in one day. Briskly shaking off the mood, she turned in the direction of her office. She was still a yard away when Merle strolled out.

''Hey,'' he said foolishly, glancing from her, then back at the door he'd just closed.

''Hey yourself,'' she returned. ''You just got yourself a promotion, Merle T.''

''Tory, there's— Huh?''

''Incredibly articulate,'' she replied with a fresh smile. ''I'm resigning. You'll be acting sheriff until the election.''

''Resigning?'' He gave her a completely baffled look. ''But you—'' He broke off, shaking his head at the door again. ''How come?''

''I need to get back to my practice. Anyway,'' she stepped up on the sidewalk, ''it shouldn't take long for me to fill you in on the procedure. You already know just about everything. Come on inside and we'll get started.''

''Tory.'' In an uncharacteristic gesture he took her arm and stopped her. Shrewdly direct, his eyes locked on hers. ''Are you upset about something?''

Merle was definitely growing up, Tory concluded. ''I just saw Tod.'' It was part of the truth, and all she would discuss. ''That kid gets to me.''

His answer was a slow nod, but he didn't release her

arm. ‘‘I guess you know the movie people left late this morning.’’

‘‘Yes, I know.’’ Hearing her own clipped response, Tory took a mental step back. ‘‘I don’t suppose it was easy for you to say goodbye to Marlie,’’ she said more gently.

‘‘I’ll miss her some,’’ he admitted, still watching Tory critically. ‘‘We had fun together.’’

His words were so calm that Tory tilted her head as she studied him. ‘‘I was afraid you’d fallen in love with her.’’

‘‘In love with her?’’ He let out a hoot of laughter. ‘‘Shoot, I ain’t ready for that. No way.’’

‘‘Sometimes being ready doesn’t make any difference,’’ Tory muttered. ‘‘Well,’’ she said more briskly, ‘‘since you’re not crying in your beer, why don’t we go over some things? I’d like to be in Albuquerque before the end of the week.’’

‘‘Ah…yeah, sure.’’ Merle glanced around the empty street. ‘‘I gotta talk to somebody first over at, um…the hotel,’’ he announced. ‘‘Be right back.’’

Tory shot him an exasperated glance as he loped across the street. ‘‘Well,’’ she murmured, ‘‘some things never change.’’ Deciding she could spend the time packing her books and papers, Tory walked into the office.

Seated at her desk, casually examining the .45, was Phil Kincaid. She stopped dead, gaping at him. ‘‘Sheriff,’’ he said mildly, giving the barrel an idle spin.

‘‘Phil.’’ She found her voice, barely. ‘‘What are you doing here?’’

He didn’t rise, but propped his feet up on the desk instead. "I forgot something. Did you know you didn't unload this thing last night?"

She didn't even glance at the gun, but stood rooted to the spot. "I thought you'd left hours ago."

"Did you?" He gave her a long, steady look. The cold water and makeup had helped, but he knew her face intimately. "I did," he agreed after a moment. "I came back."

"Oh." So now she would have to deal with the goodbye a second time. Tory ignored the ache in her stomach and smiled. "What did you forget?"

"I owe you something," he said softly. The gesture with the gun was very subtle, but clear enough.

Only partially amused, Tory lifted a brow. "Let's call it even," she suggested. Wanting to busy her hands, she went to the shelf near the desk to draw out her books.

"No," he said mildly. "I don't think so. Turn around, Sheriff."

Annoyance was the least painful of her emotions, so Tory let it out. "Look, Phil—"

"In the cell," he interrupted. "I can recommend the first one."

"You're out of your mind." With a thud she dropped the books. "If that thing's loaded, you could hurt someone."

"I have some things to say to you," he continued calmly. "In there." Again he gestured toward the cell.

Her hands went to her hips. "All right, Kincaid, I'm still sheriff here. The penalty for armed assault on a peace officer—"

"Shut up and get in," Phil ordered.

"You can take that gun," Tory began dangerously, "and—"

Her suggestion was cut off when Phil grabbed her arm and hauled her into a cell. Stepping in with her, he pulled the door shut with a shattering clang.

"You *idiot!*" Impotently, Tory gave the locked door a furious jerk. "Now just how the hell are we supposed to get out?"

Phil settled comfortably on the bunk, propped on one elbow, with the gun lowered toward the floor. It was just as empty as it had been when Tory had bluffed him. "I haven't anyplace better to go."

Fists on hips, Tory whirled. "Just what is this all about, Kincaid?" she demanded. "You're supposed to be halfway to L.A.; instead you're propped up at my desk. Instead of a reasonable explanation, you throw that gun around like some two-bit hood—"

"I thought I did it with such finesse," he complained, frowning at the object under discussion. "Of course, I'd rather have a piece with a bit more style." He grinned up at her. "Pearl handle, maybe."

"Do you have to behave like such a fool?"

"I suppose."

"When this is over, you're going to find yourself locked up for months. Years, if I can manage it," she added, turning to tug uselessly on the bars again.

"That won't work," he told her amiably. "I shook them like crazy a few months ago."

Ignoring him, Tory stalked to the window. Not a soul

on the street. She debated swallowing her pride and calling out. It would look terrific, she thought grimly, to have the sheriff shouting to be let out of one of her own cells. If she waited for Merle, at least she could make him swear to secrecy.

''All right, Kincaid,'' she said between her teeth. ''Let's have it. Why are you here and why the devil are we locked in the cell?''

He glanced down at the gun again, then set it on the edge of the bunk. Automatically, Tory judged the distance. ''Because,'' and his voice had altered enough to lure her eyes to his, ''I found myself in an impossible situation.''

At those words Tory felt her heart come to a stop, then begin again at a furious rate. Cautiously she warned herself not to read anything into the statement. True, she remembered his use of the phrase when talking about love, but it didn't follow that he meant the same thing now.

''Oh?'' she managed, and praised herself for a brilliant response.

''*'Oh?'*'' Phil pushed himself off the bunk in a quick move. ''Is that all you can say? I got twenty miles out of town,'' he went on in sudden fury. ''I told myself that was it. You wanted—I wanted—a simple transient relationship. No complications. We'd enjoyed each other; it was over.''

Tory swallowed. ''Yes, we'd agreed—''

''The hell with what we agreed.'' Phil grabbed her shoulders, shaking her until her mouth dropped open in shock. ''It got complicated. It got very, very complicated.'' Releasing her abruptly, he began to pace the cell he had locked them both into.

''Twenty miles out of town,'' he repeated, ''and I couldn't make it. Even last night I told myself it was all for the best. You'd go your way, I'd go mine. We'd both have some great memories.'' He turned to her then; although his voice lowered, it was no calmer. ''Damn it, Tory, I want more than memories of you. I need more. You didn't want this to happen, I know that.'' Agitated, he ran a hand through his hair, while she said nothing. ''I didn't want it, either, or thought I didn't. I'm not sure anymore. It might have been the first minute I walked in here, or that day at the cemetery. It might have been that night at the lake or a hundred other times. I don't know when it happened, why it happened.'' He shook his head as though it was a problem he'd struggled with and ultimately given up on. ''I only know I love you. And God knows I can't leave you. I tried—I can't.''

With a shuddering sigh Tory walked back to the bars and rested her head against them. The headache she had awoken with was now a whirling dizziness. A minute, she told herself. I just need a minute to take it in.

''I know you've got a life in Albuquerque,'' Phil continued, fighting against the fluttering panic in his stomach. ''I know you've got a career that's important to you. It isn't something I'm asking you to choose between. There are ways to balance things if people want to badly enough. I broke the rules; I'm willing to make the adjustments.''

''Adjustments...'' Tory managed before she turned back to him.

"I can live in Albuquerque," he told her as he crossed the cell. "That won't stop me from making movies."

"The studio—"

"I'll buy a plane and commute," he said quickly. "It's been done before."

"A plane." With a little laugh she walked away, dragging a hand through her hair. "A plane."

"Yes, damn it, a plane." Her reaction was nothing that he had expected. The panic grew. "You didn't want me to go," he began in defense, in fury. "You've been crying. I can tell."

A bit steadier, Tory faced him again. "Yes, I cried. No, I didn't want you to go. Still, I thought it was best for both of us."

"Why?"

"It wouldn't be easy, juggling two careers and one relationship."

"Marriage," he corrected firmly. "Marriage, Tory. The whole ball of wax. Kids, too. I want you to have my children." He saw the change in her eyes—shock, fear? Unable to identify it, Phil went to her again. "I said I love you." Again he took her by the shoulders. This time he didn't shake her but held her almost tentatively. "I have to know what you feel for me."

She spent a moment simply looking into his eyes. Loved her? Yes, she realized with something like a jolt. She could see it. It was real. And more, he was hurting because he wasn't sure. Doubts melted away. "I've been in an impossible situation, I think, from the first moment Merle hauled you in here."

She felt his fingers tense, then relax again. "Are you sure?" he asked, fighting the need to drag her against him.

"That I'm in love with you?" For the first time a ghost of a smile hovered around her mouth. "Sure enough that I nearly died when I thought you were leaving me. Sure enough that I was going to let you go because I'm just as stupid as you are."

His hands dove into her hair. "Stupid?" he repeated, drawing her closer.

"'He needs his own life. We agreed not to complicate things. He'd hate it if I begged him to stay.'" She smiled more fully. "Sound familiar?"

"With a slight change in the personal pronoun." Phil pulled her close just to hold her. *Mine,* they thought simultaneously, then clung. "Ah, Tory, last night was so wonderful—and so terrible."

"I know, thinking it was the last time." She drew back only enough so their mouths could meet. "I've been giving some thought to it for a while," she murmured, then lost the trend of thought as they kissed again.

"To what?"

"To…oh, to moving to the coast."

Framing her face with his hands, Phil tilted it to his. "You don't have to do that. I told you, I can—"

"Buy a plane," she finished on a laugh. "And I'm sure you can. But I have given some thought lately to moving on. Why not California?"

"We'll work that out."

"Eventually," she agreed, drawing his mouth back to hers.

"Tory." He held her off a moment, his eyes serious again. "Are you going to marry me?"

She considered a moment, letting her fingers twine in his hair. "It might be wise," she decided, "since we're going to have those kids."

"When?"

"It takes nine months," she reminded him.

"Marriage," he corrected, nipping her bottom lip.

"Well, after you've served your sentence…about three months."

"Sentence?"

"Illegal use of a handgun, accosting a peace officer, improper use of a correctional facility…" She shrugged, giving him her dashing grin. "Time off for good behavior, you should be out in no time. Remember, I'm still sheriff here, Kincaid."

"The hell you are." Pulling the badge from her blouse, he tossed it through the bars of the window. "Besides, you'll never make it stick."

* * * * *